Escape to the Straits

BY SARAH RENEE GREEN

Copyright © 2013 Sarah Renee Green
All rights reserved.

ISBN: 1484066235
ISBN 13: 9781484066232
Library of Congress Control Number: 2013907129
CreateSpace Independent Publishing Platform
North Charleston, South Carolina

In memory of,

My parents Cecelia & James Green, my sister Suzanne and my son Shane

My grandmother Margaret Malone who at the age of seventeen bravely sailed from Ireland, leaving her home in County Carlow to seek a better life on Quaker Hill, Pawling, New York

My ancestors, the Stephen Hopkins family who endured that harrowing journey on the Mayflower

To the best
security officers!!
Miss you!
  Sarah

Author's Note

Although this novel is based on a true story, many events and characters, and all details and conversations portrayed are a product of the author's imagination. All characters' names are fictitious.

Table of Contents

#	Chapter	Page
1	THE CIGARETTE FACTORY	1
2	THE DISTILLERY	17
3	JULI'S BUTTERFLY	37
4	THE NIGHT SHIFT	51
5	THE MEETING	67
6	ITALIAN TOBACCO LEAVES	81
7	YUCCA STARCH	97
8	THE STORM	109
9	THE MOTORCYCLE	127
10	THE PROPOSAL	141
11	THE GIFTS	153
12	THE WEDDING	163
13	THE HONEYMOON	179
14	CAPTURED	191
15	LA PENDIENTE PRISON	207
16	THE INFERNO	215
17	THE RECOVERY	219
18	THE LAWYER	231
19	THE DEPARTURE	243
20	HAVANA	257
21	THE SOLDIERS OF THE CROSS	265
22	BOLERO	277
23	DODGING THE COAST GUARD	289
24	THE CHICKEN ESCAPADES	299
25	THE SURPRISE VISIT	319
26	THE SEPARATION	351
27	TRIAL RUN	361
28	THE PLAN	367
29	THE ESCAPE	375
30	THE STRAITS AND BEYOND	391

Chapter One
THE CIGARETTE FACTORY

Daniel Milan trembled as he wiped the mist of perspiration from his brow with a handkerchief. He stood on a loading dock stretching the length of the cigarette factory, Ramiro La Vandero, and saw his best friend, Rafael Reyes, nod and meander toward the factory entrance. Daniel returned the signal and waved the handkerchief once before he stuffed it in his pocket. The dolly Daniel leaned on concealed the gesture from his supervisor, who paced at the dock's edge, awaiting a truck scheduled to arrive forty-five minutes earlier.

El Jefe, Daniel's boss, threw up his arms as the vehicle turned from Central Highway onto the alley leading to the largest of four docks. Daniel heard the rumbling truck but focused on Rafael, who disappeared into the factory so suddenly the swinging doors seemed to swallow his lean body. Daniel took in a breath, regained his composure, and turned toward the truck laden with tobacco. Clouds of exhaust swirled around its swollen wooden frame pressed by overstuffed bales, and as much steam cascaded from beneath the hood.

Two dockworkers jumped down on either side of the truck, unlatched its rusted chains, and lowered the tailgate, causing a loud crash when metal struck the cement edge of the platform. The sound vibrated in Daniel's ears. Another dockworker gripped the twine tied around a bale, and the three men heaved each bale onto the dock one at a time.

"*Vamos*, Milan," El Jefe called to Daniel with a harshness revealing his anger at the driver who garbled a lengthy explanation of how the truck broke down on the highway. After handing the old man a paper from his clipboard, the boss focused on the inactive dockworker, Daniel.

"Load up. Move those bales."

"Shut up, idiot," Daniel muttered to himself and disguised his words with a hacking cough caused by fumes drifting in the air. He glanced at his watch. Only five minutes had passed. Ten to go. He pushed the cart past towers of tobacco shading the dock's surface and with the assistance of two dockworkers lifted bales topped with palm fronds onto his hand truck. As he reached for a bale, fronds brushed his face and clawed at his bare arms, etching white scratches into his tan skin.

"Listen to El Jefe and work, lazy boy," Maximo Lopez said grinning at Daniel as he rushed over to help him lift a bale.

"What the hell do you think I'm doing?"

Maximo bent over. "Your chance is now. Go do as planned," he said, close to Daniel's ear, with his eyes glued on the supervisor. "El Jefe's mad at you. Don't stay on the dock."

"It's too soon." Daniel looked directly into Max's eyes. "We made a pact. Rafael said fifteen minutes after the signal, when the guards break for lunch."

"It'll never happen if you wait."

Daniel looked at his watch and hesitated as he pondered Max's suggestion. Then he tilted the loaded cart, kicked it forward with the sole of his boot, and wheeled it inside as he glared at Maximo.

"Remember this was your idea."

Two government police in khaki uniforms stood erect with arms crossed, peering at Daniel as he maneuvered the bales past them. He ignored their sour stares and whispered for the sergeant, Pothole, to stay put. "All I need now is for you to bust my ass."

Within the factory, paddle fans blew a warm breeze overhead, rustling Daniel's hair. He inhaled the sweet, musty scent of tobacco leaves that had recently hung on vegas and dried brittle in the Cuban sunshine. The noise of machines cutting and chopping leaves and the steady hum of an exhaust fan added to the clamor deafening him.

Despite the commotion, he stalled to waste time and greeted the production-line employees, whose frowns turned to smiles when they caught sight of him. Their hands busily plucked bad leaves and tossed them into trash barrels. They mouthed, "*Hola, Daniel*," and "*Qué pasa, niño?*" Their voices droned and faded into the monotonous tones and the steady beat of the factory at the peak hour of production.

Beyond the assembly line, Daniel's pace quickened. Casually he looked over his shoulder and gasped at the sight of the two khaki-uniformed men. They strode down the aisle, weaved in between workers, and made a beeline straight for him. Pothole, nicknamed by the employees because of his acne-scarred cheeks, fixed his dead eyes on Daniel, and Garcia, second in command, kept up a rapid pace with the sergeant.

Thoughts of aborting the plan sped through Daniel's mind. To dump the bales and head back to the loading dock seemed the only solution under these pressing circumstances. Suddenly Pothole's thick, bushy mustache and acne-scarred cheeks flashed within inches of Daniel's face. He whiffed the stench of cigar smoke on the official's breath when he sneered, "*Cuidado.*"

Daniel's reaction was to tip his head backward to escape the intruder's invasion of his space, a movement that caused him to lose his balance just as Garcia's elbow jabbed his ribs, knocked the breath out of him, and slammed him into the edge of a sorting machine. His quick thinking and agility saved him from a more serious injury when he leaped beyond the sorter and rolled down the aisle. Upon impact his boots knocked over the unsteady hand truck, and the bales toppled onto a conveyor belt and jammed it to a halt. Except for the whirring fans, an eerie silence smothered the room.

Employees who witnessed the incident shook their heads and scrambled to help. Daniel planted himself firmly back on his feet in time to see Garcia trail Pothole out of the sorting area, both laughing as they veered toward the dock where cigarettes were hauled off for export. Rubbing his arm, Daniel watched the uniformed men vanish from the dimly lit room and enter the loading dock drenched in bright sunlight.

Several concerned employees left their posts to upright his cart. Although he assured them he was fine, they returned the bales to their original stacked position on the dolly. Now ironically late, Daniel decided to proceed with the plan anyway. He thanked his colleagues and guided the cart to the storage area.

Once inside, Daniel pushed the bales off the hand truck and hid it behind one of many bundles strewn around the room. After he crossed a narrow hallway and raced down a stairwell three steps at a time, he ran outside to a building off limits to his position. He scoured the area for guards and cautiously entered the door propped open with a stick.

Out of breath, Daniel scanned the spacious storehouse filled with cardboard boxes that were bloated with cut tobacco leaves. He walked down the narrow rows to the far side. To his amazement, against a wall leaned a dirt-smeared placard printed with the faded words, "*Trinidad y Hermanos. Real Fábrica de Tabacos Partagas. Fundada en 1845.*" The old-timers were right. The sign from before the revolution still existed. He headed parallel to the sign and combed hundreds of crates. Rafael had told him to look for a red plastic tag, but among the vast number of cardboard boxes, how would he ever find the one with a marker?

From his position on the floor, Daniel peered from the top boxes down to the larger ones on the bottom. He squeezed down rows, searching and pounding cardboard with his fists as he advanced. He felt shrunken and insignificant in this maze and was about to surrender to its vastness when he rounded the corner of a center aisle and spotted the red strip hanging over the box crowning the heap. The plastic tag waved and fluttered in a current of air blowing from a vent in the wall.

Daniel analyzed how best to scale the cartons, dabbed his forehead with his handkerchief, and stuffed it into his pocket. Then, with a running start, he jumped, and by clutching the uneven sides, he shimmied up to the labeled container. He rested a moment at the top before reaching inside and sweeping away pieces of brown leaves, exposing cigarette cartons peeking out of the loose tobacco.

"Eighty packs of Popular cigarettes. My buddies pulled through," Daniel whispered and sighed with satisfaction.

While carefully balancing, he tore open the cartons, raised his pant legs, and crammed ten packs inside each pair of baseball socks hugging his calves. He unbuttoned his shirt and frantically stuffed his undershirt until he heard a door creak and saw a streak of light stream across the ceiling. The sound of boots treading on cement alerted him to the fact that guards must be approaching. Daniel plastered himself across the open container and ceased to breathe. His hand clenching the edge of the box, shook.

A voice echoed across the room. "Daniel, it's me. Pothole and Garcia are coming. Get down. Hide."

"Rafael?" Daniel let out a breath. "Hide where?"

"Come down. I'll show you."

Daniel slid halfway down the wall of cardboard, went airborne, and landed with a thud on the cement floor.

"What happened? Your timing was off." Rafael pushed him toward the sign.

As Daniel scrambled to get his footing, he put a hand on his chest to sustain the packs inside his shirt. "Max told me to leave the dock. El Jefe was angry. Then Pothole and Garcia harassed me. I—"

"Never mind. Climb up. Those boxes are empty. Get inside. The top one's open."

Daniel climbed the boxes, and Rafael ducked out a fire exit and darted along the three-story building. He circled the complex by way of the street, Camilo Cienfuegos, to the factory park where Maximo was taking his break. Rafael strode over the grass to his coworker, who sat on a bench eating Cuban bread and sipping coffee.

"*Qué pasa?*" Maximo said with a full mouth. He noticed the stern look on Rafael's face.

"Daniel's hiding in the warehouse. An informant tipped off Pothole that he suspected a dockworker went inside. Now they're looking for him."

"They know it's Milan?"

"I don't think so."

"God, I hope they don't catch him."

"He's screwed if they do."

"Will he squeal on us?" Maximo said and sipped from the paper cup.

"Not Daniel. Why did you send him into the sorting room before the time we all agreed upon? That was exactly the time Pothole and Garcia break for lunch. You sent him into a hornet's nest."

"El Jefe was mad at Milan. If he didn't leave the dock he would have been punished and delayed even longer. Rafa, we can't chance going into that warehouse. It's too risky."

"We have no choice."

Maximo stared at Rafael, popped a piece of bread into his mouth, chewed, and gulped down the last of the coffee.

"Give it half an hour. Then meet me by the sign." Rafael ran his fingers through his hair. "We've got to get him out of there."

The sun glared off the white concrete building. In the structure's shadows lurked one of Fidel Castro's force assigned to the factory. Rafael recognized the khaki shirt with a brown, red, and white badge on the sleeve.

"Oh, shit. This facility's like a fucking prison." Rafael slapped the back of the bench and pointed at Max as if about to launch a spear aimed at his heart. "Remember, half an hour."

Rafa returned to the loading dock.

Following Rafael's instructions, Daniel ascended to the pinnacle of the empty cartons, opened the lid, and quietly crouched inside. Minutes passed. He heard a scraping sound, and then the box he hid in shuddered and the underside gave way. The base of the carton beneath him also collapsed, and he plummeted down a dark tunnel of cardboard as each container's base swiftly caved in to his weight. He felt like he had been propelled from a canon, descending through a dark abyss.

Daniel's hands reached up, grasping to break the fall. His right hand groped air, while his left hand struck metal supports, slicing his palm during the downward plunge. Pasteboard bases cushioned the landing, but the impact jolted his head backward, and the back of his head struck hard against the wall of the last box. Despite the pain emanating from his head and hand, he froze, hushed and frightened that the guards had heard the racket. He sighed with relief at the stillness outside.

Daniel pressed his injured hand to his chest in an effort to stop the bleeding, but with the pressure, bits of metal protruding from the gash stung his wound. He felt the warmth of blood trickle down his arm. The blood dampened and stained his shirt and the hidden packs of cigarettes tucked against his chest. He squinted to determine the size of the laceration and raised his hand toward the light shining through the opening above. Blood dripped into his eyes and momentarily blinded him. With his sleeve Daniel wiped each eye. He wrapped his handkerchief around his hand to swathe his injury, waited, and kept still, even though his impulse was to crash out of this prison.

The warm, stuffy air smelled of stale tobacco, cardboard, and blood. Daniel bit his lower lip and rested his forehead on his knees. He winced and mumbled a prayer encouraging his friends to rescue him from this confinement. Concentrating on being free took his mind off the pain and nauseous feeling in the pit of his stomach.

He dozed. Visions of water and waves flickered through his mind. Shadows gliding beneath the surface of the ocean darkened the pale water, and Daniel forced himself awake, refusing to allow the nightmare to continue. He supposed the fearful predicament he was in triggered the old dream inflicted upon him since childhood.

An hour crept by, during which he struggled with bouts of claustrophobia, but Daniel perked up when he heard shuffling and whispers outside. Someone brushed against the box he huddled in. The sound of Pothole's scratchy voice caused him to stiffen. He heard Garcia answer his boss among mutters and conversing and realized the multitude of voices meant Castro's factory henchmen had joined in the search. Daniel hugged his knees and remained still. He dreaded the guards' wrath if they were to capture him.

Seconds seemed endless. The thundering echoes of boxes being hurled against each other created havoc outside the dark cell he cowered in. One box crashed into his own. He ducked and lowered his head further when boots stomped across the floor. They were running, and soon the shouts waned. Once again, silence enveloped the warehouse for what seemed an eternity until softer, more muted voices and lighter steps approached. He was certain the police had returned for one last look to catch him off guard.

The cardboard tower rocked when someone ascended the stack of boxes engulfing him. Each step against cardboard sent a chill of terror within him, and Daniel cringed when a figure blocked the light from shining into his lair. He peered through blackness to the entrance. His tension eased when the unknown person shifted to one side and the light clearly outlined the silhouette of a young man. It was Rafael's profile.

Relief flooded Daniel as he watched his friend's hand pat the vacant interior of the crate. Confusion abounded on Rafael's face when he strained to look inside at cardboard but focused on an endless view of ebony.

"Daniel, *amigo*, are you in here?"

"*Sí, aquí al fondo.* Down here," Daniel shouted.

"Are you all right?"

"I cut my hand. I'm stifling. Rafa, get me out."

"He's at the bottom," Rafael called down to Maximo.

"How the fuck...?" Max tapped the box.

Daniel rapped hard on the cardboard. "*Hijo de puta.* Get me the fuck out of here."

Maximo smiled at the submerged tone of Daniel's voice. "He sure is."

"Max, find a rope." Rafael pointed toward some crates.

Maximo untied and snapped a long cord from a crate, climbed up the boxes, and sat beside Rafael. He tossed it down to Daniel, who stood up and snatched the rope with his good hand. Lying atop boxes, Rafael and Maximo tugged the rope and, after several tries, eased the prisoner out of his cardboard cell. Daniel stuck his feet in the last grooves that notched the cardboard wall and at the summit reached for his friends' hands. They yanked him free, and he moaned as he slid across the boxes. He glared at them.

Rafael raised his hands. "*Oye*, we tried to get here sooner. *Verdad*, Max? Pothole and his posse were all over this warehouse. We had to wait until they left to search the machine room before we could rescue you."

Maximo, on the verge of defending himself, changed his mind when he saw the blood-soaked handkerchief and the crimson shirt sticking to Daniel's chest.

"Holy shit. You lost a lot of blood." Max turned to Rafael.

"No shit. Let's get him out of here." Rafael removed his outer shirt, tore off his t-shirt, and wrapped it around Daniel's hand. Rafa quickly put on his shirt without buttoning it and climbed down from the boxes alongside Daniel. Blood soon tinted the white shirt red. Daniel felt weak and dizzy. His head throbbed. While squinting in the bright light at the base of the boxes, he faltered and propped himself against the wall to prevent from falling to the cement.

"Don't pass out on us," Rafael said as he and Maximo each clutched an arm. Supporting Daniel, they rushed him out of the warehouse and half carried him up the stairwell to the storeroom. Rafael and Maximo lifted Daniel's hand truck to an upright position and moved a bale of tobacco beside it. Rafa removed the bloody shirt and handkerchief from the wound and told his injured friend to bleed on the bale.

"Take your knife out. Put blood on it."

Daniel, too weak to protest, slowly pulled his knife from the sheath on his belt, unfolded the curved blade, and smeared blood over the stainless steel. With the knife, Rafael cut a strand of twine hugging the bale and allowed blood to absorb into the twine.

"Let the blood drip on the floor too. That's it."

Daniel's head spun, his thoughts were fuzzy. He dropped to his knees.

"Enough. Max, get the supervisor. Tell him Daniel cut himself here, in the storeroom. Hurry." Rafael helped his friend up. "Hang in there. After this I promise we'll get you to the doctor."

El Jefe, stormed into the storeroom with Pothole and Garcia at his heels and shouted, "What happened, Milan?"

"He cut himself," Rafael answered for Daniel, who reclined on a bale and leaned his head against the wall. He noticed the contrast and pallor of his friend's face next to the brown leaves. "With a knife, cutting twine."

Rafael showed them the red-coated knife and twine. The factory official smirked and glanced down at the cement floor littered with bits of tobacco leaves and spots of blood.

"Anything to get out of work." The boss's face contorted with anger.

"Something's wrong here," said Pothole as he grabbed for Daniel's shirt to pull him off the bale. He released it at once when he felt dampness and saw the blood stained material. He wiped his hand on his pant leg and poked at Daniel's stomach.

"Were you in the warehouse?"

In a stupor, Daniel worried the guard would discover the cigarette packs in his shirt. To Daniel's relief he grabbed his shirt above the hidden cigarettes and jabbed at his stomach below them.

Daniel shook his head while cradling his wounded hand. "No."

"Of course not," Rafael piped in and turned toward Pothole. "He was unloading bales. I heard him yell and found him in here, injured. I sent Maximo for help. Listen, he needs medical attention. The bleeding doesn't stop."

"We'll take a look around," Pothole assured the supervisor. "I know these rascals are up to no good. Milan hadn't been seen on the dock for at least an hour."

"Fine." The supervisor kicked the leaves on the floor toward Rafael. "Get the son of a bitch to the doctor."

Daniel faced the factory doctor, Javier Nieves. The bastard looked like an American—light brown hair, blue eyes—but the unlucky slob was a Cuban puppet of Castro working in a factory just like him.

God, his hand and head hurt.

The physician dragged a chair from beneath the desk and told Daniel to sit down. It screeched across the vinyl floor. Daniel reluctantly sat next to the sink. The doctor examined his palm and flushed the laceration with a gush of water, coloring the sink burgundy. The faucet moaned and wobbled. He placed Daniel's hand at the edge of the sink, plucked shards of metal out of the wound with tweezers, and wiped the silver-colored splinters on a towel. Again, he rinsed the cut with water and scrubbed it gently with a bar of soap. Less blood flowed down the drain.

Dr. Nieves reached for a bottle on the shelf, and without warning his patient, squirted the injury with a clear liquid. Daniel screamed. It felt as if the doctor had poured acid on his raw flesh. Circular lights flashed before his eyes, and his ears rang from the sharp stinging sensation emanating from the slit in his palm. He jerked his hand away from the doctor and cursed him once he regained his senses.

"Fucking alcohol."

"Do you want me to treat you or not?"

"This is brutality, not treatment."

"The fun is yet to begin."

The snide bastard thought he was funny. Daniel bit his lip and stared out the window to a walkway and a view below of forklifts scooping and stacking boxes of cigarettes in preparation for export. He watched colleagues involved in repetitive factory chores, reminding him of the monotony and boredom of his own job, his own life. The miserable and painful moment he had just experienced darkened his mood even further. It had been almost three years since he started working at the factory and four since his father died. Maybe he should have become a doctor like his father wanted—but not like this one, the factory witch doctor.

Daniel looked away from the window and suspiciously watched the physician, who removed some instruments and a spool from a drawer and, with one eye closed, threaded a needle. Without anesthesia or a numbing agent, the doctor gripped his hand and sutured the gash as if his skin were torn fabric, not incised human flesh. Daniel grimaced and looked away. The pain radiated around his palm so intensely that he squeezed his eyes shut, and his thoughts wandered from the cigarette factory back to his home in Las Villas when he was thirteen.

He recalled sitting on a bench gluing rubber to the sole of a shoe in the factory formerly owned by his grandfather. Fifty pairs of shoes designed and constructed by Daniel's father lined the counter in front of the young boy, who concentrated on his task. Across from Daniel sat Daniel Milan Sr. on a stool. He reviewed a drawing of a pair of women's high heels while he severed a strip of leather with a razor. Mr. Milan set the blade on the table after making a clean and precise cut. He contemplated his words before opening his mouth to speak to Daniel.

"Son, you know I appreciate your help. It advances the output."

The boy looked up after spreading a stream of contact cement on the sole of a shoe.

"And of course I enjoy your company too."

His father stood across from him and pressed his hands on the counter.

"But the main reason you are working with me after school is to experience the tiresome job of a simple cobbler. I want you to despise making shoes and aspire for more in life. You are an intelligent young man. Your grades in school prove that."

He reached over and ruffled his son's hair.

"What I'm trying to say is that I want you to study medicine in the future. Doctors are respected in Cuba. As a doctor you will make more money than a cobbler."

Before fitting the second piece of rubber onto the shoe, Daniel laid it down.

"*Papá*, your income is enough for us."

"Ah, but this is no life. The government's constantly pressuring me to produce more for their beloved tourists. If it weren't for the extra shoes I make and sell from our house after work I wouldn't make ends meet. You deserve better, my son."

Mr. Milan affectionately gripped Daniel's shoulders.

"You're only thirteen. All I'm asking is to consider a medical career so your life in Cuba will be more bearable."

Daniel finished the shoe and set it on the counter.

"I'm tired. I'm going home." He looked up at his father and cracked a weak smile. "*Papá*, I promise I'll think about it."

Daniel closed the door behind him and walked beneath a Poinciana tree in full bloom, crushing orange petals as he stepped across the sprawling lawn to their house. Darkness beckoned, and the boy saw the lamplight from the living room shine between the boards of the house, creating a misty glow in the night air. He stepped up to the cement block, imprinted with the year 1902, which led to the back door. Daniel wiped his feet on a frayed straw mat. Maybe his father was right.

The needle pierced the tip of the wound. Daniel jerked his head upward, and his brown hair swept over his eyes. The palm of his hand, numbed by pain, was red and puffy around an uneven row of black sutures.

"Done. Twenty-two stitches." Dr. Nieves snipped the remaining thread with scissors and laid it on the counter, careful not to lose the needle at the opposite end. "You weren't such a bad patient after all."

"No comment on your medical skills."

The physician ignored Daniel's remark, wrapped gauze around his hand, and taped the wound. "I have to update your supervisor. Here. Take these with some juice." He gave the patient two aspirin and reached in a cooler for a bottle of orange juice. Ice chips slipped off the bottle as he handed it to Daniel. "Relax. I'll be right back."

The juice moistened his parched mouth and quenched his thirst. Soon the weakness subsided, but his head still ached, and his hand stung. Daniel sat back, closed his eyes, and stretched his feet on top of the desk until the doctor opened the door. He slammed his feet to the floor.

"Daniel, go home. I'll examine your hand again on Monday. Rest. Don't immerse your hand in water or get it dirty. See you in five days."

Daniel rose.

"Will you be able to get home? Someone should accompany you."

"I live only four blocks away."

The doctor's eyes were fixed on Daniel's blood-stained shirt. "Do you know smoking's bad for your health?"

"What?"

The physician's eyes widened and he raised his brow.

Daniel looked down at his unbuttoned shirt. Oh God, he saw the cigarette packs. This time he was going to jail. He waited, expecting Dr. Nieves to alert the guards. He buttoned his shirt with his right hand and shrugged.

The doctor sat down, swiveled the chair around to his desk, and with his back to his patient said, "Daniel, get out of here."

Daniel raised his bandaged hand.

"Thanks, doctor."

Chapter Two
THE DISTILLERY

"What's all the commotion?" Alma Milan asked as she stood on the back porch in the early morning light. Through a window coated with dust, she watched her son rummage inside the shed located at the eastern corner of her property. With his good hand, Daniel tossed utensils out the door. Tools, pots, pans, pipes, hoses, cans, and wood scraps sailed in the air and landed one after the other on the lawn. A cast iron pot slammed the door, swinging on rusted hinges, and banged it hard against the shed wall. The pot continued to roll along the ground and clanged into a can.

The clatter enticed curious neighbors to glance up from their chores, their eyes fixed on the peculiar actions of Alma Milan's son, although Daniel's unusual escapades were never a surprise to his neighbors. Even passersby paused on the sidewalk to peer at the young man creating a racket in the quiet neighborhood.

Mrs. Milan called to her son, "*Hijo*, not the distillery."

Daniel stooped over to view the paraphernalia. He ignored her at first but finally answered, "I need a real painkiller. My hand and head are killing me. I got no sleep last night." He wiped cobwebs off a hose with a rag. "Taking the aspirin the stupid doctor gave me was useless."

Tightlipped, Alma glanced at the house next door and saw a head bob in a window and vanish. A lace curtain swayed and closed.

"You'll have the whole neighborhood over here again."

"I don't care. I can't tolerate the pain."

Mrs. Milan untied her apron and tossed it on a chair. "I'm going to Consuelo's to hem dresses. You're hurt. No *fiesta*. Did you hear me, Daniel? No party tonight."

"*Bueno, Mamá.*"

"You'd better mean yes."

A sack filled with sewing supplies dangled on her arm as she marched out the front door at the same instant that a wagon, pulled by a pair of oxen, passed the house and rolled down the street. She kept pace with the plodding beasts until she rounded a corner.

Deep in thought, Alma was unaware that her neighbor, Emilio, spied on her as she walked out the door. A straw hat concealed his small bald head, ringed with wispy gray hair. He hid in his garage and peeked at her as she reached inside her bag and slipped on her sunglasses. Once she disappeared from view, the spry old man strode up to Daniel as he selected implements necessary for his project.

"Let me help."

The sudden words startled Daniel. "I didn't realize you were there. Thanks, Emilio."

"After all, I know the process."

"That you do. I learned it from you, remember?" Awkwardly, Daniel lifted the large pot and attempted to balance it with his good hand and the elbow of his injured hand. "It's tough doing this one-handed."

"I can see that. How did you hurt yourself?"

"Cut on the metal edges of boxes in the factory."

"You should be more careful."

"Being careful didn't matter in this case."

Daniel was relieved when Emilio questioned him no further and instead he surveyed the items.

"Forget something, Daniel?"

"No."

"The most important ingredient is missing."

"Sugarcane. I didn't forget. I'm not sure I can make it out to the fields. I'm still feeling weak and dizzy."

"I'll go for you." Emilio looked at his neighbor's bandaged hand. "Sit down." He nudged Daniel to a hammock strung between two palms by a thick rope tied around the trunks with oversized knots. "*Descansa*. Rest. I'll be back soon."

Emilio yanked a burlap sack off a hook in the shed and trudged through backyards, scattering hens and chicks as he walked. He shuffled along paths to the road leading to the government sugarcane fields on the outskirts of town.

When Emilio disappeared behind a weathered barn, Daniel flopped in the center of the hammock with his injured hand raised to avoid bumping it. As the hammock swayed, he remembered the fall in the warehouse and the sensation of the downward motion he was unable to control. He closed his eyes and felt more of the same movement. How foolish he was to think cardboard boxes would support his weight. The throbbing of his hand persisted, a pain similar to the burning sensation he'd felt the instant he'd landed, helpless and bleeding at the base of the boxes.

Daniel massaged around the wound and rubbed his wrist and fingers, numbed by the tight bandage. After he loosened a strip of gauze, the hammock rocked, and he dozed to hens clucking and foraging, and to the chirping of birds nestled above in the fronds of a Bailey palm. To his relief this nap was dreamless.

"Daniel, you awake? Here's the cane."

Emilio heaved the overflowing bag on the ground next to the hammock.

"Now I'm awake." He opened his eyes to stalks of sugarcane spilling onto the grass. The chickens scattered. As Emilio removed his hat and wiped the perspiration from his forehead with his sleeve, he said, "A jeep of Policia Nacional Revolucionaria almost caught me by the roadside. I had to dive into a field and hide behind stalks. Assholes. Too busy jabbering and smoking Cohibas to see me."

"Lucky," Daniel said while stretching and yawning.

"All these years robbing cane. Those PNRs haven't caught us and never will," said Emilio as he gathered kindling. He picked up branches and dried palm fronds strewn in the yard and stacked them under logs Daniel had piled in an ash-covered pit. Emilio encircled the wood with rocks strewn near the shed. "You're right." He glanced over at Daniel. "It is luck. *Es suerte.*"

Daniel rose to help Emilio. "No peace in our poor, simple lives. Those PNRs harass the hell out of us any way they can."

"*Si,* but we always outsmart the bastards." A sly smile separated Emilio's lips. He looked at the mass of branches and nodded his head in agreement to his own statement.

"Got any matches?"

"No."

"No? Check in the house."

"I know we don't have any."

Emilio snatched newspapers from a heap in the shed and brought them into the house. In the kitchen his calloused hands tightly rolled and twisted the paper. He turned on the gas stove and dipped the wadding in the flame. Carefully he carried the newspaper torch and with his hand shielded the flame from the wind as he hurried outside.

One swoop of the torch ignited the dried kindling and palm fronds. In minutes the wood caught fire. Emilio dropped the blackened paper on the fire. He and Daniel stared at flames lapping and exhaling an intense heat in their direction. Emilio backed away from the blaze and said, "That cute girl who lives a few doors down spends a lot of time here, no?"

"What are you talking about?" Daniel filled a kettle with water drawn from a spigot and clumsily set it near the fire. He cooled the water with chunks of ice that came out of an old freezer in the shed. "Is the heat of the fire getting to you? It's not true." Cold water splashed on Daniel's pants and sent a shiver throughout his body.

"She passes by your house any chance she gets," replied Emilio as he drenched the bottom of a small pot with water, added stalks of sugarcane he had chopped in half, and sealed the lid by tightening four screws with a screwdriver. "There. An instant pressure cooker." He flung the screwdriver into an open box. "Speaking of pressure cooker, what's her name? She's got a nice butt."

Daniel reached for the longest stalk and wielded it like a sword. He jabbed at Emilio, who sucked in his stomach to avoid the slashes, leaped to the side, and grabbed a pot lid for protection. They both laughed as he shielded his chest from the advancing stalk.

"Her name's Juliana. Stop looking at her butt, you dirty old man."

"Jealous?" Emilio smiled as he dropped the lid and knelt to inspect the ends of a hose. "I can't help looking. She always walks away from me toward your house." He stood. "You like her, don't you?"

Daniel side glanced him. "Of course I like her. She's my buddy Rafael's sister."

"I mean you really like her."

"I know what you mean, and no, I don't like her in that way."

Emilio stared at Daniel with a questioning look. "Well, she seems to like you a lot." He awaited a response, but Daniel remained silent.

When the blaze subsided, Emilio set the pot on the smoldering fire. He handed a hose to Daniel, who connected it to a serpentine pipe resting across the kettle's interior. Where the pipe exited on the opposite side Daniel attached another hose and tried to fit its end over the mouth of an old milk bottle. As Emilio watched Daniel struggle with the bottle, he said, "I know Rafael. He's a good kid, but your friend Maximo's a troublemaker."

"*Sí*. Rafael watches out for me. Max, sometimes. I knew Rafa first."

"Listen to me. Maximo's no good."

"Hey, he can be a jerk, but we tolerate the guy. That's all." Daniel remembered how Max set him up for disaster when he told him to leave the loading dock early.

Emilio stepped back with his arms crossed, admiring the assembled distillery. "Tolerate, but don't trust him." He touched the hoses to make sure they aligned properly. "Nice job. Soon you will feel no pain." He grinned and exposed a gap in the back of his mouth where two teeth were missing.

Daniel's wound ached. He curled up on the hammock and napped while his neighbor tended to the backyard operation. An hour passed, and Emilio removed the hose attached to the milk bottle and set it against the kettle facing upward to prevent the loss of precious liquid. He poured the alcohol into two glasses he'd snatched from the kitchen cabinet and prodded Daniel awake.

"The first drink's for you."

Daniel sipped. "Good. But weak."

"First batch is always weak. Drink up." Emilio's eyes brightened. "Does your hand feel better?"

Daniel swallowed. "Soon it will."

They drank the homemade liquor for the remainder of the afternoon. Through blurry eyes the pair watched friends and neighbors wander into the Milan's backyard, drawn by the scent of sweet, grassy sugarcane wafting in the air and by the sound of music blaring from a radio plugged into an outlet on the porch. Dance partners soon shimmied and shook to salsa and merengue on a plywood dance floor. At the edge of the floor a barn door supported by concrete blocks displayed leftovers spared by several neighbors. Platters of pork, black beans, rice, and fried plantains emptied quickly as partygoers sat at the makeshift table and dancers gyrated and hesitated to gobble a bite of food.

Steam spewed out of the pot. Pure alcohol dribbled into the milk bottle. As couples danced, Emilio maintained the kettle full of water, the pot full of cane, and added fuel to the fire when necessary. The more Daniel drank, the less he helped Emilio with the distillery, but Emilio didn't mind because as he toiled, he sweet-talked the female dancers, chatted with his old friend, Gustavo, and gulped out of a glass he set on an oilcan.

Daniel slouched in a chair and watched as Emilio leaned against the pole used to stoke the fire. He imagined his neighbor a guard of royalty with his trusty lance. While looking at Emilio, Daniel realized the pain in his hand had subsided and his face flushed warm from the cocktails.

"*Oye*, Daniel, got a smoke?" said Gustavo.

Daniel remembered the stolen cigarettes in his duffel bag hidden under his bed. This may be a chance to earn some money.

"*Sí*. Just a minute."

He rose from the chair, and his head spun as he staggered into the house and to his room. Some of the packs in his duffel bag had been smeared with his blood during the fall in the warehouse. He carried the bag to the bathroom and wiped the packs with a damp towel, but some stains remained. Out in the dark yard they wouldn't see the red blood dried to a muted brown.

Before leaving the bathroom, Daniel splashed water on his face to sober up and tried to focus on the cloudy reflection of his unshaven face in the mirror. He turned away and sealed his eyes shut when the alcohol-induced haze caused his features to resemble his father's. When he opened his eyes, he was surprised at how bloodshot they were. As he closed his eyes again and dabbed them with a cool, wet washcloth he heard laughter coming from outside. Daniel ran a comb through his hair and shuffled through the house to the backyard, toting the satchel. Emilio's friend saw the cigarette packs he had removed from the bag as he walked toward them.

"Selling those? How much?"

"Cheap. A peso each."

"Not a bad price. Black market's higher. I'll take a pack. *Gracias, hombre.* I haven't smoked a cigarette in months." Gustavo opened the pack, shook it, and three cigarettes popped up. He offered one to Daniel, but Daniel hesitated. Emilio's friend moved the pack closer to Daniel and coaxed him by shaking the pack again. "Take it."

Daniel popped the cigarette in his mouth, knelt down, and lit it in a flame lapping at the rock border. He inhaled with his eyes closed. When he opened his eyes, his head spun, and Daniel braced himself with his good hand to keep from falling into the fire. He felt Gustavo's heavy hand on his shoulder. When the dizziness ceased, he backed away from the blaze, stood beside Gustavo, and thanked him.

Gustavo slipped the pack of cigarettes in his pocket and used Daniel's cigarette to light the one dangling between his lips. He handed it back to Daniel and watched him puff and blow smoke in wobbling rings aimed at a cluster of stars overhead. Daniel noticed a cloud hovering at the base of the moon suspended above the horizon. The cloud drifted beyond the moon, and the backyard brightened.

Emilio carried a bucket of ice from the shed and saw Gustavo and Daniel smoking by the fire. "Selling cigarettes? I'll take a pack." Emilio set the bucket down and reached for his wallet tucked in his back pocket.

Daniel threw him a pack. "On the house." Emilio caught the cigarettes.

The other partygoers smelled cigarette smoke. When they realized Daniel had packs for sale, familiar faces swarmed around him and grabbed at the bag. In the frenzy he felt like a celebrity.

"Take it easy. One at a time."

Pesos replaced the cigarette packs snatched out of his good hand. He stuffed the money in a side pocket of the bag. The sale of cigarettes happened so quickly he was unable to calculate the quantity of money he made. Daniel zipped up the bag after he sold all the packs and announced, "Sorry. No more left."

"When will you have more?"

"I don't know."

He relished the idea of making extra cash but couldn't conceive of taking a similar risk again. The thought of spending two hours trapped at the base of twenty cardboard boxes made him cringe. He decided no amount of money was worth what he'd experienced in the warehouse. Maybe he would discuss a safer way to remove cigarettes from the factory with the gang, Rafael, Maximo, Jaime, and the Rialto brothers. Daniel was determined to hold a meeting.

As he gripped the handle of the satchel, he glanced toward the porch and was shocked to see his mother standing with her hands glued to her hips. She glared at him. Daniel flung the tote over his shoulder and headed toward her, but she stormed inside as she always did when disgusted with him. Her early arrival surprised Daniel. Usually he would have had time to sober up and clean up the mess before her return from work.

Emilio handed him a drink, and he took a swig.

"*Qué enojada está tu madre.*"

Daniel nodded. "She sure is mad."

He set the glass down and carried the bag to his bedroom. Light filtered from beneath his mother's door. He hesitated at her door but decided to let her cool off before trying to reason with her. Daniel tiptoed past, and at the entrance to his room, he put the bag on the floor and gave it a push, and it glided under his bed. As he pivoted in the hallway in darkness, he stepped on a loose tile. The tile rocked and bumped against the one next to it. Daniel froze. When his mother's door creaked open, the light temporarily blinded him. He stared at the silhouette of a robed figure in the doorway.

"I wondered what that noise was," she said.

"I just went to my room for a minute."

"What is going on out there?"

"A party."

"I told you no *fiesta*."

"My hand hurt. Emilio and I made alcohol to ease the pain. The neighbors just wandered over."

"Daniel, didn't I tell you this would happen? It always does. So you become an alcoholic just to soothe an injury. Your father never would have approved of your drinking or of those drunks in his backyard. You should be ashamed."

"My father would have done something about my injury."

"What are you insinuating?" Alma opened the door wider and moved closer to him.

"Nothing."

"Are you saying I don't care? That's an insult. I told you to rest today. You knew I had to work. One income isn't enough. You know that." Her eyes swelled with tears. Then anger contorted her face. "How were you injured, anyway? Up to your old tricks with the gang? I watched you sell those filthy cigarettes. Where did you get them?"

"Like you said, we can't live on one salary. We barely get by on two."

He turned.

"Don't walk away from me."

"You know damn well where those cigarettes came from."

Daniel headed back to the party. Why can't she admit her son's a thief? She couldn't admit it because she'd raised this thief. He reached for the glass he had left on the table and took a big gulp of alcohol. As he stepped down from the porch he caught sight of

Rafael approaching from the side of the house. Juliana appeared out of the darkness and into the moonlight beside her brother. Daniel stopped mid-step. The anger at his mother released at that instant. He saw Juli balk at the sight of the crowd and hover close to Rafael. She followed her brother and gracefully advanced across the lawn, her path lit by moonbeams. Her flowing chestnut hair shone in the light. Despite all the people surrounding them, for an instant Daniel was only aware of Juliana. As they neared, Daniel lowered the glass to his side and concentrated hard on maintaining his composure.

"How's your hand?" said Rafael.

"Better now. *Hola*, Juli."

She leaned forward and touched his cheek with hers. "I was sorry to hear of your accident." She looked at his bandaged hand.

"She wanted to see how you were feeling," Rafael said as he winked at Daniel. Juliana blushed. Rafael sensed her uneasiness and changed the subject. "Sorry those boxes in the warehouse didn't support you. I thought they were strong enough."

"So did I. I'll survive. What's happening at the factory?"

"The guards are watching every move we make, so we're staying clean for the time being. Everyone has their own version of what happened to you. We stay quiet and let them talk."

"Is there anything you need?" Juli asked Daniel, avoiding his eyes as she glanced at the dancers.

"Not really. They're taking good care of me," he said, careful to enunciate each word and avoid slurring his speech. His eyes followed her gaze. She seemed nervous.

Juliana spotted a former classmate near the table, shaking to the beat of the music.

"*Hola*, Eva," she called to her friend and tapped her brother's side. "You boys talk. I know you have a lot to say."

Daniel watched her long hair sway as she joined the other girl.

"I hinted to her that we had things to discuss. Don't worry, lover boy. She'll be back. She's been looking for an excuse to see you."

"She has? And you actually let her come?"

"I've kept you two apart as long as I could. She really likes you."

"So now I'm good enough for your sister. What changed?"

"Nobody's good enough for Juli. I'm just not going to get in the way anymore."

"Hey, I'm really not a bad guy."

"I never said you were. It's just that you've been around, and she's very innocent. She's my little sister."

"Been around? I've had a few girlfriends."

"*Sí*, and you broke their hearts."

"I'm tired of discussing this. I told you I'm not the playboy you think I am."

Daniel glanced over at Juliana, who was deep in conversation with Eva. "I respect her."

"You better."

Beyond the girls Daniel saw Gustavo take a drag on a cigarette.

"Listen, just before you got here I sold all the cigarettes I carried out of the factory. I never had such demand before. Selling at this party was better than selling on the street. Emilio's friend said it's hard to get cigarettes on the black market these days. The price has gone way up."

"You got cigarettes out? They stayed inside your baseball socks?"

"And inside my shirt, but the doctor saw them. My shirt unbuttoned while I was in his office."

"Nieves saw the cigarettes?"

"That's what I said."

"And didn't call the guards?"

"No. He sent me home."

"Without saying anything?"

"He told me smoking's bad for my health." Daniel snickered.

"You lucky bastard. That doctor's decent."

"I'm not so sure he's decent, but he didn't turn me in."

"Amazing. When can you go back to work?"

"Monday. I'm trying to tell you I just made sixty-plus pesos tonight. A month's worth of work in the factory. These people were crazy to buy cigarettes. *Te digo que son locos por los cigarillos.*"

"Sixty? You did all right. How did you get that many out without anyone seeing?"

Rafael hoisted himself up on the porch.

"Sixty-plus. Stuffed in my clothes. I gave Emilio a pack for free since he helped me with the distillery. I was thinking of devising a better way to get even more out."

Rafael noticed Daniel's unsteadiness and helped him as he awkwardly sat.

"Are you all right?"

"I've been drinking all day. A little drunk, but feeling no pain." He raised his bandaged hand.

Rafael laughed and then became serious. "Aren't you worried Javier might change his mind and turn you in?"

"He had his chance and decided against getting me in trouble. The doctor's a quack, not a rat."

"I heard he's a good doctor but lacks medical supplies to properly do his job."

"Whatever he is, don't go to him. The pain he caused me was unbearable."

"Well, I just hope he doesn't tell the authorities on you, or there will be agony added to the pain."

"Just help me figure out a way to steal more cigarettes. We'll be rich and get the hell out of the factory and out of Cuba."

"Eventually we'll have a meeting. As it stands we're lying low. Guards watch us like hawks." Rafael looked up. "Here comes Juli. She couldn't stay away from you for long." He elbowed Daniel.

"I can't believe you're actually letting me talk to your sister." Daniel pushed his glass of liquor behind him and grinned at the approaching girl.

"I may regret it one day."

Juliana reached the porch. "It was good to see Eva again. I haven't seen her since she left for Moscow. Can you imagine? She speaks Russian."

"She's been gone a few years. She should have learned something." Rafael eyed Daniel's hidden glass and pointed at it. "Where are the drinks?" He leaned over and whispered in Daniel's ear, "Be good to her. I'm watching you."

"Rum's on the table." Daniel gestured toward the center of the lawn while frowning at his friend. "Emilio's cooking up more alcohol. But it may take a while." He glanced over at Emilio, who added a log to the fire, but his mind was on the girl standing before him.

Rafael caught sight of the empty milk bottle, sprung off the porch, strode to the table, and poured amber-colored rum over ice in a glass. The ice clinked as he walked. He struck up a conversation with Emilio and Gustavo. Out of the shadows emerged a figure. Maximo sauntered up to Rafael. Emilio took one look at Max, handed his stoking stick to Gustavo, and marched away with a sour look on his face.

Gustavo hollered to Emilio, "Where are you going?" He held up the stick. "What do I do with this?"

"Stoke the fucking fire, you old bastard."

Daniel faced Juliana and stared for a few seconds. Copper highlights glistened in her hair and glowed in the golden firelight. He inhaled her floral-scented perfume and wished Rafael had stayed. He knew his best friend had surrendered on purpose.

Daniel recalled endless conversations about his fascination with Juliana during the three years of their friendship. Each discussion terminated abruptly when her protective brother prohibited their meeting, and Daniel always walked away frustrated by Rafael's stubbornness.

"Would you like a drink?" he finally asked, unsure of whether Juli drank alcohol or not.

"Not now, thank you. Maybe later." She touched his arm. "I was worried about you, Daniel. Rafa told me how you hurt yourself."

Her voice chimed like a string of bells gently ringing in a breeze. He was mesmerized by the sound and the way her plump lips defined her words.

"He did?" Daniel said. He was under the impression that any factory antics remained a secret among the ones involved and was surprised that Rafael had divulged this information to his sister. He was also embarrassed that Juli knew the details of the fall.

She explained, "My brother tells me everything. We're very close."

"Everything?"

She noted concern on his face. "Not to worry. Rafa's personal matters stay with me. Are you afraid I will betray you?"

"No. I trust you. And I trust your brother with my life."

"I hope you can trust me with your life someday. I would never say anything to harm either of you."

"I know. I'm confident in Rafael's judgment. As I said, I trust both of you." Daniel was relieved she'd clarified her loyalty.

"Here. I brought you these. Maybe they will help." Juliana reached in the macramé purse hanging by a strap across her shoulder and removed a small jar containing oblong white pills. "They're painkillers. A nurse felt sorry for me and slipped them to my father at the clinic when I fractured my ankle. These were left over."

"Thanks. Rafael had told me you hurt your ankle, but I didn't know you broke it."

"Just a hairline fracture. I was dancing and fell off the stage."

"I was sorry to hear that," he said as he lowered himself from the porch.

He'd known of her fall and had brought her flowers, but Rafael had left Daniel standing at the front door and insisted on taking them to Juli himself. When the door closed in Daniel's face, he'd decided to give up and had stopped questioning Rafael's motive to isolate him from Juli. Daniel was sure she'd never received the bouquet.

"I'm sorry I didn't thank you for the flowers. I was going through a very difficult time."

It was like she'd read his mind. "That's all right. I knew you hurt yourself. A difficult time?" So Rafael did give her the flowers.

"It was more than that." She avoided the subject and handed him the bottle. "These are for you."

Daniel reached for the vessel and watched her hand release the object. Her manicured fingernails, and fingers were like those of the statue of a Greek goddess, chiseled to perfection. He felt her soft skin as his hand glided over hers. The pills rattled inside, and he squeezed the bottle.

"*Gracias,* Juli." He set the bottle on the porch. "Thank you so much."

Daniel raised her hand, leaned forward, and delicately brushed the top of her hand with his lips. "You're an angel." He bowed. "Would you like to dance?"

Rafael immediately noticed Maximo's expression of anger and said, "When did you get here?"

"Just a few minutes ago."

"What's wrong?"

Max pointed toward the dance floor where dancers stomped across plywood sections, shook their shoulders, stepped in rhythm, danced, and twirled to the beat of blasting salsa music. "Them."

"The dancers?" Rafael was confused. "The noise?"

"No." Max hesitated before admitting the reason he was perturbed. "Daniel and your sister."

Rafael paused before he sipped from his glass of rum and looked at him, baffled by his statement. "They finally hooked up."

"Since when?"

"Since this evening." Rafael saw his sister and Daniel grinning and eying each other's dance moves as if they were the only ones on the floor. Daniel raised his bandaged hand and spun Juliana around with his good hand.

Maximo was silent.

"Do you have a problem with that?" Rafael gestured with his glass toward the dance partners.

"No. No, I don't." But Max could not conceal his flushed cheeks and anguish in the firelight. "I've got to go. I shouldn't have come anyway."

Rafael stared at Max as he garbled his words, sentences faded as if a mechanism in his brain ran out of fuel and slowly came to a halt.

"I heard the music from the street." Max pivoted.

"Wait. Don't tell me." Rafael caught up to Max. "You like Juli too?"

Max shook his head. "No. No," he uttered, wanting to believe himself. Then he nodded. "I love her."

The impromptu party was winding down. Attendees gathered their empty bowls and platters and drifted home. Dancing had sobered Daniel up, and when he and Juliana discovered Rafael was nowhere to be found, Daniel offered to walk her home.

"You don't have to walk me. I live so close."

"I don't mind."

"I have no idea where Rafa went."

"He never mentioned leaving," Daniel said. He held her elbow as they crossed the uneven ground to the sidewalk.

"He's probably helping someone. You know my brother, the peacemaker."

"At the factory we call him the Diplomat. He's gotten me and so many others out of serious problems."

"My parents dubbed him the Negotiator." She smiled. "It's not like him to just leave and not say anything."

"I'm sure he'll explain." Daniel noticed a slight limp to her step. "Is your foot all right?"

"Oh, it's fine. Occasionally my ankle bothers me."

"Do you want to rest for a moment?"

"No. Dancing makes it sore, but it doesn't matter. I love to dance."

"Here's your house. Maybe we can get together again soon. I had a great time tonight."

"I would like that. So did I."

Daniel watched as she slid the key in the lock. "Maybe you should put ice on your foot."

"Thanks. I will." Juli waved to him before entering.

Daniel returned to his backyard. Everyone had gone. He grabbed a plastic bag out of the shed and filled it with cups smelling of rum, wine, and beer; napkins and paper plates coated with a film of black beans and cigarette butts. While rinsing glasses and flatware with a hose, he wondered what had happened to Rafael. After he and Juliana danced, he'd lost track of him. Daniel was curious to know if he had left the party with one of the girls.

Daniel set a plate and some utensils on the porch so the neighbors could collect their forgotten wares in the morning and finished his after-party chores by raising the sheets of plywood off the ground. Awkwardly he carried the wood sections to the back of the shed and leaned them against the wall. For a moment he hesitated, thinking of the fun he'd had dancing with Juli. When Daniel pictured her straight nose and pout as she reeled to the music, he felt a tingling sensation.

After recalling the details of his time spent with Juliana, he realized his wound hurt again. He scooped the bottle of pills off the porch, flipped open the top, and spilled the capsules into the palm of his bandaged hand. Daniel popped one in his mouth, swallowed, and chased it with the watered-down rum left in the glass beside the bottle. He'd sleep like a baby tonight, thanks to Juli.

Chapter Three
JULI'S BUTTERFLY

Daniel awoke at noon and reached under the bed for his duffel bag. He turned the bag upside down, and pesos fluttered onto the sheets. He counted sixty-six bills, a record heist. If only time had allowed him to stuff more packs inside his clothing while in the warehouse. He wondered if there would be a next time. Daniel slipped some pesos into the fold of his wallet and tucked the rest under a tile in his closet.

Juliana's medication allowed him a sound, painless slumber and a bonus of eliminating a morning hangover. But the effects soon wore off, and his wound ached. To forget his throbbing hand, he entered the kitchen to heat a small pot of espresso that his mother had left tilted on the edge of a burner. He centered the *cafetera* on the burner, and while lighting the stove, noticed a note on the counter written in his mother's script.

Briefly Alma stated that Consuelo, her partner in the alterations business, had a job for them to hem curtains at Las Tecas Hotel on the outskirts of town. Daniel sensed a distance in her words, not only because of the curt message but because she eliminated her usual Love, *Mamá* at the end of the note. His intentions had not been to upset his mother last night. He knew her work at a hotel meant she would be out late into the night for the next few days, which would delay the difficult task of having to explain and to defend himself.

Daniel opened the refrigerator door. Hunger pangs gnawed at his stomach. On the shelf next to a covered butter dish was a plastic bowl with onions and a boiled potato. He pushed the bowl aside to see if there was fruit hidden behind it. No fruit for breakfast. He knew there was no bread, cereal, or eggs either.

The lid to the coffee pot clanged as it percolated on the burner. The brown liquid boiled, bubbled, and seeped out of the small pot like a tiny erupting volcano, overflowing onto the enamel stovetop. With a rag Daniel wiped the coffee, and with each swipe the white cloth turned a deep umber color. He allowed the hot coffee to calm and then poured the liquid into a demitasse cup. He stared outside at the backyard.

Daniel thought of Juliana's smile as she danced with him last night and focused on the grass where they had stood together. He questioned whether to involve himself in a steady relationship. The weight of uncertainty at work fostered a doubt to entangle her in the web of his life's complications.

The hammock rocked in a breeze between the two palms. For now he would allow fate to take its course. After all, it was a miracle that Rafael was the catalyst in uniting them. Daniel could not deny that he cared for Juli and had for three years. Obviously she was also interested in him. He decided to move forward and see where their feelings would take them.

As thoughts of the previous night and Juliana faded and the yard came back into focus, he realized the distillery had remained untouched. Coals smoldered in the center of the pit. He had forgotten to extinguish the fire while cleaning up last night. In the grass near the rock border, a burlap sack covered a sheaf of sugarcane stalks Emilio and Gustavo had retrieved during a midnight run to the fields after boiling down all the cane.

Daniel sipped the bitter coffee mellowed by a spoonful of sugar and envisioned the comical sight of the two drunks staggering through fields, chattering about politics and chopping stalks in the moonlight.

He licked the coffee off his lips and set down the cup. He walked outside and fed wood to faint embers, rendering the distilling process again. Pleased with how successfully the liquor had eased his pain yesterday, he anxiously awaited relief from the soreness pulsating in the palm of his hand. Vapors condensed into a soothing liquid he consumed along with his coffee as a poor substitute for breakfast.

Intoxicated by two o'clock, Daniel retreated to the hammock. He watched palm fronds sway above in the breeze and was filled with contentment in the quiet afternoon. He had plucked eucalyptus leaves and sprinkled handfuls on the fire to mask the scent of sugarcane. He had no intentions of angering his mother a second time with another party. Curious neighbors associated the scent of eucalyptus with the treatment of respiratory ailments and stayed away. Even Emilio roamed elsewhere.

Daniel savored the tranquility, and his thoughts wandered to the money hidden beneath the tile in his room and how he would spend it. Any purchases would have to be made in small quantities to avoid suspicion. Most importantly, he would stock up on food and fill their empty refrigerator. The thought of sustenance enticed his stomach to a growl, and he rubbed it. After the purchase of groceries, Daniel would take his mother shopping for new clothes. Future thefts and sales of cigarettes would allow him to buy a motorcycle and eventually a car. A strong desire to spend the money engulfed him, and as thoughts about other purchases came to mind, someone crept up behind him. Small, floral-scented hands covered his eyes.

"Guess who."

The voice, as soft as the breeze brushing his cheek, caught him off guard. "The person I want you to be is supposedly working."

He heard Juliana giggle. "Maybe that person felt more needed here than at work." She lifted her hands.

Daniel opened his eyes. "I had hoped I would see you today." He gazed into her hazel eyes, reflecting her joy at seeing him.

She circled the hammock and stood before him. "How is your hand?" When Juliana noticed the steaming distillery and the glass of alcohol under the hammock, she said, "Why didn't you take the pills I gave you?"

"I did, last night. I'm saving them for sleeping."

"I'm sorry there weren't very many."

"There were enough. I slept like a baby. My hand was pain free until I woke up this morning. Have a seat." He patted the woven rope, and she carefully sat facing the yard. The hammock swung, and she pointed to a butterfly flitting over the grass and onto a hibiscus leaf.

"I love butterflies. How pretty and graceful they are." Juli turned to Daniel and suddenly changed the subject. "Rafa told me you and your mother moved to Ranchuelo several years ago."

"Almost four years. We lived in Las Villas on a small farm out in the country."

"Where is your father?"

Daniel watched the butterfly. "He passed away when I was eighteen. My mother couldn't stand the memories, so we came here."

"I'm so sorry. I thought your parents were divorced. Rafa never told me about your father. May I ask how he died?"

"Cardiac arrest."

"Very sudden."

Daniel nodded. "I began my first job as a geography teacher at the elementary school on a Monday, and on Thursday he died."

"I'm sorry."

"Thanks." He reached for the glass and gulped down the liquor. "He wanted me to be a doctor." Daniel's eyes misted. He turned away from Juliana as if to watch the monarch skirt from branch to leaf, blinking away the blurriness. "Although he never told me, I know he was disappointed I became a teacher."

Her eyes also followed the insect while listening intently. "I doubt—"

"I often wonder whether my choice to be a teacher contributed to his passing."

"Why would you think that?"

As if he hadn't heard her question, Daniel said, "Or whether the government pushed him to an early death."

"In what way?"

"He was a shoemaker and designed women's shoes. The styles he created were popular among tourists, to the government's delight. Government representatives gave my father impossible deadlines to meet. He often stayed up an entire night to finish a pair of shoes just to please them. Then he worked the following day, exhausted."

"Certainly your father didn't die because of your career choice."

"Well, I'm not certain of anything. After he died I resented my career choice, and I despise the government."

"How long did you teach?"

"Eight months. I liked teaching, but we moved here, and there were no positions available in the school."

"So now you work in a cigarette factory."

"Don't remind me. I should have listened to my father and studied medicine. Maybe he would be alive today."

"Daniel, stop torturing yourself. It was his fate. No one's to blame." She touched his arm. "You could still be a doctor."

"That's what everyone says, but I have no time." He jumped off the hammock, causing it to sway. Juliana rocked in the bed of interlocking cords and watched him squat by the milk bottle. As he filled his glass, he felt inadequate and unworthy of Juliana. To mask this sadness, Daniel became comical and reached for a short, stubby stick on the ground. Then he stood and turned toward her.

He slipped the stick in his mouth, puffed on it like a cigar, and rubbed his chin as if stroking a beard. "Daniel and Fidel, the two evil Cubans."

He tossed the stick on the grass and walked back to her. As she laughed, he tapped her knee with his good hand. "Maybe you shouldn't get involved with a guy whose life is so messed up. You're too nice. You deserve better."

Juliana touched his cheek. "In you I see a kind, humorous young man who is doing the best he can under very trying circumstances. Let me be the judge of whom I become involved with, *señor.* Besides, I enjoy your company." She pointed to the butterfly. "Concentrate on the beautiful things in life, and your problems will disintegrate."

"I am." Daniel smiled and gazed into her eyes. "I'm looking at you. At this moment I have no problems."

Juliana looked away from the insect and studied the warmth in his eyes. He leaned forward. She closed her eyes, and his lips met hers. While holding the glass, he hugged her waist and pulled her closer to him. With arms around his neck, she clung tightly as the kiss deepened. Then she eased back, opened her eyes, and cast them downward, blushing.

He stroked her chin and raised her face. "I'm sorry. I got carried away."

"Don't be sorry. It was nice."

"You liked it?"

"Sí. *Me gustó.*"

Daniel tried to kiss her again, but she gently pushed him away. The hammock swung backward and returned in front of him. Their faces practically touched again. He puckered his lips.

"We'd better wait. What will your mother think?" Juli looked toward the house and grabbed hold of his arm to steady the hammock. "Let's continue our conversation."

"But you liked my kiss. My mother's not here."

"I want to know more about you."

Daniel sighed. "If you insist." He climbed back on the hammock, and liquid spilled out of his glass. He wiped the rope with his hand and offered Juliana a sip. She nodded, and he held the glass to her mouth as she drank. She wrinkled her nose. "Strong stuff."

"Pure alcohol." He took a swig while looking at her. "You know, I like being with you too. I'm afraid if I tell you more about me, your feelings toward me may change."

"I don't think so. From what Rafa has told me, I feel I already know you."

"Oh no. What did he say?" He knew Rafael had tried for years to discourage them from getting together.

Juliana laughed. "Nothing bad, really." Her tone became serious. "I've thought about you ever since you had dinner at our house. The time you came home with Rafa. My parents liked you too."

"I liked you before that dinner. Long before. I asked Rafael to tell you, but he ignored me."

"I never knew. I thought I liked you first. How mean of my brother."

"Don't get mad. He was only trying to protect you."

"From his best friend?"

"He had his reasons. I didn't agree but..."

"I wish you had persisted."

"To be honest, I did until one day he told me point blank to stay away from you. Rather than destroy our friendship, I did what he asked."

"That was terrible of him to interfere in our lives."

"I thought so too. I remember that dinner in May. In fact, you wore this dress." Daniel touched the material.

"I wore it today to see if you would recall. What else do you remember?" She leaned closer to him.

"Is this a test? The clips in your hair matched your blue dress."

"Blue flowers with tiny butterflies. And?"

"Butterflies? Why aren't you wearing them today?"

"I lost one."

"You didn't say much that evening. Your father did most of the talking."

"He usually does. My father, the patriarch. I was nervous. I didn't know what to say."

"Are you nervous now?"

"No, silly. It's easier now. We're alone. We can say anything we like, and no one else is listening."

"We've seen each other only a few times since that evening, but you always seemed preoccupied with something else. Like last night, I expected you to stay with your friend, Eva."

"I used to get nervous and tongue tied when I saw you. Now is different. Maybe I'm maturing. Last night I told Eva I wanted to be with you."

"You did?"

"I did."

"Tell me more about you."

"Let me see. Well, I love dancing and music. Going to the movies, puppies, butterflies." Juli glanced at the lawn. "Ice cream," she giggled. "And walking in the park."

"We've already done some of what you like. We danced last night. And today I performed magic and made that butterfly appear for you."

"Oh, you did not." She pushed him and laughed.

"I didn't tell you I'm a magician?" Daniel laughed. "Seriously, thanks for spending time with me. You really cheer me up."

"You don't have to thank me. I want to be here."

"What about the store?"

"*Señora* Estevez doesn't mind if I miss a day or two of work as long as I tell her beforehand."

"You're lucky you have an understanding boss. Mine's a tyrant."

"Why don't you look for another job?"

"I'd like to, but it would upset my mother. My first job in Ranchuelo was in the sugar refinery, unlocking railroad cars from engines. I had to lift a hook attached to a metal rope out of a hitch and pull the cars along the track to a slanting platform."

"My father took us there when we were little. I remember seeing the sugarcane drop a kilometer down to a conveyor belt."

"Not a kilometer. Maybe two stories."

"From a child's point of view it seemed that far. The belt takes the cane into the refinery and processes it into sugar."

"Syrup. Then sugar."

"At least I learned something."

"You did. Well, my mother worried herself sick I would be crushed by a train or fall off the platform. She couldn't bear the thought of losing me after the loss of my father."

"I can see her point. If I were your mother I'd get you out of there too."

"She did. One evening she visited an old friend of my father, Angel, a mechanic on the evening shift at Ramiro La Vandero and asked him to get me a job at the factory. He said he'd do anything for my father's family. The next day I was hired as a dock worker, and Rafael was the first guy I met." Daniel yawned. "Excuse me," he said and continued, "My mother believes that compared to the refinery, the factory is a safe place to work. Besides, we need the money. She has no idea of the abuse that goes on in the factory. If she only knew."

"You could explain it to her."

"I don't want her to worry."

"Rafa told me it's best to just do your job, say as little as possible, and mind your own business."

"He's right, but it's difficult."

"Things have to get better. I will pray every night for you."

"Help from above is always appreciated."

"I worry you boys will get caught taking cigarettes out of the factory. Be careful."

"We are. The extra money's how we survive."

"Still, you are risking your lives."

"I know." Daniel tried to conceal another yawn with the back of his hand. "Juli, do you mind if I take a *siesta*? I'm still feeling weak."

"Not at all. I'll rest with you for a while."

Side by side they lay in the hammock. He slept, and she dozed until she was awakened by the whistle of a train on its way to the sugar mill. Slowly she swung her legs around and slid off the hammock while holding it steady. As Juliana crossed the lawn, she searched for the butterfly, but it had flown elsewhere. "The lovely creatures never stay around for long," she whispered. On her way home she decided the next visit she would bake pastries for Daniel.

"Juli, where have you been? I've been looking for you," Rafael said as he bolted out of the house.

"Where have I been? Where did you go last night? I was at Daniel's. What's the matter?"

"We have to talk."

"About what?"

They sat on chairs facing each other at the entrance to their house.

"I spoke to Maximo last night at the party and he was distraught about you dancing with Daniel. I went with him to his father's auto body shop to have a beer and talk. I've never seen him so furious. He's upset at Daniel for being with you. I'm afraid of what he's capable of doing. I had no idea you and Max were seeing each other. I would never have taken you to Daniel's."

"I'm not seeing Max. What gave you that impression? I would have told you."

"He made it sound like you two had gone out."

"Why would he think that?" She became pensive. "One day he stopped by. You were out. He was depressed about how badly his father had treated him in front of a customer at the garage. I only listened to his troubles. We went for a walk so our parents wouldn't hear what he was telling me. That's all. Another time he stopped by to see you, but you and Daniel had gone somewhere. Max and I went to a movie. He was going to ask you to go. Nothing serious. I've only hung out with him when he came to see you and you weren't home. I did nothing to make him believe I liked him. We were together as friends. This is crazy. What will he do to Daniel?"

"I have no idea, but the more he drank the angrier he got. Max was insane with jealousy. He must have misunderstood your feelings toward him."

"Obviously. I never saw him at Daniel's party."

"He came from the back, and when he saw you two together he took me aside and confessed his feelings. He thought you felt the same. When you and Daniel danced, he was visibly upset and asked me to leave the party. Max needed to talk. His father had beer in the refrigerator at the garage. We were supposed to go there first and then to a bar, but we never left the body shop. He kept talking about how much he loved you. When he threatened to get even with Daniel, I told him to cool down, and I left. I got home at two this morning. Emilio saw him at the party too and didn't like the idea Max was there."

"I can't believe this! That idiot had better not ruin my relationship with Daniel. And it's only beginning."

"Maybe Daniel was right. We can't trust Max," Rafael whispered his thoughts.

"Daniel said that he couldn't trust Max?"

"Actually, Emilio told him to be careful of Max."

"Such complications. My concern is Daniel. Now what do I do?"

"I have to warn him."

"He's at home sleeping in the backyard. Maybe I should go too."

"No. Stay here. I'll explain this to him."

"If you say so. Rafa, be sure to tell him I have no feelings for Maximo."

"I will."

"*Hombre*, you're always drunk or sleeping these days."

"What do you expect? Alcohol numbs the pain in my hand and in turn makes me tired." Daniel climbed out of the hammock. "Juli was here."

"I know. I just saw her at home. Listen. I have to tell you about Max."

"What about him?"

"Juli."

"Juli? What are you trying to say?"

"He has a serious crush on her."

"On Juliana? When did that start? He never said anything."

"He's liked her for a while. He just told me last night at your party."

"Max wasn't at the party."

"Daniel, you were drunk. He was there."

"Give me a break. I was high, but I know who was at my house."

"Max didn't approach you because he saw you dancing with Juli. We went to his father's body shop. He poured his heart out about how much he loved her. I thought he was going to cry when he saw you two dancing. He threatened to kill you. I was shocked. He'd never mentioned her name to me before last night."

Daniel was stunned at Rafael's words. "So that's where you went last night. Go on. What else?"

"Juli swears she only talked to him when he came to see me, months ago, the time you and I went fishing. I wasn't home, so he invited her to a movie. She said for her it was like going out with a friend. After the movie she listened to Max's problems. He considered their time together a date. She only felt sorry for him."

"How sorry was she?" Daniel asked bitterly.

"Come on, man. Nothing happened. Don't doubt my sister. It's you she likes."

Rafael outstretched his arms. "I'm only trying to tell you to beware of Max. Stay away from him until he cools down. You and Juli can keep seeing each other. Just be careful."

"Hey, I'm bound to run into Max at some point. I'll straighten him out."

"You'll straighten who out? Look at you." Rafael grazed Daniel's bandaged hand with his.

"I'm recovering."

"Don't lose your cool. Let that hand heal. I wonder what will happen to our gang."

"Maximo has the problem, not me. Why should this involve what we do at the factory?"

"It may. He has a temper. And he's friends with Ricardo and Roberto. The Rialto brothers will side with him if anything happens. Jaime too."

"Let them. Then you and I will work alone."

"We need lookouts. Two can't take cigarettes out alone."

"We have to have a meeting."

"Call a meeting now? What timing."

"We used to have meetings once a month. When was the last? At least two months ago. A meeting will determine once and for all where we stand. We have to discuss the next heist."

"Discuss the next heist? Are you crazy? Remember, Maximo will be there, the jerk who wants to kill you, and the guards are waiting for you to mess up. That alcohol's fucking your mind."

Daniel kicked the kettle off the smoldering fire and stomped out the small flames. With his good hand, he tossed rocks from the circle surrounding the pit onto the glowing coals in the center. Each landed with a thump. Ash and sparks swirled in the air, settled, and extinguished in the dirt.

"Daniel, come on," pleaded Rafael. "Calm down. Control yourself."

"There's no more to say. See you at work." He stormed in the back door and slammed it hard enough to shake the porch. Rafael stared at his friend's reaction in disbelief and heard Daniel's voice coming from an open window.

"Arrange a meeting, Rafael. The usual place. The church."

Chapter Four
THE NIGHT SHIFT

On Monday morning a hangover lingered, but the pain in Daniel's hand had subsided. Juliana's painkillers were gone, but he didn't need them anymore. As Daniel walked to the factory, he thought about the conversation with Rafael regarding Max's affection for Juli. Rafael's words had taken him by surprise. At first he'd concluded that she had deceived him. But after Rafa convinced Daniel otherwise, and explained how Max mistook her concern for deeper feelings, Daniel was shocked when unexpected feelings of jealousy surfaced. He realized how important Juliana was to him.

Maybe he should have reined in his anger when he lost his temper at the end of the conversation with his best friend, but he'd been hungry and had woken up from the nap in a bad mood, and Rafael's news magnified all the difficulties in his life.

Daniel picked up his pace to arrive at the factory on time and pondered his problems. He dreaded returning to work and knew El Jefe loathed him and expected him to slip up. The pressure at the factory would intensify.

He passed several homes on his way to work. One house had a crumbling barrel tile roof and ceramic pots with aloe and fragrant herbs tilting haphazardly on a cement front porch. A row of banana trees hugged a fence enclosing the yard. Mature bananas peeked in yellow clusters from behind abundant leaves. Apprehension consumed Daniel as he looked around to make sure no one watched him bend down, reach between the railings, and pluck a banana. Pangs of hunger caused his stomach to churn when he inhaled the scent of the fruit concealed by his hand. He slipped it into his pocket and hurried toward the factory.

Daniel approached security on the loading dock at the factory rear entrance and saw Pothole scribble notes in a logbook inside the dispatch office. He bounded up the steps, reached for his timecard on a rack, and was about to clock in when Pothole caught sight of him and stepped out of the office. The sergeant blocked Daniel's passage.

"*Oye*, Milan, report to your supervisor immediately."

"What for?"

"His orders. Wise guy."

Daniel raised his eyes to the sky. Here it came. Everything was always taken out of context. "I'm only asking why." He stared at Pothole.

"Don't ask questions. Just do as you are told."

Daniel tried to maneuver around the sergeant, but he stiffened his fist in the direction Daniel stepped.

"You'll get what's coming to you," snarled Pothole.

"What are you talking about? I'm only trying to go to work. To do my job."

Daniel pushed the tightened fist aside and proceeded through the door. Curious dockworkers ceased their conversations, expecting an altercation to ensue.

"What job?" Pothole roared with laughter and spit at Daniel's heels. A swell of bubbling saliva left a wet stain on the cement. Daniel ignored him and headed for his boss's office. Rafael rushed to intercept Daniel.

"Maximo took a sick day today. Guess he's afraid to face you."

"I have worse problems than Max right now. Did you hear? El Jefe wants to see me. Pothole just made a scene when I tried to punch in and insinuated I didn't have a job. Rafa, I think they're going to fire me."

"On what grounds? You don't know for sure."

Daniel looked through a window at Pothole, who sliced the air with his hand like a hatchet aimed at him.

"You son of a bitch," Daniel said through his closed mouth, projecting the words like a ventriloquist. "Maybe the doctor turned me in after all." He focused on Rafael. "Damn, I need this job even though I hate it."

"Don't guess. Go find out. You'll go crazy trying to figure out what these devils have up their sleeves."

"Here comes Pothole. Meet you in the park during break if they don't fire my ass."

"Good luck."

Daniel formed a fist and wanted to pound the door but knocked instead. From inside he heard the supervisor say, "*Adelante.*"

He entered.

"*Siéntate*," said his stern-faced boss.

Daniel sat in a chair opposite the cluttered desk and eyed El Jefe as he paced.

"We're sick and tired of you and your friends—the jokes, sneaking around, and God knows what else you do. One of you entered the warehouse the other day. Unfortunately, we were unable to prove it." He halted, slammed both hands on the desk, and leaned forward. "With no evidence we're stuck with you. Our only solution is to move you to the night shift to work as the mechanic's assistant and separate you from your *compañeros*. What do you think of that?"

"I don't care. Do whatever the fuck you want."

The supervisor's arm retracted, shot forward, and landed square on Daniel's jaw. Daniel reacted by pulling back. With the combined force of leaning back and the unblocked punch, the chair fell over, and Daniel tumbled to the floor, clutching his bandaged hand against his chest. Blood oozed from his lip.

"Show some respect, you little bastard. Apologize or march out that door." He thrust his arm forward, pointing to the exit.

Daniel opened his eyes from where he landed and looked up at a shelf. In a daze he stared at an enlarged photograph of Fidel Castro standing behind a podium at Plaza de la Revolución. Daniel remembered being transported to that rally by bus and forced to attend the dictator's speech on a hot day in July.

The stinging of his lip reminded him of the present and the infuriated figure standing over him.

"*Lo siento*," muttered Daniel.

"*Qué? No te oigo.* I can't hear you. You purr like a kitten." The boss kicked the chair to the side. "Repeat, little pussy."

"I'm sorry."

"When are you going to learn respect for your superiors? I'll have the night mechanic work the crap out of you and drive you out of this place once and for all."

El Jefe circled the chair, picked it up, and hurled it over Daniel's head. The boss pulled Daniel up by his shirt and shoved him in the direction of the door. Daniel grabbed the knob, flung the door open, and scrambled outside. He felt El Jefe's stare sear his back until the door slammed shut behind him.

Daniel touched his tender, swollen lip. Thoughts of last week's abuse and the mistreatment he'd just experienced ushered him toward the factory exit. A beating was more than he could tolerate of any place. His hand covered the sheath containing his knife, and with his fingers followed the curve of the steel tucked inside the leather case. No one was around. What if he were to use the knife on El Jefe?

Daniel reeled and gazed at the door he had just exited. The image of his mother appeared before him. Imagine her disappointment if he were to quit his job—or worse yet, if he were to murder El Jefe. Either choice would render her life miserable. His senses returned. Before reaching the exit, he veered right and scooped up his hand truck in the storage room. For the second time in a week, blood soiled his clean handkerchief. Daniel folded the blood-blotched linen and tucked it in his pocket. Although angered by his decision, he resumed work on the loading dock.

"I have no choice. Tomorrow night I train as a mechanic on the night shift," Daniel informed a fellow employee as the bitter flavor of revenge coated his throat.

Daniel sat down, leaned against a tree trunk, and glanced up at Rafael, who was lying on a bench. He peeled the banana that had been in his pocket.

"What happened?" asked Rafa.

"El Jefe moved me to the night shift." He bit into the fruit. "To work with the mechanic." Chewing was awkward with his swollen lip.

"They desperately need people on the night shift. At least you still have a job. So the doctor didn't squeal on you."

"No. He didn't."

Three women chatted at a table nearby. They chuckled and waved to Daniel. Rafael sat up to see who they were and also waved.

"What is it about you the ladies love so much?"

"My charm." Daniel smiled and then grimaced as he touched his sore lip.

"What charm? Did you say the mechanic was an old friend of your father?"

"*Sí*. He's the one who got me this job." With a faraway look in his eye, Daniel changed the subject. "You know when someone hates you and that hatred penetrates inside you? I felt it with Garcia and Pothole and today with El Jefe." He was unable to erase the encounter with his supervisor from his mind.

"Of course. They're evil characters. We've all felt it one time or another."

"El Jefe said they're on to us. By putting me on the night shift they'll disband the gang."

"He knows nothing. He's trying to get information out of you. Communist tactics. The less you say, the better."

"I admitted nothing and told him to put me wherever the fuck he wanted."

"You said it like that?"

Daniel nodded. "He punched the hell out of me for it." Daniel touched his puffy lip and moved out of the shade.

"I can see he did." In direct sunlight Daniel's lip looked even bigger. "You needed another injury." Rafael eyed him for a reaction. When Daniel remained silent, he continued, "You've got balls saying that. Lucky he didn't fire you on the spot or do worse than give you a fat lip." He handed Daniel his cold soda can. "Here. This will help the swelling."

"Thanks." Daniel gently pressed the cold can to his lip. "Fire me? I was this close to walking off the job." He raised a pebble from the dirt. "This close. I left his office intending to go home or kill the bastard."

"Kill him?"

"I considered it."

"What changed your mind?"

"Thinking how my mother would have to struggle and the misery she'd face the rest of her life. I'll find a way to get even with the son of a bitch."

"What can you do to him?"

"Rob the factory blind. Steal more cigarettes. But now the asshole put me on the night shift away from you guys. I won't have help."

"See how the night shift goes. You may like it being away from the bosses and the army of guards, though we'll miss having you around in the day."

"You guys made work bearable for me."

"We'll see each other on our days off. Anyway, you and Juli will be hanging out. By the way, you have to talk to her. She thinks you're angry at her because of Maximo."

"I'm not mad." Daniel set the can down. "It's not her fault. It sure won't be easy facing Max under these circumstances. So he never came to work today, and tomorrow he won't be here. It's his day off."

"He's obviously avoiding you."

"Emilio said not to trust him. I'm beginning to believe crazy old Emilio was right." Daniel popped the last bite of banana into his mouth.

"I told Juli exactly the same thing yesterday. Why does Emilio dislike Max?"

"I'm not sure. Something to do with his father's body shop."

"We'll ask him. Juli's worried what Max might do to you. Hey, go talk to her, man. She's fallen hard for you." Rafael's voice imitated a girl when he said, "I know you love her too."

Daniel tossed the banana peel at him and looked down at his bandaged hand. The bandage had slipped, and dark threads peeked out of the gauze.

"God, I forgot. I have an appointment with the doctor. Catch you later." He handed the soda back to Rafael and ran toward the factory.

Dr. Nieves examined Daniel's hand to insure infection hadn't set in. When the doctor saw Daniel's swollen lip he said, "I'm not going to ask where or how you got that fat lip." He reached in a drawer and handed Daniel a small tube. "Apply this salve twice a day and the swelling should go down in a few days."

The appointment was brief. Five days later Javier Nieves removed the stitches. He poked, tugged, and irritated the tender skin around Daniel's wound as he picked out the threads. This visit was no comparison to the pain experienced on the day the doctor first treated him.

These last two visits Daniel saw the physician in a different light. Dislike turned to admiration for the man who had chosen not to rat him out to the guards. He knew the doctor had to forego a potentially lucrative reward. As he sat in front of the physician, Daniel struggled for words to express his gratitude.

Dr. Nieves spoke little as he plucked and snipped at threads binding the palm of Daniel's hand, so Daniel decided to begin a conversation.

"Thanks for not having me arrested."

"Arrested?"

"*Sí*. The cigarettes. The first time in your office."

"Oh, that. Be careful, or they'll haul you off to prison."

"I'm aware of the punishment. Why didn't you tell on me? The benefit to you would have been great."

"My conscience wouldn't allow me, knowing what they would have done to you."

"I see."

"There. Finished. Except for the scar, your hand is like new. Rub coconut oil on it if the scar bothers you. It will help the mark fade. By the way, how did you really injure yourself? I know it wasn't a knife, as you told your supervisor. The cut is too jagged."

"In a crate. I was hiding in the top one, and the bottom gave way. I fell twenty feet and scraped my hand on the way down—"

"I've heard enough," the doctor interrupted. "Go now. Keep safe. Stay healthy and honest. Maybe we won't have to see each other again."

Daniel examined his hand. "I wouldn't mind. Seeing you again, I mean."

"Well, you know I'm here if you need me."

"Thanks for everything." Daniel hesitated in the doorway and moved aside as another patient entered and sat in a chair against the wall. "Starting tomorrow I'm working the evening shift. We probably won't see each other."

"Good luck to you." The doctor pressed his foot on the metal at the base of a trashcan, flipped the lid open, removed his rubber gloves, and tossed them inside. As he turned toward the sink to scrub his hands he said in a low voice, "Believe in yourself, young man. You don't have to steal cigarettes to make something of yourself."

"My father wanted me to be a doctor."

"Then what's stopping you?"

"It's too late."

"Never too late. Hell, you're stopping yourself. You underestimate your worth. If you need advice, references, whatever, let me know."

"I'll think about it. Thanks."

Daniel resumed work. On his walk home that afternoon he thought about the conversation with the physician. Javier Nieves was unaware he had lost his chance for a medical career when his father died. Along with his death went encouragement and, although medical school was free, the financial assistance to support him while studying.

Daniel lay on the couch in his living room and applied ice cubes wrapped in a towel to his swollen lip while reading *Granma*, the communist party newspaper. He skimmed over an article about the record numbers of Cubans leaving their homeland in makeshift watercraft. In the article the government discouraged this practice and threatened to destroy small boats, rafts, and inner tubes found on beaches throughout the island. Anyone intercepted while leaving Cuba illegally would be sent to prison and severely punished. Daniel threw the newspaper on the floor. Those boat people were crazy.

He picked up a book about the United States off the coffee table. The book had belonged to his father. Daniel usually kept it hidden in a kitchen cupboard behind a sack of flour. The subject matter would be considered propaganda, and he could be arrested for having it. In this country you can be arrested if you smile wrong, he thought as he flipped the pages to a chapter about Florida. Daniel was imagining a life in Miami when he heard a tap on the door. He set the book on his chest.

The door opened. Juliana entered, set a platter on the table, and sat beside him.

"I brought you some pastries."

When he smiled a weary smile at her, she noticed a black and blue mark on his cheek and his protruding lip.

"What happened to you? Hurt again?"

He snapped the book closed and shoved it under the sofa.

"El Jefe slapped me around his office."

"Oh. I'm sorry."

She gently touched the bruise on his cheek. He jerked his head away from her.

She retreated. "Are you angry at me?"

"Why should I be?"

"I was afraid Max's behavior might cause trouble between us."

"Rafael told me you weren't dating him. You only listened to his problems. Is that true?"

"Of course it is. I kept him company because he was so down about his father. Nothing more. Did Max say anything to you?"

"I haven't seen him yet. He never showed up for work."

"Be careful. Rafa said he wants to kill you. None of this makes sense to me."

"Max and I weren't very close, but you'd think he would have mentioned to one of us at the factory that he liked you. Rafael said he was at the party. Did you see him?"

"No. He told me the same thing. They went to his father's body shop to drink beer and talk. Rafa was the first to tell me about Max's feelings toward me. Daniel, it's you I really care about." Juli kissed him on his cheek. "I think I'm falling in love with you."

Daniel, shocked by her words, was unable to react. He couldn't stop thinking about the new position and the abuse at the factory. Worry caused him to set aside any emotion he had for Juliana. Blankly he stared at her.

She repeated, "I said I love you."

Daniel sat up. "I'm sorry, Juli, but I have so much on my mind right now."

"Do you want me to leave?" She rose.

"No. Of course not. Stay." He reached for her hand. "I'm immersed in many problems right now. I had an argument with El Jefe. He changed my schedule to the evening shift. I dread working at night as a mechanic. It will be like starting over again."

"It's only a change. At least you have a job."

Daniel sensed she was annoyed with him, but he needed to talk about his troubles.

"I know nothing about mechanics."

"You'll learn."

"Do I have a choice? If I don't I'll be thrown out in the street. Unemployment's high."

Juliana leaned over to hug him, but he was unresponsive.

"Then quit," she said in a harsh voice.

"Maybe I will."

"You don't mean that. I'll let you wallow in your misery alone." She stood and eased between the coffee table and the sofa. He grabbed her hand, squeezed, and pulled her toward him.

"Where are you going?"

"To work."

"But that's later. Sorry. I'm in a bad mood." Daniel stood, reaching for her, but Juli slipped away and rushed out the door. He saw the platter on the table, lifted the cloth, and smelled the sweetness of freshly baked pastries. He could be so insensitive.

Daniel opened the door and called for her, but she was nowhere in sight. He left the door open and jogged barefoot down the broken sidewalk, leaping to avoid jagged pieces of displaced cement. With each stride the brick-colored earth seeping through the cracks reddened the bottoms of his feet. His mind raced. He repeated their conversation as he ran. She'd actually admitted she loved him.

Daniel reached Juliana's house and hesitated at the door, unaware that she peeked at him through a tear in the window shade and prayed he would knock. Her heart sank when he turned and headed home. She gripped the windowsill. Her hands slipped, and she collapsed on the floor, weeping.

It took a few weeks for Daniel to adjust to the late hours of the evening shift, but in time he realized working at night had its advantages and proved to be less chaotic and stressful. The night guards stayed to themselves, unlike Pothole and Garcia, who constantly harassed employees. His new boss and father's childhood friend, Angel, was easygoing and fair, unlike El Jefe. Daniel became acquainted with his father's friend and grew fonder of him each day.

Their first introduction resulted in stiff formality, which baffled Daniel as to why the old mechanic acted distant toward him. He assumed El Jefe had lectured Angel on how to mistreat Daniel. This deduction filled him with the constant worry of what was to come. He remembered his former supervisor's threat to have him worked so hard by the night mechanic that Daniel would choose to leave the factory. But the air cleared when Angel encouraged a serious talk while showing his apprentice the machinery.

"*Sabes, chico,* I never understood why you didn't come by to thank me for getting you the job here. I felt sorry for your mother. She was desperate and worried about you working at the sugar mill. Of course I would have done anything for your parents. Your father was the closest friend I ever had. Still, you could have at least said hello."

Now Daniel understood the reason for tension between them and explained, "I tried to see you after I was hired, but Pothole wouldn't let me stay at the factory after four o'clock. I attempted to sneak in at night several times, but the guards forced me to leave. They told me I didn't belong after hours. Your address was unlisted. I gave up trying to see you, but I put a note under your office door. You never received it?"

"No, I didn't. What office? I use this counter to write on. The workshop is my office."

"I slid the note under the door over there. A day shift mechanic told me that was your office."

The old man laughed. "Son, that's a closet. We store scrap metal in there. I haven't gone in that closet in ages. Let's look." Angel reached for a key in a drawer and opened the door. On the floor a dusty envelope lay by a copper pipe. "Is this from you?"

"I believe so."

"Well, thank you, boy. I'll read it at home. By the way, I live with my niece and her husband out by the elementary school." He wiped and folded the note and put it in his back pocket.

"My mother and I both appreciated your help. I'll never forget what you did for me. Sorry, I was unable to tell you in person." As much as he hated working in the factory, the job had helped his mother and him survive.

"It's OK. Especially now that I've finally spoken to you and I have this." Angel patted his pocket. "Come on, son. Let me show you the rest of the shop. This is where you'll spend most of your time."

Daniel looked around. Everything was gray, brown, or black. Such a dreary atmosphere. Before him was a workbench on a raised platform. Shelves lined the walls surrounding the work area. Below the shelves small drawers were stacked on a countertop and hidden by machine parts. All kinds of tools, screwdrivers, wedges, hammers, saws, and pliers covered the surfaces of several tables. Motors lay in parts on the floor by a bench separating two rows of lockers with combination locks.

"Pick a locker, and I'll give you the combination. Take one from the bottom row on that side. Those are empty."

As Daniel chose a locker, he asked Angel if El Jefe had contacted him.

"Sure he did."

"Did he tell you to work the hell out of me?"

"Yes, he did. Aren't I working you hard, boy?"

Daniel stared at him.

Angel burst out laughing. "I agreed with the asshole, but he doesn't have to know what a great time you have here at night. I'm not saying we won't do our job, but El Comandante Castro puts enough pressure on us, and son, you sure don't need another Castro in your life, do you?"

Daniel laughed. "No, I do not."

Angel taught him the equipment, and gradually Daniel became accustomed to operating and repairing machinery. He watched Angel solder and mold Russian parts to fit American-made machines.

Every night they roamed deserted sections of the factory together, oiling levers, tightening screws, and testing devices they created to make broken machinery run. During their chores Daniel delighted in hearing the older man reminisce about Daniel Milan, Sr. and the childhood they shared in Las Villas. Daniel got some insight as to why he had been such a mischievous child. He took after his father.

At night the factory became a peaceful refuge away from his former overbearing superiors, El Jefe and Pothole. Daniel adjusted well to the night shift, to his surprise. His apprehension turned to an inner calm he hadn't felt since before his father passed away.

While working on projects with Angel, Daniel often thought of Juliana. He was ready to visit her again if she was interested, and he decided to incorporate his former life into his new schedule. He had even refrained from contacting Rafael since he started his new position. Their schedules didn't coincide, and even though Daniel became content with the night shift, the change had been an adjustment.

Two weeks passed, and Daniel strolled over to the factory park on his day off to catch Rafael on his morning break.

"Where have you been?" said Rafael as Daniel approached the table.

"Working at night. It hasn't been as bad as I expected. I get along with Angel, and I have more freedom now." He sat down on the bench beside his friend. "Rafa, we've got to talk."

"I know. I arranged a meeting. Next Thursday night. I was going to leave a note on your door. Jaime and the brothers will be there. I'm not sure Max will show up. He was vague about whether he could make it or not. Are you off that night?"

"No. But I'll tell Angel I won't be in. I'll tell him I'm sick or make up something."

"My days off are Wednesday and Thursday. We're on then. And Daniel." Rafael's eyes narrowed. "You have to visit Juliana. She's—"

"I know."

"No, you don't know. She's sick over not hearing from you. She shuts herself in her room, refuses to eat, and cries. I hate seeing her—"

"I'm sorry. I'm going there now."

Rafael had a questioning look on his face. "Are you really going *now*?"

"*Ahora*. I'm going to see Juli, I said."

"Good. Then see you Thursday."

"By the way, my days off are Tuesday and Wednesday. We can get together on Wednesdays."

"Great. Catch you later."

Chapter Five
THE MEETING

Daniel strolled in the center of Ranchuelo along the Prado and searched for Carmelita, saleswoman of black-market products, from cigars to jewelry, clothing and any other requests by her clients. He knew she balked at selling on principal roads to avoid encounters with police but appeared briefly on main avenues and lured her customers to side streets to make the sale.

Daniel crossed the Prado and walked until he saw two elderly men playing dominoes at a table set up under a banyan tree outside the Liceo, a private club in the center of Ranchuelo. He asked them if they had seen Carmelita. One removed a cigar from his mouth and held it between two fingers.

"On my way here I saw her walking along Prado Nuevo. I bought this cigar from her. I'm not sure where she is now." He raised the cigar, which was burning orange at the tip, and was about to put the soggy end between his lips but stopped when the other man commented on how hard Carmelita worked for a living in the black market. They both burst into laughter. Daniel chuckled, thanked them, and walked toward the business section of town.

He spotted Carmelita carrying her gift box with a red bow on its cover. The box contained jewelry and a humidor brimming with cigars. Her scooter with a basket on the back fender leaned against a ficus tree nearby, ready in case she needed to flee in a hurry. She sashayed ahead of him on the sidewalk. Her short flowered skirt flounced, and a low-cut pink top revealed a deep line of cleavage. Discreetly she asked pedestrians to purchase her wares. Daniel glanced at her shapely, muscular legs as he rushed up to her.

"Daniel, *querido,* how are you?" she cooed like a dove.

"I'm fine, and how have you been, Carmelita?"

"I'm doing well. Don't you think so?" she asked as she strutted and twirled in front of him.

He smiled. "Yes, you are."

"What are your needs today?" She winked at him.

"Do you have jewelry in the shape of a butterfly?"

"Aha, for a new love? The secret's out. Daniel Milan is in love again."

"Again? I've never been in love, Carmelita."

"You're always with some beautiful, young thing." Beaming, she opened the box and displayed rings, earrings, bracelets, necklaces, and watches arranged haphazardly on a newspaper with prices marked in red ink beside each piece. She surveyed the jewelry and gently shifted the ornaments with her long, painted fingernails. "I'm afraid not, my love. No butterflies." Daintily she picked up a necklace with a charm dangling from it. "But I do have this heart-shaped gold locket. Would that interest you?"

"How much?"

"*Amor,* you can have it cheap. Fifty pesos."

"Forty and I'll take it."

"My dear, how can I refuse such a handsome man?"

Daniel slipped the pesos out of his wallet and into her opened hand. Carmelita stuffed the money between her breasts, wrapped the necklace in tissue paper, and pressed it into his hand.

"Daniel, *mi amor,* don't forget to tell your factory friends that new merchandise arrives next week. How about a cigar, *querido?*" she said quickly, trying to detain him. She lifted the top, and the cedar box was packed with Montecristos, Romeo y Julietas, Fonsecas, and Trinidads. The cedar and tobacco aroma gave Daniel a flashback of the moment he was imprisoned in the crates in the warehouse. He backed away from her.

"Thank you, but no. Only the necklace. I will tell my friends. I always do."

"I know you do. *Gracias, guapo.* Come see me again soon."

Daniel touched the doorknob to Juliana's house and listened for voices. The door was unlocked, but he refrained from entering. He tapped the knocker twice. Juliana opened the door and at the sight of him was about to slam it. When she saw how he sheepishly stood there, she changed her mind.

Daniel slid his foot forward to prevent the door from closing. At this gesture a wave of anger crossed her face, and Juli pushed the door with all her might but realized she was no match for his strength.

"Juli, please. I have to talk to you."

"What is there to say, Daniel?"

She ran into the kitchen. He heard a lid slam hard on the counter. As he stood at the entrance to the kitchen he saw a cloud of steam rise from a pot on the stove. The smoking pot looked like the one he used for the distillery, but this steam had no odor. His eyes lit up as he watched her grip a potholder and stand motionless in front of the stove. Daniel tiptoed into the kitchen and kissed her softly on her neck. She pushed him aside.

"I'm sorry. Please forgive me," he pleaded and stepped back. Juliana pouted, and he waited for a sign of forgiveness. "I will never behave like that again. I promise. I was being selfish."

"You were. I told you something I have never told any man before, and you ignored me."

"Like I said, I will never act that way again. Am I forgiven?" He gently turned her around by her shoulders so they were face to face.

She raised her arms, hesitated, but then hugged him. "I think you are."

"Thank you." Daniel softly touched his lips with hers, but she did not respond. He turned toward the stove. "What's cooking?"

Juli smirked before answering. "If you must know, I'm boiling cloth, not food."

"Cloth? As in fabric?"

"Yes," she said quietly. "I'm preparing my sanitary napkins for next month."

"Oh," he said. His timing was impeccable.

Juli stirred the clean white strips and swirled them in hot water with a stick whittled clean of bark. "This was the top sheet of my parents' bed." She blushed.

He put his arms around her. "Hey, we'll buy them a new set of sheets."

"That would be nice." Finally she smiled.

"Give me a kiss."

Juliana turned and quickly pecked his lips and noticed his swollen lip was back to its normal size. "Do you think you deserve that kiss?"

"Probably not. But leave this. Come with me." Daniel lifted the pot off the flame, put it on a cool burner, and turned off the stove. "Maybe soon you'll believe I deserve to be kissed."

"Where are we going?"

"I'll show you."

As he reached for her hand, she tossed the potholder on the counter, and he led her out of the house. Daniel decided without saying that he would take her to the garden of an abandoned home where he often spent time alone. Although plants in the garden were gnarled and overgrown, the bougainvillea were a brilliant pink, and the honey-scented plumeria and gardenia in full bloom wafted a mixture of perfumed fragrances with each passing breeze. The garden setting was the perfect location to make up with Juli. He was certain the flowers would entice her into a romantic mood.

Together they walked down Paseo de Abreu. Juli questioned why he hadn't stopped by to see her in the past two weeks. He put his finger to her lips.

"Hush. I will explain."

Daniel guided her to a neighborhood of large homes, several of which were abandoned by families living in exile. The couple approached a bench on the south side of a two-story stucco house with tall windows secured by decorative iron bars.

"Daniel, this was my aunt Lucia's home. I can't believe you brought me here. She died in Miami years ago. Since the day she left Cuba her house has remained vacant."

Juliana smoothed her skirt as she sat on a bench decorated with mosaic tiles of yellow sunbursts surrounded by white birds in flight. Some of the mosaics were chipped. She looked at the unkempt but familiar surroundings. "We used to play in this garden."

The bench was warmed by the morning sun. Daniel's scarred hand pressed against the warmth of the tiles as he sat beside her.

"I had no idea the former owner was your aunt. I come here to sort out my thoughts." He put his arm across her shoulders and looked at the garden. "I came here the last day we were together. I was so confused that day. But it was here I realized that I love you and want to spend as much time as possible with you."

Juliana stared at the overgrown garden and marveled about the flowers. When she realized what he had said, she looked deep into his eyes.

"You do? You really mean it?"

"I really mean it."

"That day at your house, I thought you felt otherwise."

"Sorry, for the way I acted. My problems overwhelmed me. I should have focused on you, not on my troubles."

"I thought you hated me. I had hoped you would knock on my door that day and come in so we could clear things up."

"I would never hate you. How did you know I came to your house?"

"I saw you from the window."

"I didn't realize. You should have tapped."

"I wanted it to be your choice to come inside."

"I chose not to burden you with my worries. That's why I went home. I knew I loved you too. I was just unable to express it. I'm sorry for that." He held her hand. "I was worried about my job. My thoughts were on El Jefe punching me and the fall inside the warehouse. Everything negative that happened in the past two weeks came to a head while I was lying on the couch. You showed up right in the middle of those dismal feelings."

Daniel kissed her, and she kissed him back. They kissed more and hugged hard and long. Then they stopped and stared into each other's eyes. He remembered the locket.

"I have something for you." He took the tissue paper out of his pocket and gently placed it on Juli's lap. She lifted the tissue.

"How beautiful, a gold heart. A locket. I love it. Thank you so much." She kissed him on the cheek.

"You're welcome. I'm happy you like it. Sorry, there were no butterflies. Next time I'll find you a butterfly."

"Oh, Daniel, I don't care whether it's a butterfly or not. I'm happy with this locket. Now we need a photo taken together. I'll keep it inside the heart forever."

Juli rested her head on his shoulder as she held and admired the necklace. They sat in silence until she glanced at her watch.

"I hate to leave, but I have to go home. My mother expects me to have dinner ready."

"One more gift, something you told me you like, something sweet."

"Something sweet that I told you I like? Ice cream. Sounds wonderful. I always have time for ice cream." Juliana put her two fingers to her lips, kissed them, and touched his heart. "Thank you."

"For what? Inviting you for ice cream?"

"Yes." She beamed. "And for the locket. And for bringing me here. The flowers are lovely. It's such a peaceful place with the mountains in the distance beyond the plains. Such a sentimental setting."

Daniel glanced at the tall grass growing between the stones of the sidewalk and turned to face her.

"Thank you for coming here with me."

Daniel and Rafael stood in front of a side door to Santa Rosa de Lima, the Catholic Church of Ranchuelo. The government had mandated this and all other churches to remain secured and declared that congregating for religious purposes was forbidden throughout Cuba. Angered by the Catholic Church, Fidel Castro banned religion soon after he seized control of Cuba. He accused the church of campaigning against his newly formed government.

Santa Rosa de Lima and all other places of worship on the island were locked up or destroyed. Many worshippers and priests fled, were imprisoned, or were expelled from Cuba. Castro's government also terminated all religious holidays.

To be discreet in their use of the church for meetings, Daniel and Rafael refrained from passing in front of the elementary school and clinic situated on the main route to Santa Rosa de Lima. As the sky darkened they weaved in and out of back streets and alleyways to avoid being seen near the Spanish colonial church, off limits to residents. They jogged past the cemetery several blocks away and approached the church from the rear. Rafael swung open the gate of a black iron fence surrounding the stucco building and followed Daniel into the churchyard on a footpath leading to the side entrance.

With a strike of a match, Rafael lit a candle he'd pulled out of his pocket, illuminating the padlock targeted for removal. Daniel rapidly removed the four screws that secured the latch in place. The last screw dropped into his hand, and he slipped all four into his shirt pocket. He knocked the latch aside with the screwdriver handle, and the door creaked open into darkness. Daniel turned to his friend. "Welcome to the black hole. After you, sir."

He outstretched an arm.

"Send me into doom first, as always." Rafael entered.

Daniel crossed the threshold into blackness behind Rafael and smelled a strong odor of mildew. Warm, muggy air brushed his face. They felt their way by sliding their hands along the backs of pews. Most of the seats were detached from the metal bases that had fastened them to the floor and were knocked out of straight rows like derailed train cars.

They reached a candle stand on the opposite side of the church. Daniel slipped by Rafael to open a window. Rafa reached up to the top of a brass candlestick and touched the faint flame of his candle to the wick on a mound of melted wax. One lump of wax provided sufficient light for their meetings without brightening the stained glass windows. The dim light allowed them to walk across the mosaic tile to the altar with ease, where they sat on the steps and discussed the topic of their meeting.

Ten minutes passed, and the Rialto brothers entered the church. Jaime Pascal soon followed. They saluted each other by clenching fists and sat in pews nearest the altar. It was no surprise to Rafael and Daniel that Maximo was the only member not in attendance. Daniel sat back down on the steps of the marble altar, waited, and wondered if the brothers and Jaime knew Max was angry at him.

"To hell with Max," Daniel said as he stood and glanced at Rafael, who leaned against a column. The candlelight and shadows falsely patterned an expression of gloom on Daniel's face as he spoke. "We've waited long enough for him. Let's get started. I have some interesting information to tell you guys. As you know, I've been working the night shift."

Daniel's eyes followed Rafael as he moved to a pew opposite the others. The bench rocked as he sat down.

"At first I gave up on the idea of taking out cigarettes again, but now I have access anywhere in the factory except behind the locked door of the carton storage where you guys enter freely. With a master key to that room, I'll take out a record number of cigarettes. We'll all gain. It'll be easy because night guards and supervisors smoke and drink on the loading dock and sleep for hours in their offices. My immediate boss sleeps between nine and ten. Every night they get smashed." Daniel's enthusiasm echoed in his voice.

"Sounds ideal, but the key you need is locked up in the security office at the end of the shift," said Jaime. "There's no way we can sneak it to you."

Roberto Rialto chimed in, "He's right. The key's signed in and out, and if it's missing for long, guards come looking for it."

A bat swooped down from the beams, grazing Daniel's shoulder. Then it flew past a window and up to the choir loft. Daniel ducked but resumed the conversation as if a fly had buzzed by.

"All I need is an imprint. I know a locksmith, an expert at cutting keys."

"You mean, Ramón Ramos." said Rafael. "Rambo. These guys probably don't know him. He works part time on the dock and lives on a farm by Santa Maria sugar mill. Daniel and I hang out with him."

"An excellent locksmith," said Daniel.

"An imprint we might be able to get," said Ricardo Rialto. "But remember, the guards do spot checks and sometimes search us before we leave."

"Hey, if Pothole can poke at my stomach and grab my shirt with twenty cigarette packs in it and not realize, then you guys can leave the factory with one picture of a fucking key."

A voice echoed through the eaves of the church and overpowered Daniel's words. They all turned. Daniel recognized Maximo's voice coming from near the vestibule at the main entrance.

"You were lucky that day," shouted Max. "Tell me, if you are proposing to be the only one of us to remove cigarettes, how in hell do we benefit? I like the old way. We steal and sell individually. What are you expecting? A percentage of what we sell?"

Daniel strained to see Max and wondered at what point he had entered the church and how he snuck back to the main entrance so quietly. Had he entered from the front? His eyes scanned the blackness down the center aisle and saw the pale alabaster holy water fountain but distinguished nothing else.

Daniel shouted back, "Max, you've got it all wrong. I can get enough out on my person, or I'll pass the cigarettes directly to you guys at night while the guards sleep. I'm not asking for a cut from your sales—"

Max eased out of the shadows and into candlelight. "Then what are you asking for? This sounds like a one-sided proposal to me. I think it's time we went our separate ways. Right, boys?"

Maximo walked down the aisle and approached the pews near the altar.

The brothers looked at him, and Jaime answered, "If that's what you want, Max."

"Come on," Rafael said. "Isn't there more to this than Daniel taking cigarettes out for all of us? These guys are unaware of the whole story."

"Doesn't matter. The brothers, Jaime, and I have already talked about working alone. Didn't they mention this to you two yet? Since Daniel screwed up in the warehouse we've been leery of doing business with him. That mistake could have landed us all in prison."

"You son of a bitch." Daniel glared at Max. "You told me to leave the dock early, before the time we'd originally planned. I told you it was too early."

"El Jefe would have detained you on the dock if you didn't leave. That has nothing to do with getting trapped in a stack of boxes."

Rafael stood up. "Wait a minute. For the record, I told Daniel where to hide. Neither of us knew those boxes weren't strong enough to support him."

"Rafa's right. Admit it. You're angry at me because of Juliana. You hate me for seeing her. You never told us you liked her. Did you guys know? Maximo's in love with Rafael's sister."

The three shrugged their shoulders, and their eyes shifted toward Max. They ducked when Max leaped onto a seat and sprung off the back of a pew in one motion. He flew over them and toward Daniel, arms spread wide. Rafael raced after Maximo who sideswiped Daniel as he dove out of Max's path. Daniel landed on the marble floor with a thud and rolled along the altar.

The Rialto brothers and Jaime hurried to the duo as they tumbled over and over next to the altar railing and rolled within inches of a statue of the Virgin Mary.

"Maximo, we were all friends. Why end it like this?" said Roberto.

"Don't let him fool you," Max answered between clenched teeth. "He knew I liked Juliana and made his moves anyway."

Daniel kicked at Maximo to release his leg from his grip. "Liar. I never knew."

Rafael locked his arms around Daniel's waist and pulled him away from their angry cohort while the brothers held onto Max by his arms. Jaime stood between the fighters. But Maximo's anger-fueled strength pushed Jaime aside and dragged the brothers with him to get at Daniel. Rafael and Daniel lunged at him, but Max shoved Rafael over the railing, more intent than ever to annihilate his rival.

Daniel shut out the chaos, screams, and everything but thoughts of Juliana spending time with the loser before him. With this in mind, he punched his attacker with both hands despite his recent wound. Two punches sent Maximo sailing backward and sliding across the floor. He landed against a white and gold-flecked table.

Max staggered to his feet, bleeding profusely from his nose. He held his shirtsleeve to his nostrils and peered at Daniel who was poised with clenched fists, ready to resume the fight.

"Our gang's finished, but the war between you and I will never end. You will regret this night." Max's sleeve reddened. He motioned toward Jaime and the brothers. "Come on."

Roberto helped Maximo to the side door, and the others followed single file behind them. The former gang members disappeared into the night.

Daniel extended a hand to Rafael. "Are you hurt?" He pulled him off the floor.

"No. Just humiliated."

After blowing out the candle, closing the window, and replacing the latch plate to secure the church, Rafael and Daniel stepped into the night air but hesitated before moving on.

"Be careful. They may be waiting for us behind a tree," cautioned Rafael.

"I doubt Max has any strength left in him."

"Revenge takes little strength."

At the front of the church, the brilliant colors of the stained glass windows dulled in the darkness of night. The white stucco building was topped by a bell tower that loomed eerily above them. A scooter sped by and pierced the quiet night. Rafael commented when he saw no one lurking outside the church, "That meeting adjourned quickly. I guess that leaves the two of us to fend for ourselves in the factory."

"And that's not a bad thing. We'll make more money, and I swear I'll steal cases of cigarettes. Now I have to depend on you to get that key imprint."

"I should be able to do it. Best time is Pothole's day off."

"As soon as you can. I'm running low on cash."

"He's off on Sunday." Rafael poked at Daniel's chest. "Spending all your money on my sister?"

"Some of it."

"How are you two doing?"

"I guess you could say we're a couple."

"You should have told that to Max while you two rolled on the floor."

"He would have won. You know he'll find out soon enough, wise guy."

"Wise guy? You're the one who hasn't gone a week without a fight."

"They start the fights, not me, but anyway, I intend to concentrate more on love and less on violence from now on."

"We'll see," Rafael said. He put his hand on the back of Daniel's head and pulled him as they ran to the street and cut through town.

At Paseo de Abreu they parted. Daniel had promised to pick up clothes in need of mending from one of his mother's clients. Before separating they made plans to meet briefly on the following Sunday afternoon after Rafael finished work.

Daniel jogged across the road and called to his friend, "Don't forget the imprint."

"How can I forget? I know you'll torture me until I get it to you."

Chapter Six
ITALIAN TOBACCO LEAVES

On Sunday, as Daniel bounded up the steps to the loading dock, he saw Rafael seated at the dock's edge with his legs dangling over the side.

"It's about time you got here. I was about to leave."

"I'm on time. What's your problem? Let me punch in."

"It's just that I want to get out of this fucking place. I put in my day's work and want to go home."

"Hang on." Daniel swiped his timecard. "Did you get the imprint?"

"It's here." Rafael reached for Daniel's hand, shook it hard, and passed a folded piece of paper into the palm of his hand. "Good luck. Let me know if it works. See you Wednesday."

"Hey, man, thanks. Now we're really in business."

Rafael rushed down the steps.

Daniel slipped the paper into his pocket and joined Angel in the shop. He found him talking to a man with a white beard who wore a white *guayabera*. Daniel estimated he was in his late seventies. His first impression of the pale man dressed in white was of an albino.

As Daniel approached the conversing men, he realized how frail the old man was. Both his hands trembled as he gripped the back of a chair to keep his balance. Angel introduced them. "Daniel, this is my good friend, César, who handles production. We were just discussing how busy he is, and maybe when we aren't so busy, you could lend César a hand. It will be good for you to learn what goes on in another department. What do you say?"

"Fine with me." Daniel pitied the elderly man who worked late into the night when he should have retired years ago.

"Tonight I can handle our work. How about helping César this evening?" Angel didn't wait for Daniel to answer. "Go ahead with him now. He'll show you what has to be done."

Daniel kept a slow pace beside the rickety César and followed him to a section of the factory he had never seen. His eyes lit up when he realized that helping César involved counting inventory and transporting cigarette boxes to the production storage room on the first floor. The boxes he moved contained five hundred twenty cigarette cartons.

Amazed by this stroke of luck, Daniel pushed the dolly and beamed as if he were moving gold bars down the aisles of the cigarette factory. He stopped the cart, took out the imprint of the key Rafael had given him, and stared at it. He glanced down at the boxes filled with cigarettes. With access to two storage areas, stealing hundreds of cigarettes out of Ramiro La Vandero would be effortless. That night he smuggled out thirty boxes, a small heist but an incredible beginning.

At the end of the shift Daniel sat next to César at his desk as he filled out a form on a typewriter. Over the sound of clicking keys they heard the screech of brakes, and a truck halted in front of the small loading dock outside César's office. Headlights beamed in the window. As Daniel watched the old man stand up, ease the chair back, and stretch his arms, he asked, "What's that truck delivering tobacco at night for?" Through the window Daniel saw the driver lift a canvas cover to expose bales of green tobacco. "I thought El Jefe received all the tobacco deliveries from the fields during the morning shift."

"*Es cierto*. El Jefe receives tobacco from Cuba during daylight hours in plain view. The nighttime deliveries are tobacco shipments from other countries. This load is from Italy."

"Italy?"

César limped outside, directed the dump truck to the corner of the dock, and signaled the driver to raise the back. The engine droned as Daniel stood on the dock and watched bales of Italian tobacco tumble out of the truck bed and bounce in all directions. César shuffled past him to the office to type a form indicating the factory cigarette boxes picked up by the truck. These boxes were to be distributed to stores throughout the provinces or sent to ports to be shipped abroad. César kept no record of the arriving Italian tobacco leaves.

The old man turned the knob, slid the paper out of the typewriter, and separated the pages. As Daniel walked through the door, César said, "The yellow sheet goes in our file, and the pink one goes to the driver. Would you give it to him?"

"Sure. And what about the white one?"

"That's for El Jefe. I'll put it in his mailbox before I leave tonight. This filing system has to be accurate because you never know when government inspectors will come to examine our files. They can show up at any time."

"I never knew they came at night." Daniel reached for the sheet of paper.

"They arrive like phantoms on a wind. I've seen five at a time do a surprise inspection. One night they filed out of a van, opened the door, and one rushed to the files while the other four checked on the nighttime employees."

Daniel had paused at the door to listen to César. When he mentioned phantoms, his voice quivered. Daniel imagined pale César, a phantom before him. Obediently he took the paper outside. The driver loaded cartons on the truck as Daniel handed him the form and said, "So the world thinks Cuban cigarettes are made from Cuban tobacco?"

The driver snatched the sheet out of Daniel's hand.

"Let the world think what it wants." He slammed the tailgate shut and raised the palms of his hands in unison. "The world's an ignorant place."

He climbed in the cab, started the ignition twice, and drove down the driveway. Daniel watched the truck rock over ruts in the road. The driver downshifted at the gate, halted, and then bounded for the highway.

The following day Daniel rode his bike out to Rambo's farm and sped by a huge billboard of a *guajira*. Large block letters above the peasant read "*Viva La Patria*," "Long Live Our Native Land." Daniel leaned to the side and spat on the road as he always did when he passed this or any other signs displaying communist propaganda. Beyond the billboard flat fields of sugarcane eased into pastures and a cornfield, which marked the beginning of the Ramos occupied farm.

He pedaled his bike up the long driveway past snorting, grunting pigs in a pen to the main barn, where he found Rambo pouring oil into a tractor near the entrance. Rambo closed the hood and wiped grease off his hands with a rag. He spotted Daniel. "What brings you out here, Milan?"

"I need a key made. This one's a tough assignment. I only have a drawing on paper." Daniel unfolded the paper and handed it to him.

Rambo examined the picture. "I'll give it a try. No promises, though."

Daniel smelled dried corn and hay as they entered the barn. In a room where sacks of feed were stacked against the wall beside hay bales Rambo reached over an old American-made Ilco key machine on a counter and pulled a blank key out of a can on the windowsill above. He set the blank on top of the key drawing, but the key was too short. He picked a second blank out of a smaller can. This one matched the drawing.

The locksmith placed the paper drawing on the key machine, clamped the blank beside it, and flipped on the switch. The machine purred, and he carefully guided the blade that sliced into the blank. The screech of grinding metal pierced their ears. On a buffing machine Rambo smoothed the rough edges and held the cut key up to beams of sunlight streaming through the window to inspect his craftsmanship.

"It might work. But you'll have to test it on the lock." He wiped dust off the key with a rag and handed it to Daniel. "What are you up to this time, Milan? No doubt entering somewhere you're not supposed to be. Do you ever stay out of trouble?"

"Fuck you, Rambo. The story of my life is trouble." Daniel held up the key to examine the grooves. "This baby better get me where I want to go, which is none of your business."

"I don't want to know."

Daniel slipped the key in his pocket.

"Let's get serious, Milan. What happened between you and Max? He badmouthed you the other day while some of us guys were playing basketball at the athletic club."

"I showed him who was boss. What did he say?"

"Something about a fight in the church. That you're a dirty fighter and need Rafael to help you win your battles."

"That's a lie. Max attacked me first and pushed Rafael out of the way."

"Well, he swore he was going to get even with you. He was mad."

"He's a sore loser. He'll get over it."

Daniel ended the conversation because he knew Rambo spread gossip, especially in the presence of ladies. He told anyone who would listen about the personal lives of town residents.

Daniel pat his pocket. "I'll test it, but if it doesn't work, I'm going to be pissed."

That night Daniel returned to his regular position as mechanic's assistant. The factory was dark and quiet. Angel fell asleep in the machine room with his feet propped up on a crate. Daniel left his snoozing supervisor to check on the guards' whereabouts from a third-floor window at the end of a hallway. He stared down at the uniformed personnel on the main dock. They were settled into their usual routine of drinking, smoking, and bullshitting. He was relieved they were preoccupied with each other and hurried down to the storage area to test the key Rambo had cut.

Daniel slipped the key into the keyhole, but the shaft only entered halfway. "Damn," he uttered and rushed back to the shop for a file and a can of oil. He kneeled at the door, filed the irregular surface of the key, squirted several drops of oil into the keyhole, and tried to insert it. When it refused to budge, he threw the key and watched it bounce on the cement floor.

A deep, unfamiliar voice called him, and he reeled around. In a doorway seven meters from Daniel appeared a government inspector.

"What are you doing here?"

"Oiling locks."

Daniel picked up the oilcan to show the inspector. As he set the can down, he caught a glimpse of the key lying near the door. As he stood, Daniel gave the key a light push with his boot, and all but the tip hid beneath the door.

"Greasing locks is my main duty tonight. We've had several departments complain about keys not working."

The inspector stared at him for a few seconds.

"You'd better get on with your work then, and I will continue mine."

"I have to get more oil. Have a good evening."

Daniel grabbed the oilcan, walked past him, and headed toward the machine room to warn Angel of the intruder's arrival.

The man followed him with his eyes. "You too."

Daniel ran and called for Angel to wake up. By this time the mechanic was snoring. He jumped out of his chair and knocked over the crate upon hearing the urgency in Daniel's voice. "What the hell is wrong?"

"An inspector. Pretend you're working. I think he's headed toward the loading dock. The guards are hanging out there, smoking and drinking rum. If he catches them they're done for."

"Don't worry about them." Angel rubbed his eyes, massaged his left knee, and stiffly walked over to the workbench. "They're immune."

"Immune?"

"Nothing will happen to them."

"They're screwed."

"Believe me. They'll come out of this inspection with flying colors."

Daniel waited fifteen minutes before retrieving the useless key in the storage room. As he picked it off the floor, he realized another bike trip out to Rambo's farm would be necessary tomorrow to have the key recut. Daniel dreaded riding the long distance and also remembered he had made plans to visit Juli. She'd expect a good explanation of why he had to cancel.

Daniel climbed back up the creaking stairs to the third floor window and peered down at the loading dock, certain Angel was mistaken. He anticipated a view of inspectors reprimanding guards. Instead, beyond his reflection in the glass, he witnessed guards and inspectors seated on stools taken out of the dispatch office, relaxed and chatting together like old buddies. They laughed and belted down shots of rum as smoke streamed from the tips of their cigars. One government official passed out cigars he removed from his jacket pocket. Daniel was shocked to see inspectors having a grand time with the idle factory workers. He stepped back from the window and whispered, "There's no justice in this country. Absolutely no justice."

Daniel pedaled his bike along the road leading to the Ramos' homestead early the following morning and spat as he sped past the billboard. When he rolled into the barnyard, he found Rambo scooping grain out of a burlap sack and into troughs for cows sauntering in from the fields.

Rambo immediately defended himself. "What do you expect? That key not working is no surprise. It was cut from a piece of paper."

"I'm not blaming you. I just didn't want to ride my bike all the way out here again."

The key machine screamed as the blade ground into a metal blank and sprinkled golden dust on the dirt floor. Rambo also cut a spare key on the machine as a backup since Daniel complained about returning to the farm. He filed and smoothed the sharp edges and grooves of both keys and deposited them in Daniel's hand.

"*Estoy seguro.* These will work. You won't be riding out here again for a long time. I'll bet you money on that."

"I don't have the pesos now, but next week I'll bet on anything." Daniel squeezed the keys in his hand and was thrilled to think of the quantity of cash soon to land in his possession.

He paid Rambo for the keys, and they sat on kitchen chairs on the patio and drank Havana Club, Rambo's favorite beer. Before raising the second bottle to his mouth Rambo mentioned that he had bumped into Maximo in town earlier in the morning.

"Now what did he say about me?" Daniel slouched in a chair and touched a chilled bottle to his lips.

"Nothing. He was on his way to a side job mowing and landscaping some cop's lawn. He said he had to stop by Rafael's house first."

Daniel swallowed in a hurry, coughed, and sat up straight. "Was Max going to see Rafael?"

"I don't think so. I got the impression he needed to talk to his sister."

"Talk to Juliana?"

"I think so."

Daniel guzzled the rest of the liquid. "Thanks for the beer. I've got to go to work. See you at the game."

"What interest do you have in Rafael's sister?" Rambo asked with a sly tone in his voice.

"None of your business."

Daniel jerked his bike off the ground, slammed up the kickstand, and jumped on the seat. He pedaled furiously past the billboard and spat twice on the road, once for communist propaganda and a second time for Maximo flirting with Juliana. Daniel was supposed to have spent the morning with his girlfriend. If not for the faulty key, he would have been there to protect her from Max.

He raced the bike down the country road and coasted around a sharp bend at an intersection. Without warning three shiny black Mercedes Benz careened around the corner on Daniel's side of the road and forced him to swerve to the roadside. The bike plowed into a ditch. It was like being charged by three Spanish fighting bulls bolting out of nowhere. They appeared suddenly, and each missed his bike by centimeters.

His body hit the ground hard. The bike crashed on top of his legs. Daniel's upper torso lay on a rise, and his legs rested in a rain-soaked gulley. He remained in this awkward position while he determined whether he had sustained an injury during the fall. Pain radiated in his left elbow which had struck the ground first, but Daniel knew the injury was minor. He listened to the vehicles reverse. A car door slammed shut.

Daniel glanced up into the sun and saw a great silhouette of a man towering above him. He squinted, and to his amazement Fidel Castro Ruz, Dictator of Cuba, lifted the bicycle off him.

"*Te dañastes?*" the commander-in-chief asked.

Daniel lay stunned in the shallow water of the ditch. Finally he said, "No, I'm not hurt."

A man in a black suit with a wire dangling from his ear rushed over to scoop the bike out of Castro's hands. "*Comandante, por favor, déjeme ayudarle. Señor, usted no debe levantar bicicletas. Por favor.*"

Fidel Castro pushed the bike toward the secret service agent and offered a hand to Daniel. Castro's firm grip on his scarred hand pulled him out of the ditch, and Daniel came face to face with the leader of Cuba. He stared at the beard, the brown eyes muted by sunglasses, and the rim of his camouflage cap. The dictator stood tall and powerful in his army fatigues before the startled young man. Daniel recalled an acquaintance who had caught a glimpse of Castro and described him as a foreboding man, powerful in character and strength. Daniel agreed with this description but had never expected to see him this close.

Daniel suppressed a desire to question Fidel Castro about the Italian tobacco leaves that were secretly blended with Cuban tobacco, the confiscation of exiles' homes and businesses, the imprisonment of dissidents, and the countless murders and bloodshed of innocent Cubans. He had a thousand questions to ask him in reference to his ironclad rule since his deceitful takeover of Cuba on New Year's Eve of 1959, but of course he remained silent. One wrong move on this deserted highway and the secret service could execute him and bury his body in a meadow, and forever his fate would be a mystery.

Two military men eased in between the dictator and Daniel and guided their supreme leader back to the safety of his armored car. Daniel followed them with his eyes as he brushed mud and blades of grass off his pants. The engines of the three Mercedes hummed, and the chauffeurs accelerated in unison. They moved as one down the long stretch of highway and vanished at the distant horizon. Now Daniel pictured the convoy not as charging bulls but as a black mamba with sharp fangs, slithering, hissing, and dripping venom across the island of Cuba.

Daniel cast a glance at the billboard in the distance, spat on the pavement, and moistened his scar with saliva where Castro had gripped his hand. Vigorously he wiped the wet palm on his shirt. He remembered the keys and checked his pocket. Inside he felt the cold metal. Daniel hopped on his bike and resumed a rapid return to Ranchuelo, anxious to monitor Juliana's unexpected visitor.

"I know Max was here. What did he want?" Daniel leaned forward in a chair as he sat across from his girlfriend in her living room.

"What makes you think he was here?"

"Never mind. I know he came to see you."

Juliana stroked his hand. "If you must know, he stopped by. I let him in because I thought he came to see Rafa."

"Why would you let him inside? You knew he wanted to see you, not Rafael."

"I didn't know what he wanted and didn't want to upset him anymore."

"Upset him? You're worried about that loser's feelings?"

Tears welled in her eyes. "No. I'm worried about you."

"About me? I can defend myself. I don't want him near you." Daniel saw her eyes cast down and stare at the floor. Gently he raised her chin so their eyes met. "You don't have to worry about me. What did he say? Tell me."

She blinked away the tears. "He begged me to break up with you."

Daniel pushed the chair back and knocked it over as he stood up. "That..." He made it a point never to swear in front of his girlfriend, so he cut his sentence short and headed for the door.

"Daniel, please come back. You insisted I tell you. It wasn't my choice."

His senses returned. "You're right. I did." He saw the worried look on her face, the same expression she'd had on the day she fled from his house. He set the chair upright and sat down.

Rafael walked into the room. "What was that noise?"

"The chair tipped over. That's all," Juli said.

"I didn't know you were home." Daniel directed his gaze from Juliana to Rafael. "Did you know Max stopped by to see your sister?"

"She told me, but he left before I got here. Now don't go crazy, Daniel. The guy's more of a jerk than we realized. Eventually he'll get over her."

"He will," Juli said. "Please be patient. I have no feelings for him whatsoever."

"You always say that, but he doesn't give up."

"Ignore him. His pursuit is in vain."

"Rafa's right. Pay no attention to Max. He's trying to make you angry."

"You're both right. I'm just sick of his persistence." Daniel glanced at his watch.

"I'm sorry I can't stay to discuss this further. I have to go to work. I'll stop by in the morning."

Juli gazed into his eyes. "Tomorrow?"

"*Sí*, tomorrow, and it's true I have to go to work."

"And where were you this morning, *señor*? I waited for you."

Daniel detected a suspicious ring to her voice.

"I had to go back to Rambo's farm. I wanted to come here but had to get a key recut. There was no way to let you know. On my way back El Caballo almost ran me over with his Mercedes. I should say three Mercedes. Fidel and his entourage."

"Fidel Castro?" Juliana and Rafael said in unison.

"Yes, him. The cars were speeding. They crossed to my side of the road, and cut me off. I fell off my bike and into a ditch. Can you believe it? Fidel picked up my bike and pulled me out."

"You're joking," Rafael said.

"No, it's the truth." He lifted his mud-stained pant leg as proof.

"*Hombre*, you're like a cat with nine lives. You can't have many left."

"Very funny. And my luck was improving." Daniel bent down to kiss Juliana. "I've got to go."

Rafael walked him to the door and asked if he had tried the key in the lock.

"You traced the key just fine, but Rambo had trouble cutting it from paper. The first key hardly fit in the lock. That's why I went back to the farm this morning. He cut me two keys this time."

"Let me know if they work."

"I'll test them tonight. At least one should fit, and you'll see how our lives will prosper."

Daniel waved to Juliana and knew she'd heard every word, although she pretended to read a magazine. She raised her eyes from the page as the door opened and returned his wave by blowing him a kiss.

Daniel stood in line at La Criolla, the government-owned grocery store, and clutched his Libreto de Consumo, a ration book issued by the government to every household to record monthly purchases of food and supplies. Earlier, Emilio had cornered Daniel on his way to work to tell him that the store had received products that had been out of stock for months and to hurry before the shelves emptied. Daniel had asked Emilio to advise Angel that he would be late for work. Outside Daniel's house, before Emilio headed for the factory, Daniel said, "Why do you dislike Max's father so much?"

"It's a long story. I'll tell you when we have more time."

"I'm really curious. What happened?"

Emilio paused and then said, "Everyone in the Lopez family is known to be deceitful. Some are even criminals. I've had several bad encounters with them, but the straw that broke the camel's back was when I left my car to be repaired at the body shop. A Seat Seis Cientos I bought from a Spaniard returning to Galicia. The car had a brake problem, so I left it with Rodolfo, Maximo's father."

Daniel nodded that he knew Rodolfo Lopez.

"That little car fell off the lift and onto the cement floor. It dropped and was totaled because the lift was faulty, and Rodolfo refused to reimburse me for damages. The front of the car was squashed like an accordion, and that son of a bitch had the nerve to yell at me to get the wreck out of his garage. I was furious. It left me without transportation, and like you I had to ride my bicycle everywhere. I haven't spoken to a Lopez since. No good sons of bitches."

"You were right about Max."

"I tried to tell you. He's just like his father and the rest of them. If you need help, let me know. I can handle a Lopez."

"I'll deal with him. Did you move your car out of the shop?"

"No." Emilio's eyes glazed with anger as he recalled the incident. "I told him to go to hell and everywhere else in all kinds of foul language."

"He deserved it."

"He did, but I was still worse off than him, without wheels. It made me feel better to know that he had to move that wreck. Like I said, never trust a Lopez. I'd better go to your boss. Get over to the store. Word is spreading fast."

Daniel watched Emilio rush toward the factory. Now he had a better understanding of why his neighbor disliked Maximo.

Patiently, Daniel waited in the long line forming outside the market. A woman holding her daughter's hand in line ahead of Daniel turned and stared at him. The girl whispered to her mother. The woman asked the man behind her to hold her place in line and walked over to Daniel. She asked if he was dating Juliana Reyes. Reluctantly, he told her that he was.

"What a wonderful girl. The most exquisite ballerina. My daughter," the woman touched the girl's head, "also dances. We watched Juliana perform. She always stole the show. We were sorry she injured her foot. Will she ever dance again?"

"I don't know."

"We miss seeing her on stage. Tell her Alicia and Ylenes wish her well. She has such a promising career ahead of her."

"Thank you. I'll tell her." As the mother and daughter returned to their place in line, Alicia told him it was nice meeting him.

Daniel pondered what Alicia had said and wished he could have sat in an audience during a performance featuring Juliana. This was yet another example of Rafael's interference. Rafa had guarded his sister like a pirate hoarding a treasure and had refused to reveal anything about her life. He was certain that the purpose of Rafael's silence was to discourage Daniel's pursuit of his sister. Today, during the conversation with Alicia, was the first time Daniel had learned Juli was a ballerina. His best friend's secret hurt and disappointed him. Juliana had mentioned dance but not ballet. He continued to wait in line, saddened that he was never invited to attend Juliana's recitals.

An hour later he watched Alicia and Ylenes lift bulging bags off the counter.

Daniel opened the door for them as they passed.

"Don't forget to tell Juliana you saw us. She'll remember."

"I won't," he said as the door closed. He stepped closer to the counter. After five minutes the clerk took his booklet and checked off each item as he filled three bags with groceries. The shopkeeper signed the notebook and handed it to him, along with the bags.

One bag brimmed with twisted, elongated tubers, known as yucca. Threadlike roots peeked out of a coating of soil on the pipe-like vegetable that poked Daniel's cheek as he whisked the sacks into his arms. He walked past customers chattering as they stood in a crooked row along the sidewalk. He snapped off a piece of carrot and munched as he rushed home, anxious to surprise his mother with a refrigerator full of food. Tonight after work Daniel would feast on a dinner prepared by his mother. For the first time in months they would eat a balanced meal.

Chapter Seven
YUCCA STARCH

Alma Milan awoke to sounds of Daniel in the kitchen. Drawers opened and slammed shut, and pots clanged on the stove. While standing in the kitchen doorway she watched her son strain shredded yucca in cheesecloth. He wrung the liquid from the cloth into a pitcher. Daniel had boiled the tubers, removed them from a pot, and placed them on a platter. One dropped to the floor with a splat. He scooped it up, juggled the hot vegetable from one hand to the other, washed it off, and returned it to the top of the pile. Then he rinsed his burning hands under a stream of cool tap water. Alma saw the garbage can overflowing with yucca peels that dripped dirty water on the floor. She eyed a chain of muddy puddles that speckled the ceramic tile.

Unaware of his mother's presence, Daniel poured tepid yucca water into an empty spray bottle. Liquid dribbled down the side of the bottle. He noticed movement in the doorway, glanced up, and waited for Alma to speak first. He assumed she was still angry at him because of the party.

"*Hijo*, now what are you concocting? You are always scheming." Alma recognized the sly look on his face. Even his reassuring smile did not fool her.

"I'm not scheming," he said. "I'm about to iron my pants for work."

Daniel took the bottle to the living room, where he had set up an ironing board draped with a pair of black flared pants.

"Daniel, we have enough yucca for a month. Why did you get so much?"

"Don't worry. I'll freeze some. There was a delivery at La Criolla yesterday. Finally we have food."

"Yes, finally. I prepared a stew last night. Did you eat?"

"Of course."

"La Criolla hasn't had food in weeks. I thought you got the vegetables at Rambo's farm on loan. You paid for all that?" She sank into a chair while he ironed. "Daniel, I don't like this. Your father and I didn't raise you to be a thief."

"Hell, what's the difference? He was already disappointed in me when he died."

"That's not true. He wanted you to be a doctor but left it up to you to decide. He didn't mind that you became a teacher. He was right, though, wasn't he? You should have become a doctor."

Daniel was silent.

"Anyway, you must be more discreet. The loud parties, selling cigarettes in front of everyone…government spies are everywhere."

"You worry too much. Believe me. I'm careful."

"And where did you get the new clothes?" Alma pointed to the pants on the ironing board.

"Rafael's cousin sent them from Miami. Rafa gave me the ones too big for him."

Daniel wanted to sneak away, but he had to iron his clothes for work. He hated when she grilled him.

"And the Armani cologne on your dresser?"

"His cousin. Rafa and I are sharing it. Ease up, *mamá*. I have to get ready for work."

"Am I interrupting?"

"*Tengo prisa.* I'm in a hurry."

Daniel hoped she would go to her room to sew the pile of clothing in a bag leaning against her sewing machine, but she remained seated. He sprayed some yucca water on a pant leg. The steaming iron hissed and glided over the wide leg. A cloud of steam rose from the hole at the top of the iron, and the combined scent of hot fabric and boiled tuber filled the air. As the material dried, it stiffened. He lifted the pants from the waist and examined the legs with an expression of satisfaction on his face.

"Starched to perfection."

Daniel reached for another pair. Then he glanced over at his mother, winked, and ironed the bumpy cloth around the zipper.

Alma returned the wink. "I have to admit it was nice to wake up with a full stomach. Thank you, dear, for the food."

"You're welcome. I'll try to keep the refrigerator stocked from now on."

She stretched her legs and set her feet on a stool in front of the chair. "Consuelo told me she saw you with Juliana Reyes the other day. She seems like a nice girl."

Daniel knew she was prying him for information. "I've gotten together with her a few times."

"A few times? Consuelo said you're with her on your days off."

"I also go to see Rafael. What does she know?"

"She has eyes."

"And a big mouth."

"Daniel! Consuelo would kill for you. That's how much she cares. Now be considerate."

He turned off the iron, picked up a bundle of clothes from the sofa, and went to the kitchen. He soaked a Miami Dolphins jersey and several plain t-shirts in yucca water and hung them on the clothesline to dry. His mother followed him outside and hovered around him. Daniel loved her, but she doted and nagged too much. He glanced at his watch. After pinning the last shirt to the line, he hurried past her to his room, changed and emerged in the ironed pants and a loose-fitting gray shirt, both starched to an unnatural stiffness.

"You have such a nice physique. Why hide it with those awful baggy clothes?"

"To keep the girls from attacking this body." Daniel flexed his muscles and hastened out the door.

Alma Milan shook her head. It was sad that her husband had missed out on their son as a mature young man. Tears stained her cheeks. When overcome by thoughts of Daniel, Sr. she forced herself to keep busy. After she craned to watch Daniel walk down the street from the living room window, she cleaned the house, washed her clothes in a tub, and hung them outside to dry. First Alma had to remove Daniel's crisp, starched shirts from the clothesline to make room for her clothes. When she set the last shirt on a lawn chair, out of the corner of her eye she saw Emilio strolling toward her. She had seen him earlier digging in his yard.

"God knows what for," Alma had told Daniel. "He's probably hiding contraband from the PNRs." In Emilio's yard sprouted an array of markers that protruded above the grass to define the location of his secret treasures.

"*Buenos días*, Alma," said Emilio. "I think your son is madly in love with the Reyes girl."

"Is that so? *Porqué dices eso?*"

"Because Carmelita told me he bought her a heart-shaped locket."

"Carmelita told you that?"

"*Sí*. And Osvaldo saw Daniel walking hand in hand with Juliana in town the other day while they ate ice cream."

"Osvaldo the butcher? Why wasn't he at work in his shop?"

"He was on his way to deliver meat to the police station—you know, a gesture of gratitude."

"Yes, I know. A payoff."

"Something like that."

"I see," she murmured with a clothespin in her mouth. Alma draped a wet dress over the cord and pinned it. "Everyone seems to know what my son is doing but me, and that worries me."

"No need to worry. Daniel's a good boy. He stays out of trouble, not like some of those factory boys."

Alma turned and looked at Emilio to detect sarcasm. When she realized he was serious, she said, "I hope you're right, Emilio. Well, I must finish ironing."

Daniel's shirts were stiff as dried banana leaves. Emilio watched her clutch the shirts like cardboard cutouts and carry them inside. Alma heard him laugh. Her worry over her son's escapades turned to amusement at the comical way the shirts hardened in place. She also laughed.

In the living room, Alma chuckled as she ironed the starched garments. Wrinkles quickly disappeared. After she finished, she folded the ironing board, placed it in a closet, and hung Daniel's shirts neatly in his closet. For two hours she procrastinated and then sat down at her sewing machine. Alma sighed as she slipped a torn sleeve of a blouse under the needle and pressed the floor pedal with her foot. The familiar hum of the machine always reminded her of bees buzzing in a hive as they labored to produce sticky golden honey.

Daniel arrived home from work after midnight and noticed darkness beneath his mother's bedroom door. He locked the door to his bedroom, raised the stiff pant legs that hugged his calves, and picked out box after box of cigarettes stashed inside his baseball socks. He unbuttoned his shirt, untied the rope fastened around his undershirt, and watched dozens of packs fall to the floor. During his eight-hour shift, Daniel craved this moment of relief to rid himself of packs wrapped in plastic that dug into his flesh and irritated his skin. He paused to listen and to assure that the noise of dropping cartons had not disturbed his sleeping mother. The house was quiet. He frantically rubbed his stomach and legs.

Cigarette packs filled his duffel bag, and he emptied a sport bag to accommodate the rest of the cigarettes. Once the second bag was full, he stuffed boxes into his backpack. Daniel decided to give Rafael his share of the heist at the baseball game in the morning.

He was anxious to tell his friend that both keys cut by Rambo fit the storage room lock. He reached up to put the bags on the closet shelf and noticed his starched and ironed shirts neatly hanging in a row, which brought a smile to his face.

Rafael stood up to bat and concentrated hard on the pitcher of the Santa Rosa Sugar Mill Team. The pitcher gripped the ball and slung a pitch at the anxious batter. Daniel bounced from one foot to the other on second base, awaiting a hit. From his vantage point, he saw the determination on his friend's face and took off when he heard the bat crack against the ball. Rafa smashed the ball short between first and second, and Daniel tore along a stretch of red sand to third base, slid nimbly, and kicked up a geyser of dust as both feet touched square on the marker an instant before the third baseman caught the ball and slapped it on Daniel's thigh. The pain and the slide as he momentarily looked down at his feet set him back in time to the fall in the warehouse.

Daniel stood up, wiped off his white pants stained auburn, rubbed out the pain in his leg, and shook his head to rid himself of the flashback. When the umpire yelled, "safe," a group of fans in the bleachers and a cluster of townsfolk standing on the sidelines cheered for Daniel. He distinguished Juliana's high-pitched voice above the cheers of the other fans. Her naturally sweet vocals rang out.

Daniel felt his right sock slip to his ankle and reached down, pulled it up, and tucked it firmly inside his pant leg. "Damn," he said in a low tone as he eyed the crowd. The cigarette packs had stretched the elastic of his baseball socks.

He recognized the stocky build of Rambo poised in front of the catcher, ready for the pitch, and called to him, "*Dame un regalito*. Give me one little gift, Rambo. A home run."

Crack went the ball on the wood, and the small globe whizzed over Daniel's head and sailed like a meteor over the fence in left field. Daniel shouted, "Rambo, *amigo*, you are powerful," as he raced to home plate. He strutted with confidence, and in plenty of time he lightly tapped home plate.

Rafael soon followed and jogged behind him. He ran up to Daniel and slapped his extended hand. The spectators cheered and laughed as the two danced together around home plate. When Rambo raced to home the small crowd roared. Daniel and Rafael greeted him with hugs.

"Great hit," Rafa said as he smacked Rambo on the back. "Way to go!"

As the three sauntered to the bench to allow the next hitter his turn at bat, Daniel leaned over to Rafael. "I have the packs for you in my bag, the blue one. Whenever you get a chance, slip them into your bag."

"Will do, *amigo*."

Together they sat on the bench as the applause and cheers continued. Juliana stood up and gazed admiringly at Daniel and her brother who chatted and gestured with their hands. They were oblivious to the noise as they analyzed this crucial game.

At the end of the game, the noise, shouts, and dancing by the fans in the bleachers continued until the winners, the factory team, left the field. Daniel carried his duffel bag to meet up with Juli and asked Rafael, "Did you get the cigarettes?" He shook his bag. "It weighs less."

"I got them." Rafael raised his bag. "They're in here and ready to be sold."

"Life will get better, *amigo*," Daniel said as he watched Juliana bounce gracefully down the bleachers. Instinct caused him to look around for Maximo. "I was keeping an eye out for Max. I almost forgot he works at the shop on Saturdays."

"That he does. Anyway, he hates sports, so you can be at ease today. Your rival's busy. Juli's safe."

Rafael lingered on Santa Rosa Street in Carmelita's territory. Carmelita didn't mind the young man selling cigarettes alongside her. In fact she enjoyed flirting with the young men of the town, and to her delight Rafael's company was a unique opportunity. Besides, she knew Daniel and he were good friends, and Daniel always gave her business. Since he'd purchased the locket, he'd bought earrings and a bracelet for his girlfriend and had sent several friends who also bargained for her wares. Despite the customers sent by Daniel and their persistence to lower the price, at the end of bidding she was rewarded by a substantial profit.

Carmelita surmised that Rafael's cigarette customers may become future clients of hers, so she swooned around him as he prodded pedestrians to buy packs at a reasonable price. Their clients departed, and as they stood on the sidewalk, Carmelita nudged him. "*Oye, guapo,* where is Daniel today?"

"Working second shift."

"When will he ask your sister to marry him? I can see their relationship is getting serious. Tell Daniel it may take me a while to get an engagement ring. Convince him to order one from me now. Diamond rings are hard to come by."

Rafael smiled. "That I'm aware of, the subject of marriage hasn't come up yet. You know Daniel. Although he loves Juli, he's still the free spirit he always was. I want him to be absolutely sure before he makes a commitment to my sister."

"Stop worrying. It's obvious he really loves her."

The day slipped by. Carmelita and Rafael became excellent selling partners. Rafael urged people to buy Carmelita's wares, and she coaxed her clients to purchase his cigarettes. Their street marketing strategy proved prosperous for both.

"People are spending more today than they have in a long time," she commented to Rafael.

While they discussed a new sales strategy, Carmelita pointed to a small group of students crossing the street and told Rafa to corner them. She waited for him to lure the students her way when suddenly Rafael's father approached them from behind after eying the two street vendors from across the street. Mr. Reyes grabbed Rafael by the shoulder and swung him around.

"What in the hell are you doing on the street like a bum pedaling junk?"

Carmelita gasped. "*Buenos días, Señor* Reyes."

He ignored her. Rafael stopped mid-step, shocked speechless at the sight of his father, who was supposed to have driven Juliana to work and spent the remainder of the day in Santa Clara visiting relatives.

"I thought you had more sense than this. I never want to see you selling stolen goods again."

Mr. Reyes grabbed the cigarette packs out of his son's hand, threw them inside the duffel bag, and tossed it into a trashcan in front of a dry goods store. Carmelita scrambled to snatch up the bag. She reached for a pack and dug into the cellophane wrap with her fingernails. It crinkled as she peeled the clear plastic. She picked out a cigarette, slipped it between her lips, and gestured for a young man passing by on the sidewalk to light it. Her pink lipstick stained the cigarette tip. Carmelita inhaled, blew out a puff of smoke, and witnessed the scolding. Two sisters approached. She removed the lit cigarette, balanced it on the edge of a shop windowsill, and proceeded with her sales pitch to the girls who strolled by arm in arm.

Mr. Reyes put a firm hand at the back of his son's neck and pulled him toward his car parked by Prado Nuevo. As they crossed the street, Carmelita heard Rafael's father say, "Do you have any concept of what you are doing? If you get caught, you'll go straight to prison."

On the way home, when his father had calmed down, Rafael said, "Why didn't you go to Santa Clara?"

"Because someone told me you would be selling cigarettes in town. That's why."

"Who told you?"

"And give away my source? Not on your life, son."

Rafael later questioned his sister, Emilio, and Rambo about the incident with his father, but they all denied speaking to Mr. Reyes and swore they had not revealed any information about Rafael's street sales to anyone, including his father. When Rafa caught up to Daniel, he said, "I have no idea who told my father."

"Me either. I can't even guess. Who would have said something? What gets me is no one but Juli and I knew you were going to sell in town."

"I mentioned it to Emilio because he bought a pack on my way to town, and Rambo saw me selling. That's all."

"Rambo?"

"He didn't say anything. He swore."

"Someone saw you. We can't mention our selling plans to anyone."

"The business is all yours now. My father will kill me if he catches me again. Like Castro, his spies are out there."

"That sucks. Don't worry. I'll give you a portion of whatever I make."

"You don't have to. I messed up."

"If it wasn't for you, I'd never have gotten into the locked storage area."

"Hey, you're getting just as many packs out of production storage, and I had nothing to do with that."

"And that's a lot of cigarettes. More reason to split the profits."

"Come on. You'll be doing all the work. Just make Juli happy, and I'll be happy."

"I'll do that too."

"I almost forgot. Carmelita mentioned she has sheets you ordered. They came in yesterday." Rafael decided not to say anything to Daniel about ordering an engagement ring.

"Thanks. I'll pick them up."

"You ordered sheets?"

"*Sí*. Juli wanted them." Daniel chose not to explain to Rafael how his parents had sacrificed the top sheet of their bed for Juliana. For certain this tidbit would get back to her and might embarrass her.

"By the way, have you noticed that every time you buy something from Carmelita, the next week she has on a new outfit?"

"You're kidding. You notice her new clothes, Rafa? You're that observant? I have no clue what she wears. I only know she wears her skirts short and blouses tight and low cut."

"I notice that too. But ask anyone. Since you've supported her black market business, she's bought a new wardrobe."

"Well, good for her. Capitalism is at work in this communist society."

Chapter Eight
THE STORM

Daniel took two personal days to spend time with Juliana over the weekend after she hinted that their work schedules kept them apart. Daniel promised her a weekend of continuous hours together. They sat in her dining room on Saturday morning and made plans for the afternoon while they sipped café con leche and ate guava and cream cheese pastries.

"Didn't you tell me you liked to walk in the park?"

"Yes. You remembered?"

"I remember everything you tell me."

"Everything, Daniel?"

"Yes, everything. Come on. Let's go."

"The pastries?"

Daniel returned the guava pastry to the plate and wiped his hands on a napkin.

"We'll finish them later."

Holding hands, they cut across town via Prado el Viejo. Daniel glanced over at the firehouse at the end of the esplanade and at the village where one house connected to another in a European style. He thought of Ranchuelo as an attractive town but had always felt he needed more than it offered.

Ramiro La Vandero and the two sugar mills, Santa Rosa and Santa Maria, had brought wealth to Ranchuelo. Despite hard times instilled upon Cuba by Castro's communist regime outwardly reflected in its deteriorated buildings, the architecture of Ranchuelo remained in decent condition.

Juliana and Daniel left the village and headed toward the railroad station. They stopped at the tracks when they heard the morning passenger train whistle and chug toward town. There was time to cross, but Daniel chose to play it safe and stretched his arm out in front of Juliana to discourage her from stepping onto the tracks. She was pleased with her boyfriend's protective gesture, and when she stepped back, she pulled him with her. The engine roared in front of them, and passenger cars crept by as the engine screeched to a halt.

The train blocked their view of the station. A passenger waved to them from inside a car as he stood in the aisle to exit the train. In a few minutes the train departed, and the station and passengers carrying suitcases came into view. Daniel held Juli's arm as she straddled the tracks. They crossed in front of the train station and continued to Jose Martí Park, situated in front of the school. One-horse buggies lined up under the shade of trees along the street bordering the park.

Juliana skipped on the cement ahead of Daniel. At the statue of Jose Martí she turned to her boyfriend with a serene look on her face, arms spread wide. "I used to love playing here as a child with Eva and our dolls."

"Eva? Oh, the girl at the party."

"*Sí*, my dear friend." Juli scanned the park with her eyes. "The political situation didn't affect us back then, in our innocence. But despite the oppression, I still wouldn't want to live anywhere else. How about you? Don't you love Ranchuelo, too?"

Daniel was surprised this subject surfaced after his recent thought about living elsewhere. "It's fine," he said to avoid conflict. He saw Juli so happy, and his desire for a change or for an eventual move to the United States seemed an inappropriate subject to discuss at this time. At a later date, delicately and in a detailed explanation, he would confide in Juliana about his desire to leave Cuba. Blurting out his plans now may ruin a lovely day together.

Daniel's eyes panned the square park surrounded by manicured ficus trees, and the sight of the village roofs in the distance forced him to admit that Ranchuelo was a safe, quaint place to live. But then he focused across the park at the police station constructed after Castro gained power, an ugly reminder of suppression in Cuba. He kept these thoughts to himself as he marveled at the beaming young lady before him.

Juli's arms moved in motion to her hips as she mimicked the swaying trees. Daniel leaned against the statue with his arms crossed. A young girl rushed over to Juliana as she twirled on her toes.

"Miss Reyes, please dance for us, for my sister and my *abuelita*. Please?"

She smiled down at the girl. "I'd love to."

Juliana arched her arms above her head and whirled around and around in a pirouette. With each revolution she glanced down at the child. The girl watched with her mouth wide open and tried to imitate the ballerina. Her grandmother and younger sister clapped.

Juli left this stance and leaped across the park's surface. The girl followed. Daniel curiously watched his girlfriend and the little clone glide before the audience of two. Every step and stance Juliana positioned herself in, the little shadow copied. Juli laughed, and the girl giggled. He watched her coach the young ballerina.

Before him danced his ideal vision of a woman, the special one he'd waited three years for. Daniel had told Juli the truth while seated on the bench at the house her aunt had been forced to abandon. For the first time in his life, he had fallen in love. At this moment nothing else mattered, not even his desire to depart Cuba.

But deep thoughts and sentiments for Juli vanished when he heard the girl scream and he looked up and saw Juliana leap high in the air, falter, and stumble to the hard surface. He panicked but was stunned that even her fall was delicate and graceful.

Daniel ran to the far side of the park to assist his girlfriend, who was sprawled on the cement, and was relieved when she sat up and massaged her foot before he reached her. The little girl skipped over to Juliana, kissed her on the cheek, and ran to join her grandmother, who held her sister in awe at the sight of the fallen maiden.

Daniel reached for Juli. "Are you all right?"

"I'm fine," she said with discouragement in her voice. "Just embarrassed."

He helped her to her feet. "No need to be embarrassed. Are you sure you didn't hurt yourself?"

"I'm sure."

"I didn't know you were a ballerina until I was in line at La Criolla. A woman, Alicia, with her daughter told me how well you danced and asked me to say hello to you."

"That was nice of her. I taught her daughter ballet, as I did this little girl. Alicia and Ylenes always attended my recitals no matter where they took place." Juliana signaled to the elderly woman that she was unhurt and watched as they left the park.

"*Adios*, Miss Reyes."

Juliana waved and watched the girls' small hands grip their grandmother's. She turned to Daniel. "I wanted to be a ballerina. But the fracture weakened my foot, and I was forced to give up dance." She clutched his arm to regain her footing. "Ballet was my passion, my first love before you came along." She gave him a slight smile.

"Your first love? There was someone, something, before me? I had no idea." He gave her a hug. "It's a shame. Your injury, I mean. I'm sorry you can't do what you really enjoy."

"I'm sorry too. But I've finally come to terms with it. I was confident I would be accepted at the School of Ballet in Havana and planned to perfect my moves in Moscow during the summer." Solemnly she looked into his eyes. "With this injury," Juli touched her ankle, "I gave up all hope for a career in ballet."

Daniel leaned over and kissed her forehead. "There's no chance of your foot healing?"

"The doctor told me no. This will be as good as it gets."

"We'll have to find another passion for you."

"What do you have in mind?" She smiled but before he replied she returned to a serious tone of voice. "Like your work at the factory, I'm working at a job I'm not interested in, waiting on tourists in a hotel gift shop."

"At least you're working," he said and recalled that these were the exact words she had quoted him while swinging on the hammock in his yard.

"True. Those are my words. At least I get free books and magazines. Damaged ones, that is. But it's not the same as doing what you really love."

"You have to stay positive."

"I try. But I didn't always look on the bright side. Ask Rafa. For a long time I was bitter and took my anger out on my family, the people I dearly love."

"In what way?"

"I was argumentative, antagonistic. I don't know. Ask Rafa. I was a bitch, I guess."

"I can't picture you like that."

"I'm sorry to say I was. I was so sad and upset. I apologized to them. They understood. Ever since I was a little girl I practiced ballet and was determined to be a prima ballerina. It was traumatic not to dance anymore."

The sky suddenly darkened, and the park was cloaked in shade. Daniel glanced up at a billowing gray thunderhead rapidly approaching from the west. Surprised at the rapid change of weather, Juliana said, "It's a storm." At the instant she uttered her words, the cloud obscured the last rays of sun, and rain sliced the air in torrents. Slivers of rain became javelins drenching the couple.

"Take cover." Daniel wrapped his arms around her and supported her as she limped beside him. Together they huddled beneath bushes and low palms on the outskirts of the park's square in hopes the rain would pass. He felt a chill as cold rainwater dripped under his shirt and down his back, but as Juliana snuggled closer, the coolness dissipated and turned to warmth and a glowing sensation he had never experienced before. He embraced her and drew her closer to him. The rain pounded and splattered them with earth accumulated at the edge of the cement.

Juliana's ivory complexion glistened with raindrops. The lip gloss she had smeared on as the train passed sparkled with water droplets. Daniel leaned over to kiss her, and his lips covered hers with an urgency he could hardly contain. The warmth of their bodies huddled together, and the cool wind stirring the leaves of surrounding trees, excited him and evoked a passion he described as breathtaking.

A sudden clap of thunder and streaks of lightning that brightened the sky added to his fervor. All he wanted was to disrobe her and make love beneath this natural shelter. He urged Juliana but never became forceful. Also caught up in the intensity, she refrained from allowing their emotions to be acted upon.

Juliana whispered, "Daniel, *te quiero mucho*." Her words interrupted the ecstasy he was immersed in.

"Juli, *por favor*," he pleaded.

"I want to, but we can't. We have to marry first."

He buried his head in her chest. "Marry?"

She stroked his wet hair but removed her hand when lightning struck a tree across the street with a crackling sound. They ducked down. Daniel rose to shield her body when the crash of thunder followed.

"If we live through this storm, I promise I will marry you."

"You will?" she said with a voice muffled by his weight. Talk of marriage was soon forgotten when lightning flashed and struck near them again.

Juli screamed, "Daniel, I'm afraid."

Thunder pierced their ears, and an electric charge emanated from the ground and jolted them to their feet. He grabbed her hand, and they ran to the railroad station for shelter.

The stationmaster flashed them a look of contempt as threatening as the forked lightning illuminating the sky. He groaned as they trailed a stream of water and mud to a bench far from windows reflecting the brilliant lightning. They sat and waited in silence for the storm to pass.

Daniel broke the silence. "I loved watching you dance in the park. Would you like to go dancing?" His intention was to take her mind off the terrifying storm. He chuckled at the thought of her rhythm without music to the swaying trees and how her dance moves were mimicked by the little girl. "There's a festival at Prado el Viejo tomorrow night. Would you like to go?"

"I would love to." She perked up. "I was hoping you would ask me. A band plays there every Thursday and Sunday night."

A faint smile disappeared as her eyes met his. Daniel held her hand and knew her usual bright smile lay dormant behind sealed lips because the thunderstorm had frightened her. Never had he known Juli to be so quiet. He hugged her shivering body and was astonished at how fearful he had been in the park too. He leaned his head back against the wall, closed his eyes, and pondered his fierce attraction to Juliana and the intense desire for her while cowering in the storm. Despite the cold air and wet clothes stuck to his body, he felt lingering heat. Daniel stretched his legs.

"Sorry about today. I wanted that walk in the park to be special."

"It wasn't your fault I fell or that there was a storm. I had a great time until I fell and that cloud arrived." With her finger she wiped a raindrop about to slide off his forehead. "Let's promise, from now on, to have only wonderful times together."

"It's a promise."

"Fun only, from this moment on. I really thought we were going to die in the park."

"I didn't think that, but I have to admit I was worried." His lips practically touched her ear, and his voice lowered to a whisper so the stationmaster wouldn't hear. "Before the thunder and lightning, I wanted to make mad, passionate love to you in the rain."

Juliana laughed. "I felt the same, but I told you we have to marry."

"Finally you're laughing. You must feel better." But he felt hurt because her laughter meant she didn't take him seriously. "Why wait until marriage?"

She saw disappointment in his expression. "I'm sorry. I laughed because your whisper tickled my ear." She stroked his cheek. "My parents are strict Catholics and raised us so. Although we were forbidden to practice our beliefs in a church, at home my parents taught us catechism and the bible every Sunday morning." Juli became pensive. "*Mi amor*, did I hear you say above a loud clap of thunder that if we survived the storm, you would marry me?"

Daniel imitated her tone of voice. "Those words I said under great duress. Maybe someday."

"Duress?"

"I mean the storm."

"Someday we'd better," she threatened. "I can't imagine marrying anyone else."

"You can always hook up with Maximo. He's as wild about you as I am."

"Now that's not funny." She tickled his side and pushed the cold, wet shirt against his skin. To escape his retaliation she jumped up, but to her surprise he remained seated and made no attempt to rise.

Juliana crossed the room and studied the antique photographs of sugar barons posing beside engineers with black locomotives looming behind them. Daniel watched her examine the gallery of pictures hung along the wall. The photos nearest him portrayed field workers gathered in front of train cars loaded with sugarcane, pulled by steam engines.

He looked away from the pictures and glanced out the window opposite the wall where Juli stood with her back to him. The rain was easing. Daniel thought about her statement of how Catholicism was an integral part of the Reyes household. In all their years of friendship, Rafael had never mentioned the importance of religion in his life. Of course the subject was taboo in Cuba since Castro had declared the island nation an atheist state. But he and Rafael trusted each other. Why was religion a secret in Rafa's life?

Juliana was unaware her brother had confided to Daniel that he had slept with a few girlfriends. Daniel made up his mind not to relay this bit of her brother's history, although it was perfect leverage to debate the issue of sex before marriage. Daniel was certain Rafael would consider a discussion about his sex life a breach of trust. For this reason Daniel remained silent and refused to risk compromising their friendship. Rafael cherished his privacy and deep down was a sensitive guy. Daniel respected that.

Quietly, he rose from the bench and rushed over to the unsuspecting Juliana, swept her off her feet, and lifted her high in the air. His strong grip around her waist and the rising motion startled her. Her scream pierced the quiet train station and echoed louder than her shouts during the height of the storm. As the stationmaster jumped up from his desk, his swivel chair rolled across the floor and bumped into a table. He ran to the door and flung it open. His cap blew off his bald head and glided to the wet floor as he beckoned the couple outside into a light rain.

"You immature juveniles. Get out of here right now." He slammed the door as Daniel carried the struggling young lady across his shoulders into the steamy air. The stationmaster peeked out the window into a sunny mist, shook his head with a look of disgust on his face, and vigorously wiped the mud off his cap.

Sunday night before sundown and before the band started playing, Daniel bought cotton candy for Juliana on Prado el Viejo. They watched the vendor swirl the paper cone around a circular heated tub, amassing pink strings into a puff of cotton. Juli reached for the cone and plucked at the sugar threads that quickly dissolved in her mouth. After she swallowed the melted sweetness, she said, "Eva will be here soon."

Hand in hand she and Daniel strolled across beige granite pavement contrasted by large red diamonds. They sat on a bench inlayed with a matching design in miniature, beside Rafael.

Daniel nudged Rafa with his elbow. "Maybe this will be a romantic beginning for you."

Rafael frowned. "I've known Eva all my life. She's like another sister to me. No chance."

"Hey, you never know. It's logical, you and I best friends, and I'm going out with your sister. Juli and Eva are best friends. Get it? The ideal foursome, right?"

"*Por favor*, Daniel, let it go."

Juli chimed in, "Brother, don't be mean. Eva's a sweetheart, and we both believe she would be perfect for you." She draped her arm around Rafael's neck. "You should appreciate us. You're lucky to have us here tonight. Daniel and I were almost killed in that thunderstorm yesterday. We were trapped under trees in the park in the pouring rain."

"And the lightning struck meters from us," Daniel added.

"You two are crazy. Never go under a tree in a thunderstorm. You know that."

"They were bushes, not really trees, but the point is we had a brush with death," said Daniel.

"It was a bad storm," Rafael said. "I was in town walking by the hotel and had to wait inside. Daniel, guess who saw me and followed me in."

"Not Max."

"How did you know?"

"Who else could it be?"

"He said he was over Juli." Rafael turned to his sister. "Can you believe I ran into him?"

"Finished with Juli? Just like that? I doubt it."

"That's what he said. He's still mad at you. A warning: he'll be here tonight."

"Oh, great." Daniel said as he picked a tuft of Juli's cotton candy and shoved it into his mouth. "Just what I need."

"Keep your distance."

"Tell him to keep his distance, not me. I thought he helped his father at the shop on the weekend."

"Yeah, but he's finished at four."

They watched musicians from throughout the province of Villa Clara set up and were surprised that a piano, transported in the back of a pickup truck, would accompany the usual band consisting of guitars, trumpets, bongos, and saxophones. Late-arriving employees of the government-owned kiosks also hurried to set up and sell food and drinks. Two men lifted tanks off a truck parked next to Prado el Viejo. The vats contained ready-mixed rum and an imitation Coca-Cola for Cuba Libres. From another truck green and red cases of Cristal and cases of Buca-ñero beer were unloaded and carried to booths surrounding an open space used as a dance floor.

Daniel looked across the plaza and saw two groups of teenagers. The girls sat on benches on one side, and the boys stood next to a planter opposite them. The girls giggled and pointed at one of the boys. A young man looked at the others with a shocked expression and said, "*Yo?*" His arms rose in the air in denial of the accusation, and the other boys laughed hysterically. Daniel remembered his teenage years, when his father was still alive, as happy times living in Las Villas. He hung out on the village plaza during festivals, like the teens across from him, in hopes of meeting girls.

Juliana slipped the last bite of cotton candy into her mouth and tossed the paper cone into a trashcan. Daniel asked her if she wanted something to drink.

"*Sí, por favor.* Rum and Coke."

"Rafa, a drink?"

"I'll go with you."

Rafael trailed Daniel through the crowd to the booths and passed townspeople encircling the dance floor. They said hello to the mayor and his wife, and Daniel approached a counter made of plywood and ordered a Cuba Libre for Juli. He asked Rafael if he wanted one, but Rafa preferred a beer.

"I'll take care of it," Daniel insisted. "I'm having beer too."

"You don't have to."

"I want to. My treat."

"Thanks. Have you gotten many cigarettes out of the factory lately?"

"Tons. I alternate taking them from the two storage areas, and I devised a way to sew cloth bags inside my shirt and pants. I carry out twice as many packs as before. Of course I make sure no one's around at the end of the shift. I move like a sumo wrestler. Not too obvious."

Rafael grinned at the thought of his friend, obese from cigarette packs stuffed in bags sewn in his clothing. "Only you could come up with something like that. I have to hand it to you."

"Ingenious, right? I got the idea when I saw my mother sew purses out of squares of cloth. She sells the purses to gift shops."

"You can sew?"

"She taught me."

Together they walked over to the beer booth, and Daniel purchased two cans of Cristal.

Rafael said, "Man, I wish I could work with you as a team like we planned after Max quit. The extra cash came in handy. But my father would disown me if he found out I was selling again."

"I told you, whatever you need I'll buy. I have no problem sharing this money with you. In fact, here. Take this, a little spending money." Daniel rolled up a wad of bills and discreetly handed it to Rafael.

"*Hombre*, I can't take your money. Like I said, take good care of my sister, and I'll be happy." Rafa tried to give back the cash, but Daniel moved away and tightly clutched the beer can as he raised his arms. He refused to accept the pesos.

"Come on, man. You're pissing me off."

"Keep it. It's yours. Don't worry. I'll still take care of your sister."

Embarrassment reflected on Rafael's face as his hand squeezed the money.

Daniel put an arm across his friend's shoulders. "I really want you to have it."

"Thanks. I feel bad."

"Don't."

As they cut through a crowd that had gathered in anticipation that the band would soon play, Daniel caught a glimpse of Eva near the group of teenagers. She was heading toward Juliana but then stopped, looking confused. Daniel glanced from Eva to Juliana and to his amazement spotted Max seated on the bench beside her. Maximo leaned in close to Juli, and his mouth moved rapidly. Daniel imagined him deep in a conversation pleading for her love.

Juli inched away from Max when she saw Daniel and Rafael approaching. Daniel heard her demand that the intruder leave.

Hearing this, and as Daniel eased closer to his girlfriend, Maximo's presence beside her infuriated him even more. His face reddened. He turned to Rafael and blurted, "I thought you said Maximo was over Juli."

When Rafael caught sight of Max seated on the bench, pestering his sister, he said, "That's what he told me. Daniel, don't do anything stupid."

Between clenched teeth Daniel said, "Wouldn't you say he's doing the stupid thing? Isn't he the fool?" He strode over to the bench.

"Is there a problem, Juli?" Daniel peered at Max.

"Not really." She gazed up at Daniel with a look of helplessness.

"What do you want, Max?"

"Just to say hello. I'm leaving."

"I know you are." Daniel glared at him. "That's my seat."

Maximo turned to Rafael and as he rose pulled him by his shirt to the side. "If you know what's good for you, you won't hang out with that thief or allow your sister to date him."

Rafael pushed Max's hand off his shirt. "If you know what's good for you, you'll get the hell out of here."

"Hey, I have no problem with that. I'm joining my friends to listen to the music."

Rafael stuck to Max as he eased toward Juliana and said, "Maybe we'll dance later, Juli."

Daniel swung his arm back, but Rafael raised both arms to block the punch as Daniel extended his tightened fist forward. He stopped before hitting Rafa's arms.

"Let him go. He's not worth getting in trouble over," Rafael said as he watched Maximo strut toward the dance floor, laughing and eying Juliana. He joined the Rialto brothers, who stood near the band grooving to the music, as if nothing had happened.

"My God, he's persistent. Sit down, Daniel. Have a drink." Rafael handed him his beer. He took it, set it on the floor, and asked Juli what Maximo had said.

"The usual. Ignore him. I want no part of Max. He's so irritating. The music is playing. Let's enjoy it." To ease the tension, she raised her glass to Daniel and her brother. "*Salud, dinero, y amor.*"

Daniel slowly reached down and picked up his beer. She tapped her plastic cup against their beer cans and added, "To wonderful times ahead." As she sipped the rum and Coke she noticed a look of concern cloud her boyfriend's face. He chugged his beer while staring off in the distance, beyond the teenagers who were now massed together, girls and boys mixed. Juliana lightly touched his shoulder and he leaned over to listen. The music blared.

"Please forget it. Let's have a good time."

"If you say so," he said, and she lightly kissed his cheek.

Eva had watched the incident from afar and was already aware of Maximo's interference in their relationship. When Max departed, Eva walked up to the three seated on the bench. Juliana, unaware of her friend's presence, was absorbed in Daniel and his reaction to Max.

Rafael rose and said to Eva, "You just missed the excitement."

"Unfortunately I saw it."

"You did? Maximo continues to bother Juli." Rafael focused on his sister and best friend deep in conversation.

He heard Daniel say, "How do we deal with this guy?" and decided to let them talk in private.

"Eva, come. I'll buy you a drink. They have important matters to discuss." Rafa held out his arm for her.

"Thank you, sir. I could use one."

Rafael and Eva eased through the crowd and watched the dancers while they waited in line. Upon their return they found Juliana and Daniel hugging, chuckling, and talking again about their frightful experience during the thunderstorm. Relieved that the subject of Max had changed, Rafael rolled his eyes. "Haven't you gotten over that storm yet? You're both cowards."

Daniel shot a stern look at his friend. "We're what?"

"Juli's a coward."

"That's better. I saved her life, didn't I, Juli?"

"You did what?"

"Saved your life during the storm. I took you to a safe haven." Daniel raised his eyebrows.

"Oh, that. Yes, you did. You rescued me from serious danger and guided me to the train station. Thank you, darling."

"Don't mention it."

Juliana realized her friend had arrived. She rose and greeted Eva by touching cheeks. "You made it."

"Yes. Right in the middle of everything."

"I'm sorry."

"Don't be. It's not your fault you're gorgeous and that jerk pursues you with a vengeance."

The four raised their drinks in a toast to their friendship as the sun set and splashed its final rays of red and orange light across the horizon. Juliana asked Eva why she had arrived so late. Eva admitted she had seen Maximo seated beside Juli and decided to stay back in case a confrontation erupted between the rivals.

"Besides that," Eva said, "I spent the day with my cousin and his wife who returned after a two-year sabbatical in East Berlin. They brought a crate full of East German products and wanted to know if I needed anything. They had appliances, kitchenware, furniture, and, of all things, a motorcycle. Can you believe they fit a motorcycle in there? They want to sell everything to help make ends meet until my cousin, Tómas, gets a job. They're staying with Tómas's parents until they move into their own home."

"Did you buy anything?" Juli asked.

"A set of pastel bowls. For the wholesale price. The bowls are really nice."

Daniel strained to rid his mind of thoughts of Maximo, but when he heard the word "motorcycle" mentioned during the girls' conversation, he interrupted Eva.

"Did you say there's a motorcycle for sale?"

"Yes. Why? Are you interested?"

"I'd like to see it. Is it new?"

"I think so. My cousin bought it a few weeks before leaving for Cuba. Everything was shipped days before they left Germany. A truck delivered the crate yesterday."

"Tell him not to sell that motorcycle. I'm really interested."

"Do you have that kind of money, Daniel?" said Juliana.

"I have most of it." He focused on Eva. "Maybe your cousin will take a down payment and I'll pay the rest in installments."

"You'll have to ask him. Why don't you stop by tomorrow? My aunt and uncle live near the clinic. Here's the address." She wrote the street and number on a crumpled receipt, smoothed it, and handed it to Daniel. "I'll be there in the morning to help them unpack the crate."

"Perfect. I'll stop by before work."

Chapter Nine
THE MOTORCYCLE

Daniel stepped into the garage with Tómas. His eyes widened, and he rubbed his hands together at the sight of the scarlet-colored motorcycle parked next to a large wooden crate.

"Bright red. I like that. An East German bike, right?" Daniel said as he examined it. "Eva told me about it."

"Brand new. I bought it before leaving East Berlin for the sole purpose of selling it here. I'm not crazy about motorcycles and need the cash to get settled. We live with my parents for now, as Eva probably mentioned to you."

"She did. Well, it is a beauty." Daniel eyed the blue headlight, stroked it, and moved his hands to the handlebar grips and over the red shield with ETZ-250cc written in slanted white letters. The black seat stretched over the back wheel, room enough for Juli.

Tómas dropped the keys in his hand. "Take it for a spin."

"Sure, but I already know I want it."

Daniel straddled the bike, started it, flashed the headlight twice, and eased out of the garage. On the road he veered to the right, past the elementary school to Colonel Acebo, and south toward Santa Maria Sugar Mill. He rode out of town to avoid the stares and questions and, more importantly, to evade suspicious police.

Once on open road he kept an eye out for highway patrol. When he was certain the highway was clear, he rose above the seat, rolled the throttle, sat back down, leaned forward, and cranked it up to 150 kilometers per hour. His hair blew back, and the high speed generated a wind that lifted his shirt and exposed his back as he raced past fences and trees lining the pavement.

Daniel slowed to a dirt lane and disappeared between sugarcane fields to turn around. He was pleased by the way the shocks absorbed the bumps and crevasses in the dirt. He reversed in a three-point turn and steered back onto the highway, revved the cycle, and gained speed with no hesitation. The exaltation Daniel felt riding this motorcycle was indescribable. A unique sense of freedom overwhelmed him.

He turned onto Eva's aunt and uncle's street, beaming with pleasure as the tires crunched over the stone driveway. He coasted to a stop and stretched his legs to balance the bike.

"How did you like it?" Tómas asked as he exited the house.

"Great. Let's talk business."

"Come inside." Tómas held the door open. "Eva just arrived."

Daniel waited for the night shift employees to leave before he departed the factory. He pretended to repair the motor of a packing machine while seated at the shop workbench when Angel waved good-bye to him. At half past twelve, certain everyone had gone but two night watchmen, Daniel loaded the bags sewn in his clothes with cartons he had hidden in a tool chest during his break. He packed the cartons loosely inside the sacks to allow freedom of movement, but when he waddled down the street the bags bumped, enveloped his legs, and tripped him. Daniel wrapped his arms around an electric light pole to prevent from falling and to readjust the shifting bags. The entangled sacks prevented his knees from bending and his arms from reaching his legs to release the bags. He was relieved that the street light he stood under was unlit. In his black shirt and black pants he would be difficult to spot.

Daniel shook his body and kicked out his leg in the shadows until he favorably positioned the bags and was able to plod along. Slowly he cut across his neighbor's backyard. Walking was more difficult on the grass, and the curious rooster and chickens crisscrossed in front of him and interfered with his urgency to get home.

Daniel shuffled up to the porch and sat on the top step. His oversized stomach and appendages bulged as he stretched his legs. He unzipped his pants, removed them, slipped off his shirt, and dropped the carton-filled clothing in a heap. In his briefs he hastened to his room to dress and retrieve his knapsack.

While stuffing the sack full of cigarette packs, he decided to ask Carmelita to help him sell cigarettes. It was an abundance to sell on his own, and since she sold her wares on the streets daily, her involvement would advance his sales. Surely she would appreciate the extra money, and besides, he was anxious to own the motorcycle outright. Assistance in selling the large quantity of cigarettes was a necessity. Daniel planned to go into town tomorrow to ask her and at the same time purchase a gift for his mother. After all, his patient mother, troubled by his illegal endeavors, deserved a trinket.

"*Resolver*, Daniel. That's what we all have to do."

"Make do, m*amá*? Maybe you and the rest of Cuba, but I want more in life. 'Live large,' like the Americans say. Making do doesn't cut it for me."

"But that motorcycle in the shed. You purchased a brand new motorcycle? Forty-seven thousand pesos. How can we afford such a luxury?"

"I need something faster than a bicycle and my own two feet to get around. It's a necessity. Anyway, I can afford it."

"Dishonestly."

"So who's honest in Cuba? Our government? Everyone gets conned or screwed here one way or another."

Alma ignored his comments about the government as she always did and said, "What kind of an example are you going to set for your future children?"

"Hopefully my children won't be born in Cuba, and wherever I go to live, I won't have to steal to survive."

"I doubt Juliana wants to leave Cuba. She may not follow you to America. Then what?"

"We'll see when the time comes." Daniel was tired of the constant sparring with his mother over stolen cigarettes. He knew she mentioned America because during their heated arguments, he always threatened to leave Cuba and go to the United States. He concluded that once she realized cash from cigarette sales enhanced their lives she would cease arguing every time they got together.

"Don't worry. The motorcycle's not registered in my name. The authorities won't trace the purchase to me. It's in Rambo's cousin's name."

"What a relief. It's in someone else's name, but it happens to be in our shed."

Daniel rushed out of the living room, snatched a glass jar and cloth off the kitchen table, slammed the kitchen door, and ran to the shed. The jar contained automobile polish borrowed from Angel. He removed a gray tarp concealing the motorcycle and threw it on the freezer. He wiped the bike clean with the damp cloth and dried the surface. Then he dipped an old towel into the jar and smoothed thick paste over the metal. The crisp scent of polish entered his nostrils. Daniel rubbed saddle soap, lent to him by Rambo, on the leather seat and took a moment to stand back and admire the shiny bike.

He draped the towel stained with polish over a bar connected to the rearview mirror, reached in his pocket, and placed a gold and topaz ring in the palm of his hand. The metal was cool on his scar, which was still sensitive to touch. Carmelita had helped him choose the ring yesterday, a gift intended for his mother. The blue gem matched a necklace his father had given her on her birthday a few weeks before he died. Daniel flipped the ring over and admired the oval stone before sliding it back into his pocket.

Their argument and her criticism made him feel she was not deserving of this gift. She always misunderstood his intentions.

Daniel continued to scrub the motorcycle and recalled the conversation with Carmelita after finding her chatting with a client near La Colonia Española. She had agreed to sell cigarette packs for him with no hesitation and even suggested selling individual cigarettes to customers unable to afford an entire pack. He liked the idea and left her twenty boxes to start. Knowing Carmelita as well as he did, Daniel expected some of the inventory to mysteriously vanish, but in the long run, with her assistance, pesos would generate faster, and the motorcycle would soon be paid off.

Carmelita had also convinced him to order an engagement ring for Juliana even though marriage, in his mind, was a plan for the future. She reasoned, "By the time you're ready to propose to her, you'll already have the ring in your possession."

Normally he would refuse such persuasion, but he thought about Maximo's relentless pursuit of Juli and decided an engagement ring worn on her finger was the solution to keep the stalker at bay.

Daniel glanced at his watch and realized it was almost time to get ready for work, and surprisingly he was anxious to go. He'd adjusted well and preferred the peaceful night shift. He looked forward to hauling another heist from the factory and had become bolder about stealing.

That night he found a canvas sack in the closet where Angel had discovered his note, filled it with cartons, and blatantly carried it home. His mother's annoying chickens pursued him, and to his surprise the rooster hopped on the hammock and crowed as if to tell the world Daniel was in possession of a bag of stolen goods.

"Shut up," he said, waving his free arm at the rooster. The rooster pecked at air in the direction of his arm as Daniel heaved the sack onto his other shoulder. He dropped the bag on the porch and hurried into the shed. Before he quietly rolled the motorcycle across the yard, he scattered a handful of grain on the ground for the chickens. The rooster pushed off the hammock and flew low to the spot where the grain had settled. Daniel grinned as the bold rooster tapped the hens away from the precious seeds with his sharp beak.

Daniel pushed his bike out of the neighborhood and onto Central Highway. With no one in sight, he turned the throttle, revved the engine, and sped to the countryside along the straight highway. The bike swiftly passed through a mist drifting near a soggy marsh on the north side of the road. After passing this low section of highway, he raced as fast as the bike was capable in the direction of his former home.

Daniel cut off the motor before reaching the Milan homestead and walked the bike in front of his childhood home. A lamp shone in the window of the living room.

Through sheer curtains he saw a young mother cradle a newborn in her arms. She paced in front of the window. The baby whimpered and sporadically wailed. Daniel assumed the father was asleep in the second-floor bedroom since the upstairs windows were dark. He wondered if his own mother had coddled him with such love and tenderness like this one in silhouette before him.

Staring in the window made him feel like a prowler, so he eased the motorcycle forward to get a better view of the back of the house. His father's old shoe factory loomed a short distance across the yard. The display window was lit, and Daniel sensed that the old place was inhabited by another cobbler. While looking at the building, he recalled how his mother had insisted they depart their home in a hurry after his father's death, despite Daniel's protests.

Alma Milan had allowed him no time to grieve in comfort surrounded by family and friends who also loved his father. Daniel had never properly mourned his father's death. The sudden move and the work involved in sorting and discarding his father's personal belongings, the packing and cleaning the house and shoe factory, had robbed him of time to mourn his tremendous loss.

The abrupt change had left three voids in his life: he was fatherless, the move had forced him to leave behind family and friends, and lastly, he'd moved out of his childhood home. Seeing this young mother as she gently rocked her baby in her arms gave Daniel satisfaction to know a decent family resided here. Although he had resented his mother's choice to move to Ranchuelo, now he concluded that her judgment was correct. Making a living in the country would have been impossible for them. They barely survived on their meager salaries working in town.

Daniel rolled the bike away from his old house and up an incline with a feeling of relief. He hopped on the seat and started the engine on an isolated section of road. His right foot dragged along the pavement as he drove at a slow velocity to the cemetery. Daniel stopped the motorcycle at the wrought iron gate and reached over to unlatch it. The mausoleum beyond loomed dark and eerie. He parked his bike at the side of the road and propped it up with the kickstand. With his head bent down, he shuffled through the overgrown grass to his father's grave. This was his first opportunity to return to the gravesite since the funeral.

The granite tomb was obscured by plant debris and leaves. With both hands he wiped the stone clean and the words *Daniel Milan Ortega, nació el 29 de marzo 1936, murió el 6 de septiembre 1993* appeared. Reading the imprinted words and numbers confirmed his father's death and startled Daniel into the harsh realization that his beloved father was gone forever. He fell to his knees beside the Milan family crypt that now housed the casket containing the corpse of his father. Previously deceased ancestors' bones had been removed from the crypt and were stored in an ossuary in the mausoleum nearby.

Daniel prayed. He peered up at the night sky and called, "*Papá*, forgive me for not living up to your standards. I promise to do better." A pledge to stop robbing the factory of cigarettes was impossible at this time. "Soon I will stop stealing." He turned away from the tomb and lowered his voice. "I just have to pay off my motorcycle and buy a few necessities. Then I'll study to be a doctor, as you wished, and live off my own income. I swear." He was sure his father's spirit was leery of the excuse to prolong his studies, but he was being sincere to his departed loved one.

Overwhelming emotion engulfed Daniel, but he failed to shed tears. He had expected to break down and cry upon returning to the family plot. The impact of his father's sudden death had remained bottled up inside him for so long. His grief was never verbalized with those he befriended in Ranchuelo. Now he felt at peace, and he lay down on the lid of the crypt. His hands cushioned his head, and his mind wandered to the past.

Memories of his father drifted into solemn thoughts of his grandfather, who had built the shoe factory and tended his small farm. Castro's militia had confiscated the Milans' business in 1960, which had caused his grandfather's health to deteriorate. He died heartbroken at the loss of his property and livelihood.

Daniel had always wondered why his father had agreed to work in his family's business that had been maliciously taken over by the government. But he refrained from verbalizing those thoughts to his father. Daniel had promised himself never to work for the government as a cobbler on property rightfully owned by his family, on land intended to be inherited by Milan descendants.

While dozing intermittently, he visualized his father's face, and with a start he awoke, assuming he had slumbered on the hammock in his backyard. The unfamiliar trees and hard surface beneath confused him. He remembered the cemetery and wanted to spend the night but knew his mother would worry.

Daniel leaped up, gave the sign of the cross, and rode the motorcycle home at such drastic speeds that the fuel tank swiftly lowered. The bike stalled and ran out of gas a few miles from home. He dismounted, pushed it down the highway, into the shed and covered it with the tarp. As he locked the shed, tears flowed from his tired eyes. Daniel leaned his forehead against the door. Wood splinters pinched his skin as he cried. He regained his composure, wiped his eyes, and picked up the sack full of cigarettes on the porch. Without making a sound, he entered his house.

After his days off Daniel changed his fraudulent tactics. Carrying a bag out of the factory was too brazen and risky. Instead, he sewed more bags to smuggle out merchandise in his clothing. At the end of his shift, he awkwardly descended the factory steps and shuffled onto a side street. Headlights flashed, and a car pulled up alongside him as he struggled to walk.

"Are you all right?" A man called as he stuck his head out the window. "Can I give you a lift?"

Daniel was relieved that the vehicle did not emit the roar of a military truck or jeep but hummed like a civilian's car. The voice was familiar, but he couldn't quite place it. He tried to face the man by turning sideways, but the bags inside his pant legs shifted and he stumbled backward.

To the driver it appeared that Daniel had tripped over his own feet and fell to the sidewalk in slow motion. The bulk under Daniel's clothing cushioned the fall. He seemed grossly overweight. But the shifting bags created rolls of fat where fat should not exist on a man's body. The driver cupped his hand over his mouth failing to stifle a loud laugh. While lying on the sidewalk, padded by cigarette boxes, Daniel caught a glimpse of the person amused by his clumsiness and was shocked that the good Samaritan was the factory doctor.

"Oh, Dr. Nieves, it's you."

"And it's you, Daniel. What a surprise. I thought you were an invalid in need of a ride." The doctor opened the door and rushed to assist the fallen one. "Do you know how pathetic you look?"

"I can imagine," stammered Daniel as the physician pulled him to his feet.

"Don't you think you would be a more valuable member of society if you pursued that medical career you mentioned?"

"I have a motorcycle to pay off."

"Don't give me that rubbish."

"I've been thinking about going to medical school."

"Great. Stop thinking. Act upon your thoughts. Here's my home address." The doctor took his wallet out of his back pocket, tore off a piece of paper, and wrote his address for Daniel. "I won't include my phone number. I assume you're without a telephone like the majority of citizens."

"Your address will be fine."

"Take this." The doctor handed him the paper, and Daniel slipped it into his bulging pants pocket. "My friends are doctors, teachers of medicine, or involved in the medical profession. I'm not boasting, but I'm an essential asset if you choose a career in medicine. I offer you an opportunity and when you make up your mind to become a doctor, the door will be wide open to you. Do more with your life, Daniel. This is utterly ridiculous." The doctor looked him up and down and shook his head.

"You're right. I agree."

"Here. I'll help you. I doubt you'll fit in my car." The doctor steadied the wobbly young man and walked him to the edge of his backyard. "In case you wondered, I came to the factory to treat a guard who complained of stomach pain. It turned out to be a virus. I had planned to stop by to see you but assumed you had already left at midnight." The doctor released his hold on Daniel's waist. "Can you make it from here?"

"Yes. I'll be fine. Thanks for your help. And I am considering a medical career."

Several weeks passed and on their mutual day off, Daniel and Rafael fished along the Bélico River. They stepped through thick brush and over felled trees along the embankment. To their right they tossed their lines to avoid clumps of silt collected in the middle of the river. Out of the silt grew a scraggily bush, and a delicate, unstable island was born in the calm, swollen river. Ripples glistened in the sunlight, and the swells glided over an abstraction that was Daniel's and Rafael's converging shadows.

"Rafa, what are your religious beliefs? Juli told me your parents are devout Catholics and taught you on Sundays."

"My beliefs? I believe as Fidel Castro believes."

"A communist?"

"Hell no. I'm an atheist."

"Atheist? I never expected you to tell me that. Didn't you study the bible?"

"My parents insisted, but I don't believe in any of it."

"I was disillusioned with God after my father's death, but I still believe."

"After the hell my country's been through, I don't think there's a God, heaven, life after death, or any of that. This is it." Rafael pointed toward the river, the trees, and sky.

"That's depressing."

"What can I say?"

They reeled in their lines and tossed them into the flow. Daniel eyed his fishing line where it dipped into the water. "Being here makes me want to get away, spend time in nature. Go camping or something."

"Why don't you? You've got the motorcycle. You can do those things." Rafa nodded toward the red bike leaning against a tree above them.

Daniel became pensive. "What would you say if I asked Juli to go camping with me? Your parents are going to Havana in two weeks."

"Take my sister?"

"Wait. It's not what you think. Before you answer, let me talk. Juli refuses to have sex before marriage."

Rafael leaned his pole against a rock and sat down on the riverbank.

"I have honored her wishes so far and will continue to do so as long as she chooses." Daniel set his pole against a branch and sat down beside his silent friend. "I don't know what you've heard about me with the ladies, but Juli, I love her deeply. There's a big difference here. I want to ask her to marry me." He hesitated to watch Rafa's reaction. "I already asked your father."

Rafael ceased staring at the river and looked deep into Daniel's eyes. "You did? Are you sure you're ready to commit?"

Daniel slipped his hand in his pocket, pulled out a diamond ring, and held it in front of Rafa's face. "Carmelita ordered it for me a month ago. It finally came yesterday."

"Come here." Rafael wrapped his arms around him. "You *are* ready, my future brother-in-law. Let me see that ring. What a beauty. It actually sparkles. Juli will be ecstatic. Have you mentioned this to her?"

"She has no idea." Daniel took the ring and examined it before putting it back in his pocket. "Well, she has a slight idea because I mentioned I'd marry her if we survived that thunderstorm we got caught in at the park, but the subject hasn't been discussed since. Don't say anything. I want this to be the biggest surprise of her life. Promise me."

"I promise I won't."

"I want you to be best man at our wedding."

"I'd be honored. Hey, a great spot to propose is up in the mountains by this waterfall. Few know about it. I'll give you directions. Pop the question there. How romantic that will be."

"I'm not romantic. I was going to ask her at night by the campfire. A waterfall?"

"Why not?"

"Maybe that's a better idea."

"She'll love it."

"Right before sunset?"

"Nice. Maybe you are becoming a romantic."

"We'll see if I can pull this off."

"You will. She loves romance more than anyone I know. She's always reading novels about love." Rafael looked intently at his friend. "Thanks for being so good to her. I know my parents will be happy too." He tossed a stone at the fragile island. "You just have to supplement your income another way. If my father finds out you're stealing cigarettes…"

"I know. I'm working on it. I met with Javier Nieves." Daniel chose not to elaborate on their late-night encounter but told Rafael about visiting the doctor's home one morning several days after. "He'll help me get into medical school and get me a job in the medical field while I study."

"Fantastic. You're on your way to a great career. No reason to leave Cuba now."

"Guess not."

"Juli prefers to stay here."

"I know. She never knew I planned to leave."

"Why should she know? As a doctor you'll be better off." Rafael saw a fish rise and flop sideways into the river. "Get up. Fish are jumping."

They grabbed their poles and flung the lines out into the current.

Chapter Ten
THE PROPOSAL

Juliana paced back and forth in the shade of a banyan tree where a coworker had dropped her off after work. She waited for Daniel to pick her up on the highway leading to the Sierra del Escambray Mountains. Her face lit up when she saw Daniel sail down the road on his motorcycle and skid to a stop in front of her. He hopped off the bike, embraced his girlfriend, and picked up her backpack from the ground. He helped Juli slip her arms through the straps and over her shoulders. The bright smile he saw as he approached had faded. Juliana's lips were pursed as the backpack rested snugly on her back.

"Sorry I'm late."

"I wondered why you took so long."

Daniel helped her on the bike. Juliana's hair was loosely gathered in a bun at the back of her head, a style she hadn't worn for him before. He liked the way the strands and wisps of hair framed her face.

"I packed and had to roll up the tent and blankets and strap them to those two black bars under your legs," he said as he straddled the seat.

Juli glanced down at the camping equipment beneath her slender legs. Her dainty, sandaled feet were supported on footrests.

"I thought you were going to pack yesterday."

"I was, but Angel got the bright idea to clean the shop. I stayed late to help him. I was tired when I got home."

Daniel straightened the red bandana on his forehead and reached behind his head to tie it tighter. When he finished, Juliana reached up, centered the knot in the back of his head, and tugged at the scarf. "I don't like to be kept waiting, especially while all alone on a highway."

He turned to face her. "I'm sorry. It wasn't my intention. I had to get gas too." He kissed her. "I am sorry. I won't do it again."

Daniel revved the motor.

"Hold on tight."

They took off. The red motorcycle buzzed to the hilltops. The sound lulled in the dips of spacious valleys. Juli squeezed his waist, and he eyed her from over his shoulder. Her head rested on his back as they sped past green pastures and golden hayfields. She gazed beyond the scenery in a dreamlike state. Lazy colonial towns slipped by before she could admire their charm. For a second she closed her eyes and clung to him even tighter.

Like a soaring cardinal, the East German bike flew across the Cuban countryside toward the Sierra del Escambray mountain range looming through a haze in the distance. Daniel told Juliana to lean with him at the hairpin curves. Together they slanted left and then right on the following turn. He reduced speed only for sharp bends and gunned it on straightaways. In this driving pattern, they forged on to their mountain retreat.

The motorcycle roared as Daniel steered up a path through the pasture of a farm occupied by an acquaintance of Rafael. Rafa had assured Daniel that the owner permitted passage through the property as long as the grazing animals were undisturbed. Daniel concentrated on steadying the bike during the bumpy climb up the hill. Juli clung to his waist as she was jostled on the seat. Behind her the back tire ejected a spout of dirt that sprayed her legs and darkened the grass at the edge of the trail. She looked up after examining her dirt-speckled leg and watched a herd of cattle lope away from the source of the noise that frightened them. They ran in the direction of the barn and pens in the valley below. Juliana saw a small group of livestock break from the herd and ascend a slope on the opposite hillside.

"Daniel, slow down. The cows are scared."

"If I slow down we won't make it up this hill."

"But the rancher said not to bother the animals."

"It's a motorcycle. It makes noise."

"He'll tell us to leave."

"Who will? No one's around. It's just a short distance to the gate."

When they reached the fence, Daniel dismounted the bike and helped Juli off. She pushed the bike through the gate while he secured the latch. As he gripped the handlebars, he kissed her. "Don't worry about the cows. They'll calm down."

Side by side they ascended into a wooded area. The terrain steepened as they followed an overgrown path into a pine forest and up a mountainside. Ferns hugged the bases of tree trunks that stretched high to reach sunlight. Beyond the ferns they hesitated in a clearing to gaze at the lush valley below. Royal palms dotted the valley's slopes like reed parasols shivering above the tranquil lower vegetation.

They trekked on in silence. Sweat seeped through his bandana as Daniel pushed the motorcycle through woods that became more jungle-like and humid. He thought about hiding the motorcycle and picking it up on their return but feared losing his prized vehicle in the dense forest.

He gripped a handlebar in one hand and held Rafael's map in the other. Daniel stared at the map and wondered why it was taking so long to reach the waterfall. Maybe a marriage proposal during a camping trip wasn't such a good idea after all.

"What was your brother thinking? I see no familiar landmarks. I'm not sure we're supposed to be in this jungle. There's hardly a path."

"I have no idea where we are. You and Rafael arranged this trip."

"So you're blaming me?"

"Blaming? I'm not blaming you for anything. I'm looking forward to camping. But my foot hurts. I'm getting tired."

"Why didn't you say so?"

"Because you're in such a rush."

"I just want to find the falls."

Juli sat on a boulder, removed her sandal, and rubbed her foot.

He stopped. "The good thing is we can't get lost. Straight down this mountain is the ranch."

"I'm not worried."

Daniel leaned the bike against a tree and tossed the map on the seat. "Why don't you ride the bike? Give your foot a rest."

"You'd let me do that? I thought you were mad."

"Just frustrated. You're tired." He wiped away pearls of perspiration from her lip with his finger. "Your foot's sore."

"You're strong, but I can't burden you more. It's hard enough to push a motorcycle without my added weight. That was sweet of you."

"I try." He pulled two water bottles out of his bag, handed her one, and sat next to her. Daniel touched her bottle with his. "Cheers. To a wonderful outing."

Juliana smirked. "Time alone was supposed to bring us closer together." She tapped his bottle.

"It has." He nudged closer to her and caught her before she slid off the rock. "I'd never let you fall." She gripped his arm.

A steady wind rustled the leaves in trees surrounding them. When the wind ceased and the leaves were still, Daniel noticed a whirring sound remained. He stood up.

"Listen."

"I only hear the wind."

"That's the point. Look up. The trees aren't moving. There is no wind."

She focused on his eyes. "The waterfall?"

He scooped her off the rock and swung her onto the seat of the bike before she knew what happened. "Daniel." Her voice echoed through the trees and across the valley. He pushed the motorcycle with all his strength up the overgrown path toward a sound of gushing, splashing water.

At a clearing they both gasped at the feat of nature before them. Three cascades tumbled down the mountainside and united above a pool carved out of a limestone rock formation. A platform of stone led to the pool churned by spilling water. They abandoned the motorcycle and stood on the rock shelf in awe.

Daniel whispered, "It's perfect," referring to the ideal location to propose to Juliana.

"Truly paradise, and ours for three days. Look to the right of the falls. Is that a white orchid growing on the mountainside?"

"I think so. My mother would know."

He knew she was impressed by the waterfall's beauty and ideal location for camping. Later in the day this setting would take on a more sentimental meaning to her. Daniel glanced up at the sun and calculated a few hours to sunset.

He held her hand and walked around the pool. They squeezed behind a curtain of clear liquid. A hand plunged through the stream of water—Daniel's hand. Juliana ran back to the motorcycle for her camera. Suddenly his face peeked through the cascade, and she snapped the photo. Daniel contorted his face and stuck out his tongue at Juli. She shoved him through the veil of water and into the pool. The camera captured him in midair with his arms flailing. When he surfaced he called for her to join him.

"I have to put on my bikini."

"Don't waste time. Just jump in. It feels great."

She set the camera down on a dry section of rock, stared at him for a moment, and dove in fully clothed. They treaded water face to face. With his hand on the back of her head he eased her forward until their lips touched. Still locked in a kiss, he guided her beneath the falls. The water pounded their heads with such intensity that they floated to a gentle mist beyond the deluge. For an hour they frolicked until Daniel saw the sun had lowered in the sky. It was essential for the proposal to take place exactly as the sun set. Concern showed on his face.

"What's wrong?"

"We have to set up the tent and make a fire before dark." He lifted her out of the water and set her on the ledge. Firmly, he placed his hands on the rough surface and heaved himself beside Juli. Water gushed off his body and flowed across rock and trickled into the pool. Daniel put an arm around her. "Are you happy?"

"Happier and freer than ever."

"Good." He gave her a quick peck on the lips. "Now to set up the tent and build a fire."

"Not yet. Let's relax awhile longer."

"We'll relax later. Come on." He pulled her up and, while walking backward, guided her to the motorcycle, untied the tent, blankets, and his bag and set them on the grass. Candles rattled inside his duffel bag.

"What's in there?"

"Jars and cans of food. That's all."

"Sounds like a baby's rattle."

"That it's not. I can assure you."

"Didn't think so. What can I do to help since you insist we work?"

"Let's start with the tent."

The small tent went up quickly. They gathered wood, and Juli crawled inside the tent to change. As she zipped up the entrance and vanished inside, Daniel grabbed his clothes out of his backpack and hastened to dress. He hurried to arrange the ten votive candles along the border of the pool and lit them with matches

Rafael had tucked in his bag. The white water of the falls flowed like strands of silk into the pool, and amid the froth and foam he saw the same turquoise color of the ring he had purchased for his mother. He felt ashamed for his stubbornness and decided to give her the ring for Christmas.

Daniel touched his pocket to make sure the diamond ring was still there and wondered how to present the ring to Juliana. He plucked some daisies in the clearing and formed a bouquet. He slipped a blade of grass through the ring and tied the blade around the stems to bind the flowers in place. The diamond dangled inconspicuously below the blooms. He gave himself credit for putting together this special moment, so far anyway, a sharp contrast to the exhausting climb to get here.

Daniel called into the tent, "What's taking so long in there?"

"I'm brushing my hair. I'll just be a minute."

He glanced at the western sky. Red, purple, yellow, and orange streaked the horizon and stained cumulus clouds flanking the sun. His proposal to Juli may be a success after all. Everything was falling into place. Even nature had participated.

Daniel paced back and forth across the ledge. He took a deep breath, and as he turned, Juliana emerged from the tent wearing a white sundress with small yellow flowers. Her hair was swept to one side in damp curls and tumbled over a bare shoulder down to her waist. He spotted the chain and locket delicately caressing her neck and visualized the photograph tucked inside the gold heart—a picture Rafael had snapped while the couple danced at a party. The locket swayed as she approached him.

The bouquet slipped from his hand onto the rock ledge. He scooped it up, eying the ring to make sure it remained attached to the grass ribbon.

"What do you have? Flowers for me?"

"You look amazing." His hand shook as he handed her the flowers. "Wait a minute." He almost forgot to kneel and stepped back, reeled around, and dropped to one knee.

"Daniel, are you all right?" She reached to help him. He placed the bouquet in her outstretched hands.

"Juli, will you marry me?"

"What?" Her mouth opened wide. "Are you proposing to me? These flowers mean we will marry? What a sweet way to propose."

By her expression he saw that she was stunned and confused.

"Look closer. The ring also means something."

The diamond sparkled against the stems, and she gasped. "How beautiful. Are you sure this is what you want?"

"Of course I am. Are you?"

"Yes, yes. I've waited forever for this moment."

Daniel tore the strand of grass and removed the ring from the bouquet. "Then you should be wearing this." He reached for her hand and slipped the ring on her finger. She held her hand out and stared at the diamond. Daniel stood, and she hugged him.

The pool and waterfall reflected the vivid colors of sunset. After a lengthy kiss, he said, "I promise I will make you happy."

"I'm already overjoyed." Juliana looked at the waterfall and at the flames dancing in the votive candles on the ledge.

Daniel removed a bottle of champagne from his bag and popped the cork. Foam rose in the bottle and champagne sprinkled them like a light tropical rain. They took turns sipping from the bubbling bottle as they huddled at the water's edge and viewed sundown until darkness descended upon them. They sprawled on the ledge mesmerized by the flickering candles, now the only light reflected in the pool. On cue the moon rose, and stars specked the night sky.

They discussed their future together. Daniel saw the serenity in Juliana's face as she glanced at the ring on her finger. She suggested they make a formal request of the government to reside in the house once owned by her aunt, the abandoned home with the bench and garden. He confessed his desire to become a doctor and explained how he aimed to fulfill his father's dream.

"Rafa told me you met with Javier Nieves. I had hoped it was for that reason."

"Did he also tell you I planned to propose to you?"

"Rafa knew? That he kept a secret. I was truly surprised."

"I told him not to tell you, but I didn't think he would keep it a secret."

"My parents will be thrilled. They are very fond of you. Our future is so promising. You'll be a doctor. We'll live in a lovely home. Have children. How many do you want? I'd like two."

"I'd rather hold off on having kids. Let's first get settled, and I'll get my career underway. Two? Fine. In the future."

"Where will we marry? I wish in a church. It would make my parents so happy."

"Impossible, thanks to Castro. If a church wedding is important I can get us into Santa Rosa de Lima. The ceremony would have to be brief and at night in a messed-up church."

"Too risky. A night wedding in a church locked up for years? I'm not so sure."

"We'll think of something better than a church."

"A church would be ideal."

They planned their future until two in the morning. Daniel stretched his arms and yawned. "Let's go skinny dipping before we turn in," he suggested but never expected her to agree.

"I'm not ready for that yet."

He was certain the effects of the champagne influenced her decision a few minutes later when she rose above the ledge, slipped off her panties, pulled her dress above her head, and flung it at him, shouting, "Why not?"

Daniel missed glimpsing her body when the flying dress wrapped around his face and covered his eyes. He heard a loud splash and felt the chill when a wave doused him. He bunched up the dress and tossed it on the tent.

Daniel stripped off his clothes and did a cannonball in front of her. The swell saturated the shelf of rock and fell centimeters short of soaking the tent. They splashed and swam until they tired, dried off and retreated to the tent. They slept fully clothed. Daniel curled up beside Juliana and respected her as he had promised her brother.

"These wonderful days can't be over," Juli shouted from the back of the motorcycle as they left the gate to enter the pasture. "I don't want to go back."

"I don't either, but your parents come home tonight. I have to get you back before they arrive." Daniel patted her hand. "Hold on tight. This hill looks steeper going down than it did coming up."

They bounced on the dirt path. Halfway down the hill Juliana shrieked. Daniel lurched to the right, and the motorcycle swerved off the path and onto grass.

"What's wrong?" he shouted as he eased the bike back onto the dirt.

"Look to the left. Behind you. Go faster. Oh my dear God."

Out of the corner of his eye, Daniel saw movement, something large and beige. He turned his head and focused on a Brahman bull charging toward them at a gallop. The bull's muzzle skimmed the grass, and his lowered head made the hump on his back look bigger. The animal appeared gigantic. Daniel accelerated and leaned forward. "Hold on tight, Juli."

Her arms squeezed his waist when she saw the beast's head nod and the horns lunge closer. The bull was gaining on the swift motorcycle. With his left hand Daniel reached behind his head. He struggled to untie the knot securing the red bandana. She was about to scold him for removing his hand from the handle grips, but once she realized his intention, Juli hugged the seat with her knees and with both hands helped him loosen the knot. She guided the unbound material into his hand. He held the scarf as far from the motorcycle as possible and waved the bandana in front of the bull like a cape. The bull's eyes caught the motion of the fabric rippling like a flag and raced toward the scarf. Daniel raised the bandana in the air, released it, and allowed the wind to carry the cloth across the field. To his relief, the bull changed course and pursued the red object sailing in the air. The motorcycle hurled on down the hill.

Juliana pressed her face against Daniel's back, closed her eyes, and envisioned the sharp horns about to gore them. She peeked to see the bull trailing off to the left along the hillside, chasing the red object. With his horns, the bull jabbed at the immobile scarf and stomped it with his front hoof. The motorcycle escaped. In the distance Daniel saw a man standing by the main gate at the bottom of the hill and assumed he was the occupant of the ranch. The rancher unlatched the gateway and waited for the terrified couple.

The bull, bored by the lifeless bandana, perked up his ears to the distant rumble of the motorcycle and resumed his vigorous attack. When Juliana saw the bull race toward them again she screamed, "Hurry, Daniel. He's charging us again."

The gate swung open, and Daniel sped through it and shouted, "*Gracias.*"

They barreled down the road in the direction of Ranchuelo. The bull's master slammed the gate shut, and the bovine swerved to avoid the structure. The rancher leaped on the fence and waved his hat at the animal.

"*Diablo, toro malo! La pobre pareja tenia miedo de ti. Lárgate. Vete de aquí. Vete con las vacas a la montaña, toro malo.*"

Daniel eased the motorcycle to the side of the road as they approached a passive, slow moving herd of cows being driven by four *guajiros*. "Might as well stop. They may take a while."

Juli dismounted. Her eyes welled up with tears and he caressed her. "Don't worry. We survived this one too."

She collapsed on a grassy incline, stared at the sky for a few minutes, and then sat up. She wrapped her arms around her legs as she watched the cows amble by. Their hooves clicked on the road, and a pungent smell of fresh manure filled the air. The cowboys whistled and waved their lassos, steadily moving them along.

"Our three days in El Escambray were the most beautiful moments of my life. The engagement was perfect. Why did it have to end with a bull about to gore us to death?" Juli nodded toward the herd. "Those cows were in the field on Friday. I remember them. Why would the rancher remove the cows and put a dangerous bull in there?"

"That rancher lives on this land. He can do anything he wants until the government tells him otherwise. We were the trespassers." Daniel rubbed his chin. "In life there are good moments and bad. We have to enjoy the good ones. Let the bad ones go. *Oye*, cheer up. We're both fine."

Juliana remained silent. Daniel dropped down beside her, gently eased her to the ground, and lay next to her. He watched as she stared at a cloud formation drifting across the sky.

In a solemn voice she said, "Thanks to your quick thinking and the bandana, we are here to talk about it. Did you realize how close those horns were? Centimeters from my leg."

"I heard the bull snort." He ruffled her hair, cupped her face in his hands, and gave her a big kiss. For a long time they embraced.

The *guajiros* guided the cows through a gate to a meadow on the opposite side of the road. Daniel saw the animals graze as they drifted to the crest of a hill. "The cows are off the road. Let's go home and celebrate our engagement."

"And celebrate being alive."

Chapter Eleven
THE GIFTS

Daniel knocked on the door to the Reyes' house and waited. Rafael opened the door. His hair was disheveled, and he squinted in the sunlight. Daniel noticed his puffy eyes. In a hoarse voice he said, "What do you want?"

"Sorry I woke you. It's eleven. Still in your pajamas?"

"I got a mean hangover at Rambo's last night."

"Didn't you have to work?"

"I took a sick day."

"Go back to bed. I just wondered where Juli was."

"She said something about the house. With Eva."

"What are they doing there?"

"Gardening, cleaning up. I don't know. She got all excited."

"About what?"

"Didn't you apply to Urban Reform? To live in our aunt's house?"

"It's not ours yet. I don't know if it will be."

Rafael yawned.

"Go back to sleep. You look like hell."

"Thanks." Rafa closed the door and then opened it suddenly. "Daniel."

Daniel looked up at him from the bottom step.

"I almost forgot to tell you. Max was at Rambo's. I keep running into the guy. He's such a strange character." Rafael ran his fingers through his unruly hair. "I told him you and Juli got engaged to keep him from bothering her. I'm not sure I did the right thing."

"Why? Nothing wrong with telling him."

"He got angry. He mumbled something about ruined plans. The rest of the night he was quiet."

"He had to find out sometime. Someone would have told him."

"He downed beer after beer and acted like he was a million miles away."

"News travels fast in this town."

"I thought I did you a favor but…"

Daniel saw the worried expression on his friend's face, climbed to the top step, and slapped him on the shoulder. "Don't stress over it. What can he do? I guess he still cares for Juli."

"I guess so."

Juliana and Eva yanked weeds in the garden and tossed them in a pile on the grass. Daniel noticed their purses propped together on the mosaic bench and stood at the garden's edge, listening to their chatter about the wedding. For several minutes he went unnoticed and got an earful of their opinions and plans as they were engrossed in conversation. He moved closer. Juli looked up when his shadow came into view and let out a yelp at the tall figure of her fiancé towering above her. Eva jumped up.

"Daniel, you frightened us." Juliana dropped the trowel, stood, and hugged him, careful not to touch his clothes with her soiled hands. "We were discussing where to have the wedding."

"I heard."

"What do you think? My parents' backyard? Eva agreed to be maid of honor."

"Great. Rafael's best man." He scanned the tilled soil of the garden surrounded by seedlings in tiny ceramic pots. "What are you two doing?"

"What does it look like? Getting the place ready."

"Juli, don't get your hopes up. They haven't accepted our application yet. All this work may be for nothing."

"I truly believe it will be ours. Even more repairs are needed inside. Window frames are cracked, and walls need plaster and paint."

"Inside?" He looked at the barred windows. "It's not ours."

Daniel placed his hands on Juli's shoulders, leaned close to her face, and looked deep into her eyes. "I have very good news. Pope John Paul II will be coming to Cuba in January. In honor of his visit, Castro lifted the ban on religion. We can celebrate Christmas, and even better, our wedding can be held in a church."

Juli looked at Eva with her mouth agape and then wrapped her dirt-smeared arms around Daniel.

"When did you hear this?"

"On television last night. At Javier's house."

"A dream come true. My parents will be overjoyed."

Eva stood. She and Juli danced in a circle and coaxed Daniel to join them. They spun around like three children playing ring around the rosy.

"A church wedding? I'm so happy for both of you," said Eva.

Daniel broke from the circle. Juliana glanced at the dirt stains on his shirt, brushed the soil off his back, and wiped her hands on her shorts. She slipped her hand in his. "I want to show you something." They walked to the battered gate, and she pointed to the overgrown backyard. "Picture this lawn trimmed and manicured, with a few kids laughing and playing. Isn't it a lovely vision, Daniel?"

He smiled with sealed lips. "Sounds great, but don't be disappointed if we don't get this house."

"I will be disappointed. For a short time. But I'll be happy in any house with you. You know that."

"Our first home may be my mother's house. How would you feel about that?"

"Fine, for a while. Don't be so negative. Everything's falling into place." Juli unlatched the gate and walked into the yard. "The children won't be here for a few years. How about a puppy instead? This yard would be perfect for a dog too."

"A puppy? You really want a puppy?"

"*Sí*, our first child."

"Maybe we can get a puppy."

"Soon?"

"If that's what you want." Her eager face made him crack a smile. Juliana wrapped her arms around his neck and kissed him. Eva glanced over at them and cheered as she sifted clumps into loose dirt.

They both looked at Eva, and Juli called to her, "I'm coming."

"Take your time."

"I'd better help Eva."

"And I have to go to work," he said.

"Daniel, don't worry. Wherever we are, as long as we're together, I'll be happy."

"Me too."

While Daniel rode his motorcycle to Santa Clara to pick up a puppy, Alma Milan decorated a cardboard box to put the puppy inside as the perfect Christmas gift for Juli. She poked breathing holes in the lid and meticulously tied a satin bow on top after wrapping the box in shiny green cloth. Alma sighed when the bow unraveled, but her face brightened when it finally remained in place.

Daniel had decided to give Juliana a Havanese puppy after she commented on how cute a small dog was as it pranced and hopped on a leash held by a young girl while they strolled along Prado Nuevo. A few days after seeing the dog, Daniel recognized the same girl playing with her white puppy on a front lawn in his neighborhood. He asked her where she got the dog.

"From my grandfather."

"What kind of dog is it?"

"She's a Cuban dog. A Havanese."

"There's actually a Cuban breed? I've never heard of it."

"My grandfather has two litters. There are too many dogs in his small house. If you want a puppy, call him. Here's his number. But he lives in Santa Clara."

"I have a motorcycle. I want to surprise my fiancée. She saw you walking with your puppy in town and fell in love with him."

"It's a she. Her name is Blanca. She's a wonderful dog. A puppy like Blanca will make your fiancée very happy. She's smart and loves people."

Daniel had a pen clipped to his shirt pocket but no paper. He made note of her grandfather's telephone number on the palm of his hand and thanked the girl. He called her grandfather from a telephone at the restaurant in town. A gravelly voice told Daniel he had two puppies left and would save a white male with tan markings for him.

Daniel wore one of his factory shirts with a bag sewn inside to transport the puppy on his motorcycle. Like Juliana, his mother fell in love with the little Havanese, but when Daniel called back for the last puppy someone had already adopted it. The elderly man promised if there were any future litters Daniel would be the first to know.

Daniel had difficulty keeping the animal hidden from Juli. He met her in locations outside his home, which caused her to question him. After declining to take her to his house, her annoyed expression made him realize she was suspicious of him. He changed the subject and ignored her when she asked, "Why not meet at your house?"

By the middle of December, Daniel detected cheerfulness in the townspeople of Ranchuelo. As the holiday approached, sounds of gaiety and laughter filled the streets. Homes were adorned with Christmas decorations from years past, and trees along the Prado were draped in lights. In front of Santa Rosa de Lima, children helped Father Cardona set up a nativity scene found in a storeroom in the back of the church. Years of accumulated grime and dust were scrubbed off each piece, and the crèche was displayed and admired by residents of all religions. The words *"Feliz Navidad"* echoed throughout the town, and Christmas songs were sung by carolers huddled around pianos in need of tuning.

When December 24th arrived, Daniel, his mother, and Eva joined the Reyes family for a *Noche Buena* celebration. On the night before Christmas they sat down to a dinner of roast pork, black beans, rice, plantains, and salad. For dessert, Juliana's grandmother had baked flan in a cookie tin, all part of their family tradition before Castro banned the holiday. The guests chose from several kinds of Spanish *turrón* passed around the table on small trays. The sweetness of flan and the almond, chocolate, and nougat flavored *turrón* melted in their mouths as they sipped Cuarenta Y Tres, a Spanish liqueur that had been locked away in a cabinet and removed only for special occasions.

Mr. Reyes raised his glass to toast the engaged couple and gave thanks for being allowed to openly celebrate the holy day. He mentioned how proud he was to have Daniel as a member of his family and included Daniel's mother in the toast.

"He will make a fine husband for my lovely daughter and a wonderful father for my future grandchildren. Through his friendship with Rafael we have grown to know him well."

In spite of Daniel's protest, Mr. Reyes blurted out a secret kept for several years. "I will never forget the day Daniel dove into the ocean to save Rafael from drowning at Varadero Beach."

Daniel hung his head and glanced at Rafael, noticing the embarrassment in his shaky speech when he said, "Thanks to Daniel I'm here to celebrate with all of you."

"That was almost two years ago, long forgotten," said Daniel.

"Not forgotten by us," Felipe Reyes said as his wife nodded.

Daniel remembered that day in August spent lounging on the beach with Rafael and his father. He enjoyed being near the sea but had feared the ocean since he was a child. The thought of sea creatures lurking below the surface panicked him. Rafael, on the other hand, loved the sea and teased Daniel about his phobia.

On that day at Varadero, Daniel suntanned while Rafael swam laps off shore. He got a cramp. His outcry, a moan, alerted Daniel, who ran to the water's edge. He stared at the vast sea, overwhelmed with fright as waves slapped his legs and foam swirled at his feet. Watching Rafael struggle to stay afloat, Daniel dismissed his fear, dove into the water, and pulled his friend to safety.

The difficult part about saving Rafael was the initial dive into the water. Keeping him afloat and pulling him to shore was easy. Rafa had always kept Daniel's fear of the ocean between the two of them.

Rafael raised his glass and tapped Daniel's. He thanked Daniel for saving his life, as he had many times before. Alma's face radiated pride for her son. Daniel had never told her of the episode at Varadero. Upon returning from the beach he had only said that they had a great time.

Glasses clinked, and their faces glowed in the candlelight. After dinner they set out for midnight mass, which was to be held on the lawn of Santa Rosa de Lima. The church's interior was in the process of renovation for Sunday services. Daniel and Rafael preferred to forego the Christmas Eve mass but felt it appropriate to partake in the religious fervor everyone was feeling. For them, the church was a meeting place to plan the removal of cigarettes from Ramiro La Vandero without getting caught, not a place for prayer. Rafael admitted he was an atheist, and Daniel's practices of worship had diminished after his father passed away. He reasoned that God took away his father, so why should he worship and pray to him?

The rest of the Reyes family was ecstatic to attend mass recited by a priest after years of hidden bible studies and mock masses at home. Alma Milan also welcomed mass in a church. Religion had been completely removed from her life. Work and mere survival had taken precedence since the death of her husband.

Daniel watched the joy, satisfaction, and peace radiate on their faces as they walked to the church. Church bells tolled. They sat together in the first two rows of folding chairs arranged in the churchyard. The altar was replaced by a narrow table, and on it a candelabra brightened the open air church. Seats filled quickly, and residents from Ranchuelo and the surrounding province of Villa Clara crowded around Santa Rosa de Lima and in stillness listened to Father Cardona recite mass and to the angelic songs of the choir.

When the service ended, everyone clapped and chatted contentedly. Juliana and Daniel held hands and followed the family to the street. Father Cardona carried a book of sermons against his chest. His robe flowed as he rushed across the lawn and called to the couple.

"My dear children, I hear you will soon wed."

Daniel and Juliana hesitated before the gate, surprised at his knowledge of their future nuptials and his hurried approach.

"How would you like to be the first couple to wed in Santa Rosa de Lima in seventeen years, a celebration that will involve the entire community? Your wedding will make history in Ranchuelo." The priest stared at the couple in anticipation as he took in deep breaths.

Juliana shifted her purse from one shoulder to the other and let Daniel answer.

"We had planned to have a private wedding. Friends and family only. What do you think, Juli?"

"A large wedding? The cost?"

"The church and congregation will cover the cost. The food will be covered. Your responsibility will be your formal wear and flowers."

"Maybe we could change our plans. A historic event? We'll discuss it with our families and will let you know, Father," she said.

"Do consider what a wonderful celebration it would be. The religious residents need rejuvenation in their stifled lives. What occasion is more joyous than a wedding?"

"We'll consider it father," said Daniel. "Thank you."

The couple joined the family awaiting them curbside.

"What did Father Cardona want?" Rafael asked.

Juli said, "He wants our wedding to be a town event. What do you think?"

"Fantastic," said Felipe Reyes. Sandra Reyes's eyes glistened. While strolling toward home they all agreed it would be a chance of a lifetime for the young couple.

The family acted nonchalant when Daniel explained to Juliana that he had to return home. He would meet her at her parents' house. Daniel parted, and Mr. Reyes suggested they stop to visit an old friend of his, "To wish him a Merry Christmas."

"Where is Daniel going?" Juliana said, following him with her eyes as he jogged down the street.

"He won't be long. We'll meet him at home," said her father.

Daniel opened the door, and the tan and white puppy greeted him. Juli's surprise Christmas gift was excited at the return of his master. The little dog danced in circles and kicked up his front paws at the sight of Daniel. Brown doll-like eyes peeked through silken fur at him.

Daniel chopped some chicken and scraped the pieces into a dish. He refreshed a bowl with water and set both on top of a newspaper on the floor. He reached for the decorated box on the dining room table, and after the dog finished his meal, Daniel walked him to the Reyes' home to await the group.

He played with the puppy in the living room until he heard voices outside. When he heard a key turn the lock of the front door, he lifted the squirming dog into the box and slipped on the lid. The puppy nudged his nose against the cover and peeked out, but Daniel gently rested his hand on the top to keep the animal hidden.

Juliana entered the living room. "Where did you go? Why walk off by yourself our first Christmas mass together? How could you leave me like that?"

With a glint in his eye, he slid the box across the floor. She saw the top lift up twice, and a puppy's white head popped out and knocked the lid to the floor.

"How cute. Now I see why." She picked up the Havanese pup, and he licked her face, pawed, and wiggled in happiness. Juli petted his soft fur and thanked her fiancé. "I love him. I love you." She kissed Daniel, unaware the others had gathered around them to admire the new addition to the family.

Juliana blushed. "He's like a little spark. Let's call him Chispa."

"Nice name," her father said. "Now let's open our gifts."

Rafael and Eva passed out the presents as Juliana and Daniel played with their puppy. Daniel glanced at his mother, seated in an armchair, as she opened the small gift neatly wrapped by Juliana.

"Daniel, Juli, how beautiful." Mrs. Milan slipped the ring on her finger. "It matches the necklace your father gave me. You knew this, didn't you?"

Alma rose, and the box and wrapping paper slid off her lap to the floor. She put her arms around the couple and kissed them. "How special this gift is. How special you are to me."

Chapter Twelve
THE WEDDING

    The wedding day was approaching, and Juliana and Daniel spent the morning in town making final arrangements. Carmelita saw them walking hand in hand along the street and waved with an eagerness that fizzled to disappointment when the couple's attention was focused on the antics of their feisty puppy and not on her. Juli walked Chispa on a leash and reined him in at the approach of a larger dog that sniffed the curious newcomer. Daniel grabbed hold of the leash and eased the puppy away from the big dog. They headed toward the apartment of Reynaldo, their floral designer, located above his flower shop.

    At the sight of Chispa, children gathered around Daniel, and adults accompanying them chatted about the upcoming nuptials with the dog's masters. An appearance in Ranchuelo by the first couple to receive their wedding vows in Santa Rosa de Lima in seventeen years kindled excitement and anticipation for their special day. The couple was followed and congratulated like town celebrities. Carmelita witnessed her friends' star power and scurried in the opposite direction toward a potential customer as Juliana and Daniel opened the door and climbed the stairs to Reynaldo's apartment.

    They discussed the final details for flower arrangements. Juli decided that two sprays of live white orchids would flank the entrance to the altar at Santa Rosa de Lima to symbolize the couple and the white orchid growing near the waterfall. Clear glass vases of white carnations surrounded by votive candles were chosen to adorn the tables at the reception. The votive candles were a reminder of the candles reflecting in the pool, another fond memory of their proposal. She would hold one white rose during her walk down the aisle. With a limited budget, the couple chose elegant simplicity as the theme for their wedding decorations.

Daniel handed Reynaldo the last payment in cash and they left. While descending the stairs to the street, Juliana told Daniel how relieved she was to have finally wrapped up their wedding plans. Planning the wedding had caused friction between her and her mother, which she believed would now ease.

The satin and lace wedding gown her cousin purchased in Miami as her wedding gift to the couple hung in Juliana's closet. Daniel's tuxedo, tailored by his mother with the help of Juli's mother, would be completed upon their return from town. After Daniel's final fitting, they could relax for a few days.

As they rounded a corner, Juliana expressed to her fiancé how pleased she was with the choice of flowers. To their astonishment she almost bumped into a man who veered to avoid a gap in the sidewalk. The couple halted in front of a stunned Maximo. A look of shock crossed his face when he registered who the couple was.

Cars bustled past on the street, a woodpecker chipped the bark of a Rosewood, and *tocorros* scolded in the branches of a mahogany tree. These sounds went unheard. A tomblike silence bewildered the three, who stood as if in a time warp. Juliana picked up the puppy.

"Cute dog," said Maximo.

"Thanks."

"Let's go." Daniel rested his hand on her shoulder blade and directed her off the sidewalk along the curb.

"Congratulations on your engagement." Max said, conjuring an unnatural enthusiasm in his voice.

Daniel detected a tone of sarcasm. When Juli thanked Max, Daniel's eyes narrowed. He stepped back onto the sidewalk. With the puppy in her arms, she had to walk briskly to catch up to her fiancé.

"Of all the luck," Daniel mumbled as his step quickened. "We can't get away from him."

Juli set the puppy down, and Chispa stopped to sniff a tree trunk.

"Daniel, wait up."

"What happens if he tries to come to our wedding? What do we do?"

"I meant to tell you. Max asked Rafa if he could attend."

"He did? Why didn't Rafael tell me?"

"He knew you'd say no."

"What did you tell him?"

"Everyone in Ranchuelo is invited."

"Not him."

"Why not?"

"Why not? You want him to come?"

"No. But we agreed with Father Cardona to include everyone."

"He's coming?"

"It's a community event. Everyone's coming."

"Maximo isn't."

She guided Chispa to Prado Nuevo and sat on the wall in the shade. "How can we exclude one person?"

Daniel stood in front of her. "I'd eliminate a few others if I could. Let's face it. He's made our lives miserable. He's not coming."

"It wasn't that bad."

"Maybe not for you."

Juliana could see the boy in Daniel trying to get his way, but she refused to give in. "We have no choice. We agreed. Everyone in Ranchuelo is invited."

"Call it off then."

"Call it off?"

"If he's there, no reason for a wedding. It'll be ruined."

"Do you really want to call off our wedding? Now that everything's in place."

"What happened to that small intimate wedding we planned in El Escambray by the waterfall?"

"We all agreed on a community wedding. You can't back out now. Don't you love me?"

"Of course I love you. It's not about us."

"Not about us? Who is this about?"

"Max. The problem is him."

"You cancel it, then. Tell everyone." She handed him the leash and crossed the Prado. Her arms swung at her sides as she picked up speed.

"Juli, wait." He rushed after her but before he reached Juli an elementary school teacher she knew paused to wish her well.

"Your marriage will be soon. How exciting. We wouldn't miss it."

"Yes. In a few days." Juliana turned and glared at Daniel as he caught up to her.

"See you at the wedding." The lady waved to her and Daniel as she opened her car door and climbed in.

Juli refused to look at Daniel, who stood next to her.

"Get away from me."

He stepped back. "I don't really want to call it off."

The puppy sat on the pavement with his tongue hanging at the side of his mouth and stared at his masters as if waiting for them to solve the problem.

"Do you think I want Max there? It's about our agreement with Father Cardona." She picked up the puppy and put him in Daniel's arms. The dog licked his sullen face.

"Don't you want your fifteen minutes of fame, Daniel?"

"Fame? In a few years they'll all forget it ever happened."

"We won't, though, will we?"

"How can I forget being married?"

"I hope you won't forget. Do you think we'll even see Max in the crowd?"

"I guess not."

"We'll focus on each other, right? Only on each other."

Daniel awoke at five in the morning on the big day. His stomach felt the same as the day he'd recited an oral presentation in seventh grade. His queasiness was not only due to nerves but because Rambo had elected him, against his will, to help slaughter four pigs donated by the Ramos family for the reception dinner. It made him even more nauseous to think of killing a pig. He brushed his teeth, dressed, and met Rambo at a temporary pen for the pigs at the edge of town near the church.

Rambo handed Daniel a knife. He gripped it, stared at the silver blade gleaming under the streetlight and turned it over in his hand. Rambo led a young sow to him and waited. Daniel closed his eyes and thrust the knife into the neck of the unsuspecting pig. A bone cracked, and Daniel backed away from the terrified animal. Blood gushed and spilled onto the grass. The pig screamed, wailed and fell forward on the ground, chin first. Daniel turned to Rambo, who was shaking his head.

"That's not how you do it."

"I had to get it over with. Now what?"

With the back of an axe, Rambo gave the animal a blow to the head to end its suffering. Daniel looked at the stiff, bleeding pig, legs stuck straight out of her pink body. He threw the knife to the left of the animal, and it stuck straight into the ground. The handle vibrated. Daniel reeled. "The first and last time I kill an animal."

The squealing sound of the sow reverberated in his ears. He covered his ears with his hands and walked away.

"Where are you going? This is for your wedding."

"I don't give a damn. Find someone else to be your assassin."

Daniel strolled to the abandoned house. A donkey, tethered to a stake in the ground, grazed at the side of the road, lifted his head, and perked his ears up as Daniel passed. He could care less what Rambo thought of him—a coward, probably, but he felt disgusted and nauseated by the slaughter. Killing the pig triggered in him an overwhelming melancholy.

He sat on the mosaic bench in the garden, and as the sky brightened, he focused on the yard and how manicured it looked. Juli and Eva had trimmed the hedge and fertilized the lawn. The garden was in full bloom. Even the backyard was mowed. Daniel wondered how Juli had managed to finish the yard work without his help. From what he observed at this vantage point, only internal repairs on the house would be needed.

He hung his head and noticed a loose slab of stone under the bench. He lifted the stone. If he dug a hole under it, this spot would be perfect to hide his cash. Daniel had run out of hideaways in his bedroom to stash his cigarette money. After their honeymoon he would transfer all the pesos here and would confide the whereabouts of this secret location only to Juliana.

The sun rose and crested above the horizon. Its warmth bathed his face. Clouds in the east dawned gray and illuminated to orange as if torched by the rising sun. The cloud formation plumed against a pale sky. He marveled at the striking color contrast painted by nature.

For the first time after months spent with Juliana, he questioned whether marriage, studying a difficult career, and settling in this abandoned house requiring constant upkeep was the right choice to make. Daniel grilled himself about whether he was prepared for the pressures of adulthood. He shook his head to elude such thoughts. From where were these doubts surfacing? His love for Juliana had been a certainty.

No matter. There was no backing out now. They'd already had an argument about Max, and Daniel had suggested cancelling the wedding because of him. As Juli had reminded him in town, she, her family, and his mother had devoted hours of preparation, and the entire town had become involved in the wedding. If Daniel declined to marry her, he would be shunned. Rafael would despise him. How could he think such gloomy thoughts under such an exquisite sky?

Daniel lay on the bench and placed his feet flat on the ground. The gray clouds bleached to white and billowed in the sky. His own life's journey resembled the clouds above, he had drifted along. Every decision he had made in the past affected his life. Was he making the right decision now? Daniel was happy with Juli and blamed killing the pig as the motive for doubt. Yesterday he was at ease with the direction of his life. Now he urged himself to be rid of any toxic thoughts and to rise from the bench, return home, proudly wear his tuxedo, and recite his vows to the love of his life. He knew his future bride anxiously waited for this day to begin.

Daniel and Rafael dressed at Daniel's house. His mother assisted Juliana at the Reyes' home with last-minute adjustments to her gown. Rafael stood in front of Daniel to straighten his bowtie.

"You seem tense. What's wrong?" Rafa looked up from the bowtie and into Daniel's eyes. "Having second thoughts?"

"Of course not." Daniel couldn't believe how perceptive he was. "Killing the pig messed up my mind. It was traumatic."

"Rambo said you couldn't take it. He's telling everyone."

"I expected that and don't give a damn. Never again. No way I'm eating pork today."

"Eat what you want. It's your day. Yours and Juli's. Are you sure you're ready to marry her?"

"Why do you ask?"

"I'm your friend. I know you. You're not yourself."

"The pig. I told you. Honestly I don't know. I love Juli."

"Maybe this will help." Rafael reached in his bag and pulled out a flask filled with rum. He twisted off the cap and poured them each a glass.

"You're always prepared. How do you do it?"

"I don't know. That's me. I would be nervous if I were getting married. I thought this might calm your nerves." He handed Daniel a glass. "To you and Juli forever."

They raised their glasses, downed the liquid, and drank a second glass as they awaited Rambo to pick them up in a horse-drawn carriage. Rafael offered him a mint as they climbed into the cart.

Daniel sucked on the candy and tasted the cool flavor of peppermint. He ignored Rambo's teasing about the pig and watched the white geldings from the back seat as they pranced to the church. He gaped at the hundreds of people gathered in front of Santa Rosa de Lima as they pulled up to the entrance.

"Who are all these people?" asked Rafael.

Daniel shrugged.

Rambo steadied the horses, agitated by the hordes of citizens from Villa Clara Province. Rafael stepped down from the carriage. When the crowd caught a glimpse of the best man, they clapped. Daniel jumped down. They applauded and cheered frantically at the sight of the groom. He raised his arms high in the air and bowed. Rafael stared at his friend in wonder. The showman before him was a total stranger. Rafa attributed the groom's theatrics to the influence of two large glasses of straight rum.

Daniel, Father Cardona, Rafael, and two ushers stood at the altar. Daniel clasped his hands behind his back and surveyed the polished pews arranged in neat rows. Every pew was filled with guests, as were the once dark and empty aisles. He was spellbound at the church's transformation and compared its immaculate condition to the years of neglect and the decayed state he had witnessed on the night of the gang's final meeting.

Statues gleamed dust-free, shiny brass candlesticks were topped with new pillar candles, and sunrays shafted through previously sealed stained glass windows. The stuffy odor of mildew had disintegrated into a subtle scent of perfume and incense wafting in the air. A crucifix and chalice adorned the altar, draped in a linen coverlet.

Daniel glanced at the congregation. Eyes stared expectantly at him. He shifted from one foot to the other and cast his eyes down to the familiar marble floor of the altar, buffed to a glimmer. Maximo and he had fought a few feet from where he stood. He also recalled Max's voice calling from the vestibule and his slow approach down the aisle. The closer Max got as he crossed from darkness into candlelight, the more enraged he looked. Daniel scanned the crowd and wondered if and where Max was seated. He imagined his anger had mutated to devastation by now.

Father Cardona looked at the groom, and a soothing smile lit up his face. Rafael patted Daniel's back, and they smiled at each other. Daniel touched his vest pocket. The ring, in a satin pouch his mother had sewn, was in place. Whispers, shuffling, and sounds of shoes bumping against kneelers echoed throughout the nave. A baby whimpered and let out a cry.

Daniel lurched, like the attendees to the ceremony seated in front of him, when the voices of the multitudes outside roared, announcing the arrival of the bride. He caught his mother's eye, and she nodded in a gesture of encouragement. The ushers and Rafael laughed at being caught off guard by the noise of the enthusiastic throng outside the church.

Daniel turned toward the vestibule and strained to erase the memory of Maximo and the night of the meeting. Eva and the bridesmaids beamed as they preceded the bride and her father down the aisle. Up the entrance steps, a veil flowed in a breeze. The silhouette of a female hesitated in sunlight streaming through the open door. Daniel gasped.

Juliana lifted her gown like an angel fanning her wings and caressed the single white rose during her entrance into the church. Never had his eyes captured her so formally dressed, so regal. She released the satin and interlocked her arm with her father's, and they glided down the aisle.

Pearls intermingled with lace at the bodice, and the luster of her dress in candlelight was breathtaking. Her shiny hair bounced and cascaded over delicate bare shoulders. Her image exuded purity and eternity as she slowly advanced over the mosaic tiles of the center aisle and approached the groom. Astounded by her beauty, Daniel whispered to Rafael, "Look at your gorgeous sister."

Everyone stood, and their low voices turned to chants. Father Cardona, in an attempt to hush the people, pushed downward with his hands but retreated as the outcries echoed throughout the church and the bride effortlessly drifted past the pews. She kissed her father's cheek and joined Daniel at the altar.

Once the congregation quieted, Father Cardona introduced himself and welcomed everyone into the church for this special occasion.

"What better reason to come together after so many years than to celebrate the love between Juliana and Daniel. Their nuptials mark a new beginning of religious celebration. The couple before me has opened a door into a brighter future for all of Cuba. May their life together be joyous and prosperous. Let us pray and begin the ceremony." The priest swept his arms in the air. "God bless Juliana and Daniel and all who have joined us in this holy mass of matrimony."

The candles in seven brass candlesticks glowed, and the scent of burning wax, incense, flowers, and Juliana's perfume entered Daniel's nostrils. This unique combination of fragrances would forever be associated with his nuptials to Juli.

As he stared at his bride and listened to every word enunciated by Father Cardona, he realized this was where he belonged.

Certainty consumed previous doubts about marrying Juliana. His emotion for the lovely lady beside him overwhelmed him. Daniel's eyes misted. Prompted by the priest, he verbalized his vows. The sincere words flowing out of his mouth seemed to be spoken by someone else.

His lips pressed together as he listened to Juliana's soft voice affirm her devotion to him. Before they kissed, they burst out laughing, which prompted the audience to cheer, stomp the floor, and clap their approval. They applauded away years of religious suppression. From the churchyard the cheers reached tonal heights.

The priest recited his final blessing and bid everyone to go in peace. Daniel held his bride's hand high and led her rushing down the aisle. Admirers' hands reached out to touch them. Individuals moved to the side in the vestibule and wished them well as they hastened by.

Rambo hopped down the church steps ahead of the newlyweds and waited by the carriage. With both hands he rubbed his horses' faces to calm the animals, distressed by the mob. The flighty steeds sidestepped on the asphalt. Rambo saluted Daniel as he helped Juliana climb into the carriage.

Daniel's elation retracted into alarm when he caught sight of four gray, Russian jeeps straddling the curb directly across the street from the parked carriage. He recognized the vehicles, the gray berets tilted on the soldiers' heads, and their light gray-blue shirts and dark blue pants. He knew they belonged to the Special Brigade.

Some of the uniformed men sat in the back seats and others positioned themselves on the hoods of the parked jeeps. Daniel flinched at the sight of Pothole, who stood with arms crossed as he conversed with a high ranking military man inside a vehicle. Another militia man, whose back faced the crowd, was also engulfed in conversation with his superior and Pothole. He had a Makarov pistol tucked in his belt. The butt of the gun rested against his lower back.

Pothole's mouth moved in conversation, but his attention was focused on the bride and groom entering the carriage. Daniel halted and grasped the handle to hoist himself into the cart. His moist hand slipped, but he regained his balance by clutching the seat back and thrusting himself forward. He slumped down beside Juliana. His face paled. Daniel loosened his bowtie as he watched Juli's bright smile evaporate.

"Why are they here?" She asked, but he didn't hear her. He signaled to Rafael as he emerged out of the crowd. Rafa stuck his arm inside the carriage, shook Daniel's hand, and congratulated them.

"See you at the reception."

"Ride with us," Daniel demanded.

Juliana swiftly turned toward her husband.

"Is something wrong?" Rafael looked from one to the other. "I'm driving Eva to the reception."

"We're fine. I think Daniel's worried about them." Juli nodded toward the uniforms congregated across the street.

"Who?" Rafael questioned Daniel by raising his eyebrows. He was unaware of the military presence and assumed the couple had an argument. Daniel leaned out of the carriage, faced him, and whispered, "Pothole's across the street with Special Brigade. You'll see them when we pull away."

"Oh, shit. Do you really want me to accompany you?"

"No, go on. I was just shocked. Nothing you can do. Why is factory security mingling with the military?"

"Everyone was invited," answered Rafael.

Along with his humor, Daniel detected Rafa's concern.

"Pothole's presence is worse than having Maximo in this sea of humanity."

"When crowds gather, police are around. You know that."

"Police, I know. But Special Forces? And what's Pothole doing with them?"

Juliana leaned forward to listen to their conversation. Her dress crinkled. She couldn't hear what was said. "What's wrong? Is it the police you're upset about?"

Daniel leaned his head against the back of the seat. "No." He turned and smiled at her.

"Rafa?"

"Don't worry, Juli," Rafael said as he stepped away from the carriage and told Rambo to move out the horses. Rambo had pacified the nervous team and glanced back at the pair.

"Ready?"

When the couple nodded in unison, he lightly tapped the reins against the horses' hindquarters, and the rig eased past the mass of people. Rafael took a quick look at the elite troops lulling around their vehicles and immediately caught sight of Pothole. A wave of melancholy swept through him as he focused on the carriage transporting the newlyweds. He hurried to join Eva, who patiently waited in front of the church.

"What happened? Tell me."

Daniel sensed fear in Juli's voice, although he knew she hadn't recognized Pothole.

"I told Rafa how I slipped and almost fell in front of all those people. I caught myself. You were looking at the police."

He had to lie. How could he explain that the man who harassed him at the factory now collaborated with specialized brigade to spy on him on the day of his wedding?

"You almost fell? You're worried about the military, aren't you?"

"I was, but Rafa said they're always present when there's a crowd."

"Are you sure everything's fine? I don't want anything to spoil this day."

"I'm sure." Daniel held her hand and caressed it. "It's the happiest day of our lives."

The horses trotted past the vigilant military elite and pranced down the street, closed to traffic and lined with townsfolk paving the way to the reception on the Prado. In front of Prado Viejo, Rambo reined in the equines to a halt, and Daniel sprang to the pavement. He caught Juliana in his arms as she dismounted the carriage to cheers and fanfare from the townspeople.

Hand in hand the couple graciously strolled over a red carpet to antique red velvet chairs with crowns carved at the top. They sat at an elegantly set table with a bottle of champagne cooling in a silver ice bucket, a wedding gift from Juliana's colleagues at work. The bride and groom had the luxury of sipping champagne while the attendees drank beer and wine.

The Reyes family and Daniel's mother congratulated the newlyweds, hovered around them for a while, and sat at a table next to theirs. The night was festive and joyous. A buffet table, a bar, and urns of flowers lined the wall of the Prado. The potted flowers were a gift from Dr. Nieves and his wife, Susana.

Daniel caught a glimpse of Maximo as he swaggered by. They glared at each other. Daniel looked away, and Max kept walking. Daniel knew Max's appearance was to irritate him and to get Juliana's attention. Juli chatted with Eva and to his relief missed the prowling beast.

Soon after the appearance of Maximo, the couple, accompanied by Father Cardona, cordially visited each table and welcomed the guests to their reception. Daniel greeted his cousins, Ofelia and Juan from Havana, and asked why their mother, his aunt Laura, hadn't come. They told him she had the flu and had asked them to congratulate the couple for her. She was sorry she was unable to attend.

Daniel chatted with his cousins for a while. Out of all the guests present, he spoke the longest to Dr. Javier Nieves. They discussed the flawless wedding proceedings, plans of the couple, and Daniel's promising career in medicine. Their conversation was cut short when the musicians played and enticed the newlyweds to dance. Daniel wondered if Max watched while he slow danced with Juliana. He found it impossible to eliminate his constant thoughts of Maximo. He felt ill at ease knowing of his presence at the reception.

At least the military had departed when the churchyard emptied. Two police officers patrolled the sidewalk across from the Prado. They were familiar to Daniel and posed no threat. He shifted his eyes from looking across the street and saw Rafael ask Eva to dance. Felipe and Sandra Reyes followed them to the dance floor. Emilio and Carmelita also joined in, to Daniel's surprise, and Rambo asked Daniel's mother to dance. He pressed Juli closer to him as they circled the center of the dance floor.

The reception officially ended at four in the morning, when the older folks and children departed. Daniel, Juliana, and their friends and cousins danced and drank on the plaza until sunrise.

Daniel awoke with a throbbing headache and had no idea where he was. He raised his head and opened one eye at a time. His wife lay on the sofa beside him, still wearing her wedding gown. Approximately twenty friends and relatives were sprawled on the floor and on furniture rearranged in a living room. Two chairs were pushed together, and two bridesmaids were asleep on them. Several bodies were curled up on pillows on the floor. The room was familiar to Daniel but he couldn't quite place it, until Reynaldo, the floral designer, walked in, clapped his hands, and insisted everyone wake up and leave. Reynaldo had a meeting scheduled with a client in fifteen minutes. Juliana, awakened by his voice, reached for Daniel's hand.

"What happened to our honeymoon?"

"I can't sort that out in my brain. Maybe no one could drive us to Cienfuegos. No one was sober enough."

"We have to go now. We're supposed to be alone together, on our honeymoon."

She watched the slumbering group arise in their formal wear as she smoothed her dress.

"Where are Rafael and Eva? They'll take us."

Chapter Thirteen
THE HONEYMOON

Rafael drove the newlyweds in his father's 1957 Chevrolet Impala to Cienfuegos for their honeymoon. Daniel suggested riding his motorcycle, but Juliana refused. They cuddled in the back seat, and Eva snuggled up front beside Rafael. Juliana leaned her head on Daniel's shoulder while he dozed. When they pulled up to the Jagua Hotel, he opened his eyes, nudged her, and pointed at Rafael and Eva in the front seat. "They'll be the next couple to marry."

She nodded, slid along the seat, and followed him out of the car.

"What did you say, brother?" Rafael asked his brother-in-law as he jumped out of the car to open the trunk.

"Nothing. Thanks for the ride."

Daniel lifted their suitcase out of the trunk and added, "Let's all have a drink at the bar. My treat."

"No. You two go to your room. It's your honeymoon. You've already missed one night. I never knew anyone who missed the first night of their honeymoon."

"One drink won't hurt, will it, Juli?"

Juliana squeezed her purse strap. "I guess not."

The foursome drank beer on a patio overlooking the ocean and reminisced about the wedding. As they talked, the sound of a hammer pounded. Rafael commented on the annoying noise. Daniel pointed to a tarp on the roof of a small building next door.

"They're still repairing damages from the hurricane. Did you see all the tree stumps in front of the hotel?" He ignored the pounding, and resumed the conversation. "I didn't know Emilio and Carmelita had a thing going."

"It started when we decorated for the wedding," said Eva. "They joked and laughed together. It was kind of cute. Father Cardona invited us to lunch at his house behind the church, and even he remarked about their flirtation."

"They're both unattached. She's divorced; he's a widower. So why not?" said Rafael. "Let's go, Eva. Let these lovebirds go to their nest." He pulled Eva's chair out as she stood. "Enjoy your honeymoon. We'll pick you up in a week." They waved and walked away, pressed together with arms around each other's waists.

Juliana watched them disappear behind a row of coconut palms and reached for Daniel's hand. "I'm happy they've hit it off." She looked into her husband's eyes. He touched her hair, eased her to his lips, kissed her, and whispered, "I can't wait one more minute for you."

Their lovemaking was endless. They stayed in the hotel room for three days and ordered room service when hunger overcame them. After a breakfast of tropical fruit on the morning of the second day, Juliana remade the bed and placed the pillows at the foot. She explained to Daniel that a direct view of the ocean would enhance their moments of passion and believed that opening their eyes each morning to ocean views would be therapeutic.

From an armchair Daniel watched her slim arms lift the mattress corners and tuck in the end of the sheet with ease. He was leery of disturbing their inner realm with the sight and sound of an ocean she considered dazzling and he, chilling. For a while he refrained from voicing his opinion, but as she folded back the top sheet and tossed the pillows onto the bed, he commented, "Won't our heads be uncomfortable facing that way?"

"I don't think so. We'll breathe in salt air and listen to the sound of waves breaking. The sea will be a very special reminder of our honeymoon. Won't that be so, Daniel?"

They awoke to an open sliding glass door and a view of palm trees, the beach, and a turquoise ocean. Curtains billowed and snapped in the breeze. Unfortunately the sounds of rushing water and lapping waves of Juliana's romantic ocean had fused into nightmares for Daniel. At first he kept his dreams a secret, but the following night he screamed out about being crushed and drowned by a sea monster. Juliana awoke to a loud thump and found her husband on the floor, entangled in bedding. Daniel thrashed and flailed his arms as if swimming for his life. Patiently she calmed him and guided him back onto the bed. She huddled close and locked her arms around his waist.

"It was just a dream. Go back to sleep, *mi amor.*"

"A nightmare," he corrected. "I was pounded by waves caused by a huge creature. I was going under."

She patted his arm. "Tonight you'll have sweet dreams. We're together."

Daniel forgot about the nightmare while in Juli's presence and during bouts of intense pleasure until he heard the waves of high tide crash against the shore. Visions of his nightmare returned. She rested her head on his chest.

"I've admitted this to very few people," he said and paused.

"Admitted what?" She raised her head to look at him.

"How much I love you."

"That's not what you were going to say," she insisted. "Tell me. What have you admitted to few people?"

He watched a sailboat glide beyond waves churning white against the sand.

"Can we close the sliding glass door tonight?"

"Sure. But why? Don't you like the sound of waves? Like now. It's so peaceful."

"I like the sound, but it triggers my nightmares."

"A creature was drowning you?"

"The same dream since I was a child. I fear the ocean and what lives in it."

Juliana sensed his embarrassment. "Well, then tonight we'll close the doors. The curtains also, if you like."

"Thanks. The curtains can stay open." Daniel hugged her.

Juliana loved their cocoon-like existence in the hotel room. She was reluctant to release him to answer the door for room service or for a room attendant delivering clean linen. She reached for Daniel when he slipped on shorts to answer the tap at the door.

"Juli, let go."

"I don't want to."

"We have to eat."

He returned with two bowls of *caldo Gallego,* a Spanish white bean soup, a bread basket, cheese platter, and a bottle of wine on a tray. He placed it between them on the bed.

"I hate for you to leave me."

Daniel laughed. "Juli, I left this bed for two seconds."

"And I missed you."

He poured Chardonnay into their glasses. "Cheers. I missed you too. What happens when we return to reality? It will be like after the weekend at the waterfall."

"I suppose we'll adjust." She raised her glass and it clinked against his. "Promise to take me to the shore again soon. I love it." Juliana sat cross-legged on the bed to better access the tray of food. "I'm sorry the ocean isn't your ideal honeymoon."

"You misunderstood. I'm having a great time. I'm happy by the water. I just can't swim in it."

The next day they lay nude on the bed and stared out the open door.

"Daniel, I know it's the wrong time to ask, but there's something I overheard Rafael tell Eva at our wedding."

"What was it?"

"It's bothered me ever since. I was going to let it go until we got home."

"Ask me." He propped up on his elbow and gazed into her hazel eyes as she stared at the ocean.

"He told her you had wanted to live in the United States."

"There was a time I felt that way."

"But you changed your mind because of me?"

"True. It was a goal I had but not anymore."

"I never knew. Daniel, why didn't you tell me of your plan?"

"It wasn't important. I married you and look forward to a career here. Now I want to stay in Cuba."

"Why didn't you bring this up before? It was such a shock. I didn't think we had any secrets."

"We don't have any secrets."

"On the day of the storm you said you loved Ranchuelo."

"Juli, you're wrong."

"I'm sure you did." She brushed at a strand of hair that slipped across her cheek.

"I like it, but it's not about Ranchuelo. It's the government, the harassment, the constant struggle to survive I wanted to get away from."

"I'm disappointed."

"I thought of telling you the day of the storm but was afraid of upsetting you. I knew you wanted to live in Cuba."

"Rafael and Eva knew, but you kept it from me, Daniel."

"How was I to explain?"

"A secret like that could affect our relationship."

"I didn't keep it from you on purpose."

"You know my family means everything to me. I'll never leave them, under any circumstances." Juliana sat up and clutched the sheet to her breast. "What if you decide we should move to Miami? What happens then?"

"We do whatever you want. I love you. You know that. It's not an issue anymore. We're living here." Daniel leaned forward and kissed the tip of her nose. "Did that kiss take away your worries?" He gripped her shoulders and looked deep into her eyes, "I told you I'm afraid of the ocean. I can't leave Cuba in a small boat or raft like so many do."

"You saved Rafael from drowning."

"What was I to do? Watch my best friend drown? We weren't in deep water. Don't you believe me? The only way I would go to the United States is by plane. And Castro won't allow that."

"Does Rafa know of your fear?"

Daniel felt warmth rise to his face.

"Another secret he knows and I didn't."

"Rafael and I've been friends for years. Why do I have to explain this trivia?"

"Trivia? It's your life. I'm supposed to know these things."

"Give it time. You'll know everything about me."

"Fine. But no more secrets, promise?"

Daniel sighed. "They're not secrets. I swear, I'll tell you everything." To lighten the mood he tickled her under her arms. "No seriousness on this honeymoon," he said with his teeth clenched. "Only fun."

She laughed, clutched a pillow to her body, and jumped off the bed to escape the torturous tickling. "*Por favor*, Daniel. Stop. You know how I hate being tickled. No fair."

He smirked. "Are we fine now?"

"I think so."

"You think so?"

Juli stood in front of the television console holding the pillow in front of her. "As long as you stay in Cuba and we raise our children here, we're fine."

"That's a promise." He patted the bed covers. "Come back. I won't tickle you. Do you want to see a show tonight? I have cabin fever. We've already made up for missing the first night of our honeymoon, don't you think?"

"I think so. I'm getting pale. I need sunlight. Let's go to the beach. A show sounds great."

She threw the pillow at him and grabbed her bikini on the chair. "Race you to the beach."

Daniel slapped plaster onto the wall of the master bedroom of their new home, and Rafael smoothed the paste into cracks. Juliana and Eva painted a smaller bedroom the guys had plastered a few days earlier.

"What was the best part of your honeymoon?"

Juliana rolled paint on the wall, glanced at Eva, and giggled. "Do you really want me to answer that?"

"No." She laughed. "I mean, beside the sex. What did you enjoy?"

"Oh God, everything. The moonlight walks on the beach, dancing at night. The shows, dancers, their costumes. Every day ended with an evening stroll on the beach. That is, after three consecutive days in our room." Juli dipped the roller in a tin of cream-colored paint and allowed some of the thick liquid to drip before smoothing it on the wall. "We talked, made plans. How we hoped we'd get this house. And here we are. In the middle of another dream come true. I can't believe it's ours."

"Three days in the room?"

Juliana brushed a strand of hair away from her flushed cheeks. "Well, it *was* a honeymoon."

"One hell of a honeymoon."

Juli stopped rolling. "Yes. One hell of a honeymoon."

"Everything you wanted you're getting. How crazy you were for Daniel."

"I still am. Now if he can just get through medical school." She set down the roller and picked up a wet brush to paint a window frame. "Our lives are merging perfectly. I hope the same happens to you and Rafa."

Eva set her brush on a paper towel after finishing half the frame. "We're taking it one step at a time. Who would have guessed Rafael and I would date? Your brother, my friend. I'm adjusting to our romantic feelings. I was totally unprepared and so was he."

"I suppose it's none of our business. Daniel and I wondered if you slept together yet. You don't have to answer."

Eva sat down on the floor as Juliana glided paint across the wall with the roller again. "Not yet. We've discussed it. I don't think I'll wait until marriage like you. I want it to be special, though. Like a honeymoon. Rafael's a sweetheart. He's letting me take my time." She dabbed at a drop of paint on the floor with a rag. "You know, Juli, we're lucky. They're good guys. They really care about us."

Juliana set the roller in the pan of paint, propped the handle against the side of the pan, and sat cross-legged beside Eva, admiring her work.

"We are fortunate, aren't we?"

Daniel and Rafael joined the girls for a lunch break. Daniel glanced at the wall and at the two friends seated on the floor. "That's all you did? Gossiping again?"

"Gossiping? The room's almost finished," Juli countered as he raised his plaster-stained hands and bent over to kiss his wife. "How about lunch? We're starving."

"Well, starve then."

He wiped his hands on a rag. "I was kidding. Excellent job."

"That's better."

Juliana rose with Daniel's help, reached into the cooler, and passed out ham and cheese sandwiches and soda. Rafael extended a hand to Eva and pulled her to her feet. The boys kicked empty paint buckets across the floor to use for seats. Eva sat beside Rafael and said, "When did you find out the house was yours?"

Juliana looked at Daniel to see if he was going to answer, but he had taken a bite of sandwich and was chewing.

"When you dropped us off at Daniel's mother's house after our honeymoon. Alma yelled and waved a piece of paper in the air as she ran to meet us. I thought something terrible had happened. She screamed to Daniel. He also thought something was wrong. It was a letter of approval from La Reforma Urbana."

Daniel chewed the bread, swallowed, and looked at Rafael. "They accepted us because it belonged to your aunt, a family member of Juli's. Otherwise I doubt the government would have let us live here."

"We're famous in this town. We had the first church wedding in seventeen years. How could they refuse us?" Juliana tapped her foot against his.

"Famous had nothing to do with it. Do you think communists care about fame? Supposedly we're all equal."

"Daniel's right," said Rafael. "It's hard to be assigned a home unless family had owned it. Anyway, you got the house you wanted. It doesn't matter why, does it?"

They heard footsteps coming up the stairs. Emilio and Carmelita appeared in the doorway. Emilio had overheard their conversation. "It's a beautiful home."

Carmelita added, "You should be proud."

"Have a seat," said Juli. "We'll be proud once the plumbing works."

Daniel brought two chairs from the master bedroom. "We're happy with it, but the house needs a lot of work. It's coming together slowly."

"Would you like a sandwich and a drink? Help yourselves." Juli opened the lid of the cooler.

"Thanks. We already ate lunch." Emilio set his toolbox on the chair. "I want to get started. Where's the problem?"

Daniel glanced at Juliana. "It seems to be the whole house. The plumbing's bad everywhere. The kitchen sink drain is plugged, the master bath toilet's not flushing, and the other toilet leaks."

"I get it. Let's have a look."

Emilio followed Daniel and Rafael, who grabbed their drinks and sandwiches and ate as they showed him the master bathroom.

Carmelita sat in a chair between Juliana and Eva and said, "I'm still hungry" and reached for a sandwich and a can of soda. Before taking a bite she said to Juli, "You should talk your handsome husband into buying more jewelry. I have some lovely pieces, just in."

"Thanks but we can't afford those luxuries anymore. Daniel begins medical school in three weeks. He'll only work part time at the factory. My salary was hardly enough to support me."

"What about cigarette sales? Surely a nice supplement to his income. By the way, I have a few boxes left. People aren't buying cigarettes like they used to."

"He stopped selling cigarettes a while ago. I'll tell him you have boxes left."

Carmelita tapped Eva's knee. "And you, my dear. When will you and Juli's brother be married?"

"No plans to marry. We just started seeing each other. And you, Carmelita? Do you and Emilio plan to wed?"

Carmelita shrugged and set the sandwich on a napkin that lay across her lap.

"*Dios mio*. It took a long time to find each other and in such a small town. Emilio wants me to move in with him. It's too soon, isn't it? He said it would be best for both of us. Marriage? I doubt we'll ever get married. What for?"

She took a big bite and then sipped her drink, smearing the cup rim with pink lipstick. Carmelita's eyes, thick with blue eye shadow, bulged as she asked Juli, "When will you and Daniel move here?"

"We're not sure. Hopefully, before he begins classes. It depends on Emilio and when the plumbing is fixed."

"You must be excited."

"I am. Daniel and I are very excited."

Chapter Fourteen
CAPTURED

Juliana and Daniel returned to his mother's house minutes after midnight on Saturday night after spending the evening with Eva, Rafael, and Javier and Susana Nieves listening to an orchestra of friends from Ranchuelo. They danced and proposed toasts to Daniel's career, to a long marriage, and to Rafael and Eva's relationship.

After the evening at the club, Juliana was tired since she had also had a busy day at the shop. She retired to their bedroom, slipped into a nightgown, and crawled under the covers. Juli stared at a pair of pants, a shirt, and a towel Daniel had strewn across the floor earlier. Ordinarily she would have picked them up, but instead closed her eyes. She heard talking but realized they were voices resonating in her mind as she drifted to sleep. Soon she flowed into a state of gentle dreams flickering before her sealed eyes.

In the kitchen Daniel drank a glass of milk from Rambo's farm, a beverage available only to children and elders. He savored the drink with one of Juli's *pasteles* and lingered in the living room. He decided to take the dog for a walk and opened a drawer where the leash was kept. He clipped it to the puppy's collar as Chispa hopped eagerly around Daniel and followed him outside to the deserted street.

His ears rang from a night of music blaring in the small club—understandable since the three couples had sat at a table next to the speakers. He slipped the loop at the end of the leash between his teeth, put his pointer fingers in his ears, and moved them up and down to rid himself of the tolling in his head. The movement of fingers had no effect on the annoying sound. Daniel returned the loop to his wrist and recalled the fun they'd had dancing and singing along with the band. He would suggest that they all go out again soon and would ask for the band's itinerary from his friend, the band leader.

The street was dark and empty. The puppy bounced along and tugged on the leash. Daniel gripped the cord with his hand to prevent the loop from slipping off his wrist. The puppy's tail flipped up and curled on his back as he waddled over the grass in search of an object to urinate on. A dog in a house across the street saw them and barked. Daniel glanced toward the house, where the only street light shone on a brown dog with his two paws on the back of a sofa. With each yelp the dog's breath fogged the picture window.

Daniel guided the puppy by the Reyes' home. The window shades were drawn in Rafael's bedroom, and the light was out, or he would have tapped on the window. Chispa raised his hind leg and wet the pole of a triangular Ceda el Paso street sign in front of the house. The sign was worn and faded from sun exposure, and blotches of rust bordered its gray letters. Daniel yawned as he waited by the sign for the dog to finish. Sluggishly he turned and guided the puppy toward home.

The desire to sleep suddenly overwhelmed Daniel. Now he was anxious to climb in bed beside Juli. As he trudged behind the tugging dog, Daniel remembered that in three days he and Juli would move to the house and that he needed to borrow Rambo's truck for the move. He would ask Rambo tomorrow at the factory before the end of his shift.

Daniel passed in front of Emilio's house and noticed that the windows were wide open. It was dark inside. He heard Carmelita scold Emilio. Poor man had to listen to her nagging and complaints about how he had cancelled taking her to her sister's house.

"But I was working." There was a pleading tone in Emilio's voice. "The house had disconnected pipes, dirt on the floor, and the water turned off. I couldn't walk out on them to pick you up. They were already upset about a water-damaged ceiling."

"But you promised me."

"*Lo siento.* It was impossible to leave at that moment."

"Be careful what you promise a woman. If you make a promise, be sure to fulfill it." Daniel cringed at the thought of living with her piercing voice. How fortunate he was to have Juliana as his wife. Quietly he entered his house and unleashed the puppy. The dog rushed to the kitchen to lap water from his bowl and followed at Daniel's heels into the bedroom.

The rasp and roar of Russian-made Gaz 66 trucks and jeeps rumbling on the street startled Daniel awake. Confused by the steady murmur of engines, he sat up in bed. He realized his ears were no longer ringing. The sounds came from the front of the house. Daniel squinted at the bright headlights glowing in the window and heard gruff masculine voices shouting orders.

"Daniel? What's that?" Juliana said in a muffled voice coming from beneath the covers.

"I'm not sure."

Suddenly, they heard a crash and in unison the windows in the front of the house were shattered by crowbars wielded by police. They smashed the glass until every jagged piece had dropped off the frames. Military personnel preceded police inside and entered the house from all angles. The front door crashed to the floor and split in two upon impact. Soldiers with pistols drawn wobbled across the door sections and trampled over glass fragments. Uniforms combed the house, room by room.

Juliana sprang from beneath the covers and clutched the sheets as she stared at the chaotic scene before her. Daniel jumped out of bed and halted at the sound of his shrieking mother, forced out of her room by rifle-toting militia. Alma tried to enter the couple's bedroom, but a row of armed guards prevented her. They pushed her onto the living room sofa with the butts of their guns and detained her there.

Four policemen smashed their way through the bedroom window and with crowbars raised grabbed hold of Daniel, handcuffed him, and threw him on the floor. The metal handcuffs gripped his wrists as tightly as the talons of a falcon gripping its prey. Little Chispa barked in terror in an effort to protect his bound master. Juliana scooped the puppy into her arms. From that moment until the raid ended, she froze beside the bed with her mouth agape, unable to utter a sound.

Juli wept at her inability to defend her husband lying on his stomach with a soldier's boot locked on his back. The soldier pressed him firmly against the floor. Daniel's mother gasped at the sight of her son wincing as crowbars prodded his sides and boots kicked his body. Alma Milan's screams and moans went unheard by Juliana as she stared at the shadow of pain that crossed Daniel's face.

From the vantage point of the floor, Daniel heard and witnessed every move. He forced himself to release all thoughts and emptied his mind of the agony he suffered from the blows of fists punching his immobile body. A top-ranking officer of the specialized brigade bent over and yelled down into his face. His beret fell to the floor. Daniel grimaced and squeezed his eyes shut after looking up at Juliana, who appeared to be in a trance. The puppy yapped in the direction where he lay defenseless on the floor, surrounded by ruthless combatants.

Policemen dragged him by his restrained arms on his stomach across the floor, over broken glass, across the front door, and out the main entrance. As glass chips pierced his skin, Daniel heard soldiers plunder the house in search of evidence. They decimated the tile floor with sledgehammers and ripped up tile segments with crowbars. Dresser drawers were pulled out and flung across his mother's bedroom. Living room shelves were shattered and chairs knocked over. A cherished photograph of his father was smashed against the wall, and the pieces landed next to Daniel as he slid through the entrance. They hauled him onto the front yard.

Intense pain numbed his body. Minutes before they heaved and threw him in the back of a van, he caught a glimpse of Carmelita and Emilio standing on the sidewalk. Carmelita prodded Emilio to help Daniel, but he turned to her, raised his hands, and questioned how. Just before the door to the van slammed shut and was locked with a violent click, Daniel saw a policeman wheel the red motorcycle from his backyard. The van's engine started, the vehicle lurched into motion, and he passed out.

The noise of a caravan of military trucks downshifting in front of the Reyes' home jolted Rafael awake. He put his head back on the pillow and dozed into sleep again. The commotion, screams, and breaking glass alerted him to the fact that the trucks had stopped a few doors down. In a daze it finally struck him that something terrible had happened. Rafa opened his eyes wide, flung back the sheets, and jumped out of bed. He pulled on a pair of pants and raced outside.

Carmelita and Emilio comforted Alma Milan. Upon seeing them Rafael was convinced that Juli and Daniel were in grave danger. In a panic he yelled, "What happened? What's going on?" They pointed toward the Milans' house. He sprinted past them and caught sight of his sister, who paced in the middle of the street, holding the puppy in one arm.

"Juli, come with me." With an arm around her, he eased her out of the road.

"I didn't help him. I couldn't move." She repeated to herself. "Rafa, they took Daniel. I don't know where. Find him. Please find him," she rambled. "They drove that way. North." Juliana pointed with her right hand as she shifted the puppy into her left. She groped her neck. "They pulled off my chain and heart. My locket."

Rafael saw a scratch and a trickle of blood on her chest below her neck and guided her over to the others, assuring her that he would find Daniel.

He patted Alma's shoulder. "Not much we can do tonight. Try to get some sleep. I'll go to the police station early in the morning and find out where they took him and why."

As if talking to a distant acquaintance, Alma said, "What did he do this time? What mess has he gotten himself into? I have feared this day since he began stealing and selling cigarettes. He knew the danger. Why?"

"Honestly, Mrs. Milan, he quit stealing months ago. Isn't that true, Juli?"

"They had no reason to take him. None."

"Something happened. Daniel did something. His life is in danger, and our home is destroyed. All this for a few extra pesos." Alma rubbed her ring finger, sore and absent of the ring Daniel had given her for Christmas.

"You'll come home with us, Alma. I have sleeping pills for you," Carmelita said as she stroked her cheek and moved a strand of hair from in front of her tear-filled eyes. "You and Juli have been through a lot tonight. Get some rest. Like Rafael said, we'll find Daniel tomorrow."

"I'll take Juli home. We'll come by first thing in the morning," Rafael said as he supported his sister and they walked home with the puppy circling them. Felipe and Sandra Reyes met them at the door. He eased Juliana into their arms and returned to Daniel's house to prop the halves of the front door within its frame to block the exposed entrance. When Rafa stepped inside the house and saw the destruction, he uttered, "Oh my God."

In the police station Rafael's eyes widened and he jerked his head back in disbelief when the lieutenant said, "Daniel Milan committed illegal acts against our government."

"But no criminal act was committed. There was no evidence."

"The motorcycle in his shed was all the proof we needed."

"Daniel kept the bike in his shed for someone else."

"Yes. It was allegedly in Orlando Sanchez Mendoza's name, who when interviewed swore the bike was not his. Milan purchased it and put Mendoza's name on a bill of sale. A crime in itself."

"Daniel is innocent. He committed no crime."

"Mr. Reyes, witnesses confirmed that he rode a motorcycle around town. A vehicle he was unable to purchase with a factory worker's meager salary."

Rafael became frustrated. "It was not stolen."

"Mr. Reyes, where did he get the money for a brand new East German motorcycle? You're his friend. Explain how."

"I don't know."

"Aha. A friend would know these things."

"Who turned him in?"

When the policeman peered at him like he was an oddity, Rafael said, "Where was he taken? I have to see him. His mother and wife are worried sick."

"You ask too many questions. Are you aware that the case of Daniel Milan is strictly confidential? All I can tell you is that he is detained at La Pendiente in solitary confinement. He is allowed no visitors. *Comprendes? Nadie.* Milan is a prisoner of the state and considered a major threat."

"A major threat? Daniel's an innocent man. What kind of threat could he be?"

"I am finished with this meeting, Mr. Reyes. You are dismissed or I'll detain you."

"And Daniel? When can we see him?"

"Take that up with the warden."

Juliana, Rafael, and Alma Milan arranged to meet at Alma's house to travel together to La Pendiente Prison in Santa Clara in an attempt to persuade the warden of Daniel's innocence and to petition his release. Juli arrived early at the Milan home to help Alma clean the mess and while Alma bathed, she walked out to the backyard. She reminisced about the times she and Daniel had spent together on the hammock, learning about each other and falling in love.

During the siege, the military had uprooted the two trees supporting the hammock and furrowed under their roots in search of Daniel's alleged hidden contraband. The hammock lay on the ground in a puddle of water. Juliana walked over to it and as she lifted the woven cloth with two fingers, muddy water dripped on the grass. She pulled at the knots securing it to the trees but could not loosen the interlaced rope to salvage it from its muddy grave. She peeked in the open door at the mess in the shed, also ransacked during the terrifying night.

The events of the night and Daniel's abduction had weakened Juli. She sat on a felled tree trunk to regain her strength. She was unable to sleep or eat breakfast and felt dizzy and faint in the humidity. She fanned her face with her hands and worried about her husband. Juliana knew La Pendiente had fame for its horror stories. She whispered into the air as if the wind would carry a message to Daniel, "My love. Your mother, Rafa, and I will do all in our power to rescue you."

Out of the corner of her eye, to her left, she saw movement. From behind the shed appeared a man. Smiling, she looked up, thinking her brother had arrived, but this person was shorter and stockier than Rafael, and Rafa would have approached from the opposite direction. Her smile dissolved into a frown when Maximo walked over to her. Shock at the sight of him almost caused her to fall backward. Juli planted both hands firmly on the bark and gripped the tree trunk to prevent a tumble to the ground. She pushed forward and stood, and as she did felt her left leg scrape the bark. Although weary, her inclination was to flee.

"Juliana, wait. I have to talk to you."

"You're the last person I want to see. Please leave. This is Daniel's home. He wouldn't want you here."

"What does he care? He's in prison where he should be." Maximo touched her shoulder and gently turned her to face him. "He was no good for you. Don't you realize? Daniel was a thief and a womanizer. What do you need a man like that for? I'm the one who really cares for you. I always have. I just never got the chance to tell you."

She bolted from him and pivoted to say, "How did you find me here?"

"I saw you leave your house."

"You followed me?" She took a deep breath and spoke before he replied. "Daniel's in prison because of you. You snitched on him, didn't you, Max? Get out of here."

The faster Juli walked away from him, the faster he tried to catch up to her.

He grabbed at her swaying hair, forcing her to a halt.

"Ouch. Let go of my hair." She reached around, trying to release his grip.

"Juliana, listen to me. Daniel put himself in prison."

"How can you say such a thing? There was no reason for him to be taken away. You turned him in." Tears welled in her eyes.

"Please don't cry." Max wiped a tear from her cheek with his free hand. "It wasn't me. This town's full of *chivatos*. Anyone could have reported him."

"You stole cigarettes too. Don't make yourself out to be a saint." Juli looked into his eyes. "I'm married to him. I love Daniel. Not you. Let go and leave before Rafael gets here."

"I need time with you." He eased her to the ground and kissed her hard on the lips. She tried to push him away, but he held tight and refused to release his grip on her.

Juli slapped him hard across his face and pushed him off her. Maximo reached for her hands and held them in one hand. With his other hand he rubbed his crimson cheek.

"Don't you realize Daniel's away for a long time? You'll change your mind about me. Give it time, darling." He planted another kiss on her lips.

"Let go of her," a strong voice resonated above them.

Max looked up into the tip of a machete gleaming in the sunlight. Juliana slid out from under him as she eyed the oversized knife and Emilio squeezing its handle with both hands.

"I'd think nothing of doing away with you, just to get even with your father—not to mention to protect my lovely neighbor." With the weapon he gestured toward Juliana. "Her husband and I have been neighbors and friends for years. No harm will ever come to her as long as I'm around."

"I'm not scared of you, old man."

Emilio swung the machete over his head and flung it into the ground next to Max's hand. Juliana quickly looked away, expecting Emilio to have sliced off Maximo's limb. She knew Emilio despised him and his family and supposed he was quite capable of disfiguring her stalker. She sighed, and a look of relief crossed her face when the weapon penetrated a mound in the lawn.

Emilio yanked the machete out of the ground. "Now get the hell out of here before I chop you to pieces."

Maximo vaulted over the felled tree and glanced over his shoulder as he ran to the street.

Alma, Juliana, and Rafael walked up to a sliding glass window reinforced with wire in the waiting room outside the warden's office. After noting their reason to meet with the warden, the receptionist told them to have a seat. They sat in folding metal chairs in a room with bars on the windows. One window was opened to allow fresh air into the stuffy, unventilated space. Rafael picked up a chair leaning against the wall, unfolded it, and joined the women in the middle of the room. They waited for hours. Rafael knocked on the window.

"The warden is busy. Be patient," said the receptionist.

After fifteen more minutes, the door opened. A middle-aged woman, the warden's secretary, called, "Milan." The three jumped to their feet. "The warden asks that you return in two months. Maybe Mr. Milan will be allowed visitors then."

The door closed. Juliana ran up to the door and turned to Rafael. "How can they treat us like this? After waiting for hours." She jiggled the knob and knocked, but no one answered.

"What can we do?" Rafael sat down in the chair.

"Wait." Juli sat between Alma and her brother.

"Wait longer? For what?" When she didn't answer, Rafa repeated, "Juli, wait for what?"

Alma touched Juliana's arm. "They won't let us in. We have to leave."

"I'll come back on my day off and try again. Let's go, sister."

The door opened again. The same woman called, "Rodriguez." A mother and daughter rose and walked toward the door. As they approached, the door opened wider. Before the secretary realized, Juliana sprang from her chair, pushed her aside, and disappeared down a hallway and into the prison offices. The mother and daughter stepped back as the lady shouted, "Stop. You're not allowed in here." She gestured for the two to sit. "Just a minute." And with a disgusted look on her face ran after Juliana.

Rafael glanced at Alma. "Juli didn't just run inside, did she?"

"That's not like Juli."

"I know. Let's hope they let her out."

Juliana saw a sign that said "Warden" on a door and burst inside. The warden was writing and looked up at the young lady. "Mrs. Rodriguez?"

"No. I'm Mrs. Milan." The room was cool. An air conditioning unit hummed loudly in the window behind the warden's desk.

"Milan? How did you get in here?"

The warden's secretary rushed in and grabbed Juliana by the arm. "Out. I told her to come back in two months, as you said. She pushed me and ran in."

Juli pulled her arm from the woman's grip. "Warden, please. I must see my husband."

"Mrs. Milan, your husband is in solitary confinement. Vilma, I will speak to Mrs. Milan for a few minutes. Tell Mrs. Rodriguez I'll be with her shortly."

"Are you sure?"

He nodded.

The secretary flashed Juli a dirty look and left the room.

"Sit down, Mrs. Milan. Pushing your way in to my office is frowned upon. After all, this is a prison. We have very strict rules."

"I know. I'm sorry. I'm worried about my husband."

He leaned back in his chair and pointed with his pen to a file at the corner of his desk. "See that red file? It's your husband's."

She saw on a label *Milan, Daniel* on a file at the top of a stack of red folders.

"This is Mr. Rodriguez's file." The warden held up a manila folder. "His crime was minor. He is allowed visitors." He watched as she lifted the strap of her purse off her shoulder and clutched the purse in her lap. She refrained from defending Daniel. Now was not the time to argue about his innocence.

"Maybe we can make an arrangement. How interested are you in seeing your husband?" He peered into her eyes.

"Very interested."

"Alma, I'm worried about her. God, maybe they stuck her in a cell."

"There's no reason. Juli only entered the warden's office."

"After being told to come back in two months. Anything's possible. I'm concerned. What do we do?"

Rafael jumped up and knocked on the window. After several minutes the window slid open. "My sister's inside. Can you let me in? I'll take her home. We won't bother you anymore."

"She's behind closed doors." The window slammed shut.

Rafa knocked on the window again and could see the receptionist's reflection, but she refused to answer. He paced by the window and heard her talking on the phone. Alma motioned for him to sit down.

"I can't."

A feeble man hobbled across the room and with his cane tapped on the window. The receptionist peeked out and opened the window wide when she saw the elderly man. Before she could react, Rafael leaped past the shocked man and dove through the window. The receptionist ducked, but Rafa's sneaker hit her head as he sailed over the desk, and tumbled to the floor. There was a loud crash. She cursed at him as he jumped to his feet, rubbed his elbow, and ran to the warden's door. His outstretched arm reached for the knob, and he flung open the door.

"Juli, where have you been?"

She was standing at the warden's desk. The warden pulled his hand back. It appeared to Rafael that the warden had reached for her.

"Rafa? I'm trying to see Daniel."

"You can't. Come with me." He seized her arm and pulled her away from the warden, who watched in amusement.

"And who is this?"

"Rafa, wait."

"No more waiting. Come."

She pushed her brother. "My note. I want to give him a note for Daniel." Juliana pulled a folded slip of paper out of her purse and handed it to the warden. "Please give this to my husband."

Rafael took her hand and led her out of the office. Two prison guards stopped them in front of the receptionist's cubicle and brought them back to the warden. The warden signaled with a wave of his hand for the guards to return to their posts. Rafael pushed Juli, and they rushed down the hall and into the waiting room.

The warden unfolded Juliana's note and saw a neatly drawn butterfly and words expressing love and encouragement. He stood over the trash can and ripped the paper to shreds, and watched the pieces drift into the container.

Forlorn, the three slumped on a small plot of land outside the prison. Juliana glanced up at the building at the rings of barbed wire spiking the top of a wall. A pair of *totis* circled above the turrets. Their wings, like carved ebony, dipped as they glided across the sky. The birds disappeared, and Juli focused on her brother.

"I had to see Daniel. When they captured him, I was paralyzed. I couldn't react. This time I had to try."

"He's not allowed visitors."

"I was convincing the warden to let me see him."

"Don't be so naive."

"Now we have to wait. What will happen to him in two months? Will he survive in there?"

"Daniel? The cat with nine lives. He'll survive anywhere. But we have to be persistent and keep after them until he's released. We can't give up."

"You're right, Rafael. We'll never let him down," Alma Milan said sadly but with conviction.

It was dark upon their return to Ranchuelo. Alma unlocked the front door, replaced by Emilio, flicked on the hall light, and left the door open for Juliana. Rafael drew his sister near him in a protective way as they stood next to the car. He felt tension in her muscles.

"Was that warden trying to cut some kind of a deal?"

"No."

"Are you sure? I sensed something sinister going on. Daniel would never have wanted you to…"

"How could you think such a thing? We were talking and you bolted in."

"I just wanted to clarify. Daniel will get through this with or without our help."

"But that doesn't mean we give up."

"Of course not."

"I'm scared for him."

"I am too. We have to stay strong for him." Rafa guided her to the porch. "I'm glad you're staying with Alma. You need each other's company."

"It's best. He'd want me to be with her."

Juli was pensive and weakened by disappointment. She slumped away from her brother and sat on the top step. There was no more strength in her to stand.

"Rafa, there is something I didn't want to tell you in front of Alma. Maximo followed me here earlier, before you arrived."

"Oh? And what did he have to say?"

"He said now that Daniel's in prison, he and I can be together. Do you believe the nerve? I told him I love Daniel." She looked away. "He kissed me. Emilio showed up with his machete and chased him away." She cracked a smile, but her eyes revealed a melancholy evident to her brother.

"That bastard kissed you?"

"He held me down and kissed me. Emilio scared him off." Juli saw a look of rage cross her brother's face and changed the subject of her encounter with Maximo. "Do you really think Max was the one who reported Daniel?"

"Wait a minute. He held you down? Max kissed you?"

"Forget it. Emilio took care of me." Maximo had frightened her, but she preferred to make light of the incident after seeing her brother's grim reaction. "Max reported Daniel, didn't he?"

Rafael peered into his sister's sorrowful eyes. "I'm ninety-nine percent sure it was him. And I promise I will find out." He lifted her chin just like Daniel often did when she felt down. "*No te preocupes, mi hermana.* Don't you worry, my sister."

"So you find out, Rafa. Then what? The damage is already done."

"Only half the damage is done."

Chapter Fifteen
LA PENDIENTE PRISON

"From now on forget your name. You are 1167." The prison guard tossed a uniform into the cell. Daniel picked up a pair of gray pants with black stripes down the outer sides and put them on. He touched his bare chest and stomach and felt bandages covering gashes he'd sustained while being dragged out of his house. He pulled a gray short-sleeved shirt over his head and moaned when the movement stung the dressed lesions.

Two small objects flew into the cell and landed at his feet. Daniel strained to see them but couldn't. He fell to his knees on the stones, swept the cold, rough surface with his hands, and grasped the objects: a toothbrush and tube of toothpaste. His arms fell to his sides, and he bent his head back in surrender.

A solitary figure in gray, he curled up in darkness on his bed, a cold shelf of cement. His hands were numb from the handcuffs clasped to his wrists for hours. Images passed before him as he dozed. In sleep, time regressed.

Daniel dreamed of police storming his house and Juliana gracefully approaching him in her wedding gown. A hand pulled him out of a ditch and Castro's magnified facial features manifested before him. He awoke, sat up and wondered why his usual nightmares of sea creatures had eluded him this night of mental turmoil.

Daniel set his bare feet on the floor, and his head spun. He leaned against the damp wall for support and raised his hand as a visual experiment. Centimeters from his face his fingers were invisible. In seclusion and immobilized by darkness, he became an unwilling victim of his own thoughts and questions, and analyzed the unpredictable events that had befallen him, delving deep into his mind for answers.

Had Max turned him in to the authorities? Why was he thrown in prison when he was never caught committing a crime? The police had no proof, no evidence he had stolen anything, if that's what he was imprisoned for. They found the motorcycle, but it could not be considered stolen goods. There were no grounds to hold him for long. Daniel concluded that he would be released within a few weeks.

When the dizziness subsided, he acquainted himself with his new living space. He reached across the bed, and his hands followed the stone wall, which in places crumbled. He wiped the sand on his pants and stepped slowly, avoiding a round, black hole in the floor that smelled like a sewer, and wrinkled his nose as he continued feeling along the wall. Daniel touched a sink at the end and estimated the room was six meters square at most. Intermittently, he opened and closed his eyes to relieve them of constantly staring at blackness. Objects in the cell appeared light gray, dark gray, and black. His stylish uniform blended well with the color scheme of the morbid cage he was trapped in.

Later, he heard footsteps outside. A door slammed. A small door at the bottom of the metal entrance to his cell opened, and a hand shoved in a tray holding a tin cup and a plastic bowl. Daniel dove for it. Liquid spilled, and his fingers felt the wetness as he grasped a slice of bread. He devoured the hard, stale snack and sipped a cup of hot water flavored with sugar and an orange leaf. After drinking he chewed the leaf, set the cup down, and slurped a bowl of watery broth with torn pieces of cabbage floating on top. When Daniel finished the scant meal, he slid the tray to the door and sat on the bed.

Minutes later the trap door raised, and the tray disappeared. It was replaced by a bucket of water and a rag. Water sloshed and splashed to the floor. He stripped off his uniform and washed with water from the pail and a lump of soap floating under the rag. With a worn towel Daniel dried himself and returned to the hard bed, which reminded him of the bench at the big house.

Like a tremor jolting his brain, it dawned on him that he'd never had the chance to tell Juliana that his money was hidden under the mosaic bench. How could he have forgotten to tell her? He was certain she would need the money. Daniel stared into emptiness and bumped his head against the wall with a thud. His mind raced with worries for his wife. With each thought of Juliana he struck his head against the cold, hard surface in a beat resembling the rhythmic tap of hands on a bongo drum.

Once Daniel's wounds healed he kept fit despite the deplorable conditions and stuck to an exercise routine. Upon awakening, he did one hundred pushups, sit ups and jumping jacks. He was unaware whether he was working out in the day or at night. Hours intermingled in the cell's blackness. His routine ended by leaping on and off his bed. This series of exercises tired him and allowed him a sound sleep.

Time passed, and after a bout of sleep Daniel awoke to the illumination of a light bulb that dangled by a wire above him in the center of the ceiling. He'd had no idea the light existed. Beams bathed the cell in brightness and shone like needles into his eyes. He shielded his eyes with his arm. It took a while before he adjusted to the light and was able to glance around his enclosed quarters.

Light burned during three bouts of sleep. Voices and stomping boots echoed in the hallway and halted outside his door. Keys clattered, and the door opened and slammed against the wall. Three uniformed guards glared and pounced on him as he sat on the cement slab. They yanked him to the floor. Their fists and boots hammered every inch of his body. Demeaning shouts accompanied the blows. Daniel was bounced against the hallway walls and pushed and pulled to a different section of the prison.

As he was marched and prodded along at a pace hardly maintained by his weak body, he glanced inside other cells. A row of thirty cells housed six to seven men in each chamber. Hairy, gaunt, sickly faces peeked through iron bars at him. The guards unlocked one of the gates and shoved him onto the floor of a compartment inhabited by five prisoners who lounged about and were disrupted by Daniel's impromptu entrance. He lay sprawled on the floor and looked up as he wiped blood from a wound on his face.

It appeared that only the whites of his cellmates' eyes stared down at him in the dim light. Eyes bulged out of unshaven, pasty faces, and well-defined ribs protruded from shirtless torsos. Daniel tried to speak as he staggered across the floor, but his mind and parched mouth were empty of words. He pointed to the bunk beds and finally stammered, "*Cuál es mi cama?*"

They helped him climb to a top bunk. A tin cup of water gripped by a skeletal hand touched his lips. Daniel sipped and tasted watered-down blood—his own, oozing from a cut lip. The liquid stained his lips like rouge. He flopped on the mattress and lay still on the bunk and slept for hours after the other prisoners had awakened until one of his cellmates thought he had lapsed into a coma and died. He shook Daniel and ushered him out of bed. They sat together on the lower bunk.

"*No has comido desde que llegastes. Hay que comer o te vas a morir.*"

"Eat? What's the sense?" Daniel swallowed hard and spoke slowly to form proper-sounding words. Then he blurted, "We'll all die in here anyway."

"Don't say that. Now Hector over there will die here. He always misbehaves. They keep adding more time to his sentence. The rest of us have a chance to leave someday. You have to stay strong. Of all of us you are most likely to get out of here."

Daniel tilted his head to look toward the back of the cell at what appeared to be a locked broom closet. Inside the darkness shone a mulatto face. His skin tone was almost invisible behind the tiny barred window. Hector stuck his pale pink tongue out at him. Daniel's eyes shifted back to the man he was talking to.

"Don't let Hector bother you. He'll be in that chamber for days. He can only stand in there, but he's used to it. He goes crazy and gets thrown in all the time. Soon water will drip on his head. Hector killed his wife and her best friend. One evening he got tired of hearing their laughter and gossip and shot them. At least that's what he said. They call me Horse because I killed my neighbor's horse to feed my starving children. I'll be in here longer than Rigo, over there in the corner, who murdered his friend in a drunken rampage. They argued over a bet. Can you believe Rigo gets ten years and I get twenty-five? The other two committed theft."

Horse slapped Daniel on the back.

"It's hell, but you get used to it. We have our routines. We try not to get in each other's way. It can feel very crowded in here."

Daniel nodded. He heard what Horse said, but thoughts of Juliana, his mother, and Rafael burdened his mind. How he missed them. He looked around and wanted anything but to be locked up in prison among these savages.

In the middle of the night a flashlight shone in the cell and awakened Daniel and his cellmates. Guards pointed the circular beam from one prisoner to the next and stuck a fire hose through the bars, turned on a lever, and sprayed water that gushed with such force that Rigo was knocked from his bunk to the floor. Daniel closed his eyes and turned to the wall. The torrent pressed hard against his back and stung his bare skin. He wailed along with the other inmates.

When the fire brigade guards moved to the next cell, Daniel slid off the bunk. His uniform, folded at the foot of the bed, and blanket slid with him and dropped to the floor in a saturated heap. Daniel and the other inmates scurried to hang their blankets and strip themselves of all clothing. Pale, nude men lolled about the cell, drying out to avoid contracting fungus or odd growths on their bodies common to life in the dampness and darkness of a penitentiary.

Several days after the incident with the fire hose, Horse, in a low voice, told Daniel, "I have to get out of here."

"Hey, we all want out."

"I need out of here now," he stuttered.

"How can you possibly escape?"

"I have to take a chance." His eyelids fluttered. "This place will do me in."

Horse's pupils dilated, and he had a panicked look in his eyes. Daniel leaned against the pole supporting the top bunk.

"We're like trapped vermin. Relax. There's no way out of here."

"I've had an idea for a long time. I need someone to help me with my plan."

"Plan?" Daniel eyed him suspiciously. "What's there to plan?"

"See this finger?" Horse raised his middle finger.

"What does your finger have to do with anything?"

"I want you to break it. Break my finger." He pursed his lips and kissed his finger.

"Break it? Then what?" Daniel thought this guy was a lunatic. As crazy as the others in the cell.

"If it's broken I go to the medical center. In the infirmary there are windows. It'll be easy to escape. So I was told."

"Escape from the infirmary. Not a bad idea. But I'm not going to break your finger."

"Oh, yes, you are. Here. Take it. Snap it with your hands."

"No."

"Break the bone. Go ahead."

"I can't."

"Yes, you can."

Daniel held Horse's middle finger and tried to snap it in half over his knee but couldn't. He twisted the finger while poor Horse moaned. Daniel banged it against the wall and pounded it on the bed pole. The bone remained intact.

"It's so dark. I can't see what I'm doing. Move down there. Get on the floor."

Horse knelt and put his hand on the floor with his middle finger sticking straight out. Daniel bent down to feel where the finger was, stood, and as he balanced with one hand on Horse's head, lifted his foot, and smashed the finger with his heel. Horse yelled and swore at Daniel as if they'd had an argument. Hector shushed them from the metal chamber.

Horse lifted his distorted finger.

"You broke it this time. Thank you. I'm out of here."

Horse was escorted to the infirmary and attempted to escape but was caught hanging from the window. After a beating he was thrown back into the cell.

"I almost made it 1167. Almost." He scratched his face with his middle finger bulging in a cast and sat silently next to Daniel on the bottom bunk.

Daniel stared at the bunks opposite his. "I'm sorry. I was rooting for you. I honestly thought you would escape."

Keys jingled in the lock. The door opened. A guard called into the cell.

"Prisoner 1167. Stand at the door alone."

Daniel rose from the bed and stood at the door. Eyes peered at him through the murky glass window. The door bumped him as it opened, and five guards seized him. Their shouts echoed in the hallway. They rushed him to the warden's office, where he sat in a chair with his hands on his knees. They pushed the chair in front of the air conditioner protruding from the window and shifted it so the fan blew directly on Daniel. The warden turned the knob to high. The blast of cold air was so forceful that when questioned, Daniel was unable to speak.

"How were you involved in Horse's attempt to escape?" demanded the warden.

The chilling air blasted Daniel's face like a snowless blizzard. He tried to open his mouth to speak but barely uttered the word, "No."

"That's no answer." A guard rocked the chair he sat in. "Did you break Horse's finger so he'd end up in the medical center?"

Daniel shivered and shook his head.

"Speak."

"Answer him." A second guard punched him.

Daniel leaned forward to get out of the artificial wind and stuttered, "I can't. You know I can't."

These words gave the guards an excuse to spring on him and pound him with clenched fists. The warden locked the office door and joined in on the punishment. Even though Daniel had eliminated God from his life after his father's death, silently he prayed to the supreme being. He feared death would soon overtake him and succumbed to the fierce beating in the warden's frigid office. The window fogged due to condensation, and extreme heat from outside misted the glass. From Daniel's vantage point on the floor, he imagined that the window was hazed by Satan's breath, a blast of hot air from the throngs of hell.

Chapter Sixteen
THE INFERNO

During the days of the factory gang meetings in Santa Rosa de Lima Church, Rafael learned by observing Daniel, who in turn learned from Rambo, the locksmith, how to enter any secured area by unscrewing latches or by picking locks, removing doorjambs, or whatever means necessary to secretly gain access to the locale of their choice.

All previous methods had failed, so Rafael was forced to use a lock cutter on the padlock that hugged the latch before him. He lifted the clippers he'd borrowed from Emilio and opened the wooden handles wide. The metal rested snugly around the lock bar, and he squeezed. Like a parrot's beak biting into a tropical nut, the lock snapped apart, dangled, and thumped against the door. Rafa tapped the lock off with the cutter and watched it drop to the floor. He leaned the lock cutter against the wall of the building and slowly raised the garage door to avoid that piercing screech garage doors often make. To his relief the rising door sounded like branches rubbing in the wind.

Rafael scoped the interior and waited for his eyes to adjust to darkness. He smelled motor oil and gasoline and saw a Russian Lada high on a lift. A 1956 Ford truck with its hood propped up was parked next to the Lada, and a dolly and tools were strewn on the concrete floor below it.

Rafa searched the auto repair shop for the row of rusty gasoline cans with spouts like curved goose necks. He remembered seeing them along the east wall on the night he'd accompanied Max here. There were fewer cans now, and they had been moved to a corner. He hurried over to the cans and one by one lifted each, grasping the handle with one hand and the bottom with the other. Rafael spilled their contents over vehicles, on the floor, over workbenches, and on the monkey suits hanging on plastic hooks in a closet. He shook out every drop of gasoline.

Potent gas fumes filled the air. Rafa worried that the smallest spark could ignite the fuel-saturated interior and feared being trapped inside and engulfed in flames. He exited in a rush. He finished his personal mission by trailing a stream of the flammable substance out the door. Rafael tossed the can inside onto a pile of rags and wiped his hands on a towel sticking out of his back pocket.

In one motion, he struck a match and lobbed it onto the dampened pavement, launching a flame into the garage. The torch multiplied into hungry flames lapping at the vehicles. A flash illuminated the objects in the garage, and the Lada exploded and transformed the body shop into an inferno. With the second explosion, the truck and everything inside the building disintegrated.

After lighting the match, Rafael grabbed the clippers, lingered a few seconds to watch as the fire advanced into the garage, and raced to a nearby wooded area. When the sign hanging above the doors swung and melted in the intense heat and the blaze consumed the Lada, he ran, dove on the ground, and threw the lock cutter to his right. Rafa landed chest first, knocking the wind out of his lungs. He gasped for air and wrapped his arms over his head. The building erupted in a fireball. The flash of light reflected on leaves nestled by his face. He closed his eyes when a powerful blast, equal to the detonation of a dozen sticks of dynamite, echoed through the forest where he lay.

The explosion sent chills throughout his body.

In the aftermath of the explosions, when flames sizzled and the warmth of the blaze branded his cheeks as if he lay beside a hearth, Rafael promised himself never to admit to committing this crime of arson to anyone, not even to Emilio, who had confirmed that Maximo had indeed reported Daniel to the authorities.

While lying on the ground in the flashing light of the fire, Rafael remembered the conversation in Emilio's living room. Rafa faced Emilio and behind him he saw Daniel's house through a window obscured by lace curtains.

"It all came to me while I drove my truck past the police station yesterday morning. I had just finished unclogging a drain at Cisco's house and was on my way to pick up Carmelita at church. It was as if the church bells rang sense into my brain. They reminded me of a small detail I had forgotten. Osvaldo, the butcher, told me months ago that he thought it strange to see Maximo seated opposite the sergeant in his office at the police station, deep in conversation. It was the day the butcher had delivered meat to the police."

This happened to be the same day Emilio had told Alma Milan, while she hung clothes on the line in her backyard, that the butcher had seen Daniel and Juliana walking together in town. The day Daniel apologized to Juli on the bench in the garden of their future house, when he gave her the locket and treated her to an ice cream cone.

Rafael stared at Emilio. "It *was* Maximo."

With each nod Emilio's face turned a deeper tone of crimson, his eyes narrowed. Rafa never forgot the expression of anger on Emilio's face.

Rafael rose from the ground, scooped up the clippers, and fled. He halted in a clearing and gawked at the fire glowing beyond the trees and the sparks spewing out of sable-colored plumes spiraling toward the night sky.

"Take that, you bastard," he said as the sound of fire trucks and police vehicles screamed toward the inferno.

Chapter Seventeen
THE RECOVERY

A haggard, bearded man stood in the doorway of La Pendiente Prison clutching a folder containing prison documents. He hunched over and pressed his slight body against the doorjamb for support. The brightness of the day blinded him. He shielded his eyes as he stared at the patterns of stones on the walkway and cowered at trees towering above the street and at the noisy vehicles passing beneath their branches.

The discharged prisoner labored to raise his head when he heard familiar voices to his right. He saw shadow figures in a group gathered on the lawn. Their words were incomprehensible, although the tones of their speech played over and over in his mind. He longed to move in the direction of the utterances, but his legs, like iron weights, were motionless.

"How much longer? You gave them the money an hour ago," Juliana moaned.

"The warden probably made off with the ten thousand pesos," Rafael said as he tossed a stone into the street after a truck roared by. "I wouldn't put it past him."

Alma Milan stretched her legs out on the grass. "It shouldn't be long now. I'll wait however long it takes for Daniel to be released." She looked up at the cloudless sky and sighed. "It took three months to raise the money. I hope they didn't confiscate it."

She turned toward Rafael. "Do you suppose something happened to him? My God, anything could have happened in six months."

Juliana watched a gray-haired man hobble to a small group of people awaiting him on the sidewalk. At first glance she also saw a ragged man in the doorway, but the cheers and shouts at the sight of the released prisoner made her turn her head toward the anxious family as they huddled around the liberated relative and helped him to a car parked curbside with its engine murmuring. The man flopped on the back seat and smiled weakly at the driver, who turned to speak to him and the car pulled away. Juli cupped her face in her hands and rocked back and forth. "What's taking so long?"

Rafael was about to comfort her, but she dropped her hands and pushed herself off the ground. Her hair blew high in the breeze. She gaped and pointed at the door to the prison. "Help him, Rafa. That's Daniel."

In the derelict's eyes she had recognized a faraway, melancholy look—an expression she remembered while rocking on the hammock with him when he had sadly spoken of his father.

"Daniel?"

"Yes, hurry. That's Daniel."

"No. It can't be. That's not my son," Alma said as she knelt and then lumbered to her feet.

Juliana pushed Rafael toward the timid one. She noticed that the watch she had given Daniel for Christmas was missing from his bony wrist. In haste Rafa reached Daniel, who edged along the wall, and supported him as he hobbled toward the women, not believing that this decrepit vagrant was his best friend. Daniel winced in pain as he treaded the walkway seared by the afternoon sun. He stopped to rub his burning feet and bent down to remove a pebble caught between his filthy toes.

Rafael guided him to the grass. Juliana and Alma withdrew from the horrid sight as tears welled in their eyes. They embraced and in doing so shielded the view of Daniel from each other. The man they loved, aided by Rafael, stood lost and dazed and stared at the prison looming above. They released each other and walked over to the men. The stench of the unfamiliar rags hanging loosely on Daniel's body entered their nostrils. Juli gagged and covered her nose and mouth with a tissue Alma had tucked into her hand.

Alma and Juliana stood at the kitchen window and watched the lonely figure in the backyard. Daniel hunched forward in a chair and stared at chickens and baby chicks as they scurried and poked at the grass. The rooster suspiciously eyed Daniel.

The ladies sighed in unison as Daniel tipped his head to one side to watch a hen gather her chicks into the shade. Alma patted Juli's shoulder. She picked up a bunched, wet dishcloth from the sink, wrung it out, folded it, and draped it over the faucet. She straightened a chair at the table and went outside. Juliana looked away from the window and saw the back door close.

Daniel sat for hours, entranced by the fowl. He was oblivious to his mother's presence, even when she accidently brushed him as she balanced a bag of feed in one hand and sifted mashed corn on the lawn with the other. She spoke to Daniel as she fed the chickens, but he ignored her. He was engrossed by the movement of palm shadows quivering on the fence in a westerly gust of wind.

Alma returned the bag to the shed and rubbed her hands together, sprinkling grain fragments stuck to her palms as she walked over to her son. When she tenderly touched his head there was no reaction. She looked at his clean-shaven face and gaunt cheeks and sat beside him. She recalled his first day home from prison. Alma and Juliana had bathed him, shaved his face, and trimmed his hair but it still hung shoulder length. Daniel became fearful and bolted to his room when he felt the cold scissors on his neck. He collapsed on his bed. As he lay there and stared at the ceiling they rubbed salve on his cuts and welts, souvenirs from his sojourn in prison.

Alma stroked Daniel's hair. Juliana carefully carried a tray laden with a plate of eggs, ham, freshly baked Cuban bread drizzled with butter, and a glass of orange juice and placed it on Alma's lap. While Alma held the tray, Juli fed Daniel with a spoon. He opened his mouth to ingest the food, but his eyes were fixated on the chickens. He chewed in rhythm to the clucking fowl as they pecked at seeds on the lawn. After he chewed and swallowed several mouthfuls, Daniel pushed the plate away. Alma took the spoon from Juli and coaxed him to eat a piece of ham, but he refused. Alma carried the tray back to the kitchen. As was customary, they would try to feed him the remaining morsels later in the morning.

Juliana sat at Daniel's feet and leaned her head against his legs. His attention turned to the spider-like strands of hair spread out on his pant leg and gazed as a tress slid down his leg when she shifted.

He changed his focus to the inanimate objects surrounding him. To his feeble mind they were alive. When treetops rustled in the wind they seemed to inhale and exhale. Daniel held his breath as he watched trees gasp for air. The neighbors' houses pulsed below the swaying branches as if blood gorged hearts beat beneath the roofs.

These sounds and vibrations confused and frightened him. For this reason he chose to focus on the lawn and smaller, less scary creatures like chickens. His thoughts were simplistic, and his mind had only the capability to process what he observed. During this observation he lapsed into a trance-like state.

"Come on, Daniel, man. Snap out of it." Rafael shook Daniel as he sat on the porch watching the chickens. "It's been three weeks since you left the slammer. Get over it."

Juliana opened the porch door. "Rafa, stop. Don't treat him that way."

"It's enough, Juli. He's got to come back to reality." Rafael sat down beside his friend, exasperated by the faraway look in his eyes. "It's like his mind imploded." Rafa slid closer and spoke into Daniel's face. "Let's go fishing at the river. Play baseball. Anything you want. I'll do it with you."

Daniel didn't even flinch.

"Stop, Rafa. You know what he suffered in prison. Let him be."

"Do you know what happened in there, Juli? Because I really don't know. Has he told you? He hasn't told me. Look at him. All he can do is stare at those fucking chickens. I'm not letting him go insane. I refuse."

Rafael grabbed Daniel's arms and shook.

"I said quit it." Juliana pushed her brother off the porch.

Rafael landed on his feet and walked back to her as she stood defensively beside her husband.

"Juli, you don't understand. They want to put him away for twenty years. He needs a lawyer to defend him. If he has no defense he'll end up back in prison or in an insane asylum if he continues like this. Do you want your husband put away forever in either one?"

"Of course not."

"Then don't baby him. Or encourage this insane behavior."

"I'm helping him. What more can I do?" Her eyes moistened.

Rafael lowered his voice. "Let's get him away from here. Take him for a walk. Anything to get his mind thinking again." He turned to Daniel. "*Amigo*, do you want to go for a walk? Answer me. Answer me."

"Rafael, don't. You're the one who's acting insane. You're the crazy one."

"I'm not giving up on him." Rafa paced across the lawn. "I know. I'll have Dr. Nieves examine him. Maybe he'll give us some answers. He and Daniel became good friends. I'll ask him."

"Then go. Get the doctor to come here." She put her arms around Daniel's head and pulled him to her chest as she eyed her brother. "Go. Do something about this, Daniel can't."

The next day Juli helped Daniel walk to the chair in the middle of the yard in the shade of the branches of a felled tree and carried another chair for herself. Occasionally she glanced over at her husband in hopes the old Daniel would emerge and give her some wisecrack about the government. As she looked at his absent stare she doubted he knew there was a government.

The chickens filed one after the other into the shed to escape the hot sun. In their absence she realized Daniel turned his attention to a cloth on the ground near the shed. It was the towel he had used to polish his motorcycle.

She heard voices and turned to see Emilio and Carmelita in Emilio's backyard.

"Juli, can we see Daniel?" asked Carmelita.

"Of course you can. Come over. I'll get more chairs."

"Don't bother. We won't stay long. How is he?"

"The same. As you can see."

"He still hasn't spoken?"

"No." Juliana slowly shook her head.

Carmelita looked at the grim-faced Emilio. "Do you think he'll ever come out of this, dear?"

Emilio observed Daniel, who peered at the towel. "I believe some day he will, although I see no progression."

"I'm afraid, my dear Juli, he may have permanent damage. He received some kind of trauma in La Pendiente. We may never know exactly what."

"Carmelita, Emilio, I'd rather not discuss his condition." She put her hand on Daniel's.

"Oh, my dear, we're so sorry. Let's just hope he soon recovers. We will pray for him. Won't we, Emilio?"

Juliana noticed the furrows in Emilio's forehead and how stern he acted. He wasn't the happy-go-lucky guy she was accustomed to. He touched Daniel's arm.

"Yes, we will. I'm not a religious man, but I will pray for you."

Emilio got close to Daniel's ear and Juliana heard him say, "Come on, son. Let's set up the distillery. That will cure any problems you had in prison. Remember how it helped the pain in your injured hand?"

Juli was sure Daniel blinked but didn't mention it to Emilio and Carmelita. It was probably her imagination. This would be the one time Alma Milan would welcome the neighbors and the distillery in her backyard. If Alma saw her son drinking and dancing she would probably rejoice and join in on the celebration. Maybe she would even indulge in a cocktail.

Dr. Javier Nieves examined Daniel in his room and guided him to the living room where Juliana, Alma Milan, and Rafael awaited. Susana Nieves was also present and upon arrival had set a casserole on the kitchen counter.

"Aside from a bump on his head and needing to put on more weight, I find him in decent health." Javier walked beside Daniel and gestured for him to sit in a chair.

"Mentally he has a long way to go. The bruises, cuts, and burn marks on his body signify he was abused and tortured. Obviously conditions in there were deplorable. He wasn't fed well and experienced dehydration." The doctor sat on the sofa beside his wife. "Before coming here I consulted with my psychiatrist friend, Dr. Lorenzo, who couldn't come because he was overwhelmed with patients. He told me these cases take time. Feed him well, and be here for him." Javier glanced at Rafael. "I think it was a good idea to accompany him out of the house. Little by little take him to familiar places, and eventually he will come around."

"But when, doctor? The date for his trial will be set soon. We have to prepare. He'll need a lawyer and will have to face a jury."

"Yes, Rafa, I understand. I'm unable to determine exactly when he'll feel better. Everyone heals in their own way. The brain is a very complicated, delicate organ. Unfortunately we don't have all the answers. Just give him time. Dr. Lorenzo will stop by when his schedule eases. Any other questions?"

"Will he ever be himself again? The Daniel we knew?" said Juliana.

"I think so, in time. Being detained temporarily changed him. One day the old Daniel will appear. Keep me posted." He tapped his wife's leg. "We have to stop by a factory employee's house. His daughter has a cough. I promised I would check on her."

"I hope Daniel recovers soon," said Susana as she reached for Juliana's hand and squeezed it. She did the same to Alma Milan. "If there's anything I can do, let me know."

"You've already helped. Thank you for the casserole."

With melancholy eyes Alma looked up at Dr. Nieves. "Thank you for the advice and for giving us hope."

The sixth week of Daniel's convalescence Juli started walking daily down their street with him. On Rafael's days off, he accompanied Daniel to the park, and gradually ventured further. He and Daniel slowly strolled along Paseo del Prado. Townsfolk, aware of Daniel's plight, stopped to stare as he passed. They asked Rafael time and again, "How is he coming along?"

Rafa responded, "He's getting there, little by little." When Juliana was present, she ignored their questions and only focused on her husband.

Several weeks later Rafael and Juliana decided to take Daniel on a two-day camping trip along the Ochohita River. At first Juli wanted to return to the waterfall above the ranch, but feared the bull's presence in the field and agreed with Rafael to camp by the river instead. On Friday morning they loaded their father's car with backpacks, camping equipment, and fishing poles. Daniel sat on the front step and watched them. Rafael escorted Daniel to the car. Juli slid into the front seat between them, and Rafael drove two hours through the countryside to the river. It was on this trip that they noticed a marked change in Daniel.

On the afternoon of their arrival, Rafael tossed his fishing line into the river as he sat with his head propped against a boulder. Daniel sat beside him, mesmerized by the sunlight crystals sparkling on the water's surface. Rafa closed his eyes and waited for a bite. He thought he heard grunting sounds coming from Daniel.

"Where's...my pole?" Daniel said in a wavering voice.

Rafael opened his eyes wide to Daniel standing over him. His body blocked the sunlight. Rafa was shocked at the big smile on his brother-in-law's face.

"*Hombre*, you want to fish?"

Daniel nodded.

"Stay right here. I'll get your pole." Rafael put his pole in Daniel's hand. "Take this and wait. I'll be right back."

Rafa ran up the steep incline to where Juli sunbathed in a beach chair outside the tent. She became alarmed when she saw her brother in a hurry.

"What happened? Is Daniel all right?"

"He's fine. Where's his pole? He wants to fish. He actually asked me for his pole."

She set the book on her knees. "Daniel spoke?"

"*Sí*. He wants his fishing pole."

"It's in the trunk. I..." Juliana watched Rafael yank the car keys from his jacket pocket, lift open the trunk, and grab the fishing pole, careful not to grip the hook at the end of the line. As he slid back down the embankment she finished her sentence. "...never thought he would use it."

"Me either. We'll see," Rafael called from below. "At least he asked for it."

Juli slipped a bookmark at the page where she left off, set the book on the chair, and walked to the edge of the riverbank. She stretched to see the two interacting below. Rafa helped Daniel cast his line out to the rapids of the swiftly flowing current. Her eyes glistened, and she wiped away the tears that slid down her cheek.

That evening the three huddled around a fire after eating grilled bass and *moros*, a mixture of black beans and rice, accompanied by slices of avocado. Daniel had eased one fish to shore with the help of Rafael, and Rafa had hooked four others, which he gutted and cleaned for dinner. After cleaning the fish, he opened a bottle of wine, a special order from Carmelita before the trip, and poured it into plastic cups to celebrate the catch and a tasty dinner. Although undeclared by sister and brother, Daniel's improvement was the real celebration.

The wine tasted sour to Daniel, but he slowly sipped anyway as he and Juli held hands. Rafael puffed on a Romeo y Julieta cigar, a gift from Carmelita for buying the wine. A full moon glowed above the river, and its light defined the ripples of an easing current. Rafa decided to take a stroll on the sandy road winding along the river. The sand and terrain were brightened by the moon, and he strolled as if in daylight.

The couple chose to stay at the camp. They rose from the hot fire and moved closer to the shoreline ridge to savor the cool air drifting in motion with the water. Daniel noticed the same highlights in Juli's hair as on the moonlit night of his party. His memory of dancing and their laughter returned.

"Juli," he said, "I'm…so…sorry."

"Don't be, darling. It wasn't your fault."

"It was…all…my fault."

"Don't blame yourself. Let's start over. Look at the beautiful river, the moon. Look what we have. You're getting better now. That's what counts."

"Look at…the beautiful…things in life."

Juliana smiled and leaned against his bony shoulder. With her eyes fixed on the river, she said, "Yes. That's what I always say."

Daniel smiled. "I'm looking at you. That's…what I always say."

Rafael reached into a bag in the tent, popped the cork of another bottle, and poured a rich burgundy into their empty glasses. "I love it out here. It's so peaceful. I hate the thought of going back to reality."

"Me too," Juli said. "In that reality we have a battle to face."

"You mean Daniel's trial?"

"I dread it."

"So do I," said Daniel as he kissed her cheek.

Chapter Eighteen
THE LAWYER

During conversations with friends at the factory, Rafael received several recommendations to contact a lawyer named Sonia Armas Ochoa for Daniel's upcoming trial. Among the factory workers, she had a reputation of being hardworking and fair to her clients. Rafael set up an appointment for Daniel, and Juliana accompanied him to Mrs. Armas' office in the Santa Clara courthouse.

Her small office was located on the second floor of the three-story building. Side by side the couple circled an atrium garden lush with tropical plants, carnations, and miniature roses. Sunlight filtered through the glass and onto the marble, over which Juli's heels clicked with each step. As they passed the atrium, they felt the warmth of the sun. Juliana clung tightly to Daniel's arm. Her steps, voices in the lobby, books thumping on desks, and many other noises culminated into an echo hovering above them at the top of the high ceiling.

They passed polished wooden doors, entrances to courtrooms, with guards standing stiffly outside. Restless ones accused of wrongdoing paced nervously in front of the doors before taking the final step inside. Witnesses sat on wooden benches and gripped papers, awaiting their turns before a judge. Daniel envisioned himself waiting for his own trial on one of those benches in the near future. He picked up the pace when he eyed the staircase leading to the second floor and Sonia Armas' office.

Mrs. Armas, a stout woman in her forties, greeted the couple, motioned for them to sit down, and reached for the folder of prison papers in Daniel's hand. She thumbed through the pages as she sat behind a large desk occupying half her office space. She glanced up at them after reading, and removed her glasses.

"Mr. Milan, as you may know, the prosecution is seeking to imprison you for twenty years. The attorney representing the government, Señor Arroyo, is someone I despise. The reasons I will not discuss. He also hates me with a passion. The good news is that I have never lost a case to Señor Arroyo. I am your only hope in this matter, Mr. Milan." She shook the papers in her hand. "I will study these and do some research, and we will meet here in a week. How does that sound?"

Juliana answered, "fine" and noticed Daniel staring at a photograph on a table in the corner. The picture depicted a man of high rank in an army uniform seated in a chair with three girls surrounding him. Sonia stood behind the officer with her hands resting on his shoulders. The sight of the stern-faced general sent a chill through Daniel, a warning that unnerved his soul.

While the lawyer flipped through the pages again Juliana calmly sat beside Daniel until his leg resting across the opposite knee began to shake. She tapped his knee to stop it and squeezed his hand resting on his thigh. He nodded in the direction of the photograph. She looked at the photo as he blurted to Mrs. Armas, "Nice picture."

Sonia looked up from the papers. "Thank you. My husband, daughters, and I. Manuel is a general in the army." She waited expectantly for him to comment. When he remained silent, she continued, "I assure you, Mr. Milan, his position has no influence upon my job whatsoever."

Daniel glanced at the photo and back at Mrs. Armas.

"I maintain a strict fiduciary relationship with my clients. Whatever my clients reveal remains confidential. Mr. Milan, I am essential to your defense and the only lawyer capable of standing up to Mr. Arroyo. I will defend you to the very best of my ability."

Sonia Armas stood, placed her hands on the folder on her desk, and pressed hard. "I will further study these documents. See you here next Tuesday, if that date is convenient."

"Mrs. Armas, whatever is written in those pages, there is no proof I was a thief."

"Their proof exists in the motorcycle they found in your shed and the down payment on a car you were about to purchase. The jewelry worn by your mother and wife were strikes against you. And also the abundant amount of food stocked in your freezer. All of this says you acquired money by means other than your job at the factory. Circumstantial evidence counts in this government."

"I don't deserve one year in prison, let alone twenty," Daniel said as he rose. Juliana followed him to the door.

"I will do all in my power to keep you out of prison."

Juli thanked Mrs. Armas, and Daniel rushed out of the office. He bounded down the steps, two at a time, to the main floor where the courtroom doors were now open and swarms of people recessed for lunch. They crisscrossed in all directions in the main hall.

Daniel sprung off the last step far ahead of Juli into the mass of people.

"Daniel, wait," Juliana called as she watched him approach a water fountain tucked in an alcove to the left of the stairs. He pushed hard on the handle and sipped the arc of water. Drops splashed to the floor. He wiped his mouth and pivoted to face his wife, who stood on the last step. Their eyes met as she leaned against the railing.

"I'm fucked," Daniel yelled so loudly the rushing masses stopped midstride and stared at him. A courtroom guard left a conversation with a man in a gray suit to reprimand Daniel. Juliana hurried to the water fountain and pulled her husband out of the courthouse. She bravely waved the guard away.

"Daniel, these outbursts will land you back in prison."

"Can't you see I'm doomed anyway? Sonia's husband is a general in Castro's army. He is the government, the bastards who are trying to put me away for twenty years."

"Sonia wants to help you. I liked her. She'll defend you against that other lawyer. Give it a try."

"Why can't you see what's happening here? They work together for the government."

"That's not what she said."

"Can you believe her? Can you believe anyone in Cuba? Who do you trust?"

"Who do you trust, Daniel? Do you trust me anymore?"

He looked at the main door and saw the guard standing in front of the glass watching them. "I don't know who to trust or what to do."

"You don't trust me?"

"It's not that. Juli, you're so naïve."

"Naïve? Don't you remember? Rafa told us she defended people he knows. Sonia won. She kept them from going to jail."

"What were the circumstances? Measly traffic violations and simple fines. What I'm up against is serious."

"I know it's serious. That's why Sonia's the answer. I'm sure." She stroked his cheek. "Let's go home. We'll talk to Rafa and see what he suggests."

Every night after meeting with the lawyer was sleepless for Daniel. He lay awake pondering ways out of his new dilemma. He was also perturbed at the woman he cherished lying beside him for her premature and mistaken confidence in Sonia Armas.

A few nights before his second meeting with the lawyer, Chispa licked Daniel's hand as it hung limp at the side of the bed. He felt the dog's wet tongue and furry face rub his arm. Juliana slept soundly and inhaled a series of sighs beside him. Glancing down at the dog, he remembered his money hidden beneath the bench at the house. Carefully he climbed out of bed, scooped up the leash on the table in the hall, hooked it to the dog's collar, and quietly left the house. Walking the dog would be the perfect excuse for slipping out late at night, should Juli awaken.

Daniel guided Chispa through backyards and behind trees and thicket to avoid being spotted and to prevent anything from landing him back in prison. When he reached the bench at the house he sat down. He and Juli should be living here. The approved application for this house was cancelled upon his incarceration. He looked at the lawn, once landscaped by Juli and Eva, and the house renovated by the couple and their friends and relatives. What a waste. A result of his poor decisions. The garden showed signs of deterioration, similar to when Daniel first came here alone. It was overgrown and tangled with weeds. He remembered Juli and Eva toiling and planting on the day he surprised them with the news of the pope's visit and a church wedding.

Daniel petted Chispa.

"You were our first child. You should be romping in the backyard."

He noticed the open gate, the spot where he and Juliana discussed having children, his career in medicine, and her desire to get a puppy.

Daniel dwelled on how the mistakes that had landed him in prison could have been avoided. This repeated over and over in his mind. To his credit he had tried to make his life, their lives, everyone's life better. His intentions were good, but where had he gone wrong? Had greed gotten the best of him?

"I'm sorry, little Chispa, that my life with Juli failed. We were so happy."

Gently he pulled on the leash and eased the dog to the side and out of his way. Daniel bent over, removed the stone marker from under the bench, and dug until he felt the coolness of the plastic bag. He lifted it out of the ground and examined its contents. When he wiped the dirt off the bag, the wad of pesos came into view.

"For my mother, for Juli, and for me."

He stuffed the money in his pocket.

"For my escape."

Daniel faced Sonia Armas Ochoa alone this time. Juli pleaded to join him, but he insisted she go to work. "One of us has to make a living," he told her.

He sat across from Mrs. Armas as she shuffled papers at her desk. Daniel felt uneasy as he sat rigid in the chair. He watched her lips part, and her words entered his ears in distant echoes and vibrations. Phrases she uttered, disintegrated. His mind drifted away, stunned, abandoning his body. The disturbed essence of his being floated elsewhere as his numbed body remained seated.

"What?"

She repeated, "Mr. Milan, I am truly sorry. After reviewing your papers, I consulted with colleagues and made a few phone calls. The least I can get you is thirteen to seventeen years. I can only lower the twenty-year term down a few years." Slowly she looked up from the papers as if expecting insults from the young man.

"I understand," Daniel said.

"Mr. Milan, did you hear what I told you? The best I could do would be thirteen years in prison."

"I heard."

"I am very sorry. You are so calm. I have never seen anyone this calm when given such shocking news."

"I guess I was prepared."

"Prepared? I feel you lacked confidence in me as your attorney. My intentions were to get you off entirely."

"I know. You did your best."

"My defense won't help you. Something I've never told a client before." Sonia put her elbows on the desk and supported her chin in her locked hands. "You are a fine young man. My advice to you is to leave Cuba. You did not fare well in prison. I heard. Your only option is to become an exile."

"Thank you for your honesty. I'll think it over." Daniel still did not trust her or the possibility of her husband's involvement in his case. He volunteered no information regarding his plight but knew he only had one choice.

I'm out of here. I'm out of Cuba.

"You have a beautiful wife, supportive family, and good friends in Cuba, but you must consider saving yourself. In these cases the government is ruthless. Do not delay."

Daniel stood. "Thank you, Mrs. Armas, for trying. How much do I owe you?" He touched his pants pocket where the money bulged.

"Nothing. I was unable to defend you, so no charge." She reached across the desk and shook his hand. "Good luck, Mr. Milan."

"Thank you."

In a daze he left her office. He pounded a wall with his fist and then wandered aimlessly up and down empty hallways, trying to sort out his next move. Daniel came to a sitting area, flopped in a chair, covered his face and wept.

The bus from Santa Clara dropped Daniel off in the center of Ranchuelo, where he searched the streets for Rafael with no luck. He saw Rambo hanging out with the old men playing dominoes. Rambo waved a bottle of beer at Daniel and shouted, "Milan, how are you doing? When did you get out of prison?"

At first Daniel ignored his question to continue his mission, but then hesitated and turned. "Have you seen Rafael?"

Rambo asked a man wearing a beret. The elderly man shook his head, and Rambo shouted back, "No, we haven't seen him today. Try the factory."

Daniel passed Carmelita's territory. Where was she? She would know Rafael's whereabouts. He raced up and down side streets. Carmelita emerged out of a storefront on Santa Rosa Street counting a fan of pesos in her hand and smiled when all the money was accounted for. She almost bumped into Daniel.

"My dear, how much you have improved since the days you sat in your backyard staring at chickens. What is your pleasure, *querido?*"

"Have you seen Rafael?"

"Why, no. What's wrong? Why the panicked look in those beautiful brown eyes?"

"I'm looking for Rafa. I need to talk to him."

"Maybe Juliana knows. I just saw her with the dog. Go to her first." Carmelita saw terror in Daniel's expression, which alarmed her. She dropped the cash and hesitated as the bills drifted to the sidewalk. "Calm down, my love," she stammered. "I will help you find Rafael. Just calm down."

Daniel had no time to waste and rushed past her as she bent over and scooped up the money scattered on the sidewalk.

"We'll find Rafael. I'm sure we will, my dear. Juliana just bought a bottle of…" Her words trailed off, and Carmelita raised her head to watch him jog down the street, jump the wall surrounding the Prado, and run in the direction of his home.

When he didn't find Rafa at the Reyes' house, he went to the factory. Daniel had lost track of time and realized while approaching the steps to the loading dock that Rafael's shift had ended. He recognized a second shift security guard on duty in the dispatch office and decided to go home and hide until he planned his next move.

"Daniel?" Juliana called to him as he neared his house. She hurried down the sidewalk. Little Chispa tugged on the leash. At first he shied from the approaching man in brown pants and a tan button-down shirt, but when the Havanese realized the stranger was Daniel, the dog leaped forward, tugging Juli toward her husband. The dog barked and squealed, his fur flowed and body shook with pleasure at the sight of Daniel.

"Where have you been? Your mother and I were worried."

Daniel forced a smile. "The bus from Santa Clara took forever."

She hugged and looked up at him. "What did Sonia say? She called and wanted to speak to you."

"She called me? Are you sure? I left her an hour ago."

"I'm positive. She left a message at the restaurant, and Miguelito told your mother. Something about papers. You'd better call her."

"I just came through town."

"Call her. It may be important. When is the court date?"

He glanced toward town and recited the first date that came into his mind. "September sixth." Ironically, the day his father died.

"You didn't tell me what Sonia said."

"She's going to do her best," Daniel lied and kissed her. "What else can she do?"

"You'll be fine, *mi amor*. Once this trial is over, we'll begin a new life. Find another home. Are you feeling all right? You look a bit pale."

"I'm fine. Have you seen Rafael?"

"My mother told me…" she stared at Daniel. "Are you sure you're fine?"

"I'm sure. Where's Rafa?"

"My mother said he and Eva are looking for a place to live. Can you believe my brother's in love? A family on the outskirts of town may move to Havana. Eva and Rafa might take over their home, if it's suitable."

"I wondered where he was."

"Why?"

"No reason. Haven't seen him in a few days."

"They should be back soon. My father will need the car later. It's my parents' anniversary. They're going to my father's friend's house—the one we stopped to see after midnight mass when you went to get Chispa. They always celebrate their anniversaries together. They double dated in high school."

Juliana picked up the dog and gently squeezed him. "My sweet little Christmas present." She stroked the puppy's head. "Before they go out we'll stop by to wish them a happy anniversary. I bought a bottle of champagne from Carmelita. Rafa can take you to town to call Sonia before he returns the car. Come walk with us."

"I don't think so."

She put the dog down. "Just a short walk. Down the street a ways." Juli locked her arm around his waist. "Come. Talk to me, please."

Daniel strolled along with them finding it an unbearable task. Should he tell her Sonia's devastating news? He remained silent and listened to Juliana talk about work, about Rafael and Eva and how they would marry next year if all went well, about cousins coming from Miami, and about a future that he knew did not exist for him. It would be Juli's future alone, and Daniel could not conceive of being without her. During their walk all he wanted was to confide in Rafael, and he had to make the dreaded call to Sonia. What could she want?

"Mrs. Armas, this is Daniel. Did you try to contact me?"

"Why, yes, Daniel."

He could hardly hear her voice above the chatter of patrons in the restaurant, the clatter of dishes, and chairs scraping across the floor. A group of children ordering ice cream at the counter added to the chaos.

"I forgot to have you sign some court papers. It has to look like we are preparing for trial. Can you come here tomorrow?"

"Did you say come there tomorrow?"

"Yes, I did."

Daniel became suspicious. Return to sign papers? Sonia told him his only option was to escape. He decided to oblige her. "I have some business to attend to tomorrow. I can make it on Thursday."

"That will be fine. Ten o'clock Thursday. Are you at home now?"

"I'm using a friend's phone."

Out the window he could see Rafael waiting for him in his father's car parked in front of the restaurant. His hand tapped on the steering wheel.

"Very well, Mr. Milan. I will see you Thursday."

Daniel slammed down the phone. "The bitch," he shouted, and the entire restaurant became silent.

Chapter Nineteen
THE DEPARTURE

Daniel and Rafael sat under a tree laden with unripe oranges on a rise in an isolated area outside Ranchuelo. The scent of sour oranges and felled blossoms decaying in the earth wafted in the air. A cooler of ice and beer tilted on the uneven ground between them. The distant steeple of Santa Rosa de Lima slashed the darkening sky. Streetlights along the Prado were illuminated. Daniel gazed at the faraway sections of town. His stomach churned. He dreaded departing his home forever.

Rafael took a swig of beer. "Thirteen to seventeen years was all the lawyer could get? She wants you to go back to Santa Clara to sign papers. Sounds like a setup to me."

"Of course it is. That's why I told her I'd be there on Thursday. To buy some time."

"That may not buy you much. What in God's name are you going to do?"

"Leave Cuba. What choice do I have?"

"You always wanted to."

"Not now. You know I love Juli. And to leave my mother and you…it's hell."

"Where will you go?"

"First Havana, I guess. Make enough money there to leave the country."

"Then what? The US?"

"Miami." Daniel mumbled, "I can't even speak fucking English."

"You'll learn. You always wanted to live in Miami."

"In the past. Can't you understand? Not now. Not since Juli. I've never loved anyone so deeply. I wanted everything to work out. It was all coming together. Our marriage, my career, the house, eventually kids. Can you believe it? All shot to hell."

"Juli will be devastated."

"I'm devastated." Daniel gulped down the last of the beer. It was warm in his mouth. "Rafa, there's no way I can tell her I'm leaving. You'll have to do it for me."

"I'll try. It'll be tough. You haven't told her what the lawyer said?"

"She asked me but I couldn't tell her. She knows nothing, only that I had the meeting. I walked the dog with her earlier and tried, but couldn't bring myself to tell her."

Daniel's eyes were fixed on the setting sun and lights shimmering throughout town. He dropped the empty bottle into the cooler, and it slammed against another bottle. He took out a full bottle and popped open the cap with a bottle opener Rafael handed him.

"Juli will try to convince me to stay."

"For sure."

"It's a matter of life or death. Don't think I haven't thought this through. The decision was made for me. It's a matter of survival. I can't bear prison for a week, let alone thirteen years minimum."

"I understand. I saw what it did to you. When will you leave?"

"Tonight."

"I think so. Police could surprise you at any time. Like before."

"*Sí*. It's all happening so fast."

"I never expected…"

"Me either."

They drank more beer and pondered the situation as darkness shrouded the streets and window lights flickered.

"You save yourself. I'll explain to Juli. I'll take care of her."

"I'm her husband. I'm supposed to take care of her."

"It won't be the same as you being here. I'll make sure she's safe."

Daniel was silent.

Rafael glanced at him and turned away from the look of misery on his brother-in-law's face.

"I'll give you a ride tonight."

"Thanks."

Mr. Reyes popped open a champagne bottle, and the cork sailed out of the dining room and bounced on the kitchen counter. Foam rose up the interior neck of the bottle and cascaded down the green glass. Juliana wiped it with a towel. She laughed as she watched her father pour the bubbling liquid, a rarity in Cuba, into the flutes on a glass tray. She stood at the table opposite Daniel, who observed the festivities with a distant look in his eyes.

Mrs. Reyes passed the glasses to Alma Milan, Eva, Juliana, Mr. Reyes, and finally to Daniel and Rafael. Daniel, the last to raise his glass, looked into each face with intensity and imprinted the moment in his memory. He was glad his in-laws had invited his mother and hoped they would continue to include her when he was gone.

"To many more years of matrimonial bliss," Juliana said as she toasted her parents, sipped, and quickly set the glass down when the bubbles tickled her nose.

"Has our marriage always been blissful for you, darling?" Felipe Reyes questioned his wife with a tone of sarcasm in his voice.

"Maybe not always. But I wouldn't have lived with anyone else for twenty-five years."

Felipe touched his glass to Sandra's and kissed her before savoring the champagne. "I feel the same. Now let's hope our children follow in our footsteps."

At those words Daniel downed his glass of champagne, wandered into the living room, and sat down hard in a chair. Rafael followed him with his eyes. Daniel stared at the worn carpet at his feet.

Juli slipped into the living room and gave him a peck on the cheek. "Try the Manchego cheese, *mi amor*. My aunt brought it from Spain. We're invited to her house tomorrow."

He smiled weakly. "I'm not very hungry."

It was early morning and dark outside the kitchen window. Daniel hastily prepared ham and Manchego cheese sandwiches and packed them in his backpack. Juliana's mother sent the couple home with a platter of appetizers left over from the anniversary party.

While he ate toast smothered with guava paste and popped a ham croquet in his mouth, Chispa barked and begged for a morsel of food. Daniel shushed the dog but heard a bedroom door creak open. He rushed across the kitchen to flick off the light. Juliana's pale, sleepy face peeked in and called softly, "Daniel, are you in here?"

The dog raced over to her and placed his front paws on her legs. When her eyes became accustomed to darkness she saw Daniel leaning against the counter.

"What are you doing? I heard the dog. You weren't in bed."

She eyed some unrecognizable objects on the table and switched on the light. Juli rubbed her eyes when she saw the bulging duffel bag and backpack with a sleeping bag tied to it strewn across the table.

"What's going on?"

He was speechless. Never had he expected to explain his departure to his wife. Rafael was supposed to in his diplomatic way. She'd caught Daniel unprepared. There was no time to practice the proper words. He was at a loss and stared at her.

"What is this? Daniel, tell me. Where are you going? I deserve to know."

"I know you do."

He pulled a chair out from the table and motioned for her to sit down. He sat beside her, put his elbows on the table, and leaned his forehead into the palms of his hands.

Juli watched him and pleaded for an explanation. As Daniel reached for her hand, she searched his tear-filled eyes for an answer.

"Sonia...the lawyer..."

"I know who she is. Go on."

"She told me she could get me thirteen to seventeen years instead of twenty. I would be sent to prison again. There was nothing more she could do for me."

"But Sonia said she always won against the other lawyer."

"Once it was determined there was a case to fight. But with me there was no standing up to the government, no matter what lawyer she was against."

"There's no trial? No date? Why would you lie to me?"

"I had no idea how to tell you I had to leave Cuba."

"You're walking out on me?"

"To save my life."

"You betrayed me."

Daniel gripped her hand tightly, and she pulled it away.

"You should have died in prison. At one point we thought you were dead. I could have handled that better than this deception."

Her words stung.

"I've betrayed all of us. Not intentionally."

He tried to embrace her, but she pushed his arms. "Don't touch me."

"Juli, they're coming after me. Like before. Only this time I'll be locked away for many years. Try to understand my predicament. I won't survive in prison again." His thoughts raced. Abruptly he stopped talking.

Daniel's contemplation and the circumstances angered her. "You can't do this to me." She stood. "I'm waking your mother. She deserves to know you're leaving her too."

As she ran to the door, he locked his arms around her waist.

"Juli, please don't wake her."

He swung her around and carried her to the back door. She screeched, and the dog yelped and snapped at his heels. The puppy leaped and grazed Juliana's leg with his cold nose. Daniel opened the back door and held his squirming, kicking wife until he reached the hammock, which had been cleaned, repaired, and strung on two trees at the yard's edge before Daniel's release from La Pendiente. Gently he laid her down and held her firmly as he climbed on the hammock beside her.

In her ear he whispered, "Please, Juli, understand. I have to do this. I don't want to go. Everything went wrong. I can't change that." He stroked her hair. "My mother will be devastated. Don't frighten her out of sleep. She'll get the bad news soon enough." He stopped talking and listened to her sob.

She turned and hugged him. Her voice quivered. "I will always love you."

Together, locked in an embrace, they cried.

Slowly he eased from her arms. Daniel retrieved his bags from the kitchen table and departed. She remained huddled on the hammock and never looked up as she felt him slip away.

Daniel tapped on Rafael's half-open window. When there was no answer, he called to his brother-in-law. Rafa pushed the curtain aside. "You're ready?"

"It's time."

"I have to get the car keys."

"Juli knows."

"She what?"

"I didn't tell her you were taking me. When you come back, go to her. She's lying in the backyard on the hammock. It was hell."

"I will. After I drop you off."

Rafael disappeared into the darkness of his room. Daniel leaned his back against the wall of the house and slid down until he sat beneath the window. The wall was cold against his back. He tilted his head and looked up at the stars. His parting words to Juli played over and over in his mind.

To block out the thought of their unexpected encounter, he scrutinized every step he'd taken to prepare for this unanticipated trip to ensure nothing was forgotten. The pesos from under the bench were divided. He had slipped equal portions in envelopes for Juli and his mother and set them on their night tables. Letters to each of them were tucked in with the cash. Juli would find the letter when she went to bed tonight. Daniel also wrote a letter to Javier Nieves expressing his thanks and explaining his plight.

Daniel had packed sandwiches, fresh fruit, canned food, and a flask of water. In his knapsack he'd also tossed several changes of clothing, a cosmetic bag, photographs and his address book that contained the addresses of friends and relatives in Villa Clara Province, including his aunt Laura's address in Havana. If possible he would visit her, but he knew she lived dangerously close to the coast guard station.

In spite of his haste, Daniel believed he was ready to depart Ranchuelo. He sighed at the thought of Juli lying alone on the hammock. His body ached. Suddenly Rafael opened the window wide, sprung off the windowsill, and sailed over Daniel, landing with a thud several meters in front of him.

"The keys were in my father's dresser drawer. It took forever to sneak them out without waking my parents."

"I wondered what took so long."

"I saw the sheets on my parents' bed."

"You saw sheets on what?"
"The sheets you bought from Carmelita."
"Oh, those. They were for Juli."
"But my parents…"
"I guess she gave them to your parents. It doesn't matter now."

Deep in thought, Daniel picked up his bags and trudged toward the car. Before opening the passenger side door he reeled. "Rafa, I have to go back to Juli and—"

Rafael interrupted. "Are you crazy?"
"To hell with leaving. I can't live without her."
"Listen to what you're saying. You're telling me you're going to your own execution."
"I love her. I can't abandon her like this. That's what she thinks."
"Eventually she'll understand. You have to get out of here."

Daniel ignored him and turned toward his house.
"Are you hearing me? The police could come at any time. It's suicide. You're going to die, Daniel."

Daniel walked faster. Rafael ran after him, dove for his legs, and tackled him in front of the neighbor's house, knocking him to the ground. The bags flew from Daniel's grip. Rafael held him down and slapped him hard across the face.

"Look. Fucking look up, you asshole."

Daniel raised his head and saw two police cars parked in front of his house.

"Oh my God. You're right."
"What an understatement."

They lay still until the police departed. Alma stood crying at the doorway in her bathrobe and slippers. Rafael pulled Daniel to his feet before he had a chance to rush over to his distraught mother. He picked up the backpack as Daniel grabbed the duffel bag, and they headed to the Chevy. Rafael hopped in the driver's seat and shoved the backpack on the back seat. He put the car in neutral, and Daniel pushed it down the driveway. As the car swung onto the asphalt, the tires imprinted the edge of the neighbor's lawn. Daniel pushed it past a few houses. Then he opened the door, threw his bag on the floor and jumped in the passenger's seat. Rafael started the car a block from the Reyes' residence to avoid waking his parents.

Daniel turned to Rafael as he steered down Antonio Maceo Street and passed in front of the entrance to Ramiro La Vandero.

"Thanks. This time you saved my life."

"I always wanted to return the favor."

Daniel rubbed his cheek. "You have a powerful slap."

"It was for your own good." Rafael smiled as he sped along the empty street.

"This is the most difficult thing I've ever had to do—besides being in prison. It kills me to leave. To think after my father died, all I wanted was to leave Cuba."

"Do you think this is easy for me? I'm the one who's driving you away from all of us."

"My only chance to survive."

"That's the reason I couldn't let you go to Juli. That decision would have landed you back in hell."

Rafael turned left onto Camilo Cienfuegos to Central Highway, the principal route to Havana.

"Honestly, I had no idea the police would come for you tonight."

"I worried about it. But I thought they'd make their move in a few days."

"How far do you want to go?"

"Just a few kilometers out of town." Daniel wrung his hands. "Juli said I betrayed her. She yelled at me and wanted to wake my mother to tell her I was leaving."

"She's upset. Her life's been turned upside down. You should have seen her when you were in La Pendiente. No wife should go through what she has."

"Juli never deserved this. I can't express how sorry I am. You were right about me."

"I was cautious for my sister. You're a good husband. Things just got out of hand." The road was dark, and Rafael braked as he rounded a bend. "It will take time. I'll make sure she keeps busy."

"Thanks."

Daniel recalled Juli's screams, but then her normal, soft voice came to mind.

"Keep Maximo away from her."

"That I will."

"Wait, Rafa. Turn around."

"You forgot something? We can't go back."

"No. Take me by the Lopez garage."

"Are you crazy? For what?"

"I want to see it."

"It's burned. The shell of a building's left. Nothing to see."

"I need to see it."

"It's too dangerous. The police."

"Drive to Max's garage, Rafa. I have to go there."

Rafael heard the seriousness in his voice and gave in. "You're not going to find Max there."

"I know. I don't want to find him. He got what he deserved. I have to see the damage."

"The place burned. What's there to see?"

"A garage, destroyed."

Rafael knew when Daniel wanted something there was no changing his mind. "Suit yourself, but I'm turning off the headlights as we near the place."

"Fine."

Rafael pulled over opposite the garage and parked the car off the street beneath branches of trees hugging the road. He hid the car in case a PNR vehicle or the military surprised them. Daniel left his door open as he crossed the street.

"You're getting out?" Rafael called as he also exited the car. "You're taking a big chance."

Even in the dark Daniel saw the charred interior of the garage and the white outer walls streaked in black where flames had licked through windows shattered by the blast.

"Did you hear me? You're taking a big chance. You could jeopardize your freedom. What if the military comes? They're looking for you."

Daniel paid no attention to Rafael and stared at the destruction before him. Cool, damp air and a smoky scent drifted out of the gutted building. Once his mind had cleared after his release from prison, he had puzzled over how this fire had occurred. Daniel swung around in revelation and faced Rafael, who stood in the center of the road.

"Did you set this place on fire?"

"Me? How could I cause damage like that?"

"Anyone can cause this damage."

"Why would you think I did?"

"They said it was arson. I was the only one with a motive. Max was my enemy."

"Hey, lots of people hate Max and his father. Emilio, for one."

"Emilio doesn't have the brains to execute this and get away with it. You do."

"All it takes is gasoline and a match. Damn you. Why do you have to leave? You know me better than a brother."

"You did do this."

"I had to."

"You burned down the Lopez family's auto business?"

"I knew you'd try to get even with Max. I didn't want you to get thrown back in prison."

"You don't think I would have gotten away with this? Or murdering Max?"

"You wouldn't have murdered him. You couldn't kill a pig." Rafael cracked a smile. "You couldn't have gotten away with this. You were the prime suspect."

"I was going to hunt him down. When Juli told me the body shop was set on fire, I decided that was revenge enough."

"I beat you to it. The *chivato* got you sent to prison. He harassed Juli the day before we went to Santa Clara to ask for your release. I couldn't take it."

"The bastard. He always harassed her. Keep him away from her."

"I told you I will."

Rafael refrained from telling Daniel that Maximo had held Juli down and kissed her. Even though Emilio had scared Max off, that knowledge would send Daniel on a rampage.

"You know your secret's safe with me."

"Hell yes. What American will give a shit about the Lopez family's garage?"

"How did you do it?"

"With gasoline from inside the garage and a match. I had to cut the lock to get in. The fire spread fast. It was easier than I expected." He eyed the destroyed building. "They're still investigating. The police grilled me and questioned half the town. They have no leads, no proof."

"They came to me, but I was out of it. I had no idea what they were asking me. I was unable to speak, not to mention set a building on fire. Juli told me about the police inquiry afterward. Now I realize why you didn't want to come here."

"It's a risk for both of us. Remember? You're supposed to escape to save your life. Let's get the hell out of here before we become cellmates in La Pendiente."

Daniel followed Rafael and took one last look at the garage as he jogged across the road to the car.

Rafael drove down Central Highway.

"This is fine, Rafa. Let me out here."

"I have all night. I'll take you as far as Santa Clara."

"You have to work tomorrow. Trucks pass by all night. I saw them when I rode my motorcycle out here." Daniel reached for his bag. "I want you to go to Juli."

"I'll go right to her, and I'll tell her what happened tonight—all except going to the garage."

"I'll write you from Havana."

"Let us know where you are."

"I will." Daniel reached in his duffel bag. "I almost forgot." He pulled out a bottle. "The Armani cologne. Take it. It's your turn."

Rafael tossed the bottle into Daniel's bag as he opened the door. "I want you to have it. A going away present."

"Thanks."

Once out of the car Daniel went around to the driver's side to meet Rafa, who strode toward his brother-in-law with the backpack in hand. Daniel embraced him. "No matter where I am, we'll always be friends. You're always welcome. I wish this had turned out differently."

Daniel slung the backpack across his back.

"So do I." Rafael turned away. Tears filled his eyes as he hopped back into the driver's seat. He revved the engine and called out the window, "*Oye*, remember to keep away from the military. All uniforms are dangerous."

"That's not a hard promise to keep."

As Daniel moved to the shoulder of the highway, Rafael wheeled the vehicle into a three-point turn and pressed his foot on the gas pedal. The tires screeched and left a patch of rubber twenty meters long. The old car fishtailed and sped away. Daniel watched the red streak of taillights rapidly disappear as the car raced down the highway that sliced the plains surrounding Ranchuelo. He removed the backpack from his back, dropped the bags on the side of the road, and sat in darkness.

Chapter Twenty
HAVANA

At sunrise Daniel hitched a ride with a truck stacked full of fruit crates. He shared his sandwiches with the driver. When the driver let him out in the city of Colon, he gave Daniel a sack brimming with mangoes.

His second ride ferried him all the way to Havana. The truck was loaded with boxes of produce from a farm outside Union de Reyes. Daniel was grateful for the ride and relieved he hadn't spent any cash so far. Since he had no specific destination, the farmer let him out before reaching Cuatro Caminos Market in Havana. Daniel left the mangoes on the seat.

"*Oye*, you forgot your sack."

"It's for you."

The farmer thanked him and told him to stop by the market. The farmer sold his produce there every Saturday. "Maybe you'd like some part-time work."

"I might take you up on that. I need the money."

Daniel wandered up and down streets until he came to a residential area. After hours of crisscrossing neighborhoods looking for a place to live, he caught sight of a "For Rent" sign hanging under the second story window of a house on Oviedo Street. The second floor, constructed of slabs of raw, blond wood, was recently added on to the original house. It was unclear to Daniel what was advertised for rent, so he knocked on the door to ask.

A middle-aged woman wearing a faded pink bathrobe with a belt tied snugly around her thick waist answered. Her hair was wet and slicked back. Daniel breathed in a scent of talcum powder as the door opened, confirmed by a chalky streak on the woman's neck.

"Yes? What can I do for you?" she said.

"I saw the for rent sign. Do you have a room to rent?"

"I'm sorry. Not now. We forgot to remove the sign. My daughter returned home and is staying in that room. Besides, you may not like the idea of climbing a ladder and entering your room through a window. An inconvenience, but my daughter and grandchildren don't seem to mind."

"I wouldn't have minded either. Thank you anyway. How long will she be here?"

"I have no idea. Isabel's separated from her husband. She always goes back. I don't know when that will be."

"Thanks anyway."

As he crossed the lawn to the sidewalk, he glanced at the backyard and saw a small, weathered, gray building constructed of wooden slats and a shingled roof. He was curious to know what the shed was used for, so again he knocked on the front door. Daniel felt anxious and worried about not having a place to spend the night. The same lady smiled when she saw him standing before her.

"*Sí?*"

"I wondered what you use the shed behind your house for and if you would rent it to me."

"You wouldn't want to live there." She chuckled. "It was a pigeon coop. The family who lived here before raised homing pigeons. Their way of communicating. It hasn't been cleaned and is not suitable to live in."

"I'll clean it. I need a place to stay. I just arrived in Havana and have nowhere to go."

She saw a look of desperation on his face.

"Take a look first. It's very messy. You may not want to bother."

"I'll check it out."

The lady was right; it was a mess. The building was smaller than it appeared, and Daniel had to stoop while inside. But it was well hidden, and this hovel would keep him off the streets and away from police patrols searching for him. He returned to the house and told her he was interested. A look of doubt crossed her face. She went inside and came back with a broom, pail, and rags, handed them to Daniel, and told him there were more cleaning supplies in the garage.

He first carried his bags and set them beside the shed. Then he carted the cleaning utensils and began to sweep and scrub his new home. Twenty minutes later the lady and her daughter came out to the coop and introduced themselves to their new tenant.

"I'm Maria Soraya, and this is my daughter, Isabel."

"*Encantado*. I'm Daniel," he said as he shoveled debris off the floor and into a wheelbarrow parked at the door. Before they arrived, he had scraped dirt from under a wire mesh that stretched across the floor of the small room and had peeled wire off the walls. Daniel felt anti-social but forced himself to stop working and speak to the ladies as a courtesy.

"Thank you for letting me stay here."

"It's not much. It will only cost two pesos a day. I'm sorry you have to pay anything, but the pesos will cover electricity and water. I'm sure you will use the water out here." Maria Soraya pointed to a spigot extending from an outer wall of the house.

He glanced up at the lightbulb stained brown in the center of the ceiling. "I'll need light and water. Nothing else."

"Isabel has a mattress in her room for the children. They can sleep with her. Would you help her take it down from the second story? With it you can cushion the wire. It will be more comfortable to sleep on."

"Thank you. I'll finish scrubbing the walls. Then I'll help with the mattress."

Isabel eyed him in a peculiar way. He wanted them to leave. His only desire was to curl up on the mattress, climb inside his sleeping bag, and sleep. Daniel felt nauseous and didn't want to be here. He longed for Juliana and his home.

As he heaved the mattress out the second floor window, Isabel tried to strike up a conversation. "Where are you from, Daniel?"

He watched the mattress slide down the ladder and flip over when it struck the ground. Briefly, he told her he was from Santa Clara. He had no desire to divulge information about his life to his landlady's daughter. Daniel sensed the two women would gossip about him later.

When she questioned why he came to Havana, he pretended he hadn't heard her. He hesitated and said, "I'm really tired. I'll catch you later."

Daniel climbed out the window and eased down the wobbly ladder. As he descended he thought she wasn't bad looking. A bit plump like her mother, but her turned-up nose was cute. Her manner of dress reminded him of a younger version of Carmelita. Daniel stepped off the last rung of the ladder with eyes cast downward, unaware that Isabel gripped the top of the ladder with both hands to keep it steady for him.

In the pigeon coop he threw his sleeping bag and a sheet on the mattress, flopped down, and remained there for forty-eight hours. When he awoke he remembered how he and Juli had snuggled in the hotel room on their honeymoon. How he relished the times spent with her. They were too few. Loneliness engulfed him as he lay in the claustrophobic shed. Daniel yearned for the warmth of Juli's body beside him and the comfort of being with the woman he loved. Memories consumed him, and for long intervals he stared at the ceiling and at the lightbulb he'd forgotten to clean. The dim light didn't matter. Unlike in prison, now he preferred darkness.

During daylight hours his t-shirt hung like a curtain over the window by his bed to block out sunlight. At night a streetlight cast beams into his new space and decorated the ceiling with diamond patterns filtered through a steel grate in a small window near the ceiling.

Just before dawn fear of being incarcerated aroused him, and Daniel imagined the shed a prison cell. The ceiling patterns were similar to shadows cast by the iron bars of his cell in La Pendiente. His face, neck, and chest were drenched. His eyes scanned the ceiling for a leak, but the window was dry, and beyond the grate stars glimmered above the trees. It wasn't raining. The moisture on his body was perspiration.

He reached in his bag for a towel. It chafed his neck and chest as he wiped off the sweat. He wondered if his mother had washed the towel in his yucca starch concoction as he dabbed his forehead with the stiff fabric. Daniel hung the towel on a nail and lay on the bed. He examined the crudely built rows of wooden boxes along the wall where pigeons once nested and preened on perches jutting from each box. Dried bird droppings clung to the perches and to the rafters above. Eventually he would hose down the walls and ceiling, but now he craved sleep.

Sleep was impossible lying on his back, so Daniel turned to his side. Every time his arm scraped against the wall a splinter stuck him and pinched until he plucked it out with his fingernails and flicked it away.

Twice during the night, he left his sleeping bag to urinate behind a stand of cypress trees. At the spigot he washed his hands, rinsed his face, and hurried back to the comfort of his sleeping bag. Hours later an overwhelming thirst drew him back to the spigot to gulp metallic-flavored water.

On the morning of his third day in the capital, Daniel's eyes opened, and he gazed at a glass of orange juice on the windowsill. The scent of freshly baked bread teased his stomach into a rumble. He spotted a section of a *Granma* newspaper wrapped and neatly folded next to the glass. A crust of bread peeked out of the paper. Daniel lay still to give himself time to adjust to the morning's gift of sunlight shining in on the mattress. The t-shirt shading the window had fallen during the night, and a sleeve was caught on the nail below the sill. The shirt hung at his eye level, covering the towel.

During his morning slumber, he'd awoke intermittently and heard children speaking softly outside his dwelling and the voice of a female coaxing them to keep quiet. Now a girl and boy screeched and chased each other around the yard. He assumed the two, Isabel's son and daughter, had left him breakfast on the windowsill.

Daniel sat up, and as he reached for the glass, he noticed small slits of dried blood on his arm. He got up and moved the mattress out from the wall to avoid more nightly splinter stabbings. He sat in front of the window and drank half of the liquid warmed by the sun. The oranges had been picked prematurely; the juice's aftertaste was slightly sour, but it quenched his thirst.

As Daniel ate the bread, he unfolded the government newspaper section featuring a photo of Castro speaking at a microphone and skimmed over the article. A girl's voice called from the backyard. "He's awake. The bearded man's awake, Chachi."

With her four-year-old brother scrambling at her heels, she ran over to the shed. They gazed at Daniel from the doorway while he ate. Their wide eyes followed each movement of his hands as he crumpled the newspaper into a ball. Their eyes closed when he pitched the paper orb past their faces into a corner of the coop.

"Did you leave the juice and bread?" Daniel was unsure whether he would get an answer from the shy kids.

The girl blushed and rocked on her feet with hands clasped behind her back. "Yes, we did. My brother and I did." She poked her little brother's shoulder. "My mother baked the bread, and we squeezed oranges for you."

"Thank you very much. It was delicious. And thank your mother for me, will you? Is her name Isabel?"

"*Sí. Isabel es el nombre de mi mamá.* And my name too. We will tell her."

They ran to the yard. The boy, with his choppy stride, lagged behind and struggled to catch up to his sister.

The children were Daniel's only contact for days. While he slept they would leave him a meal accompanied by coffee, juice, or a mug of beer. He counted on the young ones to provide him at least one meal per day. Since his arrival in Havana, his appetite had diminished, and one meal sufficed.

One afternoon Chachi and Isabelita tossed paperback novels belonging to Isabel onto the mattress and quickly returned to the yard to play. They kept their distance and seemed reluctant to come inside. Daniel called to them from the window, "Why do you fear entering my home?"

The kids hovered outside the door. Chachi rubbed his forehead and swayed to and fro. Isabelita stepped forward, peeked inside and said, "Because it's dark and scary in there."

Chapter Twenty-One
THE SOLDIERS OF THE CROSS

Daniel spent several more days inside the coop reading Isabel's novels and dozing in between, until boredom overcame him. One night he ventured out of the shed and took a short jaunt through the backyards of the houses on Oviedo Street. The following night he loafed in the backyard, but during the early morning hours he boldly explored the rest of the neighborhood.

Despite his long hair, beard, and cap brim dipped low on his face, Daniel worried his image would be fresh on the minds of police, so he cautiously strolled the streets. During these nightly walks he noted houses with CDR signs posted on doors or windows. The Committee for the Defense of the Revolution was a group of civilians who observed and reported anyone disloyal to the communist government. He stayed clear of houses advertising residents involved in the dictator's citizen spy network.

On the street Daniel hovered close to trees and bushes and hid when a car or person approached, actions similar to his final days in Ranchuelo. He admitted it was gratifying to be out of the pigeon coop, to stretch his legs and breathe fresh air. With this feeling of freedom, his legs picked up a more rapid pace, and he encircled the neighborhood at a jog and leisurely returned to the shed. After exercising he chose to stay outside rather than confined to the stuffy coop, and he flopped down in an old car seat in the middle of the yard. Daniel raised his face to an invigorating breeze.

Lounging in Maria Soraya's backyard reminded him of the comfort of his own backyard and how he lay on the hammock for hours staring at treetops and a sky thick with soaring clouds. He smiled as he recalled the yard parties, especially the night Juli accompanied Rafael, and his enchantment at her radiance in the moonlight. After his infatuation with her for three years, Daniel realized that night was when he actually fell in love with her. He tipped his head against the back of the seat, looked up at the stars, and sighed.

One night during his wanderings in the neighborhood, he heard music and singing coming from a house at the end of Oviedo Street. His curiosity piqued, and he crouched beneath a back window of the house. Daniel peeked inside and saw approximately fifteen women and men, mouths opened wide, singing a religious song with fervor at a small altar bearing a wooden cross. At the song's end, the group huddled together and embraced.

Hunched over, he eased closer to the window. A woman wearing a scarf on her head backed away from the group and mumbled in a language unrecognizable to Daniel. Her words were uttered in guttural tones and harmonic syllables. This peculiar behavior stunned and interested him.

The woman fell to her knees and clapped her hands together, raising them high above her head in prayer. The ties of her scarf loosened from around her neck, and the striped fabric swept the floor as she walked on her knees. Two other women fell to the floor at her side, speaking a similar language. Their eyes bulged and were fixed upon something beyond the room. From Daniel's viewpoint it seemed as if they peered into the hereafter.

Suddenly, a light flashed on and the back door opened. Daniel reeled. A man dressed in a white shirt and white pants stood at the top of the steps. At first he appeared tall, but when he eased down the steps, the man was centimeters shorter than Daniel.

"Is there anything I can help you with, brother?" he said in a soft, deep voice as he sized up the unkempt young man at the base of the steps.

"No." Daniel stood up straight and stepped away from the window. He noticed that the sleeves of the man's white shirt were embroidered with a swirling design. The realization that he was caught trespassing and illegally peering into a private home struck him like an arrow piercing a target. Hopefully, this man wouldn't alert the police. Daniel would run if necessary. He apologized to the man for looking in the window and started to walk away.

"Come in and join us," he called to Daniel. "Recruits are permitted on the days of the week. Today, Wednesday, you are welcome. On Saturday, our Sabbath, and Sunday, services are private to members only."

"Recruits?"

"We prefer discretion in our religious practices. The government only recently eased restrictions on religious ceremony. Our religion was criticized even before the ban."

"What is your religion?"

"We are the Soldiers of the Cross. We communicate directly with Christ, as you witnessed through that window."

"Is that what they were doing? What language were they speaking?"

"An ancient dialect. Why don't you come inside?"

He opened the door and gestured Daniel to enter.

"We are about to feast on a kosher meal. Please, dine with us and join in blessing our food. You could use a home-cooked meal. Are you hungry, brother?"

"Yes, I am."

He reached for Daniel's hand. "I am Guillermo Santos, minister of our parish. My wife is Matilde. We are the hosts. Welcome."

"It's a pleasure," Daniel said and followed him inside, feeling skeptical but craving human contact and a good meal. The women milled about in long dresses and looked plain with no makeup or jewelry. The lady with the scarf on her head walked over to greet him.

"I am Guillermo's wife, Matilde. Please have dinner with us, Daniel."

When the group coaxed him to join them at the dining room table, he declined. They accepted his choice to eat alone. Matilde prepared a plate for him, and Daniel carried it to a corner of the living room, where he gobbled down the food. She heaped more on his plate.

After dinner the minister recited some parting words, blessed the members present, and bid them to go out into the world with love and peace in their hearts. Everyone departed by the front door except Daniel, who slipped out the back and hastily returned to his hovel. Before he left, Guillermo invited him to return the following week.

"Maybe you have something to discuss. You seem bothered, brother. We will help you work out your problems, if you allow us."

The minister decided Matilde should approach "the troubled young man," as Guillermo called him. A week later the religious couple discussed Daniel while in their kitchen.

"He's thin, pale, and very pensive. My dear, he needs guidance. You, my love, are the kind, caring counselor he needs. You are a good listener. Console the young man if he shows up again tonight."

Matilde placed flatware in a drawer and gave her husband a peck on the cheek. "Anything for you." She walked toward their bedroom, removing the apron around her waist to change into appropriate attire for the religious gathering.

While Guillermo addressed the group seated in rows of folding chairs in the living room, he glanced out the window to see if he could spot Daniel peeking in. The young man was not at the window.

"Maybe Daniel felt uncomfortable and decided against coming," Guillermo said to his wife while they dined with the members.

Matilde was serving bread pudding for dessert when she heard a knock on the door. She handed a dish to her husband and answered the back door.

"*Bienvenido*, Daniel. Come right in. I have a plate of food awaiting you."

Matilde winked at her husband, hurried to the kitchen, quickly filled a plate, and poured a glass of lemonade for the late guest. She accompanied him to the living room while the others ate dessert and drank coffee in the dining room.

"This is for you. Please sit down, unless you would rather join the others in the dining room."

"This will be fine."

"Please, go ahead and eat. Are you hungry?"

Daniel nodded as he sipped the lemonade.

"Do you live nearby?"

"Down the street, behind a house."

He felt uneasy as Matilde stood near him. He held the plate and sat in an upholstered chair. She sat in a folding chair at the end of the first row and leaned forward.

"Are you in trouble, Daniel?"

He shrugged as he chewed.

"We will not report you, no matter what you have done. Our goal is to help those without religion or who are confused and have nowhere to turn. That is what our congregation is about. We explain to the wayward how God will always be there in good times and bad. The supreme being stands beside us as we convey his message. Is there anything we can do for you?"

"You have been kind to me. You've already done enough." Daniel pointed toward his plate with his fork. "Thank you for the food."

"The least we can do."

Matilde glanced in the dining room, met her husband's eyes, smiled, and turned back to Daniel. "Where is your family?"

"My mother's in Ranchuelo, my father passed away, and my wife…" To Daniel's surprise he choked on his words. He set his fork on the plate, wiped his mouth with a napkin, and forced back the tears. For years he was careful when he mentioned Daniel Milan, Sr., for his father's name stirred emotion within him and caused an unexpected melancholy. Now the mention of Juli's name overwhelmed him. At this moment he was unable to speak of his beloved wife. He coughed into the napkin and concentrated hard on saying her name.

"Excuse me. My wife, Juliana, is also in Ranchuelo."

"You are here alone? Visiting?"

"I'm preparing to leave Cuba. You see, I have to leave. I'll be sent to prison again or killed. I…"

She interrupted and held her index finger to her lips, quieting him like she would a child. "You don't have to tell me. I only want to know if you need help coping with this drastic change in your life."

Daniel nodded, and this time uncontrollable tears welled in his eyes. Matilde leaned forward, embraced him, and softly said, "That is exactly what we will do. Help you cope. We are here for you. Do not worry."

When Daniel first arrived in Havana the coop became his security blanket. Although primitive and uncomfortable, it was shelter, a place to escape from cruel government forces determined to imprison him. After meeting twice a week with Matilde, Guillermo, and the members of the Soldiers of the Cross, a change came over him. Anxiety and the fear of capture and imprisonment dissipated, and the passage of time masked his longing for Juli.

A month flew by, and the city of Havana became interesting to him. He was ready to venture further, to explore beyond the pigeon coop, backyard, and streets of his new residence. After a session with the Soldiers of the Cross and confiding with Matilde about his fear of adjusting to life in a foreign country, Daniel decided to tour the night spots near the Malecón, a promenade skirting the ocean, frequented by strollers and tourists registered to hotels lining Fifth Avenue.

The city of Havana had been an enigma throughout his lifetime. He'd refrained from visiting the capital in earlier years for lack of money, and the one opportunity as a teenager to travel there with his parents he became ill with a virus. Now, as a resident of Cuba's capital city, he was long overdue to explore it.

Daniel left the Santos' house in good spirits, reached the coop, and immediately removed his shirt in preparation for a shower under the garden hose. Usually he bathed in the early hours of the morning while the Soraya family slept. This evening Daniel had passed Isabelita and Chachi riding their bicycles along the sidewalk as he set out for Guillermo's house and calculated it was now almost nine o'clock. After playing hard, Isabel's children should be asleep and Isabel and her mother in their respective rooms preparing for bed.

He flicked the light switch on, stripped off his pants, and tossed them next to a shirt strewn on the mattress. Beneath the ceiling bulb, brightened to an intensity he thought impossible even after endless scrubbing, Daniel noticed his muscular biceps and calves and solid stomach when he pressed his fist into his firm flesh. Jogging, sit-ups, and push-ups at night and the unusual but healthy meals at the Santos' home had helped him gain weight and get back in shape. For the first time in weeks, he felt upbeat and more determined than ever to leave Cuba to begin a new life.

His conversations with Matilde and her assurance that English classes abounded in South Florida had boosted his confidence. Spanish was spoken on the streets, and Spanish speakers were hired for jobs in Miami, unlike in other US cities, where English was a necessity for job hunters. This also reassured him. Soon he would devise a plan for his escape. In the meantime, he would familiarize himself with Havana and its nightlife before the day of his departure. Daniel examined his face in the small mirror propped against the wall on a shelf.

He had shaved his beard before dining at the Santos' home, to the surprise of the Soldiers of the Cross, who at first did not recognize him as he entered the house. Shaving again was unnecessary. He removed his briefs, wrapped a towel around his waist, reached up for a bar of soap and shampoo in his shaving kit tucked inside one of the pigeon boxes, and stepped outside on grass dampened by dew. The dampness cooled the bottoms of his feet.

Daniel draped his clean clothes on the wheelbarrow leaning against the house, removed the towel at his waist, and hung it on the wooden handle of the wheelbarrow. He turned on the spigot and followed the green, coiled garden hose with his eyes until he spotted the nozzle where water gushed out. He whisked it up. Water flowed warm on his skin at first but cooled as the sun-warmed water flushed from the hose. The even flow soothed and relaxed him.

He set the hose over a bush and aimed the jet of water at his legs to free his hands while he rubbed the soap into a thick, white lather over his body. Daniel shampooed his hair and stood ghostly in the dark. He held the hose above his head to wash away the suds into a spongy mass of bubbles swirling at his feet and rinsed his shiny body of lather. Still holding the hose above his head, he dipped his face under the nozzle and happened to glance up at the house.

A figure stood in a window on the second floor. Details were vague, but the body form reflected in the windowpane was clearly the outline of a robust female. He was startled but pretended not to see her, sprayed his body once more, and dropped the hose to the ground. The force of the water caused the head of the hose to bounce and writhe on the grass like an angry reptile. Daniel quickly leaped away from the serpentine tube, grabbed the towel, and modestly covered himself from the voyeur gaping at him from the window.

Isabel peered down. How brazen, he thought. Her upper torso loomed in the center of the window with no attempt to conceal herself. He scooped up his clothes and elected to dress in the confines of the hut. As he rushed into the coop, Daniel felt her scrutinize his body. At the door he ducked, turned, and plopped down on the mattress, allowing the clothes to fall out of his arms. He lay there thinking of Isabel blatantly observing his body. Daniel grimaced and shook his head in disbelief.

An hour passed. After dressing he strolled down the street and thought about how violated he felt, debating whether to go into the city or not. He concluded that drinks and music would do him good and decided to walk as far as possible instead of paying for a taxi, and then he could opt for public transportation if necessary.

A car pulled up alongside him. Daniel worried and refrained from turning around. Paranoia had pursued him ever since the ravaging of his home, siege, and his imprisonment by ruthless military. He glanced over at the driver, and to his relief a member of the Soldiers of the Cross offered him a ride. Daniel blushed because he had forgotten the gentleman's name.

"Where are you headed, Brother Daniel?" the driver asked.

"Near the Malecón. You can drop me anywhere you're going."

"Come on. I'll take you all the way. It's only a short distance from where I'm headed. I have to pick up my daughter at a friend's house."

"I appreciate the ride." Daniel entered the car.

He looked at the young man dressed in jeans and a white shirt and sniffed the scent of cologne drifting around him.

"You must feel better. Are you more comfortable in Havana? Dressed to go to the clubs, I see."

"I'm adjusting. I always wanted to come to Havana. Leaving my family behind was the difficult part."

"Painful, I'm sure. It's good to see you are getting out and enjoying life a little. Not a cure, but a good remedy."

"I think so."

A bicycle with a reed basket tied to the back of the seat cut in front of the car. They swerved to avoid the bicyclist, who never saw them.

"That was close. There are always obstacles to watch out for on the streets of Havana. Bikes, motorcycles, donkeys. You have to be alert and drive defensively."

"So true. I didn't know you had a car. You always come to meetings on foot."

"You wouldn't have known. We are forbidden to drive on the Sabbath, and I choose to walk to Guillermo's home during the week, although we are allowed to use our vehicles. It's a personal thing."

"I respect that."

"Shall I leave you off before Túnel de Linea? The Johnny Club is not far from there. Maybe you would like to begin at El Johnny, a popular place with young people."

"A night club is a good beginning."

"It's inside a hotel. Walk straight ahead, and it will be on your right. You can't miss it. You'll hear the music."

Daniel exited the car, thanked the man, and told him he would see him at the next meeting. He was still unable to recall the man's name and strained to think of it as he strolled along the shore toward the blaring of rock music and loud chatter.

Daniel inhaled the salt air and listened to waves lapping against the rocks during a brief silence at the end of a song. A border of rocks, like dark shadows, scattered haphazardly below the seawall. White crests splashed against them and vanished into darkness. For the first time since he arrived in Havana, Daniel felt a glimmer of happiness. His gait quickened, and he sprinted toward the nightclub.

Across the water he saw lights of the coast guard station and of houses near it, one of which was owned by his father's older sister, Laura, who had kept her residence overlooking the ocean. As he glanced at the twinkling lights in the distance, he decided to pay her a visit soon to get reacquainted. Daniel bounded up the steps of the hotel and into the Johnny Club, where he strode to the bar and ordered a whiskey on the rocks.

Chapter Twenty-Two
BOLERO

Daniel hung out at the bar at El Johnny and talked to the bartender. The music blared. He danced a few dances with two different girls who were intoxicated and giddy. In their company he acted suave and cool, but inside Daniel ached for Juli. As time progressed he began to dislike the two who swooned over him and argued over who would dance with him next.

The whiskey clouded his mind, and the loud music caused his ears to ring. He felt enclosed by the throng of people crammed into the club and smothered by the two immature women shamelessly pursuing him. Daniel slipped away from the girls and eased toward the door unnoticed, he thought, until the curly-haired one sang out, "*Dani, adónde vas?*"

In slurred words the other one answered, "He's at the other end of the bar. I'll bring him back."

Daniel squeezed up to the bar, ordered a whiskey, and saw the girl stagger toward him, holding her drink before her. The liquid sloshed and spilled on a couple chatting at a table, and she stopped to apologize. At the instant of the apology, Daniel slapped a few pesos on the bar, grabbed his drink, and hopped down the steps at the back entrance. Outside, he raised his face to a cool breeze carrying a tang of salt-scented air.

He was stunned at his inability to be in the presence of women. Not one female in the club compared to Juli. Daniel thought he heard the voice of one of the girls calling him, but when he turned around he saw a sultry Dominican lady speaking to a man in a *guayabera* seated on a railing, puffing a cigar and absently staring at the ocean.

"*Aquí estoy, querida, admirando el mar.*"

Aquí estoy tambien admirando el mar, thought Daniel. I'm also admiring the sea, as free as the seagulls scolding humanity above me. He breathed deeply and sipped his drink as he marveled at the lights of Havana trailing along the shore into the distance. He strolled along Fifth Avenue to the sea walk. Motorcycles, old American cars, and trucks whizzed past on Malecón Avenue even at this late hour.

While seated on the Malecón seawall, Daniel gulped down the last of the whiskey. Carefully, he crossed the street when the congestion of traffic slowed and bar hopped until his body and mind were numb of sensation. The next thing he knew the sharp rays of the sun stung his face. He opened his eyes to gulls calling, traffic rolling by, and the chatter of fishermen across the street baiting hooks and tossing their lines into the swell below. Their fishing poles swayed in a gale. Waves slapped the rocks, and water sprayed the men, pavement, and several cars as they sped by. They wiped their eyes with their sleeves and resumed fishing.

Daniel sat up to get a better view of his surroundings. He had no inkling of where he was, but with each glance he remembered that early in the morning he had fallen asleep on this bench outside the last bar he visited. The smell of stale beer and remnants of cigarette smoke emanated from the locked door behind him. A sign with the word "*cerrado,*" hung on a nail and bumped the door as it swung on the handle in a breeze.

Daniel's temples throbbed, and dizziness overcame him. He rested his head against the back of the bench and touched his pocket, where he recalled stuffing all his cash before leaving for Centro Habana. He believed the cash was safer on his person than hidden in the unlocked coop. To his dismay the wad of money had diminished.

Last night was the first time he'd drank heavily since his wedding. In his sobriety it struck him that half the cash brought to Havana was wasted on a one-night binge. For his careless stupidity, Daniel slapped his forehead and held his left hand suspended in front of his face. His scar had thinned to a jagged white line and faded into a crease in his palm. Beyond his hand he glimpsed at clouds drifting across the sky and recalled the mosaic bench at the house in Ranchuelo where he hid his cash.

Now Daniel sat on a plain wooden bench in Havana, miles from Juliana, alone and aching to be with his wife. And now, like at the dawn of his wedding, his body pulsed with anxiety. Loneliness plagued him. He looked away from the clouds. It was incomprehensible how he had once questioned his betrothal to Juli.

Daniel regretted his poor decisions that had resulted in their separation. But he had to resume his life. He contemplated his most recent dilemma, his dwindling cash. The priority now was to earn enough money to buy his way out of Cuba.

Slowly he stood and crossed the street to the seawall to view the ocean. He stretched his arms high in the air. A mist of water sprayed and cooled his face. The dizziness subsided. The whiskey had been sympathetic and spared him a full-blown hangover. The taste of alcohol coated his mouth. Daniel wanted to return to the coop to brush his teeth and bathe but decided it was crucial to first pass by the market to see if the farmer who had given him a ride to Havana had any work for him.

His gait picked up as he walked the Malecón. A young man a few inches taller than Daniel strolled in the opposite direction with his eyes cast downward. He practically bumped into him. Daniel swerved, and as the man's arm brushed Daniel's shoulder, his straight, light brown hair lifted in a gust of wind. The male pedestrian was barefoot, shirtless, and wore a pair of khaki shorts, but what caught Daniel's attention was an American flag tattooed on his lower left leg above his ankle.

"Hey, man. What's happening?" Daniel asked the stranger.

With a big smile and protruding upper teeth, the stranger answered, "*Nada. Paseando no mas, y tú?*"

"The same. I like your tattoo. Anyone bothering you about that?"

"Police don't notice, and I don't give a shit. I've been jailed twice trying to leave Cuba. I was discouraged but got this tattoo to remind me not to give up."

He turned his leg so the flag was more visible to him and looked down at it in admiration. "Glad you like it."

"We need to talk. Are you busy?" Daniel gestured for him to sit on the wall.

"I'm going to see friends who live along the Almendares River. They don't know I'm coming."

"We have something in common," Daniel said as he guided the young man to the wall away from people promenading the expansive walkway. They sat down.

"Since you're being so open, just between you and me, I have to get out of Cuba, too. I'm in Havana for that reason. I was in prison for six months. Now the government wants to send me away for years. My only alternative is to leave."

"And go to the United States? I don't blame you. What were you in for?"

"They accused me of stealing cigarettes from a factory. I never got caught but landed in prison on suspicion."

"Did you steal cigarettes?"

"That's beside the point. They never caught me in the act."

"You stole the cigarettes."

"Thousands, but the point is I got away with it."

"Until?'

"Until a *chivato* turned me in."

"Do you know who?"

"I thought I knew, and then my neighbor, Emilio, and friend, Rafael, verified who it was." Daniel stared across the water. He realized he had not spoken their names in weeks. "Rafael's my brother-in-law. He got even with the guy."

"What did he do to him?"

"Burned down his father's auto body shop."

"That's a big deal."

"It was. I was so mentally disturbed after being in prison I didn't grasp the magnitude of the fire until Rafa brought me to the garage before coming here. What about you? How come you couldn't escape?"

"I never planned it well. I set out for Key West in a friend's boat. Cuban Coast Guard got us in their sights and knew what we were up to. They towed us back to shore and threw us in jail." He shielded his eyes from the sun as he looked toward a speedboat gliding along the horizon. "The second time was at night. I left with a group of refugees in a trawler. I thought we were free. We were celebrating below deck with some of the crew, and the next thing we knew coast guard boarded and loaded us onto their boat. Before being arrested the captain dropped anchor, and the trawler sat off shore for months until he was let out of prison. The owners of the boat thought the old captain and crew were out to sea all that time."

"How long were you in the slammer?"

"Two months each time."

"How did you get such short sentences?"

"I talked my way out."

"You talked your way out both times?"

He nodded and smiled a wide smile.

Daniel patted his back. "You're just the man I'm looking for. This time we'll plan an escape with precision. What do you say?"

"Sounds good to me. It's worth trying again. With a guy like you, I know this time I'll succeed."

"We'll think it out very carefully. First we have to make some money. *De acuerdo?*"

"How can we make money?"

"We'll start at the market. Cuatro Caminos. I know a farmer who might have work. I'm on my way there."

"That's a beginning. You're on."

"What's your name?"

"Bolero."

"I'm Daniel. Daniel Milan. Bolero, we have some planning to do."

Daniel and Bolero lifted crates of fruit and vegetables not sold that morning onto the farmer's truck parked at the end of a row of vendors at Cuartro Caminos Market.

Bolero also tossed empty crates up to Daniel, who stacked them in the flatbed. Bolero wiped perspiration off his forehead. Moisture stained the back of Daniel's t-shirt and when he swallowed there was no saliva in his mouth. As he caught a crate, he hesitated to tell his new friend he would buy him a beer when they finished.

At midday Daniel jumped off the truck. The farmer reached for pesos in his pocket, counted them, and handed the cash to Daniel and his friend. The pay was meager, but Daniel believed this work could lead to more jobs around the market and beyond. He had expressed this to Bolero in an effort to keep up his spirits while they had tediously loaded the truck.

"If you want more work, come back next Saturday, six o'clock in the morning to unload my truck. I'll also recommend you to other vendors," said the farmer. "Crops have been plentiful lately. Maybe you'll get hired for more part-time work. It all adds up."

They belted down a few beers at a bar on the way home, and Bolero accompanied Daniel to the coop. After, they planned to stop by Bolero's friend's house on the Almendares River.

"You live in here?" Bolero asked Daniel. "From the front it looked like a chicken coop."

"Almost. Homing pigeons were kept here. Now it's for this homing pigeon." He made a fist and thrust his thumb forward, pointing to himself. "The one who will never go home." Daniel flopped on the mattress. Admitting verbally that he would never return home caused him to stare out the window deep in thought. Then he rolled over, sat up, and told Bolero, who stood in the doorway looking at the dim interior, to come inside. "*Mi casa es tu casa.*"

Bolero ducked his head at the door, entered the shed, and sat at the edge of the mattress. "I'll take the small room I live in over this place any day. At least my room's inside a house."

"Where do you live?"

"Outside Havana, but I'm moving to my friend's place on the river. Antonio, the guy you'll meet. He's a fisherman."

Daniel looked around. "This is a sorry place to live in. But the PNRs and Castro's spy network haven't found me here."

"True. They wouldn't think to look for you in a pigeon coop."

"That's why I like it." He stood and bent over. "I'm going to wash up and change these filthy clothes. Then we can go."

"Where do you wash in here? Where do you eat?"

"I wash with the hose outside by the house. I eat in here. I'm fed by my landlady's family, and another family who lives at the end of the street. They're members of a religious group called Soldiers of the Cross." Daniel reached for his towel hanging on a nail. "They've been good to me. In fact, I give them credit for saving my life. I was messed up when I first got here. I had a hard time coping, especially with leaving my wife."

"You're married? You seem like a bachelor, that Don Juan type of guy."

"Maybe I was at one time. I'm very much in love with my wife, Juli. Leaving her behind has been torture."

"I guess it would be."

Daniel quickly changed the subject. "I'll hurry up and wash."

"Take your time."

"I'll take a full shower early in the morning when they're all asleep." He pointed in the direction of the house. "Last night Isabel watched me shower from that window. She's the landlady's daughter."

"You should like that."

"I felt violated."

"Men don't feel violated when a woman looks at them."

"Well, I did. I was naked."

"So what?" Bolero laughed. "Introduce me to her."

"She's married."

"I don't care."

Daniel and Bolero hung out with Antonio and some of his fishing crew on the flat tin roof of Antonio's house on the shore of the Almendares River. They drank beer in the shade of an overhang as the river flowed murky after a downpour during the night. Smells of river bottom mud and damp vegetation entered their nostrils in an occasional gale that swept up river from the ocean.

Antonio's boat was moored to a dock in plain view of the roof where they sat. The boat pitched from side to side and rocked when a small ship steamed by, creating a wake and a series of waves hammering the hull. Occasionally a fisherman eyed the boat in a protective manner. It was in this relaxed atmosphere that the men became acquainted. This day began a bond between Daniel, Bolero, Antonio, and his crew.

The following Saturday Bolero awakened Daniel in the coop and together they boarded a "camel," a cheap form of public transportation made out of a trailer truck with benches hammered to the floor of the truck bed. They arrived at the market before sunrise and sat in the dark on the lowest shelf of a booth, awaiting the arrival of the farmer. The three-tiered structure they sat on was empty but later would display produce to be sold.

"For now this job will do. Eventually we'll need more than the few pesos we earn as market laborers," Daniel said as he sipped the cup of coffee Bolero had bought at a café and handed him as they mounted the camel. The coffee had cooled during the open-air truck ride. It was tepid on Daniel's tongue and had a bitter flavor.

"I know. We already had this discussion. Let's do this for now. Something better will come along. Be patient."

"Patient is my middle name."

The farmer arrived at six thirty, and they unloaded his truck and neatly arranged tomatoes, eggplant, squash, beans, carrots, melons, papayas, oranges, and bananas in shallow bins to be handled, squeezed, and inspected by customers looking for the plumpest, ripest fruits and vegetables. Daniel stepped away from the booth and watched an elderly woman select a melon, press it, and sniff it for ripeness.

Daniel stood in front of a Spanish woman who occupied the booth next to the farmer. She sat on an empty barrel and waved a fan to cool her face in the still air of the market. She was born in Seville and sold olives marinated in an herbed oil and vinegar solution. The Spaniard snapped the fan closed and tapped Daniel's leg with it. She offered him and Bolero *churros* and hot chocolate, and they passed some to the farmer, who accepted with a smile. The Spanish vendor delighted in providing breakfast to those occupying booths surrounding hers. The homemade *churros* and chocolate always brought her a thank you and praise, which she reveled in.

Daniel munched on the serrated sticks of fried dough sprinkled with sugar and sipped the thick chocolate beverage. The light breakfast gave him a burst of energy after experiencing a lethargic bout during the monotonous unloading of the truck. When Daniel and Bolero popped the last bits of Spanish pastry into their mouths, the farmer led the young men to the fishmonger, who needed help cleaning and gutting a recent catch.

At the end of several hours of odd jobs, Daniel and Bolero smelled worse than the river stench they complained about at Antonio's house. Vendors stashed away their goods, and the market closed in the middle of the day. The two friends thanked the Spanish lady and bid farewell to vendors they'd befriended. They caught a camel to Bolero's home to shower and change out of their sweaty clothing.

Daniel felt more at ease bathing in private in an enclosed bathroom and free of worrying about Isabel ogling his body when he washed in open air. He rubbed soap on his shoulders, neck, and arms and massaged his aching muscles as the warm water flowed over his skin. When he shut off the water, the pipes moaned.

Bolero slightly opened the door and tossed clean clothes and a frayed towel onto the lid of the toilet. The color of the towel had faded to light gray but maintained yellow spots and a few yellow threads of its original color. Daniel scooped up the rag and dried his body first and then vigorously toweled his hair. While drying himself he thought how he and Bolero should be cautious about revealing their plans to depart Cuba.

Bolero lay on his bed flipping through pages of a pornographic magazine his landlord had left at the door to his room and raised his eyes from the page as Daniel peeked out the bathroom door. His wet hair was disheveled and spiked straight up at the crown of his head.

"Let's be careful who we tell about our plans. In fact, don't even discuss leaving Cuba until we know the people well enough and are sure they're not spies."

"That makes sense. I've known Antonio and his crew for years. We can trust them."

"Still, let's wait awhile before we mention it."

"That's fine. I can keep a secret if it makes you feel better."

Daniel opened the door wider to allow the steam to clear. The old towel wrapped around him and tied at his waist barely covered his buttocks. "It *will* make me feel better." He faced the mirror above the sink and reached for a comb on a small glass shelf under the mirror. "I think it's best we wait."

"I feel good about the fact that you trusted me with your secret to leave Cuba the first time we met." Bolero flipped a page.

"It was intuition, I guess." Daniel eyed himself in the mirror as he smoothed his hair and glanced at Bolero's reflection. "*Oye*, you trusted me too."

Chapter Twenty-Three
DODGING THE COAST GUARD

Daniel decided it was time to visit his aunt Laura, despite the fact that her house was dangerously close to the coast guard station. He mounted a bus on Oviedo Street, rode to the bus stop at Túnel de Linea, and flagged a taxi to drop him off as near to the entrance of her home as possible. A cap shaded his face, and he sat low in the back seat. Occasionally he stretched to peek out the window as they rode along the coast. Daniel caught a glimpse of a huge cement platform where boys dove and jumped, one after the other, into the water. In the distance men fished from inner tubes and rowboats drifting near the platform.

A tall building with picture windows housed the coast guard. All vessels entering and leaving the open ocean could be viewed from the building free from obstruction. Daniel saw a uniformed guardsman at the water's edge with a pair of binoculars glued to his eyes, observing boats gliding across the bay. Below where the lookout stood, Cuban-made speedboats awaited a swift embarkation.

Coast guard personnel could mobilize in an instant to board, search, and confiscate crafts that failed to return on schedule. Daniel recalled a conversation with Antonio and his buddies. They'd assured him that despite the guardsmen's enthusiasm to capture wrongdoers, they could easily be bought for the right price.

Daniel knew he was taking a chance by visiting his aunt but made up his mind to be cautious and heed Rafael's warning to avoid anyone in a uniform. He would go to extremes to prevent a confrontation with military personnel. For certain any encounter with the coast guard would be disastrous, and to willingly walk up to the wrong house in this neighborhood could be a fatal mistake. He double-checked the house number written on a piece of paper in his shirt pocket to verify that the taxi pulled up to his aunt's place.

Aunt Laura's house was the fourth and last on a rise overlooking the sea. It rested tranquilly beside three similar two-story dwellings taken over by Castro's militia years ago. The owners had been forced to leave and their former residences now housed offices used by high ranking military and coast guard personnel. Daniel was amazed that Aunt Laura had the gall to convince authorities to allow her to stay in her beloved home with the spectacular view. She was determined to live there forever and fearlessly shooed the military from her doorstep. Daniel chuckled when the thought came to mind about how he could have used her on the night he was arrested.

His mother told him that the only reason soldiers returned to Laura's home was to sip her freshly brewed coffee and delight in her pastries and an occasional gourmet meal. They never again attempted to remove her from her residence. Laura lived safe, secure, and exempt from eviction.

Daniel remembered his aunt as a stern and strict disciplinarian with his cousins, but he had always liked and respected her. His parents had visited her once a year. For some reason she and her family had stopped coming to their home in Las Villas. Daniel assumed it was because her son, Juan, and daughter, Ofelia, had grown and had their own interests, her husband passed away, and Aunt Laura did not drive. Juan and his wife, Ofelia and her boyfriend had attended his wedding to Juliana, but Aunt Laura had a bout with the flu and was unable to attend.

Daniel paid the taxi driver and glanced around before sprinting to the front door. A lamp shone in the living room, and a newspaper was tossed on a table as someone rose from a chair at the sound of the knock on the door. He looked up and down the street as he waited. A man in uniform walked along the road in the distance, and a swimmer did laps in a pool at the house next door, but Daniel felt unthreatened.

Aunt Laura opened the door and stared questioningly at him. "You're not coast guard or anyone I would know, are you?"

"I'm your nephew, Daniel. Do you mind if I come in?"

"Daniel? Why, no, not at all. Come in. How you have grown." She gave him a quick embrace and touched both his cheeks with hers. "What a surprise!"

"I'm sorry I didn't let you know I was coming. I'm preparing to leave Cuba and have to be careful."

She sat in a chair and gestured toward a carved wooden love-seat for him to sit. As he sat down on the firm, floral design of the cushion, he noticed that the window shades were partially drawn and the room was dark and cool, although outdoors the sun shone bright in a clear sky.

"In trouble, are you?" Laura asked as she picked up the newspaper, folded it, and returned it neatly on the table.

"You may say so. I was in prison for six months. I found out that I'll be put away for longer if I go to trial. There's no alternative but to leave."

"And your wife, will she join you?"

"I hope so."

"I'm sorry to hear of your difficulties. How is your mother?"

"Doing fine before I left."

"Trouble always seemed to find you."

"Excuse me. What do you mean by that?"

"As a boy you were a hell raiser. I never understood why you behaved so badly."

"A hell raiser? I was a kid."

"And a wild one at that. I'm sorry to say this, Daniel, but I never cared for your antics very much. Maybe now I should give you the benefit of the doubt. You have grown up."

"Never cared for me? Give me the benefit of the doubt? I was imprisoned. I suffered."

"We are living in hard times, Daniel. The government is not tolerant of wrongdoing."

"That wasn't the case." He shifted, rested the foot of one leg across the knee of his other, and gripped his shin with both hands. Why had he felt so compelled to visit his father's older sister? He'd never expected her to insult him like this. "I liked you. You were strict, but I never disliked you. This is very uncomfortable. I just wanted to say good-bye." He stood and bent to look out a window to make sure uniforms were not wandering nearby so he could leave.

"Daniel, I didn't mean to insult you. Sometimes I'm too straightforward. Please, sit back down. Would you like a drink? I have pineapple soda. Would that be fine?"

"I should really go."

"Have a drink. I would like to talk to you. Please."

"There's no more to say." He headed for the door.

"Don't leave. Please sit."

At her urging he returned to the loveseat. He was thirsty and came so far to see her. Daniel decided to stay. "Pineapple will be fine."

He sat, and a breeze brushed his face as she rushed by to the kitchen. The material of her dress skimmed the top of his hand. It was obvious she felt as uneasy as he did. He heard a tap at the kitchen window and saw a guardsman waving to get Laura's attention.

"I wondered if you would come for your café con leche. I'll prepare it." She poured coffee into a cup followed by a spoonful of sugar and stirred. "Just one moment, Daniel."

Daniel shrunk in the loveseat and listened to their conversation as the man spoke to her through the window.

"I arrived back on shore late this morning. Last night we were delayed. We made several arrests at sea."

"Boat people?"

"*Balseros.* Rafters. We're intercepting refugees on a daily basis."

"They are brave."

"Stupid is more like it. What could be worse than drifting alone on the ocean on a raft?"

"Nothing. I couldn't, no matter how bad my life was in Cuba." Laura heated milk in a pot on the stove, poured it into the cup of coffee, and passed it through the window. "There you are, Capitan. Have a pastry with your coffee." She reached for a coconut pastry on a plate beneath a glass dome, placed it on a paper plate, and passed it through the window. He thanked her and told her to have a nice day.

Daniel eyed the guardsman as he strode across the lawn. Below the window shade, Daniel saw only his legs as he stepped up to the porch of the house next door. When he sat in a chair to take his break, Daniel caught sight of the entire man in uniform.

Laura called to Daniel from the kitchen. "Sorry. I'm taking longer than expected." He surmised that in an attempt to make peace with him she continued to say, "Ofelia told me your wedding with Juliana was lovely. The biggest event of the year. I'm sorry I missed it."

Carefully she carried two crystal glasses full of pale yellow liquid fizzing at the top. Daniel smelled the sweet scent of pineapple as she handed him a glass. Before he sipped, he said, "Are you really sorry you missed the wedding? After our conversation I'm not sure I believe you."

"I wasn't feeling well that weekend. Yes, I did want to attend. The family hardly ever gets together for joyous occasions. Our reunions seem to be at funerals. The last one was your father's in Las Villas. I hated burying my younger brother."

"I still can't accept his death."

"Of course not. He was your father and a good one."

She set the glasses on leather coasters on the table in front of them.

"Daniel, I wasn't trying to provoke anything by revealing my true feelings. I had to get it off my chest and clear the air. As we sit here, I like you more and more."

Daniel tightened his lips, and his eyes shifted. In his expression Laura saw the boy she remembered.

"I suggested to your parents to have another child. They never listened to me. An only child becomes spoiled, I told them."

He gazed out the window at the guardsman on the porch.

"And you were spoiled."

He turned and looked at her. What could he say? Daniel had forgotten about his mischievous childhood. "That was fifteen years ago. I've changed."

"I see you have. But as a child you were naughty."

"I don't remember everything I did."

"You don't remember putting burrs in Ofelia's hair, throwing water balloons at us from a tree, taking a chunk out of your cousin's wedding cake, and hiding under the table and stabbing guests with a fork? I could go on and on."

"I'm sorry. Is there anything I can do to make up for those bad times?" Daniel felt uneasy but was sincere in his offer. He had made a mistake by coming. He felt out of place and wanted to go back to the coop. He had expected a pleasant visit with his aunt, but her persistent criticism put him in a solemn mood.

"Not that I can think of. I apologize for being so blunt. I've wanted to tell you my feelings for a long time. How unfortunate that I'm telling you this before your departure. I would like to get reacquainted with you. I am sure my opinion of you would change."

"Maybe it would," Daniel said as he looked out at the ocean.

Laura followed his gaze. "Do you still fear the ocean? I remember you did as a boy."

Daniel noticed the sharp color contrast between the green lawn and turquoise water and focused back on his aunt. "I do. I still have a hard time going into the ocean. It started when I was a child with nightmares about sea monsters."

"Your fear began before your nightmares."

"What do you mean? When I was four I'd wake up screaming after a dream about a whale with huge teeth. My mother comforted me. Sometimes I'd run and jump in my parents' bed. That's when my fear began."

"My dear, your fear started before the nightmares." She saw curiosity and surprise on his face. "You don't remember what happened to you?"

"No. What happened? I have no idea."

"It was a cloudless day in April. During a visit to Havana your father took you deep-sea fishing on your uncle Silvio's boat."

"I don't remember a boat trip or ever coming to Havana."

"You wouldn't remember. You were barely four. Your cousin Carlitos went too. He was much older."

"Carlitos was killed."

"Yes. Many years after the trip during a rebellion against the government." Laura shifted in the chair.

Daniel took that moment of hesitation to say, "My parents never spoke of this."

"It was best forgotten because the trip created tension in their marriage. Let me finish. Your father hooked a large shark. He reeled in the man-eater and pulled him on deck."

"How strange. My father never went deep-sea fishing that I knew of."

"You'll see why. Although he kept the shark far from you and Carlitos, it swung and writhed with such force that its tail knocked you down and swept you beneath the railing and into the water."

Aunt Laura caught her breath and took a sip of her soda.

He stared at her. "That happened?"

"I'm sorry to say it did. I told them you were too young for such an excursion. Your poor father was so shocked to see you fall overboard. He let go of the pole. Once freed, the shark thrust its massive body off the edge of the boat and landed next to you in the water. Your father jumped in behind the shark to rescue you."

"I can't believe this."

"It happened. Fortunately the shark only wanted to escape. Silvio saw its shadow swim away from the boat. Your father lifted you out of the water and up to Silvio and Carlitos, alive and unharmed. You screamed and cried until they docked at the marina. Your father held you and cried along with you."

"Was I hurt?"

"Not a mark on your little body. Daniel rushed you to the emergency room to make sure. Physically you were uninjured. Subconsciously the fall and encounter with the shark terrorized you."

"I never knew. Now my fears and nightmares make sense. They never did before."

"That close call put a strain on your parents' marriage. Your mother took you and moved in with her parents for several months. They never stopped loving each other, but Alma was unable to understand why your father took such a chance."

"I'm lucky to be alive."

"Yes. If anything had happened to you, it would have destroyed them. You were dearly loved by your parents."

"Loved by my parents." He felt compelled to add, but not by you, but he didn't.

"I was so relieved you were unscathed. You were so cute and innocent then."

"Aunt Laura, you enlightened me today. This truth may help me cope with my phobia. Thank you."

Daniel was shocked by the news and needed to be alone to sort out all that his aunt had divulged, from her dislike of him as a child to the incident with the shark. He swallowed the last of the pineapple soda.

"And thanks for the drink. I really have to go now."

"Daniel, I would like you to come back and have dinner with me before you leave."

He looked into her deep-set eyes and lined face. "Are you sure?"

"I'm sure. Try to let me know a day or two before so I can prepare a savory meal for you."

As he rose she embraced him.

"I realize you've been through a lot. I am proud of how you have matured. My opinion of you has truly changed for the better."

"I'm glad."

Instead of riding a city bus back to his hovel, Daniel walked the Malecón. Deep in thought he passed by the coast guard station, forgetting to stay vigilant in the presence of military. He longed to sort out his thoughts and to review the details of the fishing trip. There was a reason for years of fearing the ocean and for his frightful dreams. There was justification for his embarrassment as he stayed on the beach, even when coaxed by family or friends to swim. Daniel preferred the hot sand to a dip in the cooling water and cringed when they dove into the ocean without hesitation.

Understanding his phobia brought relief, but he still questioned why his parents kept such a critical secret from him. As witnesses to his nightmares, wouldn't they have realized that knowledge of the fishing trip and his plunge into the sea would have been therapeutic to him? A shark almost crushed and devoured him. He was baffled that such a crucial subject never surfaced in conversations with his parents.

His feet pounded the sidewalk. Daniel questioned his purpose in life. According to his aunt, he was a spoiled kid in trouble all the time, but now, as an adult, his behavior had improved. What had improved?

He was a married man and still in trouble. Imprisoned, a fugitive on the run, and soon to be an illegal immigrant forced to leave his country and his life behind. What in God's name was he doing? Daniel didn't blame his aunt for disliking him and was grateful she'd told him about the fishing trip. Her comment about disliking him hurt, but for her, verbalizing the truth was necessary and a consolation. From his perspective he was probably dealt everything he deserved. Was it karma? Or payback time for being a brat?

For a short distance, he sprinted along the promenade. Then he sat on the seawall and raised his knees to cushion his forehead. Daniel remembered assuming the same position, enclosed twenty feet below, inside a stack of boxes in the warehouse, another low point in his life. He gazed at the ocean he had always feared and focused on the horizon where sky met water at the Straits of Florida.

Chapter Twenty-Four
THE CHICKEN ESCAPADES

Several days had passed since Daniel visited his aunt. He lost his appetite and lay on his mattress. He knew this time his dark mood would be short-lived. Bolero would soon cheer him up and force him to leave the coop. Daniel sat at the edge of the mattress and reached for his wallet in the pocket of the pants he'd worn yesterday, which were lying in a heap on the floor. During this recent isolation in the coop, thoughts of Juliana lingered on his mind.

He opened his wallet to view her picture as he did every day. In the photo she posed with a hibiscus in her hair. He had picked the flower in a café courtyard and tucked the stem behind her ear so the pink blossom grazed her temple. How beautifully the bloom accentuated her eyes. That day in June he'd stepped back and snapped her picture as she gently smiled at him. It was his favorite photograph of Juli.

Before departing on that fateful last morning in Ranchuelo, Daniel had slipped an enlargement of the photo of Juli and a portrait of his parents taken on their wedding day into his backpack. He'd also tossed in a couple of snapshots of Juli and him clowning around the pool at the waterfall.

Since his departure he had received several letters from Juliana and his mother. Rafael always added a short message at the bottom of the last page of Juli's correspondence. Daniel knew Rafa despised writing and was amazed he wrote even a few words.

Sheer joy brightened Daniel's face when he heard from them, and he always answered immediately.

The Soldiers of the Cross made it possible for him to communicate with his family. His first letters were sent from Guillermo Santos's address and mailed as if written by Guillermo or Matilde. Subsequent letters were sent with the return addresses of other members' homes. In this manner Daniel safely stayed in touch with his family. Any other way would have been too risky. The government allowed the religious group a certain freedom denied anyone else since they helped wayward citizens. For this the authorities refrained from tampering with their incoming or outgoing mail.

Daniel kept Juli's letters hidden beneath his mattress and read them over and over again. His eyes glided from word to word. He admired her graceful, whimsical handwriting. Her script reflected the essence of her being. Words flowed across the page as he imagined Juliana, the ballerina, leaping across a stage.

Daniel remembered the tiny picture of the two of them dancing tucked inside the locket he had given her. His photo was in his wallet. He peered at the picture and was embittered by the thought of the gold heart torn from her neck on the night he was imprisoned and shuddered to think a soldier's fingernails had ripped her delicate skin. He closed the wallet with a snap, rose, and shoved it in his back pocket.

Daniel dressed and walked to the front yard. The Soraya house seemed empty. He knew Isabel's children were at school. Isabel and her mother were probably at Café Estrella, where Maria Soraya worked and her daughter filled in as a waitress. His eyes followed the steps of the ladder leaning against the house, stretching to the window frame of Isabel's room. The window was closed.

Loneliness overwhelmed him. When this happened he feared sinking into despair as had happened after his release from prison. He thought about visiting Guillermo and Matilde, but they were also at work. If not today, Daniel would have to visit them soon. It had been weeks since he had stopped by their home.

He looked away from the ladder and out to the street when he heard a loud engine and saw a truck bumping on the pavement. He was about to round the corner and return to the backyard to relax under a tree and plan his day when the truck veered across the lawn and careened toward him. Daniel dove under bushes at the base of the ladder.

While sprawled on the ground, he looked up and recognized the driver, Ernesto, one of Antonio's fishing crew, and Bolero in the passenger's seat roared with laughter. Daniel cursed them as Bolero hopped out of the cab, offered his friend a hand, and pulled him off the ground. Daniel wiped off the dirt and grass that clung to his pants and touched his back pocket to assure his wallet rested inside. He continued to swear. "You reckless shits, you could have killed me."

Bolero moved both hands in unison up and down in the air to quiet Daniel's vulgar mouth. "Daniel, shut up and listen. Ernesto stole this truck a few miles from the market after he and Ignacio delivered fish they caught last night. The truck driver left it running while he pissed on the side of the road. Ernesto jumped in and drove off. It's full of chickens."

Daniel had heard the commotion of the birds before Bolero mentioned them.

"I can see, hear, and smell they're chickens," Daniel blurted, still angry they had almost run him over. "What in the hell are you going to do with stolen chickens?"

"We have to do something fast. They're from the government-owned farm outside Havana."

"The PNRs are probably on your tail right now." Daniel's instinct was to run from this volatile situation. He looked down the street for military vehicles and turned toward the coop to get his belongings and leave. There was no way he would chance going back to prison over stolen birds.

"The driver of this truck would have to walk miles to place a call to the police, but still we don't have much time," Bolero said as he watched Daniel round the house. "Daniel, come back. Chickens could generate the bucks you need. If we sell them, think of all the cash. That's why I got involved. For you. You want more money, don't you?"

Daniel stopped in his tracks when he heard the words "more money."

When Bolero realized he'd gotten Daniel's attention he added, "We have to do something fast. Unload the chickens, hide them, and abandon this truck out on the highway."

"Unload? Unload where?" Daniel said as he peeked around the corner at the shed. "If the coop were bigger it would be ideal." Daniel saw Bolero glance at the house and said in a loud voice, "Not there. We can't."

"Is anyone home?" asked the fisherman.

"I don't think so."

"Well, then let's put the birds inside."

"Impossible. My landlady will kill me."

"Remember," said Bolero, "you can live at Antonio's house on the river."

Daniel started to say, "The chickens will destroy the..." But stopped midsentence. "Who cares? Let's go."

He joined Bolero and Ernesto and hauled the crates of four white hens each, off the truck. As he carried a crate across the lawn, Daniel plotted on how to pick the lock of the Soraya house. He reached the front door and tested the doorknob, and to his surprise the door opened. Bolero dragged two crates along the grass to the doorway, where he swung open the gates. The fowl ran into the house and fluttered around the living room. Daniel raced to close the dining room and closet doors to contain the birds within one room.

While the chickens huddled in a corner, the three men moved the furniture out of the living room and stored it in the dining and kitchen areas. Daniel worried the birds would damage the curtains and raised them by tucking the ends into the curtain rod stretched across the top frame of the window. He rolled up the area rug, heaved it on his shoulders, and dropped it next to the dining room table.

Bolero and Ernesto released more crates of brooders into the house. The poultry squawked and flew, and plumage drifted like large snowflakes in the air. Crates emptied, and the room became a mass of panicked, white-feathered bodies with bobbing heads and pecking beaks.

A large hen rose above the flock, scratching and digging into the wall as she climbed. Others flapped their wings and mimicked her behavior. Daniel hoped the ascending birds would refrain from reaching and shattering the window. As he watched them scramble upward, he remembered the small flock of hens and chicks and the bold rooster in his backyard in Ranchuelo. He had felt at peace watching his mother's brood forage in the grass. The frenzy, chaos, and clucking noises here made him nervous.

Daniel cringed when a group of birds stepped aside and smeared feces across the floor. He decided to sneak out and seek the solitude and quiet of his dwelling. While Ernesto and Bolero gawked at the sight of three hundred chickens in Maria's living room, Daniel eased toward the entry. The two men, mesmerized by the muddle before them, pivoted at the same time when the front door flung open with a swish and four chickens scurried out onto the lawn. Daniel froze before reaching the door. They heard a shriek, and Isabel appeared in the doorway, stunned, with her mouth wide open. She glowered at the three men and screamed when flustered chickens brushed her bare legs.

"What's going on here? Oh my God, no. My mother's house. How could you?"

It now made sense to Daniel why Maria Soraya had left the front door unlocked. Isabel was home, in her room. He tried to calm her down. "I can explain," he said as Bolero and Ernesto chased the four escapees around the yard.

"How? How can you possibly explain this mess?"

As Daniel approached her, she pouted and thrust out her chest. He sensed sexual tension along with her rage. She wrapped her arms around his waist and cried. He raised his arms and then patted her back.

"I will pay your mother for this. It will only be for a few days. I promise."

Isabel buried her face deep in his chest and mumbled, "No one gave you permission."

"I know. The truck broke down," Daniel lied and used the truck as a legitimate excuse for their bizarre use of the living room. "We had no choice. The chickens would have died in the sun."

Bolero gazed at the woman snuggled up to Daniel as he carried two hens by their feet and released the birds into the flock.

"*Verdad*, Bolero? We had to put the birds inside. Or they would have died."

Bolero looked away from the birds and at Daniel with a questioning expression.

With his head, Daniel motioned for Bolero to come over. Bolero lifted Isabel's head off Daniel's chest, looked into her eyes and said, "That's right. We would have lost the whole flock. In a society where people are starving, would you want this to happen?"

Isabel wiped her eyes and shook her head but soon regained her senses at the sight of white birds overrunning her mother's parlor and erupted into anger.

"You'd better pay my mother and clean up this house. I'm not the one who's going to tell her about this. You'll have to. It was your bright idea, Daniel." She reeled and marched out. "I can't stand this stinking mess."

Isabel stepped onto the ladder and shook the structure as she stomped up to the window of her room. At the top she straddled the windowsill and yelled down to Daniel, "You'll be lucky if she lets you live in that coop anymore."

Daniel peeked out the door and smiled as Isabel glared at him and waited for his next move. He pushed Bolero toward the truck. "Raise the hood and act like you're fixing something."

"The hood doesn't stay up."

Daniel unlatched the hood and raised it. "Hold it up. I'll pretend to repair the fucking engine."

"It can't take long. We have to get rid of this truck. If the PNRs catch us we'll…"

Daniel finished Bolero's sentence, "All go to prison. To hell with the truck. Get it the fuck out of here."

Ernesto started the engine. Bolero heaved himself into the cab with such energy he bounced several times on the passenger's seat. Daniel slammed the hood and vaulted away from the cumbersome vehicle. All four tires sliced the grass into clumps of sod as they sped across the lawn and headed out of town. From her perch on the windowsill, Isabel called down to Daniel. "I thought the truck broke down."

"It did. I fixed it."

"What do you know about mechanics?"

"I had a friend who owned a body shop."

Daniel faced his landlady in Café Estrella. He stood at the counter and watched Maria multitask. She flipped a Swiss cheese sandwich on the grill, wiped the counter after a heavyset customer waddled to the restroom, and set a pitcher of milk in the cooler. Daniel searched for the right words to break the news to Maria Soraya about the chickens. How do you tell a woman, meticulous in every way, that her living room had been converted into a chicken coop? From the moment he met her, he had labeled Maria as a clean freak. In that way she reminded him of his mother.

If not working in the restaurant, Maria immersed herself in housework or locked herself in the bathroom and soaked in the tub for hours. From a downstairs window of her house one morning, Daniel watched her dust, mop, pick up papers, and throw out the trash. She never stopped. On the other hand, her daughter hibernated in her treetop sanctuary, reading novels and accomplishing very little beside minimal care of her kids and part-time work at Café Estrella.

Maria Soraya ceased wiping the counter as if she remembered something, looked up, and screeched when she saw him. "Daniel, I didn't expect you. Can I get you lunch? Is something wrong?"

"Not really. Can I speak to you over there?"

He pointed to an empty table by a mirror on the wall. He chose an isolated table with no customers seated near it.

"Why, sure. Would you like a drink?"

"No thank you. I'm not thirsty."

"You're never this serious. What's wrong? Is it Isabel or the children?"

"No. They're fine."

Daniel pulled the chair out, allowing her to sit down, and sat on the opposite side of the table. With his feet he eased his chair back, for he was unsure of Maria's reaction to the news he was about to tell her. Would she lash out at him, scream, or have a heart attack? He had no idea what to expect.

"Well, what is it? Tell me, Daniel."

"I promise I will pay you for this."

"Pay me? For what? Something broke?"

"You see, we had a truckload of chickens and nowhere to put them. They would have died in the truck in the heat so…"

"So? What? What did you do with them?"

"Well, that's what I came here to tell you." He stretched and pushed the chair further from the table. "They're in your house."

"In my house?'

"Only in the living room."

"In my living room? As if that was fine. Are you crazy?"

"It will only be for a few days."

"A few days? Chickens? How many?"

"A few hundred."

"A few hundred?"

"Three. Three hundred."

"*Tres-cientos*? Why didn't you put one thousand in there? What would be the difference?" Her voice rose to a high pitch, and the customers at a table by the window glanced over at them. She stood. "How could you?" Maria sounded just like Isabel. "I have to go home."

"Mrs. Soraya, I think it's best if you bypass the living room. Just a suggestion," Daniel said timidly. "Everything's fine, and what isn't I will pay you for. I'll pay you anyway for the use of your living room. I promise. We'll clean everything. In three days you won't know it was filled with chickens. Take my word for this."

She eyed him suspiciously. "Who is we?"

"My two friends will help me. Please relax. Finish your work here. In a few days your home will be normal again."

She sat back down. "You were such a good tenant until now. Did living in that pigeon coop affect your brain, child?"

Daniel smiled a smile of relief. "My brain has been traumatized, but I doubt the coop affected it in any way."

Isabel stayed protectively close to her mother and escorted her into the house for the first time since chickens occupied her living room. Music blasted on the radio in the kitchen. Her mother reached for the knob to lower the volume.

"Stop worrying I'll have a heart attack. I know the living room is full of birds. Do you think loud music will hide the noise of a hen house? Daniel said he will pay me well. It will be an inconvenience for a few days."

Maria Soraya set her purse on the counter, shuffled around a living room chair to open the refrigerator, and removed a package of meat and a sack of vegetables from a drawer to prepare dinner. Isabel sat in the chair and watched her mother peel a carrot. She was surprised at her mother's serenity knowing her living room had substituted for a chicken coop. Behind the closed dining room door clucking, dying, and defecating chickens crowded the most formal room of Maria's house.

Before leaving Isabel said, "Anyway, it's best you stay away from that room."

Mother and daughter were unaware that Daniel listened to them from an opened kitchen window and strained to see them from the car seat in the backyard. He detected no unusual behavior between the two. It was imperative to keep the Soraya household peaceful because that would assure the safety of their precious chickens. In turn, chicken sales would generate a profit and complete the first phase of his scheme to raise money to depart Cuba.

The following morning, as soon as the family left home, Daniel, Bolero, and Ernesto began the slaughter. In the yard three axes leaned against three blocks of wood, and pails to catch blood lay strewn on the lawn. Daniel's stomach felt queasy thinking about his job as a butcher for the next two days. He remembered how traumatic it was to kill the pig, but in this case a large sum of cash was the end result, whereas the pork was only the protein portion of a wedding feast, the portion uneaten by Daniel. He would probably refrain from eating chicken for a while too.

Bolero constructed a small pen out of thin boards and chicken wire he stole from a farm near his former residence. As Daniel grabbed a hen by her neck and carried her squawking toward the chopping block, he said, "You tore down a farmer's pen to house these birds for a few hours?"

"Not a few hours." Bolero herded a flock in the direction of Ernesto, caught one, and held it in his arms. "What did you want me to do? This helps a lot. Or we would have to run back and forth into the living room to catch hens one at a time. Does that make sense?"

"One at a time, no. We could have taken the mattress out of my coop and put more in there than we can keep here."

"Now you tell me."

"You never asked."

Bolero gave him a dirty look and held the hen's neck on the block. "I'll get the pen back to the farmer."

All three men lifted their axes and swung at the same time. In one swoop metal severed skin, bones, flesh, and wood. Blood splattered, and the three headless bodies ran in circles, crashed into each other, and fell together in a pile of white feathers.

"Oh no," shouted Daniel. "Did you see that? You've got to be joking. Is this what I have to watch at every killing?" He thought about his nightmares in prison. Beside sea monsters he'd dreamed of dying, bleeding, squealing pigs. Would chickens haunt his nightmares now?

The three young men stared at each other with mouths agape. Bolero looked at the dead birds in a heap and muttered, "I think that was a fluke."

They moved their cutting blocks farther apart and continued the killings. Each death was unique, but never did three deceased birds run headless or bump into each other again.

They took a beer break. Daniel took a *siesta* on the mattress in the coop while Bolero and the fisherman plucked feathers, filled a cooler with carcasses, and sold whole chickens in the Miramar section of Havana. Many residents there were foreigners and were pleased to purchase fresh meat.

Daniel awoke and toiled on with butchering. The two returned with their pockets full of pesos and gave Daniel his cut. They handed him some bills to cover for the use of Maria Soraya's premises and joined in on the slaughter. As they labored, fewer birds occupied the living room. It became more difficult to catch the remaining ones.

Before the Soraya family returned home, the three assassins cleaned up all traces of the slayings. They wrapped whole chickens in newspaper and stuffed them in Maria's refrigerator and in coolers full of ice stored in the dining room. At the end of the day, one hundred and four live fowl paced the living room. The friends were tired and decided to end the remaining birds' lives the following morning.

While Daniel tossed seeds on the tile floor to nourish and quiet the birds, Bolero and Ernesto sat at the dining room table and watched Daniel through the half-closed door. Bolero folded his arms on the table and rested his head on his arms. In a muffled voice he said, "I can't chop one more head, look at more spilled blood, or pluck one more feather. I hate the smell of raw chicken."

After a final cleanup and securing the door to the house, they retreated to the pigeon coop, hung out, and showered individually under the hose.

"Hurry up before Isabel comes home," Daniel joked. "She'll have a field day watching three of us from her window."

Bolero called to the naked fisherman as water splashed his cinnamon-colored body, "Ernesto, let Daniel go last. Maybe Isabel will arrive by then and get her usual thrill."

"Very funny," Daniel said as he kicked Bolero with his bare foot. "You're the one who likes the idea of her peeking from the window. You go last. You wanted to meet her. Anyway, she won't be home for at least an hour. Maybe longer if the café's busy."

After showering they reclined on the mattress for a while and heard voices and the back door slam.

"Sounds like they're home," said Bolero. "Everything's clean, including us. They can't complain. Shall we meet up with the boys at the house on the river?"

"That sounds fine, but I'm exhausted. I'm not staying out late," Daniel said as he yawned.

"We'll bullshit. Have a few beers. It'll be an early night," admitted Bolero.

"Tomorrow I have to go fishing early," said Ernesto.

Bolero wrapped an arm around Daniel's neck. "Tomorrow you and I can handle the rest of the chickens. Right, *amigo*?"

"Killing chickens has become as normal as taking a shower. Not that I like it," said Daniel as he removed Bolero's arm from his neck.

"I hate it. I can't wait till it's over."

The three joined Antonio and four other fishermen on the roof. They met Antonio's brother and girlfriend, who kept to themselves at the table. Antonio carried beer on ice in a pail and set it on the table for the three newcomers, and they kicked back in chairs and lounges, facing each other.

Daniel listened as the fishermen spoke of a recent catch, the abundant schools of fish swimming in the Straits of Florida, and how they were unable to store the massive haul on Antonio's boat. Reluctantly they had to throw half the catch back into the sea.

Daniel's mind flashed to Maria Soraya's living room and the chickens scurrying around. He imagined the room air tight, sealed like an aquarium and fish swimming with mouths opening and closing and bug eyes staring out windows. Maria would have a heart attack for sure if her living room were stocked full of fish. At the thought he chuckled and watched the current of the river carry cans entangled in seaweed along as a pleasure boat buzzed past. Fish would be more lucrative than chickens. Why not purchase fish from Antonio and have Bolero sell the fresh catch?

"Who do you sell fish to?" Daniel asked Antonio.

"Markets, sometimes individuals. Why?"

"I was thinking after selling the chickens I'd like to buy fish. Bolero and I could go door to door and sell fish like we did chicken. Buying your catch would save you from having to deliver the fish. We'd take it right off your boat and pay you on the spot."

"Sounds like a good idea, but we can't short the markets. They've been our customers for years. We're thinking of buying another boat to haul more fish ashore."

"Now you're talking. Maybe something can be worked out in that respect too."

Daniel had thought of buying a boat to leave Cuba in. It would save Bolero and him money if Antonio ferried them to America. Bolero and Daniel, in turn, would let Antonio keep the boat. This would cost less than paying a runner to take them to the US. Daniel was anxious to mention his idea but cautioned against prematurely divulging his plan. First, he would have to discuss buying a boat with Bolero.

"It's something to consider," Daniel said as he winked at Bolero. "We'll keep each other up on any business deals, *de acuerdo*?" Daniel raised his bottle of beer, and it clinked against their bottles.

"*De acuerdo*," they all repeated so loudly passengers on a sailboat looked over at them and waved. The group on the tin roof waved back and shouted to the sailors.

Bolero changed the subject and told Antonio he would move in to the river house next week. "Would you mind if Daniel moved in my room too? He'll sleep in a sleeping bag for the time being."

Bolero looked over at Daniel and smiled a devious smile. "He's sleeping in a chicken coop behind a house on Oviedo Street. He wants out of there as soon as possible."

Daniel corrected him. "Pigeon coop."

"I forgot, pigeon coop. The chicken coop's in the living room."

Daniel smirked at the confused looks on some of the fishermen's faces. "It's a long story."

"It sure is," Bolero said as he gulped beer and barely swallowed before he burst out laughing.

"Ernesto told me," said Antonio. "I can't believe that lady let you put chickens in her house."

"Surprisingly she did," said Daniel.

"I bet you didn't know her daughter watches Daniel from a window while he showers under a garden hose," said Bolero.

Daniel rolled his eyes and chugged the golden liquid. "Here we go again."

"What kind of a place do you live in, Daniel?" said Antonio.

"Very unique."

They all roared in laughter and bombarded Daniel with questions. In the distance they heard the sailboat answer in cheers.

Antonio stopped laughing. "You can move in too. It sounds like you need to get out of that place or move in with the girl in the window."

Daniel mumbled, "I'm married. She's married. You're right. I need a more normal environment."

Bolero answered, "What's normal for you, *amigo*?"

Daniel shook his head and finished the last swallow of beer. "I can honestly say I don't know what normal is."

Antonio saw a forlorn look cross Daniel's face and ended the teasing. "Don't worry about a mattress. I have an extra bed I'll put in the room. Both of you can split the rent."

"Sounds great. Thanks, Antonio," said Bolero. "What do you say, Daniel?"

"Fine. I probably won't move in for a few weeks," he answered while Antonio stood in the kitchen door to fill the pail up with more beer and ice. Daniel thought it best to give his landlady a two-week notice since she had been so tolerant despite the zany request to abandon her living room to three hundred chickens.

"Two weeks will be enough notice. It's not as if I'm paying a huge amount in rent." He smiled a weak, tired smile. "I'll have one more beer. Then I've really got to go. I'm beat."

Daniel found himself in the center of his landlady's living room with headless hens cackling from their necks and bumping into his legs. One flew past him, and another grazed his face with a wing while in flight. Feathers drifted and swirled on him like snow from an avalanche. A white feather landed in his mouth. He pulled it out and batted at feathers bombarding him. He heard giggling. Daniel opened his eyes to Bolero standing above and tossing pesos on top of him. Bolero shook the last of the money out of a plastic bag.

"Wake up, sleeping beauty."

"You asshole. I was dreaming feathers were falling on me." Daniel sat up, rubbed his eyes, and gathered his thoughts as he entered into the reality of the moment. He scooped up the cash on his bed and counted the money.

"Not feathers. Cold, hard cash. Most of the chickens are sold."

"How many are left? I want to give some to Maria Soraya and four to the Soldiers of the Cross for being so good to me." Daniel put Ernesto's cut aside and handed Bolero half the pile of money before him. "Great job, *amigo*. You're the best salesman I know."

"There's still more than a dozen in the refrigerator."

"That's plenty. I've got to get up and start cleaning the living room. It's disgusting. Will you help me?"

"Sure. I'll borrow a floor cleaner and buffer from my friend in the cleaning business. The job will go faster. The tile will really shine."

"Perfect. I'll pick up some paint. I know we won't be able to scrub out the deep scratches in the walls. It should take all of today, maybe tomorrow. We'll give the living room back to Mrs. Soraya, spotless and freshly painted. A little of this, and she'll be happy." Daniel shook the pesos in his hand. "Very happy."

Just before Daniel turned the living room over to his landlady and Isabel, he saw worried expressions on their faces. Thank God she never saw the room at the height of the chicken infestation.

Maria Soraya was stunned and ecstatic when she peered inside. The walls and floor looked new. She liked the way Daniel had divided the room into two sections. He had rearranged the sofa and loveseat into a conversational area and created a separate reading nook with a table, two chairs, and a bookshelf beside them. She also thanked Daniel and Bolero for the cash.

That evening Daniel and Bolero carried a cooler with the four remaining chickens to Guillermo's house. Matilde answered the door. She was pleased to see Daniel and his friend and eagerly accepted the chickens.

"I'll roast them for the members' dinner this evening." She gave them each a peck on the cheek. "That was very kind of you."

"It was the least I could do after all your help."

"Why don't both of you come for dinner? Daniel, it's been a long time since we've seen you. Come at seven."

Daniel glanced at Bolero. "Sounds fine to me, and you?"

He knew Bolero was incapable of turning down a home-cooked meal.

Daniel and Bolero walked back to the coop after spending the afternoon on Antonio's roof chatting with the fishermen.

Daniel changed into clean clothes and splashed some cologne on his neck.

"You know, Bolero, the Soldiers of the Cross are wonderful people, but they have some strange ceremonies. Don't be surprised."

"What strange ceremonies?"

"It's difficult to describe. You'll see."

"It doesn't matter. I'm starving. I haven't had a home-cooked meal in ages."

The two young men were greeted at the door by Guillermo, who welcomed them, as did Matilde and the other members present. They sat down in the last row of chairs and politely listened to Guillermo's lecture. Daniel knew it would be a few hours before everyone sat down to dinner. He chuckled at the thought of Bolero's astonishment at the lengthy lectures and bizarre rituals of the Soldiers of the Cross before dinner would be consumed.

Out of the corner of his eye, Daniel saw Bolero shift in his seat. He crossed and uncrossed his legs and stretched one leg in the aisle. His legs were too long to stretch them forward. Daniel had learned patience while in the company of his religious friends. They had also stressed to him the importance of sharing and kindness toward others as essential deeds members practiced daily.

Daniel noticed two new recruits seated two rows ahead and assumed they were related. They were in their forties and looked like brother and sister. When Matilde and the other female members left the seating arrangement to pray directly to God, Daniel turned to face Bolero for a close look at his reaction to their religious exuberance. From Matilde's mouth blurted the ancient dialect, and the other women also garbled an incoherent language. Bolero's eyes bulged as female members threw themselves to the floor and flopped around as if in the midst of seizures.

Bolero stood and whispered to Daniel, "This is crazy. What's going on? I'm getting out of here."

Daniel expected Bolero to be shocked but never thought he would walk out, especially since food would follow the liturgy. The hosts would be insulted if Bolero left.

"Sit down. You can't leave. Once this is over, we'll have dinner. Respect what they believe."

"How do I respect something I don't understand?"

"Trust in their faith. That's all."

"This is weird." He bent down behind the chairs and headed out of the room.

Daniel grabbed him. The women resumed in a hypnotic state, but audience members turned around.

"Sit down. You're not leaving." Daniel pulled his friend and forced him back to his seat.

Bolero pushed Daniel's hands aside, sat with his arms crossed, and purposely elbowed him. Daniel ignored the gesture.

"What language are they speaking?"

"Those words aren't spoken anymore. It's an ancient tongue. Be quiet."

For the remainder of the ceremony, Bolero stared at the back of the woman in front of him. Her hair was braided and twisted on her head. The women who mumbled the strange language and stared with dead eyes made him uneasy. Bolero was unable to watch their unusual actions.

Daniel heard Bolero's stomach growl and nudged him.

"I can't help the fact that I'm starving."

"Shut up."

When they all gathered around the table and dinner was served, Bolero admitted to Daniel that the meal was worth the wait. While Bolero ate two bowls of rice pudding for dessert, Daniel chatted with Matilde in the kitchen. He admitted to her that he was able to cope better in his new surroundings and was more comfortable in Havana than when he first arrived. His new friend had introduced him to other friends. Daniel explained that he and Juliana corresponded frequently through letters thanks to her and Guillermo and the use of their address. He also told Matilde that he had found work and was preparing to depart Cuba before the year's end. Repeatedly he thanked her for her advice, kindness, and patience with him.

After Daniel and Bolero said good-bye to the members and Santos family and while walking through the backyards to the shed, Bolero asked why Daniel had spoken to Matilde for so long. Daniel explained that she was the one who had consoled and counseled him when he first arrived in Havana. As a result of her advice, his sanity was preserved. "I owe her and Guillermo more than I can afford."

Outside the coop they discussed meeting at the roof the following day, and Bolero expressed his satisfaction with the meal and with meeting such kind people despite their strange rites. Bolero headed for the house on the river. Daniel opened the door to the coop. As he lowered his head to clear the entry, the sensation of someone else present seized him.

Chapter Twenty-Five
THE SURPRISE VISIT

Daniel flicked on the light, and on his mattress Isabel snuggled in the sleeping bag. She smiled slyly. "I've wanted you for a long time. You never paid attention to my advances. Now I'll make it obvious. Daniel, come lie with me."

"Don't do this, Isabel. You're married. I'm married. I can't."

He bent down and backed out of the coop. Outside the shed he stood erect before the doorway and faced the yard. "Go to your room with your kids. We'll forget this ever happened."

"They're with their father."

"He's here? More reason to leave. If he finds us together he'll kill me."

"Stop being paranoid. They went to Varadero Beach for a long weekend and won't be back until Monday. We have plenty of time."

Isabel clutched the covers to her body. Her clothes lay at Daniel's feet by the door. She rose on her knees loosely holding the sheet. She reached for Daniel's hand gripping the doorframe and allowed the bedding to slip and expose a breast to allure him.

"Don't," he warned her in a tone more to convince himself.

"You want this as much as I do."

"No."

"When were you last with your wife? It has to be several months now."

Isabel moved forward on her knees, and the sheet entangled around her waist. She stepped off the mattress, wrapped both hands around his neck, and pulled him to her. She sealed her lips to his. Daniel kissed back and fell with her onto the mattress. He yanked the sheet and groped for her breast. She reached for his pants zipper. Daniel pushed her hand away, rolled off the mattress, and threw the sheet back on Isabel, covering her voluptuous body.

"I love my wife. Get out. Go."

He wiped his mouth of her fruity lipstick and walked outside to wait on the car seat until she dressed. She buttoned her blouse as she exited the coop. From the darkness of the yard he said, "I'm hopeful my life with Juli will continue. I want her to join me. A fling may ruin that dream."

Isabel buttoned the last button. "Keep your hopes up high, Daniel. Maybe she doesn't love you as intensely."

He paused. "That remains to be seen." He was sure Isabel had no idea how those words stung the core of his being. He despised her for saying what she did.

She approached him, sat on his lap, and pinched his cheek. "You're a man. You are weak." As she rose she rubbed her buttocks across his legs. Daniel pushed her. Isabel flashed him a dirty look, sashayed to the front of the house, and ascended the ladder to her room. He heard her high heels pound the rungs and the top of the ladder bump against the window frame as she climbed.

Daniel stayed in the car seat for fifteen minutes. He refrained from taking a full shower that night but gave his body a rigorous sponge bath in his swim trunks. While cleansing he imagined Isabel staring down at him but never looked up at the window to confirm his suspicion. Daniel made up his mind to leave this house. He would tell his landlady in the morning.

The day after Isabel's attempted seduction, Daniel washed his clothes in a bucket and hung them out to dry on a clothesline strung from the backdoor to a tree in the yard. He secured a pair of pants to the line by clasping each pant leg with a clothespin. He heard a vehicle pull up in the driveway and Bolero's voice calling him. He wondered what his friend was up to now. His voice had an air of urgency to it.

Daniel dropped the remaining clothespins on wet clothes in a plastic basket as he passed it and strode to the front of the house. The ladder lay on the ground next to the house hidden by shrubbery, a sign Isabel was out of her room and most likely at the restaurant with her mother. A gray SUV with patches on the hood where paint had worn away was parked in the driveway. Bolero opened the back and told Daniel to come see what he had. Daniel shook his head as he looked at stacks of cardboard boxes containing cartons of a dozen eggs.

"Don't tell me you stole these. I told you I won't get involved with stolen goods anymore. It's too risky."

"Calm down. I didn't steal them. I bought them. I thought we could sell eggs before going into business with Antonio. But you have to help me deliver them this time and pay me half the price of these boxes. We'll split the profit. What do you say, *amigo*?"

Bolero opened a box so Daniel could see the eggs.

"I borrowed my cousin's SUV. We can use it to sell them in rich neighborhoods. This time I have a truck, and we won't have to lug coolers up and down streets. I have it till noon."

Daniel stepped away from the vehicle. "They're not stolen?"

"No."

"Fantastic. Let's go."

"We'll sell half today and the rest tomorrow. With two of us we'll finish long before noon."

"Fine. We'll put half in the refrigerator. Maria won't mind. I'll give her a dozen to make her happy."

Daniel bent over to reach inside, and as he slid a box toward him to lift it out, Bolero said, "Why didn't you fuck her?"

Daniel froze with both hands on the side of a box staring at white eggs peeking through cardboard. "Excuse me? What did you say?"

"You should have screwed her."

"Screwed who?"

"You know." Bolero pointed to the window of the new addition to the house. "Your landlady's daughter, Isabel."

"I know who you mean. I just can't believe you asked what you did. How did you know what went on in the coop last night? I never told you."

"When I said good night to you, I was about to walk to the street. I heard a woman's voice coming from inside. I decided to see who it was."

"You mean you spied on me?" Daniel stared at his friend in disbelief. "You're sick."

"I was just curious. I left after you went outside and sat in the chair. When she sat on your lap, I left."

"Wasn't that kind of you. You left when nothing happened. Would you have stayed if there had been action in the coop? You pervert. I don't have to explain my private business to you."

"Why not? I'm your friend. Obviously you love your wife very much."

"Or I detest the landlady's daughter. It's none of your business. Don't ever spy on me again."

Daniel carried the box to the house, unlocked the door with a key he had from when the chickens were in the living room, and took the eggs inside. Bolero saw his friend's face red with anger. He carried two boxes and sheepishly followed Daniel into the kitchen.

"I don't know why you're so mad. No harm was done." Bolero reached in a box and handed the cartons to Daniel, who put them on the bottom shelf of the refrigerator. "You didn't have sex with her."

"You had the nerve to…forget it. You're right. No harm was done." Daniel slammed the refrigerator door, and the old model Frigidaire shook. Jars and bottles rattled inside.

"Let's sell eggs. Yes, I adore my wife very much, you sneaky bastard."

Bolero started the SUV, shifted, and it lurched forward. He laughed. Daniel braced his hands against the dashboard and gazed out the windshield.

"Careful with the eggs."

When they reached El Vedado neighborhood, Bolero parked in the street along the sidewalk. They alternated houses as they sold door to door. When Bolero passed Daniel, who headed for the truck to pick up more cartons, Bolero peered at him square in the eye and turned his head sideways with a big smile to get a reaction. Daniel ignored him, remaining silent and in a serious mood, intent only on selling eggs to make quick cash.

There were a few refusals, but by eleven o'clock they'd sold all but one box Daniel held. He headed for a house on the corner barely visible behind a high hedge when Bolero laughed and danced past. Daniel opened the box and pelted half a dozen eggs at him. Bolero winced in pain and ducked behind the hedge. Daniel saw his red striped shirt flash as he slinked behind the hedgerow. He snuck up on Bolero and plastered him with more eggs. Bolero ran for the truck.

Daniel felt satisfaction to see him smeared in egg attached to broken shells that dripped down his shirt and slid to the ground. He crept behind the truck and through the open window cracked the last egg on Bolero's head as he sat in the driver's seat. Bolero lowered his head too late and yelled, "Enough! You already got me back." He scooped shell and yolk out of his hair and threw it out the window at Daniel.

"It's eleven fifteen. I've got to clean up the egg on me and the mess in here and get this truck back to my cousin. Are you satisfied now? Will you talk to me?"

"I've got the perfect place for you to shower. Maybe you'll get seduced in the coop and I'll spy on you." Daniel bolted to the passenger side and hopped into the truck. "Now we're even."

"You're paying for the last box of eggs."

"That's what you think. They're yours."

Selling eggs became lucrative for the two friends preparing for their parting day. They found handling eggs a delicate matter but were more pleased with this task than killing and selling chickens. The chicken sales gave them a huge financial gain, but they both agreed that one episode of stealing, hiding, and slaughtering chickens was enough.

They kept in contact with Antonio and met daily at his house on the river. Daniel and Bolero had postponed doing business with him until one evening, while they relaxed on the roof and sipped cocktails, Ernesto remarked, "I know an old fisherman who retired. He has a boat in dry dock and thought he would fix it and fish again. He got arthritis bad, and his wife is sick, so he put the boat up for sale. It needs a lot of work, but we know an experienced marine carpenter. Maybe you two would be interested in starting a fishing business."

"And I can't afford another boat yet," added Antonio.

Daniel's eyes widened. "Maybe. I mean, maybe we would be interested in buying the boat. What do you say, Bolero?" He looked over at Bolero, who munched on pork rinds.

"I say tell them our plan."

They looked from one to the other, and Antonio turned toward Daniel, questioning Bolero's statement.

"Why not?" said Daniel. He had spent long hours over the past month in conversation with Antonio and his friends and developed a deep camaraderie with them. Most of their conversations entailed fishing trips, women, or how much they despised Castro, his government, and the bleak economic state of Cuba. They all revealed in one way or another their reasons for hating the atrocious condition their country was in. Daniel allowed them to talk and listened intently. He hadn't mentioned it to his friend, but like Bolero, Daniel had become confident in the men on the roof. He believed they were trustworthy enough to divulge their secret plan to leave Cuba.

"Bolero and I are trying to make enough money to leave Havana. We don't need a business. We need a boat to carry us to the United States." Daniel moved his chair closer to the others. "I have to leave or I'll get thrown back in prison. Bolero wants out of here after two failed attempts at leaving. My idea—maybe it will interest you—is to purchase a boat and have you drop us off on American soil. After, keep the boat for your own use as payment."

"What about the US Coast Guard? They patrol all around Miami. They have radar and special planes to spot exiles," said Antonio.

"We'll end up in Miami, but I was thinking of landing near the Florida Keys, in a less populated area. I'll study it further. Maybe you have some suggestions."

"You know if you reach American soil they have the 'wet foot, dry foot' policy. You have to jump out of the boat and swim to shore. Once on land they can't force you to return to Cuba. If they take you into custody from the boat there's a strong possibility they'll send you back," said Ernesto.

"Though I heard that Cuban-Americans are vocal and fight to keep exiles in America," commented Daniel.

"They do, but the US government has gotten stricter about its immigration policy," said Antonio. "Too many rafters and small boats leave Cuba daily for the States."

"Like Bolero and I discussed many times, we have to plan this trip very carefully, said Daniel."

Bolero agreed.

"Do you want to look at the boat?" Ernesto said as he put his hand into the bag of pork rinds and popped one in his mouth.

"As soon as possible," said Daniel.

"I'll make the arrangements."

Several days later Daniel and Bolero were loading the cousin's SUV with boxes of eggs. "Go easy or they'll break," remarked Daniel as his friend roughly placed the last box on top of the others.

"I'm being careful. You're just picky."

"Not really. Who broke the most eggs so far?"

"You did when you threw a dozen at me and cracked some on my head."

"That doesn't count. You pissed me off. For the record I only cracked one on your head. You deserved it for being a pervert."

Daniel and Bolero both reached up at the same time to close the back of the vehicle when Daniel glanced at a slow-moving car coming down the street. Guillermo and the member of the Soldiers of the Cross who had given Daniel a ride into Havana, Pedro Jimenez, walked alongside the car as they talked to the driver. Daniel finally recalled Pedro's name. It popped into his head when he saw him next to Guillermo.

Guillermo pointed toward Daniel and Bolero, or were they pointing to the neighbor's house? Daniel's eyes followed the ladder up to the window of Isabel's room and scanned the house to see if Maria Soraya awaited visitors, but no one was around. Daniel walked up to Guillermo as the car turned into the driveway.

"There's someone here to see you," said Guillermo.

Daniel peered into the car and was shocked when he realized Rafael was in the driver's seat of an old Ford. "Oh my God," shouted Daniel as he rushed to open the car door before Rafa put the car in park. "I didn't recognize the car."

"I borrowed my uncle's. How are you?"

"I never thought I'd see you again." They embraced, and Daniel called Bolero over. "Meet Rafael, my good friend and brother-in-law. You've already met Guillermo and Pedro."

Suddenly the car shook and there was a pounding noise coming from the trunk. Car keys jingled in Rafael's hand as he ran to the back of the car. "I almost forgot. I brought you something." Rafa turned a silver key in the lock and raised the lid with exuberance as if opening a treasure chest. A girl with long hair concealing her face sat up.

"Why did you wait so long to let me out? It's hot in here."

"Juli?" Daniel rushed to the back of the car but hesitated before her. He reached out and touched her silky hair. The strands slid through his fingers as he combed the tresses away from her face. Her eyes blinked. When they opened they were a lustrous green, like jade in the bright sunlight. He was captivated. They embraced each other. Tears welled in his eyes as he lifted her out of the trunk and spun her around.

"You came too?" When he set Juliana down she faltered on her bad foot, and Daniel caught her in his arms. "Your foot."

"It's fine. Just numb from lying in the trunk."

Bolero crossed his arms, leaned against the truck, and watched the couple. The independent, boyish bachelor Bolero thought he knew clung to this ravishing young lady. Despite her foot giving out, she was dainty and reclined against Daniel for support. Standing side by side, Bolero deducted that they fit together like two links in a gold bracelet. Juliana leaned over and massaged her leg. Her hair flowed across her shoulders, and she looked at Daniel as he bent to rub her foot. Daniel's eyes followed her every movement. Bolero had never seen Daniel so infatuated and happy.

"She's your wife?"

"This is Juli, Bolero. Yes, she's my wife."

Demurely she rose, stepped forward, and outstretched a slim arm to shake his hand. She touched his cheeks with hers. "Very nice to meet you. I understand you and Daniel have become good friends. I'm glad for that."

Daniel introduced Juliana to Guillermo and Pedro, and the two left to join the other members at Guillermo's house. Rafael explained to Daniel that he only had Guillermo's address, the reason he stopped at the Santos' home first.

"I can't believe you're here. What a surprise."

"We had to be secretive and didn't want police to follow us or your freedom to be jeopardized in any way. Juli and I got in the car and headed for Havana after talking about how much we missed you."

"Your mother started out in the trunk with me, but the fumes made her nauseous," Juli said as she slipped her arm around Daniel's.

"After a few miles in the trunk she signaled me by tapping. She got in the back seat, and I turned the car around and drove her home," said Rafael.

"Alma so wanted to see you." Juli gave him a peck on the cheek.

"How is she doing?"

"She was fine before riding in the trunk and sends her love."

Daniel beamed as his eyes fixated on Juli and Rafael standing before him. He winked at Rafael and Bolero, wrapped his arms around Juli, and slid her along the car to the opposite side, where he gave her a big, long kiss.

"And how have you been?"

"Missing you, but fine. And you?"

"Better than when I first arrived in Havana. I've missed you so much."

"My life is empty with you gone."

"I'd give everything to get in this car and go home with you."

A somber look shaded her joyful expression.

Daniel lifted her chin, kissed her, and said, "Let's enjoy the time we have together. Promise me?"

She nodded. He gently squeezed her, and they kissed once more. With arms interlocked they sauntered back to where Rafael and Bolero were conversing.

Daniel tapped Bolero on the back and said to Juli and Rafa, "Excuse me for one minute." Daniel and Bolero walked to the SUV. "Do you mind selling eggs by yourself today? I haven't seen them in months."

"No, I don't mind. Spend time with them. You've wanted to be with Juli for a long time."

"Thanks. And Bolero, would you mind letting me use your room at Antonio's so I can be with Juli in a decent place? I can't take her to the coop. Besides, Isabel might intrude. You understand, don't you?"

"And where do I stay?"

"The coop."

Bolero wrinkled his nose but handed Daniel the keys to Antonio's house and climbed into the SUV. He waved to Juliana and Rafael and told them he'd see them later.

Daniel signaled him to roll down the window as he started the vehicle. "Don't mention Isabel to either of them. Especially that night in the coop. Nothing happened, but Juli would never understand."

"Fine."

"We'll get together later. Thanks." He patted Bolero's shoulder.

Bolero drove forward, on the lawn, and leaned out the window. "She's absolutely gorgeous."

Daniel agreed and turned to see if Juli had heard, but she was talking to her brother. He walked back to his visitors.

"Where is he going?" asked Juli.

"He has some business to attend to. So what do you two want to do?"

"Anything, as long as it's with you."

Daniel and Juliana watched Rafael kick up sand on Santa Maria Beach as he dashed from his towel to the turquoise water for a swim. He waded into the cool water, caught a wave, and body surfed. He stood up and punched at the next wave as it curled and tumbled toward him. Rafa dove over the surge, and it continued to roll and churn the sand to the shoreline.

Rafael wanted to give the couple time alone. He bounded for the water as they snuggled together on one towel and rubbed suntan lotion on their bodies. Daniel and Juliana watched his graceful strokes as he swam in the clear water. Twenty meters out he submerged in deeper, darker water, rose, and splashed with a euphoric look on his face. His contentment was a result of being united with his friend, seeing him together with his sister, and having this special reunion take place by the shore. Rafael felt invigorated and ecstatic but knew his elation was temporary.

Daniel propped up on one elbow and stroked Juli's face, glistening with suntan oil, as she lay on her stomach. As she lowered her sunglasses, he kissed her eyes and said, "What have you been doing all these months?"

Juliana readjusted her sunglasses and glanced down the beach where tourists basked in the sun. "Mostly work. I spend time with my family, your mother, and Eva, and then back to work. Everyone treats me well, but it's not how I want to live."

He saw tears trickle down her cheeks and wiped them away as she said, "I want you to be with me."

"You know that's what I want too. Remember, no tears. We're going to enjoy the next couple of days."

"We will." Her lips pursed together.

"How has my mother been? Is she adjusting to me being gone?"

"Like I told you in my letter, she was depressed in the beginning. I was worried about her, and she was worried about me. Thank God for her. We comforted each other. Alma wanted to come along, but riding in the trunk didn't agree with her. It wasn't just the fumes. She was scared of police, and I don't blame her. She wept when we dropped her home and knew she'd lost the one chance to see you. Your mother said she'll always love you."

"Be sure to send her my love. I'll write her."

"She and Consuelo set up a shop in Consuelo's home. Now clients come to them to have clothes mended. Once in a while they're commissioned to work at hotels. At least they're not running all over town like before. Their business is doing well."

"I'm glad. That will help since she's without my salary."

Daniel sat up when he heard Rafael call to them. "What does he want? Oh, he's pointing to porpoises over there. Two surfaced. We see them," Daniel called and waved to him. "Thanks."

Two arched gray backs and tails were visible. Daniel shuddered when the mammals submerged and looked away when one resurfaced. After their brief visit, the porpoises dove underwater and eased their way down the coast pursuing schools of fish. Daniel tried to erase from his mind old thoughts of sea monsters and embrace the images of the graceful porpoises but found it difficult, even after his aunt's revelation.

"I'm sorry you had to ride in the trunk."

"Rafa stopped the car a few times so I could drink water and stretch or I never would have stayed in there. It was a tough decision to come because of the risk to you. We just had to see you."

"Thanks. I couldn't be happier. It's worth the risk."

Juliana filled him in on the news of Ranchuelo. "Emilio had gallbladder surgery, which sent Carmelita into a panic. He's recovering, and she dotes on him day and night. He borrowed your equipment from the shed to assemble the distillery and drank alcohol for the pain, like you did. He gave me a jar of homemade alcohol to give to you. It's in my suitcase."

"That was nice. Has Max bothered you since I left?"

"A little in the beginning. I ran into him once in town before he moved to Santiago to work in his uncle's garage. His father retired early and lives off government money. They never rebuilt the garage; it's still a burned-out mess."

Daniel and Rafael had never told Juliana the truth about who committed arson. They pledged to keep the secret between them forever.

"Well, that's a relief. I don't have to worry about him harassing you anymore. And what about Javier and Susana Nieves? How are they?"

"They live in the same house but he transferred to a clinic in Santa Clara. He's much happier there. Susana's four months pregnant."

"Nice. Congratulate them for me."

"I will. They ask about you all the time."

"I have to admit I miss all of them and envy their stability. I'm in limbo here."

Juli put her finger to his lips. "Stay positive, like you say. Their lives aren't as stable as you think, but like all of us they're doing their best while living under communism. In the long run, you'll probably be better off than any of us."

"Come with me to America. We bought the boat I wrote you about. It just needs a few repairs." When Daniel saw a solemn look cross her face he said, "You don't have to give me an answer now, but promise me you'll think about it. We're meant to be together."

"I know we are." She kissed him and changed the subject of departure, forever on their minds. "Do you feel like swimming?"

Her eyebrows rose when she said, "Remember how much fun we had in the shallow water on our honeymoon? Do you still fear the ocean? How will you make the trip to the States?"

"Aunt Laura gave me insight as to why I've feared sea monsters all these years.

I'll explain to you in a letter. I'm not as afraid but wish I could fly to Miami." He looked at the brilliant blue sea. "The ocean is beautiful, though, isn't it?"

"It is. So beautiful. Your mother told me about the fishing trip with your father and uncle."

"She what?"

"The time the shark knocked you off the boat. Alma told me."

"My mother told you? That was kept from me all my life. The first time I heard about it was from Aunt Laura a few weeks ago."

"You don't remember?"

"Not at all. I only remember nightmares. When did she tell you?"

"While you were in prison. Our conversations were only about you during that horrible time."

"You know more about me than I do. I won't have to write you a letter."

"Write anyway. I love getting your letters. I'm always so worried about you."

"Don't worry about me. As you see I'm fine." Tenderly he nudged her with his elbow. "I'll swim with you close to shore."

"Then let's go. I need to cool off."

As they approached the surf, Rafael swam underwater, surfaced at their feet and splashed them. They kicked water back at him, and he escaped to deeper water. "Come get me, Daniel."

"I'm fine right where I am." Daniel added, "Unless you start to drown."

"Very funny," Rafael answered. He submerged and surfaced with arms raised as if he were drowning. "Help, help."

"This time you can drown."

The three strolled to El Catamaran, a thatched-roof bar on the beach in front of the Marazul Hotel, to have a drink. They ordered rum punch. Daniel asked Rafael what was happening at the factory.

"It's not like before when we goofed on the guards and stole cigarettes. It's all about work. Even breaks are boring. All the guys take separate breaks."

"What about Pothole? Is he still chasing you down?"

"He tries. I avoid him. The doctor left the factory."

"Juli told me Javier works in a clinic and his wife's pregnant."

"I see him in town once in a while. I fill him in on what you're doing. You may hear from him. I gave him Guillermo's address. Rambo still works part time. The Rialto brothers are still at the factory even though their leader, Max, moved and works with his cousins."

"He's working at his uncle's garage?"

"In Santiago. The brothers told me he likes it there. So you don't have to worry about him bothering Juli."

"That is a relief." Daniel smiled and winked at his wife.

"Eva and I moved in together. We got the house, and I almost forgot to tell you, poor old César died. He dropped dead at his typewriter."

"That's too bad. I felt sorry for the old man."

"It was sad," said Juli as she finished her drink. "All his grandchildren were at the funeral crying. He adored all of them."

She set her glass on the bar and asked Daniel if the Great Theatre was nearby.

"Not far. Why? Would you like to see it?"

"I've always wanted to. That's home to the National Ballet."

Rafael said, "Oh, no. She's going to get all nostalgic and weepy on you. Her goal in life was to dance at the Great Theatre of Havana with the Cuban National Ballet, and then like a klutz she fractured her foot and ruined her dream." He waved to the bartender and ordered another drink.

"Daniel, don't listen to him. I'm not going to get weepy. I'm curious. And for your information, Rafa, I applied to the ballet school in Camaguey and got accepted."

"Were you accepted by the school in Havana?" said Daniel.

"I'll never know. While recovering I tore up the application. I filled it out but never mailed it. At that point it wouldn't have mattered if they accepted me or not. I knew I would never dance ballet again."

Daniel guided Juliana along the bustling streets to the Great Theatre of Havana. In awe she observed the baroque building with its façade adorned with marble statues. She peeked inside and gripped Daniel's hand tightly. "Our lives are filled with suffocated dreams, aren't they? Now it's all about the future."

"I'm sorry you never fulfilled your dream of becoming a ballerina, but if you had we probably never would have gotten together."

"True," she said as two slim, long-legged girls with their hair gathered in buns, toting ballet slippers tied together and swung across their shoulders, passed them and bounced down the steps. Daniel glanced at Juli and was certain he detected a look of longing on her face.

She looked away from the ballerinas. "You're right. We probably wouldn't have gotten acquainted."

"Maybe you would have preferred it that way, considering all we've been through."

"You're wrong. I wouldn't have skipped having you in my life for the world, even with all the pitfalls. I'm sorry for making you take me here. It was for no other reason than to see the place. I heard it was such a lovely building, and it is."

To her surprise the receptionist allowed them to view a practice session. Although Daniel had no interest in ballet, he enjoyed watching Juliana observe the leaping ballerinas. The music stopped, the dancers curtsied, and Juli said, "That was wonderful. Let's go."

"Don't you want to see more? It's not over yet."

"No. I saw enough."

He reached for her hand. "Come. We'll walk back to the beach along the Malecón, but first I have a surprise for you."

"You do?"

While walking through a shopping district Daniel spotted a leather shop.

"Do you mind if we stop here first?"

"Not at all. What for?"

He chose a money belt from a shelf and paid the store clerk. Now he had a place to secure his pesos while he was in Havana.

Juliana and Daniel passed in front of a building that seemed to have caved in on itself. The façade was a pile of rubble that spilled onto the sidewalk. Daniel guided Juli around the debris and chunks of cement. They walked past Pizzaria Vitanova, crossed the street, and arrived at a two-story blue and white building, Coppelia Ice, a popular ice cream parlor in Havana.

"Ice cream. So this is your surprise."

Before walking beneath the large blue Coppelia sign, they looked up and saw customers seated in picture windows on the second floor, gazing onto the patio below as they ate ice cream from large bowls. Inside, the couple joined the end of a long line for locals formed under a circular ceiling. Daniel noticed a line of tourists who reached the counter quicker than the Cubans. Tourists placed their orders in a timely manner because they paid more for their ice cream. Castro's government charged the wealthier foreigners more and forbade locals to intermingle with them.

"I had to invite you to Coppelia's for a cool dessert on a hot day," said Daniel.

"I'll eat ice cream anytime. You know me well."

"I thought it might cheer you up."

Together they approached the counter in the center of the room. Juliana studied the floor with its colored tiles radiating from the round counter like sunrays. Daniel handed her a bowl of coconut ice cream, the special of the day, and chose mango for himself. He scooped a spoonful into his mouth.

They climbed the steps to the second floor and sat at a table by the window overlooking a garden, away from the tourists. They were silent as they ate the cold treat. Below, a man wearing a Canadian maple leaf t-shirt wiped his daughter's mouth with a napkin. He chatted with his wife, who fed ice cream to their infant son seated on her lap. Each time a spoonful of sweetness touched the baby's tongue, he giggled.

Daniel turned away from the foreigners. "How do you like your ice cream?"

"Delicious," Juli answered after taking a bite. He detected an abruptness to her answer.

There was silence.

Juliana slammed the bowl on the table, and the spoon fell to the floor.

"I can't do this anymore."

Daniel glanced at the spinning bowl, at her face, and tried to comprehend what she meant. "You can't do what anymore?"

Juli stood. "This. All of this." She waved her arm at her empty seat and across the table at him. She snatched the bowl, emptied her ice cream into a trash bin, set the bowl on top of the trash container, and rushed down the steps.

"Juli, what's going on?"

Midway down the curving stairs she answered, "Nothing, Daniel. Everything's perfect."

He followed her to the patio and stood baffled in the doorway as he watched her storm past tourists.

"Juli, don't do this. Don't ruin the little time we have together."

"I have to get Rafa. We have to leave."

Daniel pursued her as she wove in and out of tables filled with customers.

"Why? These days are all we have."

People relaxing in the tranquil garden stared at the agitated couple. Daniel followed as she eased away from the tables and nosy customers to an unoccupied area at the edge of the leafy patio. She paced, brushing her arm against burgundy-veined leaves.

He grabbed a chair at an empty table, set it in front of her, and indicated for her to sit. Juliana sat, leaned forward, and cupped her face in her hands, concealed by a veil of hair. Daniel squatted beside her. Then he walked over to the Canadian and asked by pointing if he could borrow a chair from his table. The foreigner lifted the chair into Daniel's hands and said, "Of course. Can we help?"

Daniel did not understand the English words but got the gist of what was said and answered in Spanish, "Thank you. She'll be all right."

Daniel set the chair on the stone surface and sat facing his wife.

"Don't cry, Juli. I'm sorry. I shouldn't have taken you to the Great Theatre. It must hurt not to be able to dance on stage anymore."

She lifted her hands from her face. "No, it's not that. I'm having a wonderful time with you. We belong together. I can't bear to say good-bye again."

"I can't either."

"Now is perfect. In a few days we go our separate ways. We're a couple. We should be planning our lives together." She looked away from him at the delicate white flowers on a gardenia bush. "I can't stand it."

"We can have a future, just not here."

"And what? I say good-bye to my family, venture off to another country, and never see them again? A very difficult choice to make, don't you think?"

"It may not be the case. Your family might get tired of being hungry and lacking necessities and follow us to Miami. Russia abandoned Cuba. Cuba's a mess. It's only going to get worse."

"If they decide to join us in Miami, will Castro allow them to leave? Do you really want to raise children in Miami with the drug problem, the crime? I'm not so sure I want to go either."

"Miami, New York, Los Angeles, a small town…we'll go wherever you want. Just come with me."

"We'll see."

"Is that all you can say? We'll see? I'm your husband. You're supposed to want to go where I go."

"I'm your wife. You're supposed to stay with me."

"If I stay the phrase 'until death do us part' will come true."

Bolero met Juliana, Rafael, and Daniel at Antonio's house. He was curious as to why Rafael and Daniel spoke but Juliana was quiet. Daniel followed Juli to the tin roof, and Rafael and Bolero walked to a neighborhood cafe for lunch after Rafa changed out of his swim trunks. He was hungry after the horseplay in the ocean and had missed out on ice cream at Coppelia's. Rafael also sensed tension between the couple and wanted to give them time to sort out their differences.

As Juliana reclined in a lounge, Antonio signaled from the window for Daniel to come into the kitchen. A few minutes later, Daniel returned to the roof with a tray carrying a pitcher and two glasses. With each careful step toward Juli, a clear liquid with limes and mint leaves swirled in the glass pitcher. He set the tray on the table and poured the liquid, followed by ice and green rinds, into the glasses. He reached into the pitcher, plucked out mint leaves stuck to the sides, and dropped them into the glasses.

"*Mojitos.* Antonio made them for us. A belated wedding gift." Daniel passed her a glass, lay on the lounge beside her, and touched his glass to hers.

"I'm sorry for everything."

"You can make a better toast than that." Her glass clinked against his and she said, "To us."

"To us."

Daniel handed her his glass, lifted her, and whisked her into the house. He stepped over beach bags and towels piled in the hallway and carried her through the threshold of Bolero's bedroom like he did on their honeymoon in Cienfuegos. When he gently set her on her feet before him, she put the drinks on the night table. He unzipped her cover-up and untied her bikini top. They stared into each other's eyes as they slipped out of their bathing suit bottoms.

Juli reached for his hand. "You always say you're sorry. I'm not blaming you." She pulled him into the shower stall of the bathroom. Together they lathered their bodies with soap, rinsed, and collapsed wet onto the bed. They made love and drank *mojitos* for the remainder of the afternoon.

Daniel joined Rafael, Bolero, Antonio, and two fishermen on the tin roof while Juliana dressed. He thanked Antonio for the pitcher of mojitos. Antonio handed Daniel a jigger of homemade rum. Daniel felt his face flush as he downed the liquor. Antonio offered him more.

"Enough for me. Juli and I are going to dinner. You better slow down too, Rafa. You're coming with us."

"With you and Juli to dinner? No thanks. I'm happy right where I am." He kicked his feet up and lay back in the lounge chair. "You two go and have a good time."

"We don't mind if you come along."

"Thanks, but I'm comfortable and like this view just fine." Rafael raised his shot glass and gazed at the boats sailing along the river.

Daniel and Juliana strolled along the shore of the Almendares and walked to the inlet where the river spilled into the ocean. Juli screeched as lizards scurried across the sidewalk in front of them. One escaped a second before her shoe raised and almost crushed the rubbery little body. The reptile scooted to the opposite side and disappeared into the grass.

They passed old wooden fishing boats bobbing against makeshift docks. Many of the houses lining the street had boats parked in their driveways. Some sat high on trailers. The majority of boats in dry dock were in disrepair.

Daniel pointed to the marina before they crossed the avenue, Calzada de Linea below Túnel de Linea, a slight detour to avoid nearing the coast guard station. Before crossing Avenida Malecón they ventured past warehouses and docks where a worker diligently painted a motorboat brightened by two spotlights shining at each end of the craft. He dipped a brush in a bucket, slopped paint on the bow with one hand, and puffed on a cigarette with the other.

The couple strolled past boathouses and reached the Restaurant 1830 beside Túnel de Linea. They entered the Spanish-style mansion situated on a peninsula overlooking the sea. A host seated them at a table adorned with a white tablecloth one row from the windows facing the ocean. Daniel motioned for Juliana to take the seat with an ocean view and pulled the chair out for her. As she unfolded a napkin and set it on her lap, she said, "I'm sorry I made such a scene at Coppelia."

He picked up a menu and scanned the list of appetizers. "I understand your frustration. I feel it too."

"I should have warned you of what I was thinking."

"It was a surprise, but forget it." Daniel read the dinner menu. "What would you like to order?"

"I just want to tell you I'm sorry."

"It's over. We made up, didn't we?"

"Yes. But I needed to tell you. I'm having a good time."

He lowered the menu. "Me too. What do you feel like eating?"

"The snapper looks good. Daniel, this is quite a fancy place."

"I know. You deserve it. I think I'll have the chicken cordon bleu."

"That sounds good."

"Do you want wine?"

"How about sangria?"

The waiter approached the table with a pencil and pad of paper in hand. Daniel gave him their food choices.

"And a pitcher of sangria."

"Appetizers?"

Daniel looked at Juliana. "Do you want an appetizer?"

"Dinner will be plenty." She glanced up at the waiter. "Thank you."

"That should do it," said Daniel as he reached for a piece of warm bread.

The waiter lifted the glass globe in the center of the table and lit the candle inside. Their faces brightened, and Juli marveled at the colors reflected on the eastern sky as the sun set. "Unfortunately we can't see the sun from here. I bet it's beautiful."

"Rafa and Bolero must have the perfect view of the sun overlooking the river."

"Surely they're not paying attention to a sunset."

"If they each had a beautiful lady across from them, I bet they would."

After dinner Juliana and Daniel danced until one in the morning at La Tasca, a club situated on the coral terrace outside the restaurant. A live band blared out a fusion of Spanish and African sounds from the seaside stage. Music echoed across the water. The couple hesitated at the edge of the dance floor, away from the crowd, after a slow dance. Daniel locked his hands around Juli's waist and stood behind her. Together they stared at the moon reflecting a silver path across the dark ocean.

"I wish we had stayed up at the waterfall and never returned to Ranchuelo," Juliana said as she gazed at the moonlight shimmer on the water. The reflection of light began at the horizon and ended at the shoreline. "There, we had a simple, lovely existence with no worries. Remember the spectacular sunset? And at night the moon was full like this. Do you remember?"

"Of course I do. I'll never forget. And I'll never forget that charging bull."

"You had to bring that up. That was frightening. It took me a long time to get over that near-death experience."

"Thank God for the rancher who opened the gate."

"Another reason we should have stayed up on that mountain."

Daniel moved to a chair facing the water and eased her onto his lap. "Ideally we would have stayed there. In reality the proper procedure was to marry and face life's problems. Our fate."

"Our fate? That sounds terminal." Juliana rose and sat on the wall to face him. "Where do we go from here?"

"You know how I feel, Juli. I don't want this to end. It's your decision."

"Do you think I want this visit to be our last?"

"I hope not."

"I don't, but what do I do?"

"There are choices. You have to make up your mind what your priorities are."

"Choices? You and my family are my priorities."

"In that order?"

"Equally."

"It can't be equal."

"I'm in love with you and I love my family."

The tempo of the music grew louder. The guitarist strummed harder and bongos pounded forcing Daniel to raise his voice.

"Let's stop here or it may turn into an argument. Come dance." He reached under her arms and lifted her.

She frowned. "You're ignoring a vital issue in our lives."

When the blaring music and applause ended, Daniel lowered his voice and sat back down. "I'm ignoring it because I can't solve this problem. Only you can."

"So put all the pressure on me, Daniel."

"Put all the pressure on you? Of course there's no pressure on me?"

"I have to make the final decision whether to go with you. You have no choice but to leave."

"So I have no pressure in my life right now."

"Daniel, don't you realize your decision is confirmed?"

"Because I want to live. I'm forced to leave Cuba." A look of frustration flashed across his face as he stood. "Come let's dance."

Juliana sighed as he reached for her hand. They glided on the dance floor to a fast moving samba. Music for the next dance followed immediately. The couple swayed into El Danzón, a formal Cuban dance, provocative and sensual. The pair locked hands, faced each other, and glided close together. Without moving their hips, they patterned an invisible square on the dance floor.

"How do I choose between you and my family?"

"You don't."

They danced on in silence until the orchestra played the final song.

On their way back to Antonio's, Daniel said, "The bus stop is here if you'd like to take a bus. Does your foot hurt?"

"No. I have comfortable shoes on. I'd rather walk. I miss our walks together with Chispa."

"So do I. How is he?"

"He's fine, so cute, but every once in a while he whines. I wonder if he cries for you. I believe he misses you."

"It's possible. Dogs don't forget people."

They held hands, and she leaned her head on his upper arm as they continued into the night at a lover's pace. A trade wind blew up the river from the ocean and cooled the air. Daniel thought about his departure from Cuba.

"I'd like to take you tomorrow morning to see the boat we bought."

He sounded so proud of the purchase that she immediately answered, "I'd like that. The boat you leave Cuba in?"

"Once it's repaired and seaworthy."

Juli started to speak but changed her mind.

Daniel said, "How long will you stay here?"

"We both have to work day after tomorrow."

"Can you extend your stay?"

"I'd love to. I'll ask Rafa."

When they reached Antonio's house, Rafael, Bolero, Ernesto, and a few other fishermen were still talking and drinking on the roof. Antonio handed Daniel a rum and Coke.

"*Toma una Cuba Libre.* Every Cuban's wish, a free Cuba."

Daniel drank and laughed with them for half an hour before joining his wife in the bedroom.

"Thanks, Bolero, for giving up your bed," Daniel said before going inside. "Where are you guys sleeping?"

Rafa slurred the words, "Right here," and smacked the lounge he lay on. Bolero commented that he would probably stay on the roof instead of going to the coop. To Daniel, Bolero looked comfortable enough in the chair with his feet propped up on a crate.

"The coop? A chicken coop?" said Rafael.

"Never mind," said Daniel. "I'll explain it some other time." Knowing Bolero he would probably tell Rafa all about the pigeon coop tonight.

As Daniel closed the door, he heard Bolero describe the pigeon coop, and the two drunks laughed simultaneously. The shed was once a safe hideaway, but now it was an embarrassment. Daniel hoped Rafael would refrain from telling Juli about his first home in Havana, the hovel he longed to abandon. Hopefully in his drunkenness, Rafa would forget the conversation about the pigeon coop.

The next morning Daniel found Rafael on the roof curled up in a lounge chair with a tarp from the boat covering him, but the chair Bolero had occupied was empty. Daniel assumed Bolero had changed his mind and walked to the coop during the night.

Daniel and Juli ate toasted Cuban bread smothered with butter and drank café con leche on the roof while Rafael slept. After breakfast they hopped on a city bus, which dropped them off a block from the warehouse where the boat was stored. They crossed in front of the building constructed of cinderblocks.

Juliana squinted and looked away from the bright whitewashed walls. Blades of wheat-colored grass grew out of soft, white sand in the parking lot. "This sand looks like sugar." She slipped off a sandal to touch the powdery substance with her foot, wiggled her toes, and striated the soft mound. She slid her foot, coated with sand, into the sandal and skipped to catch up with Daniel.

He pointed to an old cabin cruiser propped up on cement blocks on the side of the building. She touched the blue hull and yellow trim of the boat as she examined it. Daniel climbed two steps up to the deck and reached for her hand.

"Want to see inside?"

"Let's see."

From the outside the cruiser was an old model wooden boat in fair shape. But once inside and on the deck, Juliana concealed her shock at the disrepair. She forced herself to remain calm and quiet, for she knew Daniel was proud of the boat and would be bridled by any negative comments.

"What do you think?"

"I think it has potential." She looked around. "Daniel, there's a hole in the floor," she blurted, unable to keep from mentioning this obvious hazard. She halted before the loosened, splintered boards surrounding a gap in the floor.

"Be careful. Don't fall."

"I won't. The steps into the cabin are broken." Juli bent to look past the steps and peeked inside. "The cabin is torn apart. Are you sure this boat can be made seaworthy?"

"I'm positive. Those are minor repairs. It's the engine that will be costly. We estimate it will take three months to complete. Juan, the carpenter we hired, works on it after his full-time job and on his days off. It's a slow process, but he's already begun working." Daniel indicated the polished boards in the stern.

"I just want you to be safe and sure before taking this boat on the ocean."

"What do you think? This guy knows how to repair watercraft. It's his profession. We'll test the boat many times before the final voyage." He saw a concerned look on her face. "Don't worry."

"I am worried." With her hands behind her back, she leaned against the railing. "Why don't you use Antonio's boat?"

"Because they're fishing on it every day. He has to keep his customers supplied."

"How will you cope with your fear in this small boat?"

"It's not that small. I understand my fear now."

"You may be out there for days."

"I'll drink Emilio's homemade alcohol during the trip," he admitted. "It's not an ocean liner, but I'll be all right in it for a day or two."

"It's not a cruise ship by any means." Juliana gripped the sides. "It is sturdy, though. I guess when repaired it will be fine."

Daniel gazed at the sailboat resting on a trailer behind his boat and carefully stepped over the gaping hole on the deck to reach Juli's side. He embraced her. "You know, there's nothing I'd like more than for you to take this voyage with me. Juli, please come with me to the United States. I promise you the day we travel, this boat will look brand new. I've seen how the carpenter has built and repaired boats. He's very talented."

"I—"

"Wait. Let me finish. You don't have to answer me now." He squeezed her shoulders. "When the boat is ready, I'll give you a week's notice. Decide then what you want to do."

"I'll think about it. But I have to say how difficult it would be to leave my family."

"I know. You told me, and I understand. Say no more. I'll send you a letter one week before I leave. We know I have to leave. Whether you choose to join me is your decision."

Her eyes were sorrowful, and he worried that her choice would be to stay in Cuba with her family. The thought hurt, but he refused to argue anymore. Daniel could only try to persuade her once more before the voyage.

"You have to admit we're having a good time together."

She hugged him. Tears welled in her eyes.

The only way Daniel could convince Rafael to stay in Havana another day was to hide the keys to his uncle's car.

"You know how El Jefe feels about missing work. He'll find a way to punish me. Where did you hide the keys?" Rafael pressed the handle of the locked car door and pulled.

"Tell the bastard you were sick or hallucinating or something."

"Come on, Daniel. Where are the keys? We have to leave."

Juliana stood in the doorway watching the two argue. It was like old times. She smiled and knew Daniel would win this round.

"You see that boat pulling away from the dock?"

Rafael heard the motor gurgle and Antonio and his crew talking. He strained to see the boat chug away from the dock.

"They're on the boat? The keys to my uncle's car are on the fishing boat?" Rafa slapped the window. "Damn you. You know I want to stay, but the hell I'll face at the factory isn't worth it."

Daniel put an arm around Juliana. "I have to have my girl for one more day."

Rafael turned and leaned against the car with his arms crossed. "Fine, but I'm not selling any more eggs. I'm taking it easy today. Where on that boat are the keys?"

"Hooked onto Antonio's key ring. They're safe, but you won't get them until tomorrow at noon when they return."

"Wonderful. That means we leave late tomorrow. You'll have tonight and most of tomorrow with your sweetheart."

"You know I appreciate that. By the way, you won't have to sell eggs. Bolero already made plans to pound the pavement in La Vibora. He doesn't mind selling alone."

"That's what you think."

The last day of their stay Rafael went to the beach, and Juliana and Daniel stayed in bed until eleven o'clock and joined him just after the fishermen returned. As the couple approached Rafa, who was chugging a bottle of Bucañero beer at El Catamaran bar, Daniel reached in his pocket and tossed the car keys to him. In one motion Rafael set down the beer bottle and caught the keys in the air before they crashed onto the bar.

"Rafa, you're free to leave whenever you want."

Chapter Twenty-Six
THE SEPARATION

The air was thick and humid, and a light drizzle shone on the body of the Ford and moistened Rafael's hair as he jammed their bags in the front seat. "Juli, the trunk is wet. You're not riding back there. Just stay low in the back seat. We shouldn't run into any PNRs since we're traveling so late and in such lousy weather."

Daniel looked at his watch, a gift from Juliana. "It's almost nine o'clock. You never know with the police. Just be careful. I'll ride with you out to National Highway."

"That's kind of far at this time of night," said Rafael.

"I can always catch a bus back," Daniel said, but he knew no buses traveled to the outskirts of Havana at this hour.

Daniel and Juliana huddled and whispered in the back seat. Rafael flicked on the windshield wipers as a sprinkle misted the glass. He stopped the car before approaching the highway and looked in the rearview mirror at the couple holding each other ever so tightly. Daniel glanced up at Rafael's reflection and saw his eyes fill with tears. As Daniel released himself from Juli's arms, his eyes met hers one last time. He opened the door and slowly got out of the car.

Rafael rolled down the window. "It's starting to rain. Let me take you back."

"That's absurd. Go ahead. It's better if you go now."

Daniel reached in the window, hugged Rafa, and glanced back at his wife. She stared at the floor. As the car pulled away, he waved. Rafael made a less dramatic exit than he had on the night Daniel left for Havana. Daniel watched the red taillights turn onto the empty highway and fade into a fog shrouding the countryside. He felt as abandoned and lonely as when Rafael had fishtailed in the old Chevy and sped away from him on that long, gloomy night outside Ranchuelo.

Rafael pulled into his driveway in Ranchuelo and ran around to open the door for Juli, who slept curled up on the back seat. Daniel had locked the back door when he got out of the car. As her brother helped Juliana out of the car, she mumbled, "*No sabes el dolor que siento*. Rafa, you don't know the pain I'm feeling."

He held an umbrella over her head and cupped the handle in her hands as he reached for the bags in the front seat. Suddenly headlights flashed at them. A jeep sped down the street, growled, and bounced across the lawn, crushing the glistening grass. The front fender cornered them against the Ford.

"Oh, no," said Juli, "not again."

Rafael dropped the bags on the pavement with a thump and told her to stay calm and not to reveal where they had been. He tossed the car keys on the front seat and quickly whispered as he eyed the police exiting their vehicles, "Remember, only yes and no answers. We visited a cousin in Havana."

Two uniformed agents snuck up behind them. The tall one asked, "Where were you two the past four days?"

Rafael realized the agents' vehicle had been parked in the driveway next door, camouflaged by the neighbor's collection of cars.

"Visiting a cousin in Havana."

"Are you sure you weren't visiting Daniel Milan in Havana?"

"I'm sure," Rafael said as Juli stared at the streetlight reflected on the side of the jeep.

"And you, Mrs. Milan? What do you have to say? Did you see your husband?"

"No. Of course not. I have no idea where he is," she said in a low tone.

"Come with us."

One shoved Rafael toward the jeep, and two others took Juliana by the arms and lifted her into the back of the vehicle. She saw her parents peering out of their bedroom window. Before the jeep pulled away, her father appeared in the front door and ran barefoot down the steps and onto the road, hollering for them to stop. The driver steered in the direction of the police station.

Mr. Reyes shook his head and closed the car doors. He noticed the keys on the driver's seat, scooped them up, and carried the wet bags into the house. He removed his pajamas and threw them hard on the unmade bed as his wife stood at the window wringing her hands. His muddy feet dirtied the dampened ceramic tile. He slipped into pants and a shirt and sped to the police station as fast as his car would go.

Daniel walked past palm trees, shacks, and small farms. He welcomed the rain because his tears dissolved into the raindrops spraying his face. The deluge obscured the countryside. He followed a footpath along the road, kicking aside leaves bigger than his feet and trampling spongy pine needles sun-dried to a rust color. Half a coconut, tilted, and filled with water, lay in his way. Daniel sprung forward on his left foot and kicked the coconut with his right. Liquid sprayed, and the brown shell landed with a thud and bounced in the center of the road. At a steady pace, he splashed through puddles agitated by the downpour. He leaped over potholes brimming with water and approached a more populated area. The sounds of rain pelting roofs and gurgling down drainpipes annoyed him.

He slowed down in front of a stand of young palms. Their trunks were ringed and slick with moisture. High in the sky Daniel heard the hum of a plane—or was it the moan of thunder?

When he glanced up at the overcast sky, bougainvillea branches thick with red blooms stretched sinisterly above him. The color reminded him of pig's blood at dawn. Beyond the flowers, cloud formations hung eerily in the gray sky.

Daniel reached Antonio's house, stomped up the steps, and stretched out in a lounge on the tin roof. The downpour saturated his already drenched clothes as he shivered and listened to rain patter on tin. With eyes closed he imagined thousands of spoons dropping on steel drums. The noise deafened him. He cupped his hands over his ears.

Bolero looked out the window, tapped on the glass, and motioned for him to come inside. When Daniel declined, Bolero called from the door, "*Oye, amigo, está lloviendo fuerte. Porqué te quedas afuera mojándose?* Don't be a stubborn asshole, Daniel. It's pouring. Come inside."

Bolero pushed and pulled in an attempt to move him from the lounge, but Daniel refused to budge. He looked into Daniel's blank eyes staring in the direction of the river.

"Are you in a trance? Don't tell me you're going to start speaking an ancient language like the Soldiers of the Cross people."

"Just leave me alone. The rain feels good. I like being out here."

"You're joking."

"No. It's cool and refreshing. I love the rain."

"My God, you're losing it."

Bolero rushed out of the driving rain and back into the dry interior. The door slammed. He grabbed a dishtowel tucked into the refrigerator handle and rubbed his hair. Ten minutes later, while Bolero reclined on the sofa and read a magazine, a loud clap of thunder echoed across the sky. Startled and wide-eyed, he sat up and saw lightning flash in the window. The rapid glow brightened the blackness outside.

At the same instant, Daniel witnessed a streak of lightning slip out of the sky. A ball of light severed the limb of a prominent evergreen on the bank of the river. He heard crackling, an electric, wood splintering sound, and a second boom of thunder. He jumped off the lounge despite being weighted down by his rain-soaked clothing, and tore into the house, followed by splattering rainwater and a cool breeze.

"Close the door," yelled Bolero. "It's cold, and you're letting rain in."

Daniel stood motionless on the floor mat like a soggy vagabond with the expression of a lost and lonely soul on his weary face.

"Now how do you like that rain? God found a way to get you inside. He frightened you in here. You're lucky you didn't get struck by lightning. I'll get you some dry clothes. Wait right there. Antonio won't be happy if you track all that mud and rain into his house. I'll be right back."

Bolero grew accustomed to selling eggs alone. Every morning he loaded his cousin's SUV with boxes and waved good-bye to Daniel, who lay on the lounge asleep or deliriously belting down shots of rum. Upon his return in the afternoon, Bolero divided the money evenly between him and Daniel. He knew Daniel had spent a large portion of his savings while Juliana and Rafael visited. He understood Daniel's reason for spending his cash and was aware that the unexpected reunion with his wife and brother-in-law may be his last.

Willingly, Bolero peddled eggs and ignored his friend who wallowed in what Bolero described as a severe case of self-pity due to heartache, a phase that would eventually pass. The reality was that Daniel wrestled with despair over Juliana's departure and was tormented by the possibility of entering another deep depression.

During a drunken stupor on the roof, Daniel remembered his belongings left in the coop. Three weeks had passed since he'd told Maria Soraya he would reside elsewhere. Purposely he abstained from mentioning his new locale in an effort to discourage Isabel from paying him an unexpected visit. His cloudy mind obsessed over the idea of collecting his few but precious items.

Daniel staggered and wandered up and down streets and across lawns in an alcohol-induced confusion and became discouraged with himself when he forgot the way to Oviedo Street. He was retracing his steps when he recognized Guillermo's house and knew he was on the right street. Upon arriving in front of the Soraya home, Daniel cheered and told Maria, who appeared in the open living room window, that he would pick up his property and permanently move to a friend's house.

"Just one thing, Daniel. Please put the mattress back in Isabel's room for the kids."

"No problem," he said as he tripped while walking to the coop. He turned to see if the landlady had seen him stumble. She called to him as he caught her eye.

"Have you been drinking, Daniel?"

"No, just not watching where I step."

The coop seemed smaller and stuffier than he remembered. He bent over and packed photographs, and clothing that lay strewn on the mattress and draped over wooden rafters. He stuffed the rest of his belongings in his bags and slipped them under the makeshift table.

Daniel rolled and tied his sleeping bag. Then he lifted the mattress through the narrow door of the coop and carried it to the front of the house. Again he tripped, on the edge of the cushion. As it opened on the grass he landed in the center of the mattress, lay on his stomach, and laughed. Daniel was thankful his body had struck a soft surface and that no one was watching.

Before he dragged the pad to the base of the ladder, he sat for a moment until his head stopped spinning. He pushed it up the ladder and called to Isabel. There was no answer, so he continued shoving the bulky object up to the window. Daniel was relieved to see that no one was inside when he peeked in the window and concluded that Isabel, with the kids' help, could properly position the cushion in the room when she returned home. He opened the window wide, squeezed the sides together, and watched the mattress flop to the floor.

The next thing he knew a hand grabbed his arm and pulled him off the ladder, through the window, and onto the mattress. Isabel, in a pink frilly bra and panties, jumped on top of him. She sucked his lips and wildly kissed his neck. Daniel scanned the room to make sure the kids were not present. A stray thought of Juliana entered his mind—the realization that his wife would decline to take the voyage with him to the United States. Isabel's lack of inhibition and urgent kisses dissolved the melancholy shadowing his mind. The excessive consumption of alcohol and her perseverance defeated Daniel. This time he succumbed to Isabel's seduction but throughout their lovemaking he imagined Juliana enveloping his body.

Afterward, he rolled off the mattress and stood above Isabel as he dressed. He zipped his pants and picked up his shirt off the floor. As Daniel slipped his arms into the sleeves, he told her he had to go.

Isabel watched him. "Can't you spend the night? The kids are at their grandmother's."

He eased toward the window to climb out but hesitated in front of the curtain to say, "I really have to take my things to my new place…" Abruptly Daniel stopped talking when he heard the familiar roar of engines on the street and screeching brakes. With a glance out the window, his eyes narrowed in disbelief. Military trucks and police cruisers veered and halted in front of the house. He dove onto the mattress.

"It can't be the police." He faced Isabel. "Help me. I have to hide."

As they moved the mattress to the other side of the bed they could hear her mother say, "No, he's not here. I have no idea where he is."

"Hide under the bed. I'll distract them," Isabel said. She threw some toys and clothing on the mattress to block the view beneath the bed and lay down. The outcries of male voices came from the lawn, and footsteps ascended the ladder. A man hesitated on the ladder, below the window, and called down to his superiors. The soldier, in his early twenties, peeked in the room and caught sight of Isabel lying under the covers.

"Anyone in here with you?" he said in a firm voice.

"I'm all by myself. Care to join me?"

She lifted the sheets, exposing her nude body. His face reddened. "I'll have to pass miss." He averted his eyes from the salacious woman and scoped the far side of the room, his eyes avoiding her nakedness. He advised the police in the yard that the fugitive was not up here and climbed back down the ladder.

Daniel remained under the bed until the platoon departed. He sat with Isabel for hours, visibly nervous. He whispered to her about his prison sojourn and his apprehension of being incarcerated again until he felt safe enough to leave. The near collision with the military and witnessing their relentless pursuit had sobered him.

Daniel rushed down the ladder, grabbed his bags from the coop, and jogged to Antonio's house. While traversing backyards thoughts raced in his mind. He realized how urgent it was to leave Cuba as soon as the boat was ready. Tonight's close encounter with the police had snapped him out of his anguish over Juliana's departure from Havana.

After the incident at the Soraya home, Daniel requested to buy a portion of Antonio's catch while Antonio prepared his boat for a fishing excursion. Antonio agreed, and later, on the roof, Daniel told Bolero to stop purchasing eggs. Tomorrow fish would be their new and hopefully most lucrative commodity to sell.

"Don't waste any time between houses because fish will spoil faster than eggs," Daniel advised Bolero.

Bolero returned to the high-class neighborhoods to sell red snapper, flounder, and tilapia hauled in a cooler. He cursed the offensive smell and the fact that he had to peddle fish in the afternoon after the fishing boat docked. His cousin's SUV was unavailable to him at that time. He swore under his breath as he trod up and down streets in the hot sun but never verbalized these complaints to Daniel. Bolero was relieved at Daniel's return to normalcy, evident in how gingerly he paced at the end of the day to join Daniel on the roof.

On an overcast day, Bolero headed for Miramar and watched Daniel veer in the opposite direction to the warehouse to check on the progress of the boat. To mask his identity, Daniel grew a beard and sported shades and a cap during necessary but brief appearances on the streets. He refrained from jaunts in public places such as selling fish to avoid being detected by police.

On the day Bolero sold fish in Miramar and Daniel worked on the boat, Soldiers of the Cross member, Pedro, paced up and down streets in search of Daniel. He found Daniel as he returned from the warehouse with a look of satisfaction on his face, knowing boat repairs were moving steadily along.

"Mr. Daniel, I finally found you. Matilde asked me to give you this letter. Since you left the Soraya home, the Santos family lost track of you. Matilde felt this may be an important message."

Pedro handed him an envelope and at one glance Daniel recognized Juli's handwriting.

"Thank you. It is quite urgent."

"Matilde wants you to know that police officers have asked Soldiers of the Cross members, including she and Guillermo, where you reside. They all decline knowing you. Military constantly patrol Oviedo Street and the neighborhood. She suggests you stay away but wants you to have the address of our new parish. If possible, she and Guillermo would like to see you before your departure."

Daniel looked up from the envelope. "Yes. Tell her I will try to stop by the church. Thanks again, Pedro, for taking the time to look for me. I really appreciate it."

"No need to thank me. I'm always on the streets in search of those in need."

The letter explained how Juliana and Rafael were sequestered by military and taken to the police station for hours of interrogation on the night of their return from Havana. The grilling questions concerning Daniel's whereabouts had exhausted her. Brother and sister were mentally battered, but fortunately not physically harmed.

Juli admitted to Daniel that under pressure she'd blurted to the interrogator that they had indeed visited Daniel. She mentioned only the address of the Soldiers of the Cross and blamed herself entirely for caving in to the interrogator's demands, for Rafael never once admitted to seeing him. She expressed her remorse, and fear for Daniel's life and pleaded for him to depart Cuba as soon as possible. Juli warned that detectives would trail him until he was found, dead or alive, and ended the letter with lamentation, a plea for forgiveness, and expressed her endless love for him. This was the first time she had urged him to leave Cuba.

Weakened by the tone of her letter and Juli's deep concern, Daniel crossed the street to the bank of the river, sat down, and read one phrase over and over again. In large block letters on the last line she'd written, "*I will travel with you to America.*"

Chapter Twenty-Seven
TRIAL RUN

After the harrowing arrival of military at the Soraya home and as a firsthand witness to their steadfast hunt, Daniel avoided the streets. He sought refuge at Antonio's house or at the boatyard. A month later, one morning at the boatyard, he dipped a paintbrush into a can, coated it with blue paint, rotated the brush so the stream of paint stuck to the bristles, and slathered the bow of his boat with even strokes. Daniel wanted the project to move along at a faster pace, so he worked alongside Juan.

While Daniel painted the boat, Juan was in the process of replacing the old motor with one removed from a wrecked cruiser belonging to a tour boat operator. Juan hailed his accomplishment by dancing on deck when the motor purred.

"I have to test it in water to find out if the motor's any good and of course whether my work on the boat is watertight."

"Fine with me," said Daniel. "Take her for a trial run. There's time today."

"We have time, but we need a vehicle to haul the boat on my trailer."

"Bolero's cousin has an SUV, hitch and all."

"Where's Bolero?"

"Selling fish in Reparto Flores."

"Let me inspect my work first. Tomorrow we'll take her out in shallow water."

"In case she sinks?"

"She's not going to sink."

"Confident son of a bitch, aren't you?"

"I must admit, I'm one of the best at repairing watercraft in Cuba."

"Tomorrow we'll find out."

They launched the boat. Daniel anxiously watched from shore as Bolero and Juan drifted away from the partially submerged trailer hitched to the SUV. The carpenter started the engine. It coughed and expelled a fog of exhaust that skimmed the waves and dissipated in the air. Daniel inhaled a scent of burned oil and worried the engine had overheated. Soon he realized singed oil was a minor flaw, as Bolero yelled from inside the boat, "It's sinking! It's sinking!" as water swirled around his bare feet.

Juan corrected, "It's not sinking. There's a crack in the bow. I must have missed it." He struggled to steer the boat around as the engine neglected to respond.

Daniel paused and waded up to his waist to assist the sailors. He hoisted himself up at the bow to see the water accumulated on deck. "Damn, will it ever be seaworthy?"

"Of course it will. This is why several trial runs are necessary before the final launch," the carpenter answered immediately.

Daniel and Juan yanked the boat onto the submerged trailer with the aid of ropes hanging from the sides while Bolero heaved at the stern. The carpenter fastened the craft securely to the trailer.

"Don't think this was the fault of my craftsmanship. My work stayed watertight. The leak was probably from a crack caused by the boat being stored out in the elements for many years."

Daniel patted him on the back. "Don't worry, Juan. We know it wasn't your workmanship. We have total faith in your abilities. Right, Bolero?"

"*No hay duda*. Absolutely no doubt."

A few days later Daniel described the second launch as perfection. The motor turned over immediately, and the boat glided on the choppy waves. He cheered from shore, and Bolero pumped one arm and shouted from the boat. After an hour of sailing, they neared shore, and Bolero called to Daniel, who seemed bored as he followed the craft's movements while seated on a boulder in a barrier of rocks.

"Come join us on the boat."

"Not yet. I'm not ready. Maybe next time."

The happy expression on Bolero's face turned serious. "Come on, Daniel. You have to get used to this boat. We're going to spend a long time on it."

"I will, just not now. Another time."

Bolero turned to Juan as the steering wheel revolved and he guided the boat to deeper water and east toward Havana Bay.

"I worry about him. He's the one who is forced to leave Cuba."

"What do you mean you're worried?"

"Daniel fears the ocean and has since he was a kid, from what his wife and brother-in-law told me."

"He does? So that's why he stays ashore. I just thought he wanted to watch the boat operate from that vantage point."

"No. Daniel is genuinely afraid of being where we are right now."

"My God, that's not good. He may be on this boat for days before he gets to the US."

"I know. That's what I'm trying to tell him. He should get used to it now, but he won't. Daniel's got a stubborn streak in him."

"We'll get him on the boat next time even if we have to tie him up and throw him on."

"That will be the only way. He told me that before our trip he'll be high as a kite and will stay that way until he touches American soil. Daniel's saving alcohol his neighbor at home distilled for the trip across the Straits."

"Poor bastard. How could anyone not enjoy being out on the ocean like this? Sailing along, free as the wind."

"Daniel's the only person I know."

The third time they tested the boat Daniel gazed at the turquoise water with a combination of worry and anger on his face. His hands were clasped together and restrained behind his back. Bolero approached him from behind and tugged at the rope wrapped around his wrists.

"Enough, Bolero. Untie me. You proved your fucking point. I'm on the boat. If the thing takes on water I won't be able to save myself and will sink along with it. Now untie this rope."

"Can you swim?"

"Of course I can swim. I learned in pools. Don't be an asshole. Untie me."

"Fine." Bolero loosened the knots and slipped the rope off his wrists. "Now don't do anything crazy."

"What do you think I'll do, jump in and swim to shore?"

"I mean to me. Don't do anything crazy to me."

"I'd like to murder you and toss your body in the ocean to those fucking sharks I fear, but I need your company on the trip. Believe me, if I truly didn't want to come aboard I would not be here right now."

"You fought pretty hard."

"You guys tied my hands."

Juan smiled as he listened to their bickering. "Are you sure you two should travel together?"

Bolero gave Daniel a bear hug and lifted him high.

"See that big, blue ocean? In a few weeks we'll cross those Straits."

"Put me down, you bastard."

"No matter what the circumstances, we always seem to remain friends. But he truly loves me more," said Bolero to the carpenter.

"The hell I do." Before Daniel walked away from Bolero he punched his arm, and sat on the lid of a storage bin.

"Keep your hands off me. Concentrate on getting used to this boat."

Daniel stared at the polished floor. "I'm trying. I'm trying."

Chapter Twenty-Eight
THE PLAN

Daniel and Bolero gradually purchased supplies for their voyage. Antonio told them to bring only necessities: clothing, food, and drinks, mainly water. The plan was to launch the boat from a less populated area outside Havana where few coast guard, military personnel, and police patrolled.

"Springtime, especially March or April, is the best time to set sail. The waters are calm, and hurricane season hasn't begun," said Antonio.

Daniel and Bolero watched him on the tin roof as he wove threads of jute to repair a hole in a fish net.

"Now is the perfect time."

They agreed to have Antonio at the helm and Ernesto as his crewmember. Two men besides Juliana, Daniel, and Bolero would make the voyage. The additional travelers had aided in a plot to assassinate Fidel Castro in 1981. During the attempt a bodyguard was wounded. The fugitives were tired of fleeing and hiding from the military and while conversing with friends of Antonio had expressed their desire to leave Cuba. The friends had in turn informed Antonio.

One evening on the roof, the six conspirators conjured up a plan of escape while sharing a bottle of rum. With a map stretched on a table, Antonio charted the route with a red pencil. He and Ernesto would drop the five migrants off on a deserted island off the Florida Keys, known by locals as Ant Key. They would remain on the island until dark and row an inflatable raft to Lower Matecumbe Key, the closest key of the island chain, and when possible hitchhike to Miami.

"We'll launch our boat directly south of the Keys." Antonio pointed to the map. "Somewhere on the shore of Matanzas Province."

Days after this meeting, Daniel and Bolero officially signed the boat over to Antonio. Antonio saw how pleased Daniel was to learn Juliana would join him on the trip. The value of the boat would cover the cost of Juli, Bolero, and Daniel's voyage.

The other two passengers conjured up three thousand pesos each, making the voyage especially lucrative for the fisherman. Antonio would pay Ernesto double time for participating. He and his first mate calculated a return to Havana two days after his passengers were safely on the small atoll. The actual travel time would depend on wind, weather, and luck.

To Cuban maritime officials it would appear Antonio departed on a lengthy fishing trip and in reality would fish on his return from the Florida Keys. If the Cuban Coast Guard questioned his lengthy absence, Antonio would produce a substantial catch as proof and cash for the guardsmen if needed.

After buying supplies for their trip, Daniel and Bolero joined Antonio on the roof early one evening. Daniel set a bag on the table and pulled out a flashlight. He slipped in two batteries and flashed a beam of light in Bolero's face. Bolero raised his arm to cover his eyes.

"Do you boys feel confident about this trip?" said Antonio.

Daniel waved the flashlight and shone the light at the trees near the river. "Our plans are made. Now we have to execute them."

"We've gone over the details a hundred times. I believe we're ready," said Antonio.

Bolero sat in a chair and looked up at Daniel and Antonio seated at the table. "You can have the best plans, but something can always go wrong."

"Haven't I told you not to think like that?" Daniel said as he flashed the light at Bolero.

"Stop." Bolero turned his head away from the beam. "I'm just being realistic."

"Think positive."

"I do. I'm just saying we have to be prepared. Anything can happen."

"Listen, I'll do all I can to get you out of Cuba," Antonio said as he passed them each a beer from a cooler. "Everything's in our favor. Once we drop you off it's all up to you to get to Miami."

Daniel pointed the beam of light straight up to the sky, flicked off the flashlight, and said, "We'll get to Miami even if we have to walk."

"You'll walk," said Bolero. "I'm hitchhiking."

The men tipped up their beer bottles and drank.

Antonio removed the bottle from his lips. "You never answered my question." He looked from one to the other. "Are you confident about this trip?"

Daniel eyed Bolero. "I am. I'll board that boat, plastered. I don't know about the negative one over there."

"Hey, you're the one who's scared. Am I confident? I guess."

"You both have to be certain."

"We are," they said in unison.

"Then two weeks from today's date, March twenty-third, we'll set sail."

"You're on," Daniel said as he tapped his bottle against theirs.

"Since the departure date has been chosen, I've got a surprise for you."

"What?" said Bolero.

Antonio shook his fists in the air. "Does this ring a bell?"

Bolero leaned forward. "Maracas. A jam session?"

"You guessed it."

"A farewell party for Daniel and me?"

"One of many we'll have in the next two weeks. In exactly one hour this roof will make South Beach look dead," said Antonio.

"The roof's going to rock, Daniel. Just you wait." Bolero bolted into the house. It sounded like a scuffle ensued inside his room as he searched for his maracas in a closet.

"I found them."

Antonio whispered to Daniel, "Since the day I met him I've witnessed that grown man steadily regress back to childhood."

"I never knew him as an adult," Daniel snickered as he glanced toward the house. Bolero stood in the window with a wide grin and shook his maracas at them.

Daniel was amazed as he watched the familiar faces and members of the band set up their instruments and take their positions on the roof, converted into a stage. He had no idea any of them were musically inclined. He saw Antonio grip the conga drums with his calves and tap the stretched hide, alternating from the palms of his hands to his fingers. Ernesto shook his entire body as he played the claves. Juan, the carpenter, and Antonio's cousin raised their clarinets high and dipped low as they blew into the wind instruments. Antonio's uncle clutched a trombone and on cue belted deep tones into the air. Two flutes whistled and a saxophone bellowed random sounds, played by members of Antonio's fishing crew. Bolero wildly shook the maracas and called across the roof to Daniel, "We play. You sing."

"Don't be funny," Daniel said as he eased down the steps and off the roof. "You know I can't carry a tune."

As the orchestra blossomed and their jam session melded into true music, Daniel felt useless and out of place standing empty-handed alongside the band. At the bottom step, he watched neighbors pour out of their houses carrying chairs, buckets, and stools to sit on. Daniel stared at the audience congregating in the vacant lot below the roof.

A skinny fellow balanced a bench on his head and held it in place with both hands. His wife hurried behind him on tiptoes, stretching her arms high to reach the bench in an attempt to help her husband, and four children scurried like ducklings in single file to keep up with their parents. Couples danced at the base of the roof. Daniel's backyard parties were no comparison to this event.

A lady with skin shining black as the night sky approached him. "Man who cannot carry a tune, can you dance?"

Daniel let go of the railing and reached for her hand. "Yes, I can."

Her white gauze skirt flowed as her lanky body gyrated and twirled. Her lean shoulders shook in rhythm to a mambo. He felt at ease and enjoyed dancing with the energetic woman. He guided her to the far end below the roof stage, jumped up, and pinched Bolero's leg.

"Ouch," he blurted and kicked at Daniel's arm. Without missing a beat, Bolero shook the maracas, and Daniel resumed dancing with the lovely lady of Haitian descent.

"Maybe I can't sing, but I can dance," he called to Bolero who stuck out his tongue as he watched Daniel and his partner move to the center of the dance floor. Her rhythm and gliding reminded Daniel of Juli. In fact the memories became so vivid that after five dances he thanked her and said, "I'm taking a break."

She smirked but continued to dance alone. As he wove in and out of shaking and swinging couples, her voice rang above the music, "White man, you *can* dance."

He laughed. His arm raised and his hand curled into a fist in a salute to her comment. "I'll be back."

Daniel needed to retreat from the blaring music, crowded dance floor, noisy onlookers, and especially from memories of dancing with Juliana. He passed the audience and tables of food and drinks being set up and headed to the peaceful river to gather his thoughts.

On the bank of the Almendares he sat beside the pine tree that had been struck by lightning on the night of Juli and Rafael's departure. Its broken limb brushed the ripples lapping against dock pilings. The severed branch, splintered and separated at the trunk, arched into the river. Pine needles released into reflections on the water and were swept away by a fleeting current.

Daniel watched the vast river in motion and the lights flickering on the opposite shore. The moon surprised him when a sliver of light timidly bowed from behind silver clouds. He leaned against the wounded tree and envisioned Juliana, the ballerina, in the sky staring down at him. She stood erect and leaped the treetop silhouettes on the far shore. She spun in a pirouette, her eyes fixated on him. He imagined himself as the object she chose to spot to prevent disorientation during her turns. Her eyes pierced him like spotlights. Daniel closed his eyes and opened them as a full moon obscured the ballerina.

Besides the image of Juli, the simple question Antonio asked them on the roof haunted him. *Do you boys feel confident about this trip?* Did Antonio mean confident about crossing the Straits of Florida, arriving alive and unharmed in the United States of America? Daniel's truthful answer was no. How could a man frightened of an unpredictable ocean and apprehensive of a new beginning in a foreign land feel confident? Why did Antonio use the word "confident"? If he had said "prepared" or "ready," Daniel would have immediately answered yes.

Their boat was moored at the far end of the dock next to Antonio's fishing boat. It rocked from side to side and was shrunken by the expanse of river. To Daniel the boat struggled against small river waves bullying its bow toward shore. How would the craft fare on an open ocean? In all these months of preparation, Daniel had never felt doubtful of this voyage until now while overlooking the river.

"What's the matter?"

Daniel turned. Bolero towered above him.

"Nothing. Why?"

"You were dancing, and then you were gone. What are you doing here? Didn't you like dancing with that beautiful mambo princess?"

"We had a good time."

"Then why did you leave?"

"To get away from the crowd. To think. I'll go back and dance."

"I thought something was wrong."

"No, everything's fine."

"Wow. Look at that moon."

"Beautiful." Daniel followed Bolero's gaze. "Hey, Bolero, have you seriously thought about the finality of this trip?" He focused on the roof and saw a boy, a neighbor's son, shaking Bolero's maracas.

"What do you mean?"

"I mean, do you really want to leave all of this? You seem so much a part of Antonio's life, the fishermen, the band. Sit for a minute."

Bolero's feet slid down the embankment in sand, and he plopped beside Daniel.

"That's not a jam session; it's a concert. I thought you were just going to have fun, but you guys are talented. That orchestra's a *típica*. You could make money with that sound."

"I doubt it. We've been doing this for years. We're just out for a good time."

"You're happy here. Why leave?"

Daniel's last two words, uttered when the band stopped playing, rang out loud. Silence swooned over the crowd for an instant before a rage of applause and screams echoed in the neighborhood.

"I love it here, but I need to settle down in my own home, get a steady job. A career would be even better. I'm lazy here and tired of hopping from job to job. Haven't you noticed? Sometimes I hang out on the roof all day. Before you got here I hadn't worked for weeks."

"You don't really need much money to live on. Do you?"

"I don't. But my parents do."

"Where are your parents?"

"You saw the room I rented outside the city. They live forty kilometers past that house. Way out in the country."

"You never talk about them. Why don't you ever go see them?"

"I do sometimes. But it makes me sad. Their house is in bad shape. My father's not well. My mother cares for him. He was in prison like us, but for longer, and he got sick in there. Malnutrition weakened his heart, and he has kidney problems. They depend on me. My sister married and moved to Venezuela."

"I thought you just wanted a new life in America."

"I do. But more importantly, money I earn there will support my parents. I gave them most of the chicken and egg money."

"Nice of you. When I get a job, I'll send my mother money too." Daniel saw the clouds drift farther away from the moon. The brilliant globe shone in a sky black as licorice. "Do you think we'll make it across the Straits in our boat?"

Bolero took his eyes off the moon and studied the blue boat. "I'm worried, but I believe we'll make it. We have to. If I don't my parents won't survive either."

Chapter Twenty-Nine
THE ESCAPE

Daniel and Bolero borrowed the SUV one morning in mid-March to locate a spot for the launch. They drove in the direction of Matanzas, approximately sixty miles east of Havana, to search for an isolated beach or marsh to use as a sailing site. On their way they crossed the Bacunayagua Bridge. Daniel felt nervous looking down at the rocks and trees in the chasm below and flinched when an oil truck passed them at a high rate of speed. Bolero sped across the bridge oblivious of the speeding truck and gorge beneath them.

They continued beyond the city of Matanzas until Bolero drove off the highway and reached a paved one-lane road. From there he branched off on sandy byways leading to the sea. Down one lane they encountered a section of beach that was too rocky. Another beach was rocky and packed with locals swimming and fishing. They continued to comb the coast for the perfect hidden launch site where military patrols would not be cognizant of their illegal embarkation.

Open white beaches stretched pristine and endless. The water swelled with snowy, crested waves rolling ashore like falling cobalt dominoes. Daniel and Bolero were in good spirits and talked of beginning new lives in America. Daniel expressed his paranoia and fretted about being found and thrown in jail in Havana before departing. He felt fortunate he had so far eluded the squad assigned to capture him. He desired tranquility, freedom, and an existence when being alert to his surroundings was a gesture of the past. Daniel repeated many times how thrilled he was for Juliana to join him in his new life in America.

The young men were hungry. The sun heated the interior of the vehicle and parched their throats. Hot air and dust blew in the open windows. They dismissed pangs of thirst and hunger to carry on their mission. After several hours of searching Daniel said, "We haven't eaten all day. I'm starving and thirsty as hell."

"We'll eat once we find the right beach."

"Don't you have to get this vehicle back to your cousin by noon? It's late. I know twelve passed a long time ago."

"He's off today and was going to help a friend work on his car. He let me have this baby all day."

"Nice, but still we have to eat at some point. Let's search another time. You know there's lots of coast to cover."

"I know, but it would be nice if we found a spot today. Everything else about this trip is ready. Don't you want to get the hell out of Cuba once and for all?"

"Of course, but I want to eat."

Daniel became weary from riding and bouncing up and down bumpy roads and began to doze. His head wobbled as the truck rocked. When Bolero slowed the SUV, Daniel's head fell forward, jerked, and then leaned against the back of the seat.

He dreamed of their departure from Cuba. In the dream he embraced Juliana as they huddled in their boat rolling over waves during a storm. The small craft rose and dipped and was tossed from swell to swell. Bolero wore a captain's uniform and hat and told them to hold on tight; American shores were just beyond that big wave. Daniel accidentally released his grip on Juli and grabbed the side of the boat to keep from being swept overboard. As the boat rose, Juli slid toward the railing. He crawled along the deck and reached for her hand, but she slipped beneath the railing and into the ocean. A spray of water cooled Daniel's face.

A loud voice woke Daniel as he was immersed in anxiety and doom over Juliana's fate in his dream. He wiped droplets off his face and licked the saltwater that was dampening his dry lips. His eyes opened to Bolero holding a cup and standing by the open door of the parked SUV. His giggling friend tossed the rest of the water from the cup into Daniel's face. "Wake up. I found the perfect beach."

A splash of seawater slapped his face, and salt stung his eyes. He blinked. "You are such an asshole. I don't understand you. I was dreaming, and you do this to me?" He pulled out his t-shirt, rubbed his face, and dabbed his eyes with the shirttail. Still in a daze, Daniel looked down at the money belt snug around his waist and touched the dampened cloth bulging with all his money tucked inside. "You got my new belt wet." He wiped the belt with his shirt.

"You're always dreaming. Just dry the belt." Bolero pulled him off the seat and out of the vehicle. "I'm telling you, *amigo*, this spot is perfect."

Daniel's shirt hung out in the front and remained tucked in his pants in the back. He stumbled in the sand after Bolero to a deserted beach hidden by sea grapes, sea grass, and a thicket of pines interspersed with coconut palms. Daniel plopped down in the sand and looked at the brilliant ocean canopied by an azure sky. The sun sparkled and shimmered bright on the waves. The water was almost inviting—but not enticing enough to dive in.

Daniel decided that as soon as he arrived back in Havana, he would buy some potent marijuana for their voyage to ease his persisting paranoia of the sea. Juli would understand. Despite his aunt's enlightenment of his fears and the forced practice run in the boat, he still felt nervous. Emilio's alcohol wouldn't be strong enough or last long enough.

"You're right, Bolero. This is it. It's isolated and the beach isn't very wide. The boat will be in the water fast. There's a drop-off, and I can see that the water's deep along here. We'll be out to sea before we know it. It will be early in the morning. Your cousin will drive off quickly. No one will ever know we were here. This is ideal."

"Am I wonderful or what? Can I pick the beach?"

"Oh, you're wonderful. You can pick the beach. Now let's get something to eat. I'm famished."

Bolero took note of the location of the hidden beach—off Buena Vista Road, but the sign to the road leading to the beach was missing, probably knocked over during a hurricane. Take Buena Vista to the large banyan tree and turn left. Then follow the bumpy road to the ocean. He finished writing and tossed the pen in the console.

"OK. We found the beach. Now we can eat."

"Finally, now that it's almost dinner time."

"I'll drive back down Buena Vista. There's got to be a town nearby."

After Buena Vista, Bolero steered onto a paved road and soon entered a small village. As they drove past a cluster of houses with thatched roofs they caught occasional glimpses of the ocean behind scrub brush and trees.

"Over there, a *bodega*. Forget the restaurant. Let's just buy some food and eat by the water. There's a beach behind the store. I'm starving."

"Fine. Whatever you say, master." Bolero pulled into a parking space at the front of the store. The SUV shuddered when he turned off the ignition.

The bodega smelled of roast pork, ham, pungent Swiss cheese, and freshly baked bread. The smell of pork still turned Daniel's stomach as thoughts of killing the pig came to mind. Chicken wasn't appetizing either.

"You can have pork or chicken if you want. I'm ordering beef."

"Beef's fine. I'll eat what you like."

They ordered two *churrasco* steaks, black beans, rice, plantains, and flan for dessert. They bought several bottles of water, and beer, fruit, and snacks for a small gathering on the roof later in the evening. Antonio had fulfilled his promise to organize parties and jam sessions on the roof until the day of their departure. Tonight a party with close friends and the fishing crew was planned.

Daniel unzipped his money belt and paid the cashier, an elderly woman whose husband meticulously sliced cold cuts behind the deli case. She asked the two customers where they were from but never allowed them to answer. She rattled on about how she and her husband had owned the bodega for forty-three years, and even though the government took the majority of the profits, the couple had no intentions of leaving their store.

The young men thanked her and stepped into the bright sunlight, rounded the corner, and walked along the cinderblocks of the bodega. They headed for a stand of palms growing by the water. There was a sandy rise up to the trees. Below the rise the sand was damp.

"Those palms have a perfect view." Daniel gestured by raising the bag toward the trees. "Let's sit up by the trees where it's cool and dry."

"Maybe I'll go for a swim after we eat," commented Bolero as he lagged behind Daniel. They stepped off the cracked sidewalk, and Daniel passed through an opening in a low wall, stepping carefully to keep sand out of his sneakers.

"Swim if you like. I'm taking a shower when we get back."

Out of the corner of his eye Daniel noticed movement, a figure in dark colors. Daniel cocked his head to see who lingered in this isolated part of town. A man in uniform was about to cross the street on his way to his cruiser in a parking lot but changed his mind and hesitated when he saw the two strangers.

"What business do you two have here?"

"*Vamos a comer el almuerzo.* We're about to have lunch." Daniel hoped his explanation would suffice and that the policeman would continue in the direction of his parked car. Daniel continued toward the palm trees. A sudden surge of caution overwhelmed him, and when Bolero stopped, Daniel whispered, "Keep walking."

The man yelled, "*Alto, los dos.* Show me your identification."

Daniel stopped and turned around. With Bolero blocking his view of the official, he whispered, "We're fucked. Be ready."

The policeman walked across the sand and approached them. "I said show me your identification."

Daniel shifted the bag to his left arm to reach in his back pocket for his wallet. He leaned, balanced on his left foot, and rapidly lashed out with his right foot. The movement was swift and flowed in one motion. He kicked the unsuspecting officer square in the chest and knocked him hard to the sand.

"Run," yelled Daniel.

The officer groped his chest with both hands as he lay on the sand. He looked upward and gasped for air. Daniel and Bolero held tight to the heavy bags and tore down the beach, weaving in and out of bushes and trees. The policeman caught his breath, sat up, yanked his pistol from his belt, gripped the handle, and fired at them.

"He's shooting up in the air to scare us," Bolero said between breaths.

"To hell he is. A bullet just whizzed past my head. Run for your life."

The officer pumped out more shots.

"He's pissed. You didn't have to kick him so hard."

"No. I should've just given him my ID and landed in prison for the best years of my life."

"Oh, yeah. They're after you, aren't they?"

Daniel shook his head in disgust at Bolero. "There's no more to say. Just run."

He calculated the height of a felled tree and sailed over the trunk. Bolero followed. Rocks and plant debris on the other side slowed them down.

"Stay in the water as much as you can. The cop has probably called for assistance. They'll bring dogs. The dogs will lose our scent in the water."

Bolero splashed in water lapping at the shore and tripped on a rock. Daniel blocked his fall by leaping in front of him and cringed at the thought of the bag of food getting saturated and spoiled.

"Hold on to that bag. It's our lifeline."

"I was going to dump it somewhere. It's hard to run with this bag."

"Keep it, no matter what."

They trekked on. The beach thickened with mangroves. They trudged over gnarled, twisted roots and advanced more rapidly in the water at the edge of tangled trees and their complicated root systems. As the water deepened they drifted with the current, holding the sacks of food and drinks above the surf, until their feet touched shallow water again. Daniel waded to a small beach nestled in the mangroves.

"Bolero, you do realize this is it. I can't go back to Havana. Police will confiscate your cousin's vehicle and question him and everyone else we know. They'll stake out Antonio's house and patrol the neighborhood. If I go back it's all over for me."

He sat down to rest and to catch his breath. Bolero dropped down beside him.

Daniel looked deep into his friend's eyes. "You could go back. You haven't done anything wrong except associate with me."

"I'm not going back either. I'll stick with you. Just what do we do now? We found the beach to launch the boat, but the boat's in Havana."

"Forget about the boat. I don't know. We'll think about it. First we have to escape the immediate threat, police chasing us. Do you have any money on you?"

Bolero lifted his shirt to reveal a money belt identical to Daniel's. "I liked your belt and had to buy one too. All my money's right here."

"Great. That's a good beginning, *amigo*. Maybe we'll buy another boat, a smaller one."

"Smaller?"

"We can't afford anything else."

"But your fear?"

Daniel poked him. "Let's go."

Bolero trailed Daniel into the water and around more mangroves. They treaded through water a foot deep, splashed, and churned up silt. Daniel halted in his tracks. He thought he heard a sound not connected with the noises of nature and the surrounding coastal environment.

"Quiet. I heard something."

"You did? What?"

"I know it wasn't a seagull. Listen."

Far down the beach they heard howling dogs and masculine voices shouting encouragement.

"I knew it. More police, and dogs are after us now. Sounds like four or five dogs, and for sure they're Belgian shepherds. Move into the thickest part of these trees and stay as low as you can. Go under water as they get closer. We have to keep them from smelling our scent or we're dead men."

"Oh, God," moaned Bolero.

From where they crouched, the thick, intertwined leaves and branches obscured their view of the beach. Daniel hoped for the same limited visibility looking from the beach to the water.

Fright consumed both fugitives, and when the dogs barked meters away they held their breath, closed their eyes, and submerged their heads, rippling the water as little as possible. With arms outstretched in front of them, they suspended the precious bags above water but kept them hidden by vegetation.

They held their breath for what seemed like an endless amount of time. Slowly they rose out of the water, hoping not to come face to face with the savage beasts trained to kill on command. They exhaled, opened their eyes, and stared at leaves and twisted branches instead of lunging, growling police dogs. They faced each other and smiled.

Yelps echoed, and the wailing of canines in pursuit faded as the agile animals dashed down the beach. Their simple minds were focused only on capturing the escapees.

"Be careful. They may return," Daniel said in a hoarse voice as he waded to shallow water. "I need a drink so bad. This saltwater has dried my throat. I can hardly talk."

They both gulped out of plastic water bottles.

"Even though we're dying of thirst it's better to save the water as long as possible." Daniel screwed the cap on the bottle. "You never know. We may need it more later on. They could trap us in these mangroves for days."

"They could. I realize anything's possible when I'm around you."

"What's that supposed to mean, Bolero?"

"Nothing bad. Just anything is possible. Now what?"

"I have no idea."

"Do we stay here?"

"I don't know. At least the dogs passed us by. We can't stay here forever. I'm not sure if we should continue or go back. I don't know this area," Daniel said as he headed for an opening between mangrove trees.

"Me either," said Bolero as he followed.

Daniel pushed a branch aside. "There may be an army back there waiting for us."

"Well, then let's move forward."

"But the officers and dogs are that way."

"Let's go inland."

"They'll pick up our scent faster."

"God, let's just go out to sea and get this trip over with."

"In what? Are you going to swim? Because you know I'm not. I'm hardly able to float in a boat out there." Daniel gazed at the calm ocean. "Thank God the weather's clear."

"So what? We're stuck here anyway."

"No, we're not. Let's just walk some more. But stay in the water."

"Fine, and then what?"

"Bolero, I told you. I don't know."

The sun lowered in the sky. The sunset must have been spectacular because they saw glimpses of orange and pink through the trees to the west, and the same colors reflected on the water. Daniel sadly recalled the sunset that was part of his gift to Juli at the waterfall on the eve of their engagement. How life had changed since that night of romance and planning their future. He relinquished this beautiful memory from his mind and returned to the reality of being hungry, hunted, and uncomfortable in sopping wet clothes.

Daniel trudged along, with Bolero right behind him. He looked to his left and saw a black obstacle bobbing under the plants and put out his arm to stop Bolero. "I think there's a dead baby whale over there." He pointed ahead and to his left. "Look, hidden under those branches. What is it? Go look."

"Go look? Are you scared?"

"I'm nauseated."

Bolero waded past Daniel to the object jounced by the motion of the waves. From a few meters away, Bolero observed the black blob and shouted back, "You asshole, it's not a baby whale. It's an inner tube."

He lifted the branches and leaves partially obscuring it and untied the rope that kept it moored in place under the trees. He gripped the frayed end of the rope and jerked the inner tube toward him. Then he towed it over to Daniel, who was still unsure of the object he'd suspected to be a dead creature from the depths of the ocean.

Bolero rested the cumbersome bag of food and snacks on the rubber that had been warmed by the rays of the afternoon sun. As he held the bag in place he said, "Why don't you hop on? We can ride this along the shore for a while."

"That's using your brain." Daniel handed the bag to his friend and boosted himself up on the tube as Bolero steadied it. Daniel held Bolero's bag while he climbed aboard.

"This thing is huge. Imagine it came out of a tire. How big was that truck?" Bolero said as he balanced and reached for his bag.

"Massive, for sure."

"Whose inner tube do you suppose it is?"

"How the hell would I know? Some idiot. The sad part is someone was going to leave Cuba on this, and we took their means of escape. I read in *Granma* that small crafts like this are scattered all along the coastline of Cuba ready for the right moment for the illegals to set sail."

"To set sail for the United States. Sad for them but lucky for us."

"We're not leaving Cuba on this."

"You're right. Too dangerous. We'll float on it and maybe reach a marina and buy a rowboat."

"A rowboat? A marina? Out here in nowhere?"

"Anything's possible."

They rounded a corner where thick vegetation led to a long, narrow beach. Bolero spotted another craft resting on the sand. "It's just like this one, only there's a slab of wood on top."

"It looks like they tied the plywood on with jump rope." Daniel touched a wooden handle at the end of the rope. "And it has oars. Someone else was planning an escape. What a way to travel across the ocean."

Bolero got so excited he jumped off the inner tube and ran splashing to the object. In the process he almost flipped Daniel over. But knowing Bolero, Daniel anticipated his intention and touched the water with both feet before he was thrown from the inner tube.

He caught his bag in midair and rescued it before it hit water. "Be more careful. This is all the food and drinks we have."

They examined the strange craft and sat on it. The oars fit into hollowed-out wooden blocks nailed and glued to each side of the plywood.

"Ingenious," commented Daniel. "I've heard of exiles escaping in all sorts of floating devices, even cars rigged to float. But this is crazy."

"I have friends who escaped in a tube." Bolero stared at the inner tube, plywood creation and slowly whispered, "Someone—I mean two people are making their escape on this."

"What did you say?"

"This is exactly what we need. A raft and a backup."

"Exactly what we need? That's not a raft, and forget the backup. There's no way I'm going out to sea in either one of these flimsy, poor excuses for boats. Never."

"What are you going to do then? This is our only option. I vote we climb aboard and head out to sea before the police and dogs come back and catch our asses."

"Oh, no."

Bolero dragged the plywood inner tube to the water, hopped on, set the bag beside him, and began to row toward the "baby whale." He scooped up the rope from the water and tied it around the block anchoring the oar. He steered the primitive crafts out of the mangroves.

"Come on, Daniel. Or do you stay behind as dog meat?"

Daniel clutched the bag to his chest and watched his friend drift on the still water. He glanced at the distant horizon and up at the colorful sky highlighting the day. He shook his head. "I can't. I can't."

Bolero ignored his words and rowed further. "I'll leave you behind. We have no choice now. This is our only chance to leave. Now or never."

"Go. You go. I can't. I'll die of fright out there at night."

"You're admitting you're scared?"

"I'm scared, you bastard. Are you happy now? You always wanted to hear me say that, didn't you? Well, I'm scared. I'm scared. I'm fucking frightened. Have a great voyage all by yourself."

"Daniel, shut up. Quiet."

"Fuck you."

"No, really. Be quiet. I think I heard the dogs."

Daniel listened. "You just want me on that piece of shit."

"No. I wouldn't joke about that. I heard the dogs."

Sure enough, the barking was far down the beach, but dogs, followed by their military masters, were returning. Bolero changed direction and pushed the oars forward. The "baby whale" floated behind and bounced off the plywood craft.

"Get the fuck on this tube, and we're out of Cuba."

Daniel waded to the floating Bolero and tossed the bag on the wood. He hoisted himself up, grabbed an oar, and gripped it with both hands. Furiously, they rowed out to sea.

There was a flash of light at the final dip of the sun. The red, purple, pink, and orange finale of the sunset perished and muted into a gray sky at twilight. A massive cloud hastened darkness and obscured the shoreline. Nature assisted them in their getaway.

Daniel let go of the oar and stretched his legs. He listened to the muffled sounds of barking dogs in the distance. He strained to see the location on the beach from where they had set sail and pinpointed the narrow stretch of sand, pale against the low trees mantled in darkness, at the water's edge. He stared at shadows moving to and fro. They leaped and sprayed water in a frenzy and bounded along the shore, in and out of vegetation.

"Bolero, look. Dogs on the beach and in the mangroves. They're at the spot where we found this inner tube. The police would have captured me, or their dogs would have torn me apart." He felt a chill crawl up his spine.

Daniel removed his wet pants and shirt and laid them on the plywood to dry. He watched a troop of about ten men in motion. Some clutched rifles, and others tended to the panicked canines that banded together like a pack of wolves on the prowl.

Deep in thought, Bolero also focused on the activity on the beach. "This raft was a gift from God. He rewarded you, and you're not even thankful. You're lucky I went back to pick you up."

"Thankful? You have no idea how grateful I am. I just told you the dogs would have torn me apart." A sudden gale chilled his arms. Daniel folded them. "You wouldn't have left me anyway. Rowing away from me was a bluff on your part."

"A bluff? It was not. I knew we had to get away from those dogs."

"Well, we escaped them, didn't we? Now we have to survive this trip." Daniel kept his eyes fixed on the police. "They're unaware we're out to sea. They're still searching the mangroves. If they were to alert the coast guard, we'd never be able to resist."

"They can't see us. It's too dark."

"Saved by the gray cloud." Daniel reached for a bag. "Let's eat. I'm beyond hunger now."

They ate in silence. Sounds of barking dogs running down the beach and shouts of their commanding masters faded into the sounds of waves gushing against the rubber of the inner tubes.

While they ate, the crafts hardly moved on the windless ocean. Daniel wrapped up the food for tomorrow and put it back inside the bag. "You'd be wise to allow that food to last as long as possible. There are no bodegas or restaurants out here. Our money is worthless."

"I'm so hungry, but I'll save half. We still have the beer, fruit, and snacks we were going to take to Antonio's."

"I may need a beer."

"Why? Do you have to get drunk to be out here?"

"Are you saying I'm afraid again? Didn't we already have that discussion? How can I be afraid now? I can't see anything beyond this raft. I just may want a beer. Tomorrow, in daylight, I'll get drunk."

"At sunrise, when we see sharks and whales."

"Don't start. It's hard enough without your comments." Daniel reached for his oar. "Now that we ate and have energy, start rowing."

"I'm tired."

Daniel gave him a sharp look. "Row while we have the strength. We've got to make progress in case the coast guard was alerted."

"But the police didn't see us."

"Row."

"Fine."

Bolero picked up his oar, and they rowed in unison into blackness. Twenty-five minutes later Bolero lifted his dripping oar out of the water, set it beside him, and curled up on the inner tube. Daniel tried to stay awake as lookout, but his eyes closed, and he slumbered beside his friend.

Chapter Thirty
THE STRAITS AND BEYOND

Daniel awoke to sunshine warming his face and to the motion of the raft drifting on a forceful current. He glanced at the backup inner tube and was relieved it was still in tow.

Bolero lifted his head. "We're moving."

Daniel sat up. "It must be the Gulf Stream. We're out in the Straits."

"We won't have to row as hard as yesterday."

"No, but we should row to get to America as fast as possible. We barely have any food or drinks. We were so organized and well prepared for this trip by boat. From one minute to the next, here we are, out in the middle of the ocean, on a fucking inner tube."

"No one knows where we are. They'll think we're dead."

"We'll write everyone as soon as we reach the States," Daniel said and became pensive. "And to think Juli was going to join me."

"She'll come later."

"It'll be hard for her to get out of Cuba with all the restrictions."

Daniel looked across the endless water. The low waves rolled, and the repetition mesmerized him. Melancholy surged within him at the realization of months, maybe years without Juliana. Thoughts of her became obsessive and shifted to anxiety as he stared at the water surrounding him. The idea of drifting on this tiny, open raft in the middle of the ocean tormented him. He blurted, "Oh my God."

"What's wrong?"

"Nothing. I'm trying to get a grip on our predicament. Everything happened so fast. I'm facing my worst nightmare. Doing exactly what I feared the most. And when will I see Juli again?"

"Hang in there. Don't dwell on it. We'll be all right."

"Hopefully," said Daniel.

Daniel shifted his position. "Can you believe I actually miss the pigeon coop? That stuffy little shed was a haven compared to this. The mattress was so much more comfortable than this slab of wood. Here we can't even stand up, stretch, or move. We might tip over. Wasn't the coop comfortable compared to this?"

"I have no idea. Well, I looked inside and sat on the mattress for a while. Anything's better than this."

"What do you mean you looked inside and sat on the mattress? You slept there when Juli and Rafael were in Havana."

"No, I didn't."

"Yes, you did. I saw Rafa on the roof, but the chair you were in was empty. You went to sleep in the coop, didn't you?"

Bolero's face reddened. "No."

"No?"

"When I got to your landlady's house, I saw the ladder leaning against the wall, so I climbed up and asked Isabel if she wanted company. She said she did, so I slept with her. I never wanted to sleep in that smelly pigeon coop."

"You did what?"

"I slept with Isabel. No one knew. Her kids were with their father. The mother was in the lower part of the house."

"Oh my God. Did you have to tell me that? You slept with her?"

"Well, you asked where I went. You didn't want her. What's wrong?"

"Nothing. Nothing at all."

Bolero had a puzzled look on his face.

"Forget it." Daniel propped up his elbow, cradled his head in the palm of his hand, and stared at the ocean. "For your information, the pigeon coop didn't smell. I cleaned and disinfected it and kept it that way."

Forty-five minutes passed, and Daniel sat in his briefs at the edge of the raft and washed himself in the saltwater while keeping guard for sea creatures. He dipped his feet, rubbed water on them with both hands, and then stretched out to dry in the sun. The sun was so intense he draped his shirt over his head and spread it tent-like to shade his face. He ignored his sea mate, who also washed himself on the opposite side of the raft.

Rowing was unnecessary, for the Gulf Stream and air currents whisked them along at a steady pace. They decided to save their energy for later on in the voyage. Daniel dozed at the rocking of the inner tube. A flock of seagulls squawked and scolded as they flew above. Once the birds disappeared, silence abounded. Splashing waves were the only sounds.

Suddenly an explosion shattered the silence. The cruel blast echoed like thunder across the sky. Daniel jumped so far he slid off the side of the tube and into the water. His shirt fell into the water with him, and he snatched it up as it floated away from the raft. With shirt in hand, he desperately groped at the slippery edge.

"What in the hell was that?" Bolero yelled and ducked when the blast echoed across the water. He saw the look of panic on Daniel's face as he clung to the plywood. Bolero stretched to pull him up. With his friend's help, Daniel heaved himself back on the raft. Water from his body saturated the wood and spewed streams that trickled over the side. Both men were stunned and looked behind them in the direction where the thunderous sound originated. The spare inner tube was flat and bobbed on the surface with a gaping hole in its side.

"That's the end of our backup." Daniel watched a wave lift the flattened tube. "It scared the hell out of me. I thought the coast guard fired at us."

"Me too. I was sure the police had called the coast guard. What a relief."

"A relief if the inner tube under us holds out. Imagine trying to float on that black pancake. The hot sun must have caused it to blow up." Daniel reached for the rope attached to the flattened tube and pulled it onto the raft. "You never know. It may come in handy, even like this."

Bolero watched the black rubber flop on the plywood. "Poor baby whale."

"Poor baby whale?"

"I liked the idea of him drifting behind us." Bolero picked it up and examined the hole. "That's the end of it, though. At least the inner tube under us has wood covering it and is cooled by the water. It shouldn't explode."

"I hope not."

The following day was overcast, and the ocean rolled succulent, like pale green gelatin. Daniel had shivered during the night. When he awoke he slipped on his clothing, which was still damp after the unexpected plunge into the water. He scrunched his shirt stiffened by salt in an effort to soften the material before it touched his skin but the rigid material chafed his back and chest.

Bolero passed Daniel a beer, and they toasted their voyage. They sipped warm beer and ate black beans and rice for breakfast. Only drinks, snacks, and fruit peeked out of the plastic bag. As they chewed they watched waves undulate around them.

Daniel shifted to the right and then to the left and stretched his legs out to relieve a cramp in his calf. He raised his uncomfortable shirt and scratched and rubbed his irritated flesh.

"Be careful, Daniel. You're rocking the raft."
"How do you get comfortable on this thing?"
"You sit still."
"I can't. My skin itches. I have a cramp in my leg." Daniel covered his head with the shirt. "The wind died down. We should row."
"Row? To where?"
"America, of course."
"Which way?"
"How should I know?"
"Then let the current carry us."
"Lazy bastard. Do what you like." Daniel lay down, propped himself up on his elbows, and peered straight ahead at the sea. "How much longer can we do this? It's been two days, and all I see is endless ocean."
"I don't know." Bolero propped up on his elbows and stretched his legs on the wood. His feet hung over the rim. He followed Daniel's gaze. "We just can't give up."
"Giving up has never been an option."
"For me either."
The two seamen heard a loud splash in the distance. Two geysers rose fifty meters in the air several kilometers from them. Bolero grabbed Daniel's arm.
"I saw."
"What made the water rise like that?"
"The hell if I know."
Bolero's question was answered when two gray phantoms, each the size of an asphalt parking lot, rose in unison approximately one kilometer from the inner tube. The sailors stared with mouths wide open at the sight of the giants, rocking the raft as they rose to their knees. The men leaned forward at the same time, paralyzed by the bizarre occurrence. Together they witnessed the "parking lots" sail above the surf on shiny wings.

Each monster had a slit of a mouth and two eyes wide apart. They glided above the waves, raised their wings skyward, and dove into the water, hitting the surface with precision. With wings spread apart they advanced underwater toward the raft at a high rate of speed. In comparison to their gigantic bodies, their short, narrow tails whipped in the milky sky before following the massive entities into the ocean depths. The great dives created three tidal waves preceding the creatures to the raft.

"Holy shit."

Daniel blinked and shook his head. The forgotten memory of the shark had, for the first time in his life, unfolded before him. He snapped out of the past and stared at a wave on a course to slam into the raft. He grabbed an oar and shouted for Bolero to do the same. "Look out. A wave. Steady the raft. *Cuidado.*"

The first surge rose twelve meters. Daniel stretched the oar out with his right hand in an attempt to balance the raft as they rode the wave. With his left hand he grabbed for the plastic bag containing the remaining food and drinks as it slid along the plywood. Two cans of beer plopped into the froth. He refrained from reaching for them and squeezed the oar with all his strength. Bolero held tight to his oar and helped Daniel salvage the few belongings from being washed away.

The raft steadily climbed, and water soaked the two passengers. In a trough they dropped with a thud and jerked forward to encounter the next wall of water. They held tight to their oars and stabilized the raft as it mounted another gigantic wave. They hollered as the vessel ascended, struggling with the oars to stabilize the tube as they reached the peak of the wave. In an instant they dropped and crashed hard in the trough. The force of the water jolted them onto the hard wood surface. Daniel bit his tongue when his oar handle swung and jabbed him in the cheek. When he swallowed, he tasted blood and winced at the acute pain in his mouth.

Once again they scrambled to clutch the oars. The raft pitched through a series of smaller waves preceding the third. The final breaker collided into the raft with more height and strength than the previous ones.

Daniel shouted above the roar, "Don't give up, Bolero. Hold tight to the oar. One more wave."

"Giving up is not an option."

The inner tube tilted on impact. The ropes holding the plywood loosened, and the wood shifted and overlapped on one side. Bolero released his oar to tighten the rope.

"Wait. It's not over yet. Look. The monsters are coming for us."

The ocean around the raft turned from light green to the color of pewter. As far as Daniel could see, shadows crept toward them below the surface. He felt the sensation of movement beneath him.

"There have to be four or five of them. A section of one is under the raft. Oh my God. Please don't rise and flip us over."

"Oh no. We survived the waves, and now this," Bolero cried out as he gripped the oar and witnessed massive sections of marine animals gliding, submerged all around them. Their journey below seemed like an eternity to the sailors. Waves of normal size kept the raft in motion. Neither the appendages nor the torsos of the sea creatures disrupted the inner tube. The surrounding ocean brightened to green again, to the rafters' relief.

The beasts blackened the water ahead. A tip of a wing lifted out of the water half a kilometer to their right like a gesture of farewell, and the giants swam on.

"Manta rays. Fucking giant manta rays," Daniel said as he lifted the dripping oar, set it on the wood, and collapsed. He spit red saliva on the foam accumulated around the raft. "How much more can we take?"

"You're bleeding."

"The oar hit my cheek. I bit my tongue."

Bolero handed him his wet handkerchief.

"Thanks. I have one." He reached in his pocket for his handkerchief and pressed it to his tongue. His blood stained the linen cloth.

After adjusting the sheet of plywood and securing it to the inner tube with the jump rope, they stripped and spread out their clothes to dry.

"I thought we were going to die," Bolero said as he opened a bag of pork rinds and offered some to Daniel.

"No thanks." Daniel pointed to the red mark on his tongue. "When I first caught sight of the manta rays I remembered the incident with the shark when I was a kid and went deep-sea fishing with my father and uncle. I pictured exactly what had happened on that day. It's like the manta rays triggered a vision of the past I had completely forgotten. My memory of the incident came back."

"Juli told me you were four when a shark knocked you off the boat. It makes sense why you feared the ocean all your life."

"Strange, but since this trip I'm not afraid anymore."

"True. At the sight of those rays you would have frozen instead of reacting like you did."

"It was as if I faced my nightmares head on. Awake. And the terror can't get much worse than what we experienced today."

Daniel reached into the bag Bolero held, chewed carefully, held up a half-eaten chip and said, "We only have one more bag of these and one of plantain chips, some bananas, and grapes. The liquids are running out. I worry more about starving to death or dehydrating out here than battling sea monsters."

"I worry about starving too. *Amigo*, you've come a long way."

"We've come a long way."

"Certainly a long way from Cuba. What do you think? A hundred kilometers, at least?"

"I have no idea." Salt from the pork rind stung the wound on Daniel's tongue as he chewed. He lisped the words, "All I know is we're lucky to be alive."

"Lucky is an understatement." Bolero offered him more chips.

"No thanks. The salt burns. Save some. Don't eat all of them."

"I'm hungry."

"More reason to save them. How will you feel in another day or two?"

Without answering Bolero scrunched the bag closed and tucked it under the flattened inner tube. Exhausted by the feat with the giant manta rays, the two travelers fell asleep at the first infusion of darkness.

On the fifth day, they cowered under their garments from the scorching sun. Sweat pearled like dew on their sunburned foreheads. Sundried skin on their arms peeled and flaked. Their scraggily, uncombed hair blew into dreadlocks in the wind, and their beards, although hot, protected their cheeks from exposure to lethal sunrays.

Despite weariness from tedious drifting and weakness from lack of food and water, when a cloud shaded the sun they picked up the oars and rowed with a vengeance. The raft surged forward. Daniel squinted toward the horizon hoping to catch a glimpse of land, but all he saw was the vast body of water.

On the sixth day Bolero pointed to a white cruise ship inching along in the distance against a clear sky. Daniel screamed at the boat in desperation. "Wave your shirt. Maybe they'll see us."

"The ship's too far away. We're only a pinpoint, kilometers from them."

Daniel ignored Bolero, kneeled, and scraped his knees on the rough surface as he flapped his shirt in an arc above him like a flag. The inner tube rocked.

Daniel worried the raft would tip over and sat back on his heels. "You're right." He sat all the way down and tossed his shirt in front of Bolero. "The passengers on that ship are swimming in pools, getting drunk, and gorging themselves on food. What do they care about two assholes drifting on a raft?"

Daniel picked at the splinters in his knees and remembered Dr. Nieves plucking bits of metal out of the palm of his left hand with tweezers. He turned his palm up and examined the old wound. The jagged scar was a pale thread on his tan hand. Like a second lifeline, it curved parallel to the line he was born with.

In the middle of the sixth night, cold, stinging raindrops awakened them and splattered their faces and shirtless bodies. Daniel scrambled for the bag of empty containers, saved in hopes of collecting rainwater. The last few days were spent sipping sparingly out of remaining beer cans. Now, they listened to the harmonic sound of drops pattering into cans. Daniel carefully peeled back the tin tops with his pocketknife. The plastic containers that had once held steak, beans, and rice also became useful as miniature cisterns steadily filling with drinkable liquid. Even the deflated inner tube held water.

As Daniel marveled at the precious clear liquid rising in the vessels, he reminisced about his homemade distillery and Emilio patiently awaiting drops of pure alcohol to accumulate in the milk bottle. He remembered the feeling as the alcohol seethed his throat, slid down his esophagus, and settled warm at the pit of his stomach. How it had eased the pain in his wounded hand.

Daniel glanced up at the rain streaming down and opened his mouth wide to catch the droplets. The rain soothed his cut tongue, cracked lips, and parched throat. Bolero copied his friend. As the two positioned themselves like wide-mouthed baby birds pleading for nourishment on a bare, floating nest, the large, sparse drops multiplied into a deluge.

Satisfied by the rain, Daniel curled up, chilled and shivering on the wet raft, and dreamed of Juliana dancing before him in Jose Martí park, leaping and twirling pirouettes. He embraced and guided her under the low trees, and as the drops pelted him on the raft, he smiled.

"*Despiertate.* Wake up. We're here to save you. *Son cubanos?*"

Four Cuban-Americans stared at the pathetic sight before them as they leaned over the railing of a boat with the words *Brothers To The Rescue* painted on the side. Daniel and Bolero lay half dressed, still, and in fetal positions on the raft as it bobbed and slowly advanced at the urging of waves knocking into it.

Their ribs protruded above sunken stomachs. Out of emaciated bodies, arms lay entangled, limp and devoid of muscle. The containers, empty of liquid and blown over in the wind, were spread out on the raft. Cans rolled back and forth from one man's body to the other, clanging together and rolling in repetitious sounds of tin striking wood.

The boat gently pulled up alongside the floating plywood. Air had seeped out of the barely visible inner tube. A film of saltwater skimmed across the wood with each ocean swell. With a hook at the base of a long pole a Brothers to the Rescue crewmember eased the raft toward their boat.

"Watch out. To your right. A shark. A big mother."

He poked at the fin with the pole and pushed at the leathery gray back circling the raft. At the prodding, the fin submerged. The pole hooked an oar, and the raft was pulled alongside the cruiser.

"Are they dead?"

The crewmember slid the pole back on deck and balanced one foot on the plywood and the other on a support on the larger craft. He secured the raft with a rope. Once the inner tube was stabilized, he knelt beside the rafters, touched their mouths, and felt for pulses.

"They're breathing. They're alive."

He tapped Bolero to consciousness and as he carefully lifted him to his feet he noticed the tattoo of an American flag on his leg. He guided him to the hands of a heavyset man reaching over the side of the boat. With the assistance of the other men, they heaved the migrant on board.

"*Amigos,* you sailed into the Gulf of Mexico. You're lucky a Mexican fishing vessel alerted us to your location."

Delirious, Daniel raised his head at the sound of voices and scanned the ocean with eyes half closed. He mumbled one word at a time, "Which way to America?"

"You passed it. But don't worry. We'll get you there," the heavyset one said as he opened two bottles of water.

The man on the raft helped Daniel to his feet and onto the boat and continued to support him with both hands. Daniel propped himself against the railing on shaky legs. The rescuer positioned the weakened traveler so he could clearly view the crest of the sun in the eastern sky. Sunrays gleamed across the water.

"America is that way, in the direction of the rising sun and a new day."

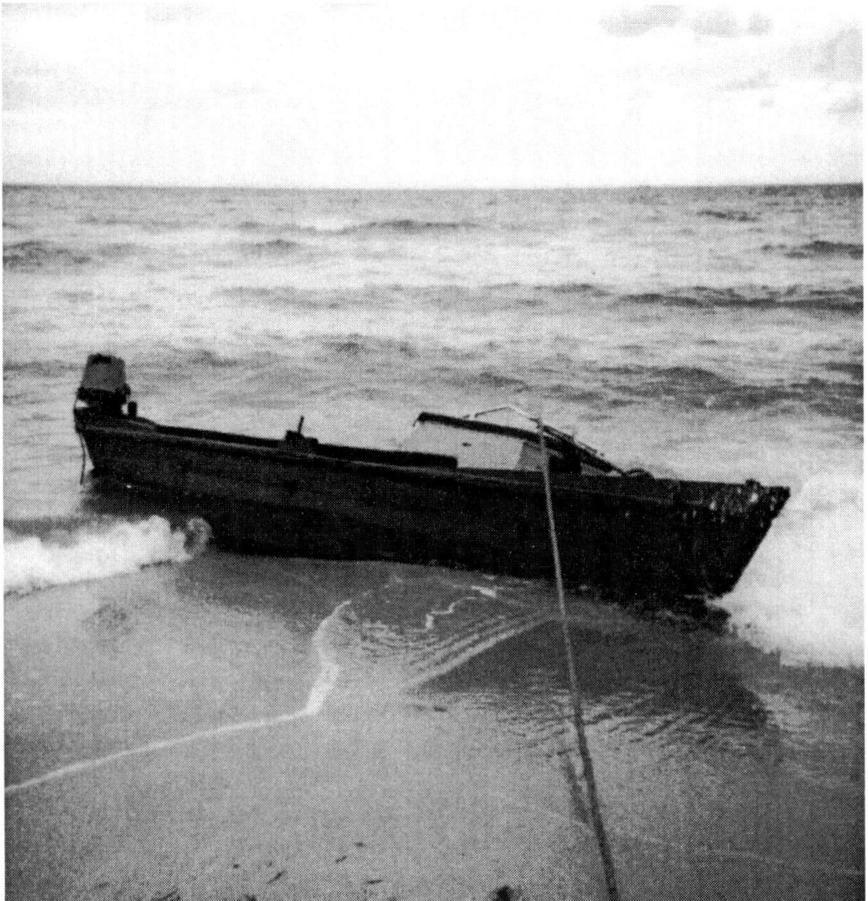

Acknowledgments

Thank you Abraham Fuentes for offering me the original idea for my novel, *Escape to the Straits*, which was supposed to have been a short story for creative writing class.

My sincerest appreciation to Alicia Chipy for her guidance, advice and editing and who, along with her mother, Alicia Ramos, patiently answered my questions about Cuba. And to Dolly, Alicia's Havanese, where the idea to include a puppy in my story came from.

A heartfelt thank you to Setury Sanchez Gil for taking time from cooking in that stifling hotel kitchen to explain to me about the difficulties of life in communist Cuba, for patiently drawing maps of Havana, and for providing photos taken in the province of Villa Clara. The best of luck to you in your nursing career.

I am grateful to Esperanza and Lesbia Varona for meeting with me and for providing information on Ranchuelo.

Many thanks to the hotel banquet servers, the girls from Santa Clara, who with enthusiasm painted a descriptive picture for me in Spanish of their homeland.

My gratitude to the staff at CreateSpace for their kindness, editing and helpful suggestions during the process of publishing my manuscript.